PERMANENT INTERESTS

James Bruno

This is a work of fiction. Names, places, characters, and incidents are either the product of the author's imagination or are used fictitiously, and any resemblance to actual persons, living or dead, business establishments, events, or locales is entirely coincidental.

PERMANENT INTERESTS

Also by James Bruno

CHASM
TRIBE

For Tosca, Lara and Annika
Always at my side and in my heart

We have no eternal allies, and we have no perpetual enemies. Our interests are eternal.

-- LORD PALMERSTON

PROLOGUE

The Carabinieri officer retched in a garbage can. His two colleagues kept a wary distance from the corpse which was sprawled across the small alley, arms outstretched, one leg twisted, doll-like, away from the body, visibly broken in several places. A ragged gash ran from ear to ear as if inflicted by the indifferent violence of some rabid beast. The victim's eyes were torn out, one brown orb thrown carelessly four feet from the body, the other apparently stepped on and crushed near the victim's head. The immediate catalyst for the sergeant's instantly losing his supper, however, was the sight of the dead man's genitals stuffed in his mouth. The Carabinieri had seen mutilated bodies before. The rising violence among growing north African youth gangs in Italy often defied human comprehension: beheadings, cut-off ears and noses, disembowelment. The case at hand could have been written off to such third world gang warfare but for one thing. The dead man was white, in his early fifties and clothed in a conservative, dark-blue pin-striped suit.

"*Gesú!*" exclaimed the youngest cop, Vellario, an erect, handsome boy of nineteen, as he crossed himself. His sick buddy wiped his mouth with his handkerchief.

Sergeant DiLazzara, a grizzled forty-something veteran of Italy's finest, shook his head. He helped his nauseous subordinate to regain himself.

"Stinking Africans," Vellario spat.

"I don't know," DiLazzara said, his eyes still transfixed on the carnage.

Vellario looked at him with surprise. "Who else then?" he asked with a shrug.

"This is not the result of rage, or even of drug-induced madness. They knew what they were doing, whoever did this."

"So?"

DiLazzara finally took his eyes off the slain man before him. He waved away flies that were beginning to swarm in greater numbers over the blood-soaked scene. "This is a case for those superior horse's asses in the detective division. Let them figure it out."

The three policemen regarded the body as if it were unholy or radioactive. An ambulance and forensic specialists were on the way. "Leave it to them. They're the experts. They specialize in the dirty cases," the sergeant said.

CHAPTER ONE

"Son of a bitch! Son of a bitch!" exclaimed the tanned, sartorially resplendent defendant upon hearing the "not guilty" verdict from the jury foreman. He hit the table with his fist in a gesture that combined triumph and relief.

"Ernie! Ernie! Come here, I want to hug you, you little kike bastard," he shouted to the small, quick, toupeed man who had defended him successfully now for the third time against the Feds. Enveloping the little lawyer in a bear hug, the exuberant defendant lifted him off the floor. "I love ya! I love ya! They don't come better than you, pal!" he shouted in his throaty baritone.

Albert Joseph ("Big Al") Malandrino had been here before. And he beat the rap each time. But this time he had made no secret of the fact that he was scared. The charges -- murder, assault, extortion, arson, conspiracy to defraud -- were more serious. The government's efforts to nail him were more thoroughgoing and meticulous than before. Wiretaps, confessions of former associates, intercepted mail, compromising photographs. They had puzzled out Malandrino's activities over a period of years and carefully pieced together a picture of sophisticated and ongoing criminality. The DA put his best lawyers on the case.

"Albert Joseph Malandrino epitomizes all forms of evil in modern society," the prosecution had declared in its summation. "A man whose vile self-aggrandizement and cynical flaunting of the law has resulted in crack babies, murdered teenagers, blighted neighborhoods, thieving politicians and a deterioration of the moral standards of our society."

That's not the way Malandrino and his lawyers saw it, however. Albert Joseph Malandrino was a pillar of the community, the jury was told. A man devoted to family, church and community. A patron of charities and the arts. An example to the youth. A successful businessman admittedly given to occasional unorthodox, though not illegal, methods. Yet another Italian-American leader persecuted by culturally insensitive authorities.

"Let's get the hell outta here, Ernie." Malandrino put his arm around Ernie Feinstein and the two skipped out of the courtroom like kids off to summer recess after the last day of school.

Outside the courtroom a mob of reporters awaited Malandrino.

"Mr. Malandrino! What do you have to say now that the trial is over?" "What are your plans, Mr. Malandrino?" "Is the government persecuting you, Mr. Malandrino?"

Malandrino paused, taking stock of the crowd of reporters, admirers and gawkers. Jerking his chin upward, he straightened the lapels of his crisp, form-fitting Armani suit. And with the righteous air of a Renaissance prince who had vindicated himself before Inquisitorial persecutors, proclaimed, "Let the people know...Let the people know that before God I am an innocent man. Why the authorities choose to squander the taxpayers' money on show trials against honest citizens such as myself is a mystery and a scandal. It is obvious that certain people with political ambitions are trying to make a name for themselves by conjuring up some all-powerful crime organization that they call 'mafia' and randomly selecting successful Italian-Americans such as myself as the alleged ringleaders. Well, it's all bunk! Why don't they go after the real criminals. The drug king pins who poison our youth. The muggers on our neighborhood streets who assault the elderly. The gun runners who supply the street gangs. That's what I want to know. And so do *you*!"

The crowd erupted in applause and cheers. Tough-looking blue-collar youths from Bensonhurst and Astoria pumped their raised fists as in an atavistic victory salute. Frumpy middle-aged housewives waved miniature American and Italian flags. Beefy hard-hatters bellowed, "Atta way, Al!" Reporters shouted questions simultaneously, adding to the cacophony.

Big Al drank it all in. He loved adulation. What he loved even more was rubbing it in the Feds' faces. Big Al pulled it off again. Made fools of the Establishment. All those Ivy Leaguers with their superior airs. All those hypocritical political bigshots all for crime-busting, yet not too proud to take in campaign "contributions" -- whether over or under the table. Upper class sissies with clean finger nails and smooth complexions who never had to sweat for a living or defend themselves on the lists of city streets. Al knew life. He had the scars and quickness of mind to prove it.

But for weeks after the trial he grew increasingly irritable and listless, sulking for hours alone in the paneled study of his modest Flushing ranch house, not emerging for days. He was convinced that the Feds were listening in and observing his every move. He put on weight. He took up

an old habit: scarfing down cannolli on weekend
afternoons while watching ball games in his darkened
living room. When he did emerge, it was usually after
midnight to visit his favorite call girls, sometimes two or
even three at a time. In one of his trials, Malandrino was
labeled an "obsessive-compulsive" by some high-falootin'
overpaid society psychiatrist. Big Al was a man with big
appetites. After he lost Angie to breast cancer three years
earlier, Al Malandrino's behavioral checks fell by the
wayside.

After a month of self-neglect and fifteen additional
pounds, Al came to. The Feds were defeating him whether
or not they were actually surveilling him. This he could not
tolerate. Since boyhood, he had looked after his family and
those who worked for the family. Nabbed at age ten for
hijacking a crate of prosciutto with his buddies, Al had
vowed that he would never be beaten down by the "Ameri-
gahns" in providing for his family. He had to get back to
business, though discretion would be the watchword. No
more business over the phone! Big Al commanded.
Meetings would take place only at locales chosen by Al
himself, usually at the last minute. No blabbering to wives,
girlfriends, drinking buddies, etc. Neighborhood social
clubs were to be used solely for recreational purposes. No
business discussions in cars, a prime target for FBI
bugging. Al was getting so paranoid that he wanted to
know who talked in their sleep, who had drinking
problems, who played around. Al fired one security capo
after another.

Finally, Al thought to hell with the goddamn Feds. So
what if they were under every bed, listening behind every
wall. Al would play it straight for a while until he found
more secure means of carrying out his business. As a first
step, he realized that what he needed was a professional to

take over security of his "family." Somebody from the outside, totally removed from "Our Thing." So removed, in fact, that Al concluded he needed a non-Italian. This way, the man would be absolutely free of family connections, however indirect, with the mob or anybody who knew someone in the mob; a man who would be devoid of the emotional response (i.e., revulsion by most, sympathy by a few) that Italian-Americans had toward the "Mafia." What Al wanted was a straight-arrow, all-American boy who was ambitious, yet guileless, loyal but detached and, most important of all: incorruptible.

Al put an ad in the help wanted sections of several southern newspapers: "Security supervisor for major northeast construction firm. Must have five years related experience, including expertise in communications security. Excellent promotion prospects and benefits. Start: $55K. Al-Mac Construction Co., Inc., Teaneck, NJ, (201) 493-0980, Mrs. McNamara."

Al figured his best recruitment prospects lay in the nation's hinterland -- anywhere but metropolitan New York. And by advertising in southern regional papers using one of his legitimate enterprises, the chances of the FBI taking notice were minimal.

Of the hundred-odd résumés that came in, one in particular caught Al's attention: "Charles Taliaferro Wentworth, Spartanburg, S.C., 28, four years in the U.S. Marines -- two in "comsec" (communications security), two as an NCO in the Marine Security Guard detachment at the U.S. embassy in Rome; four years as a security officer with the Department of State in Bogotá and Rome. Bronze Medal for service in the Second Gulf War. Single. Hobbies: boxing, fishing. Working knowledge of Italian and Spanish.

Al decided to give the young man a call.

"Charles Wentworth? This is Albert Malandrino, president of Al-Mac Construction. I've got your résumé here. Impressive. I need to get somebody for the job who's real good. Not only who's got the skills, but somebody I can trust one-hundred percent. First, I want to ask you if you're serious about this job. "

"Well, er, uh, yeah. I mean yes. I mean of course. Real serious."

"Good. You got a few minutes so I can ask you some questions?"

"Yes, sir."

"Great. Okay. First, how do you approach your work? In other words, what's most important to you in carrying out your duties?"

"Discipline, sir," Wentworth answered crisply. "Both in myself and in my subordinates. Without discipline, order falls apart and the job doesn't get done, or, at least, not right."

Already Al was taking a liking to the deferential young man with the soft drawl. "What about your relationship with your superiors, what's the key factor in getting along with your boss?

"Loyalty, sir," Wentworth responded. "Without implicit trust, orders don't get carried out properly and things begin to go out of kilter."

On the personal side, Wentworth explained that he had left government some months before in order to settle down with a girl from his hometown and go into business for himself. But he called the engagement off after realizing that he'd become too worldly for Spartanburg. He found as time passed that he had precious little in common with his fiancée. To top it off, the last recession put the kibosh on his efforts to crash the business communications equipment wholesale trade. Returning to Uncle Sam was out of the question. He was fed up with low-paying, bureaucracy-freighted government work. Wentworth wanted change. He wanted to work in a big city. He wanted a challenging job with room to exercise initiative and make improvements.

Al wanted to meet Wentworth. He felt instinctively that he had found his man. One last question. "I notice that your middle name is Taliaferro. Do you by any chance have Italian blood in your family?"

"Oh, well, sir. That comes from my mother's side. You see, her great, great granddad was Gen. W.B. Taliaferro. He was a distinguished Confederate commander during the Civil War."

"Oh," Al said, "Way back."

"Yes, sir, way back."

Al flew the young man up for a personal interview at the gray, lusterless, yet functional office at his construction company in a Teaneck industrial park.

"You gotta understand. Doing business here in New York...New Jersey...is cutthroat. Especially the construction business. There's always more bidders than contracts. And it's the guy who's there firstest with the mostest that gets ahead. The slow-pokes, the dummies, they fall by the wayside like pins in a bowling alley. This is what a businessman faces here, you follow me?"

Wentworth nodded assent with a bemused smile. He hadn't been instructed in such a patronizing manner since high school.

Al began plodding mechanically back and forth like one of the bulldozers featured on calendars dotting the colorless office walls.

"Besides the competition, you got all kinds of rules:
Federal -- all that environmental crap. You know, if it
wasn't for those goddamn hippies in the '60's and those
flaming-ass liberals in Congress, we wouldn't have to put
up with all this shit today. I always said that George
Wallace was right. We should've put those goddamn
protesters in jail. That would've given them something to
think about…"

Al could see Wentworth beginning to fidget and stare
out the window at the bleak office-scape dotted with single-
story block buildings housing enterprises with names like
Coralsco Heating Co., North Jersey Electrical Supplies,
Inc., Dutch Boy Wire & Tubing.

"But that was before your time, huh, Mr. Wentworth?"

"Chuckie, my friends all call me Chuckie."

"Good, I like that. We're all on a first-name basis here.
Call me Al. Where was I, anyway?"

"Rules and regulations," Wentworth replied.

"Oh yeah. You also got your state and city governments
to deal with. Some rules are okay, but most are on the
books to screw the honest businessman. They all want
their pound of flesh. But the worst bastards are the unions.
Just like you got heaven and hell, angels and devils, you
got businessmen and unionists."

Al's large face flushed, his neck arteries pulsed as he
picked up speed in pacing the room and decrying the
injustice in the business world. Obviously, this was a
sensitive topic for the boss and Wentworth focused on his
every word.

"Businessmen -- actual angels I admit we aren't. But we
create wealth for the nation and jobs for the people. And
that's the American way!" Al swung around on his heels
and directed a stubby finger at the young man's face to
drive home his point.

"The union devils, on the other hand, suck the blood out of free enterprise. And they sap the spirit out of the working man. I'll tell you something about myself. When I was sixteen, my uncle got me a union job in construction. I couldn't believe what I saw. You had one guy who would only screw in light bulbs. Another guy would install wire, but wasn't allowed to connect it to a light socket...not in his 'job description.' I swear, if the first guy saw a beam about to fall on the head of the second guy, he wouldn't lift a finger. Union rules would prohibit it. Not his job!"

Al's earthy manner and overblown descriptions reminded Wentworth of the good ol' boys back in Spartanburg -- minus the quick Brooklyn clip and Italian cadence that underlay Al's speech.

"Here I had this cushy union job. I was making good money, good benefits and none the worse for wear either. Whether I busted my ass or merely showed up to work and went into a coma, I got paid. Hey, can't beat that right? Got it made for life, right? So what'd I do? I quit. It was crazy! This is what communism must be like, I thought."

Wentworth was struck by Al's passionate commitment to his principles. His delivery blocked out everything in the listener's mind but the issue at hand. The young man felt that he was witnessing the performance of a great actor, a Brando, or a DeNiro.

"So, I decide to go into business for myself. I'll keep the unions out and make more dough doing better work faster. I start small: landscaping, building repairs, that sort of thing. Just me and some buddies. Mac McNamara was one of them -- Al-Mac Construction, get it? -- he's gone now but his niece works here. She's the cute dish who arranged this interview. I'll introduce you. In any case, we grew and grew and kept the troublemakers in the unions out. And we got contracts, including from the government."

"But how did you actually pull it off, what with the power the big unions wield, not to mention the bigger established competitors and all the government red tape you mentioned earlier?" Wentworth wanted to know.

Big Al's big brown eyes flitted suspiciously from wall-to-wall as he fell uncharacteristically silent. "Next chapter, Chuckie," he declared as he slapped the young man on the back and gestured toward the open door. "Let me buy you a cup of coffee and then I'll introduce you around."

Chuckie Wentworth and his boss made the rounds. Gruff, broken-nosed job foremen, urbane smooth-talking accountants, simple laborers, thirtyish divorcée secretaries who cast lascivious glances at Wentworth's behind. While such people were all to be found in South Carolina as well, these were different. Tougher, blunter, shrewder, pushier. And he found no comparison with government people either, the latter generally ranging from sycophantically ambitious to smarmily officious.

Al tasked Wentworth first with revamping the security guards. Too much equipment and stuff disappearing from warehouses and job sites. Next, look into procurement methods. Seems we're paying higher prices than we should be for supplies. After that, payroll. Does everybody on the books really show up for work?

Wentworth plunged into his work. He uncovered a scam in the guard force: they were ripping off supplies and selling them. Big Al fired the guard force. Wentworth drew on his embassy experience in contracting for a new force with an aggressive, up-and-coming firm. Wentworth personally scrutinized the background of each guard. Contract terms called for regular training of the guards and recertification. The company was indeed overpaying for

everything from paper towels to axle grease. Fire the
company purchaser, Al ordered, and an accountant while
we're at it. Sure enough, payroll and personnel didn't jibe.
Make it jibe by firing the goddamn goldbrickers and their
foremen, commanded Big Al.

In their place, Wentworth recruited ex-military NCOs
and enlisted men. "Great job, Chuckie, here's two grand as
a bonus. Spend it all on broads and a good time."

Wentworth was pleased with his new job and the turn
his life was taking. True, his greatest youthful ambition
had never been to live in or around New York City. He
shared the same biases many rural Americans, northerners
and southerners alike, have against New Yorkers. Indeed,
they were brash, pushy, shifty. But the more he got to
know them, the more he felt kindred to them. Folks back
home were more solicitous, mannerly. Yet they spat when
telling a good raunchy joke just like New Yorkers did. And
once a New Yorker took a liking to you, you had a friend
for life; not so different from southerners once you got
down to it. He began to realize that most differences were
superficial. It was a matter of adjusting to dialect, body
language, and temperament.

His thoughts about Al were at once warm and perplexed.
The boss was a big-hearted bear of a man, yet, like a bear,
potentially dangerous, Wentworth felt. He was a
tempestuous and emotional man; almost like an
overindulged child. Thus far, Wentworth only saw his
good side. He wondered about the bad, the flip side of
character that we all possess in varying intensity. It also
struck him that Al may have many things to hide. For
example, Wentworth knew next to nothing of his boss's
personal life. Was he involved with someone? Did he
have kids? Mother? Father? And the way the older man
would suddenly screech to a halt when discussing certain

subjects that aroused Wentworth's curiosity. Finally, the way he just thrust a two thousand dollar bonus on his new minion after a mere two weeks on the job floored the young man. That was almost a month's net take-home pay when he was working for the government. Working for the government was like Al's description of how it was to work under a union: whether you busted your ass or merely showed up for work comatose, you got paid all the same. Wentworth liked the private sector.

CHAPTER TWO

CONFIDENTIAL
TO: SECSTATE NIACT IMMEDIATE
FROM: AMEMBASSY ROME
FOR THE SECRETARY
DEPT PLEASE PASS WHITE HOUSE
SUBJECT: AMBASSADOR MORTIMER MURDERED
REF: BALDWIN-CROFT TELCON 5/21

1. CONFIDENTIAL - ENTIRE TEXT.

2. ROME MUNICIPAL POLICE INFORMED THE
EMBASSY AT 0545 TODAY THAT AMBASSADOR
ROLAND MORTIMER'S BODY WAS FOUND IN AN
ALLEYWAY OFF THE VIA VENETO. POLICE
REPORT THAT THE AMBASSADOR BLED TO
DEATH AS A RESULT OF A DEEP GASH ACROSS
HIS THROAT. BODY WAS MUTILATED. NO
SUSPECTS HAVE YET BEEN APPREHENDED.
ROBBERY IS APPARENTLY NOT A MOTIVE SINCE
THE AMBASSADOR'S MONEY, WRISTWATCH, ID,
ETC. WERE NOT TAKEN. NO TERRORIST GROUP
HAS CLAIMED RESPONSIBILITY. AMBASSADOR

WAS NOT -- REPEAT NOT -- WITH SECURITY
DETAIL.

3. BODY CURRENTLY AT POLICLINICO UMBERTO
I HOSPITAL. AS OF 0700 LOCAL, WE HAVE
RECEIVED NO -- REPEAT NO -- PRESS QUERIES,
BUT EXPECT NEWS WILL BREAK ANY MOMENT.

4. DCM HAS NOTIFIED MRS. MORTIMER HERE.
RECOMMEND DEPARTMENT CONTACT FAMILY
MEMBERS IN CLEVELAND ASAP.

5. MINISTER OF INTERIOR AMBROLINI HAS
INFORMED DCM IN TELCON THAT HE WILL
PERSONALLY LEAD THE INVESTIGATION. DCM
WILL MEET WITH AMBROLINI AT 0730.

6. WILL REPORT FURTHER DETAILS AS THEY
BECOME AVAILABLE.
BALDWIN

As senior watch officer in the State Department's 24-
hour Operations Center, Bob Innes had acquired a finely-
tuned sense of what constituted news important enough to
bring to the immediate attention of the Secretary of State
or, in this case, to wreck his sleep at quarter-to-two in the
morning.

Innes had been sitting at his work station waiting for
Rome's tragic message to flash on his screen. He had
already been informed of the news by Robin Croft, a junior
watch officer working the night shift. She had received the

call about the ambassador's murder from Joe Baldwin, the
Deputy Chief of Mission, now Chargé d'Affaires.

Innes didn't mind phoning the Secretary in the middle of
the night -- even to bear bad news -- so much as having to
deal with the boss's overprotective and scatter-brained wife.

"Hello, Mrs. Dennison? This is Bob Innes at the Ops
Center. I'm terribly sorry to disturb you at this hour but I'm
afraid that something has come up that Mr. Dennison really
should know about right away.

"Yes, I know this is the second time this week that we've
had to disturb the Secretary after hours.... No, it isn't the
Middle East again.... Uh, no. I'm afraid that you won't be
able to help me on this one.... Well, if we do wait till
morning, I'm afraid the press might get wind that the
Secretary of State was caught with his pants down on a
very important matter."

The one sure way of getting past Mrs. Dennison, Innes
had learned, was to imply that public embarrassment would
come to her husband if he were not told immediately of a
late-breaking development. He stifled a smirk at the
thought that Secretary Dennison indeed may literally have
his pants down.

Innes gave the Secretary a concise readout on the
murder.

"This is tragic. Just tragic..." Secretary Dennison said
in his patrician New England voice, barely thickened by the
vestiges of sleep. "Was anyone with the ambassador?" he
added quickly.

"Apparently not."

"What about his security detail? Where were they?"

Innes hesitated. "It seems that the ambassador gave
them the slip."

"Gave them the slip?!"

"Er, yes. He had a habit of doing so."

Innes heard an extended sigh from the other end of the line. He pictured Dennison sitting on the edge of his bed, rubbing his brow in despair.

"All right. I'll want a full briefing first thing in the morning. Tell whoever is running things over there at this hour that I will personally handle this with the White House. Got me?"

"Yes, Mr. Secretary."

"One other thing."

Innes readied pen and paper as he cradled the receiver on his shoulder.

"I want the full police report, autopsy report -- both translated into English -- with photos, and a detailed listing of every item on his person at the time his body was discovered. I want it delivered to my house along with the classified traffic."

Innes winced. Why the Secretary of State would want all the gory details struck him as strange, but his was not to reason why.

"Yes, sir."

Innes knew that hell would be paid by those responsible for embassy protection, from the embassy security officer right on up to the chief of diplomatic security at the State Department -- who was number two on his list of officials to be notified this early morning.

"Mr. Innes?" Damn. It was her again.

"Yes, Mrs. Dennison?"

"Now, we don't want to receive any more calls from you tonight, you hear? I don't know what it is, but it can wait five more hours, y'understand now?" she drawled in her unapologetic Alabama delivery.

"I'll try not to, ma'am." Click. "Dumb cracker!" he cursed after hanging up.

Upon being told the news, the only thing that Ralph Torres, the Department's head of diplomatic security, could bring himself to utter was an uninterrupted string of emphatic "Goddamn"-s.

Innes could hear Torres struggling to control his breathing. "How in hell could Kobalski let that…that neophyte out of his sight?" he seethed. Leonard Kobalski was Embassy Rome's RSO – Regional Security Officer. "This has gotta be an al-Qaida hit all right. Those friggin' Italians are worthless against terrorism!"

Innes could see where this was leading to. It was called "CYA" in bureaucratic parlance: Cover Your Ass. The buck was already passing at lightning speed. Lesson number one in government: Career comes first. And accept accountability only when glory is at stake.

It was this kind of behavior in the senior ranks that caused Innes to be increasingly disillusioned with his career. At 34 and with eleven years in the Foreign Service, Innes had advanced fairly rapidly until he hit a dead stall in the upper end of the middle grades. With a wife and two small kids and no marketable skills for the private sector, Innes had pretty much come to the conclusion that he was a government lifer. On the bureaucratic treadmill, drawing a decent wage and benefits, but going no place fast. At least the Foreign Service, one of the few remaining bastions for the generalist, offered a unique line of rarely boring work, lots of world travel and still a modicum of prestige.

Innes's shift in the Ops Center ended at 8:00 am. Slouched at his work station, he looked at his watch. Ten minutes left. Innes rubbed the fatigue from his face with the palms of his hands and yawned deeply. He couldn't recall whether he had made love with his wife this month. A nurse also working shifts, she was always returning home either while he was asleep or on his way to work.

"Passing ships in the night..." he murmured to himself. "God, I hate Washington."

"You say something, Bob?" asked Robin. Her curly, flaming red hair accentuated a coed's face that beamed energy and ambition.

"Nah, just going crazy is all," a wan smile creased his boyish face. He wondered if, ten years from now, Robin would join the ranks of the brainy yet barren career spinsters who were now filling the upper ranks in greater numbers.

During the 30-minute drive back to his home in Herndon, Innes recalled Ambassador Roland Mortimer and his reputation in Washington. As was the case with most of his recent predecessors, Mortimer was a wealthy businessman and political activist who had contributed generously to the President's party during the last election, a squeaker which was delivered in no small part due to 200,000 swing votes Mortimer had captured -- some alleged stolen -- in his native Ohio.

Mortimer extolled family virtues, having fathered six children with his wife of thirty years. He was a gregarious, red-faced bear of a man who loved being around people and letting his hair down in posh watering holes after particularly strenuous political fund-raisers or long, boring business meetings. Having worked his way from poverty to wealth in the construction equipment parts distribution business, Mortimer liked to boast to his politician friends that he had spent his life "building America," a slogan that his party adopted during the last general election. Mortimer never ran for office himself, preferring to back politicians who would be indebted to him once in office.

What the public didn't know about Roland Mortimer -- apart from the fact that he was a diplomatic neophyte who didn't know the difference between a démarche and a declaration of war, who called hide-bound European prime ministers by their first names, and who slapped monarchs on the back as he would business cronies -- was that he was a hard-drinking, loudmouthed lout whose faux pas and lecherous escapades caused the Department no end of embarrassment. The professionals were constantly having to cover up his indiscretions. Two weeks after arriving in Italy, he had been detained briefly by hotel security guards in Milan after having chased a 16-year old girl from an official reception to her room where he tried to break in the door. The Italian prime minister personally intervened with the publisher of a major Rome newspaper which was preparing to report that the American ambassador regularly had prostitutes delivered to the embassy guest house. When asked at a press conference about policy differences between Italy and the United States over aid to the former Soviet republics, Mortimer blurted, "Fuck 'em! The Russians lived by communism. Let 'em die by communism!" The latter statement was followed by a quick retraction and "clarification" from the embassy. And feeling forever constrained by security restrictions, Mortimer often eluded his protective detail for unescorted walks in shopping areas or drives to the countryside in his red Fiat Spider.

The Italians knew the score. They were the inventors of modern statecraft. The U.S. embassy was merely bypassed whenever important policy issues arose. The Italian ambassador in Washington was an urbane diplomatic professional with close ties to White House and congressional figures. The American and Italian leaderships alike either picked up the phone or used Italy's Ambassador Orlani whenever they had anything serious to say to one another. The American embassy in Rome was good at issuing visas and attending to incarcerated or deceased Americans, but not much more. Like a gargoyle on a lesser cathedral, Mortimer was shown respect but was otherwise paid little attention.

As he drove with his windshield wipers at full speed through a cascading spring rain storm, the thought crossed Innes's mind that perhaps, just perhaps, our bungling boor of an ambassador had brought foul play upon himself in a very direct way. Considering some of the sleazy denizens he associated with and his penchant for being in the wrong place at the wrong time, anything was possible. That moron may cause us as much trouble in death as he did alive, Innes thought.

CHAPTER THREE

The flight to Rome made Bob Innes nauseous. Air travel never agreed with him. Flying government-mandated economy class with its insipid food, knee-capping seat proximity and concentration camp congestedness merely ensured he would vomit if the trip was longer than six hours.

"You all right Bob?" asked Innes's fellow traveler to his left. "You're looking green around the gills, boy."

"I don't know if it's the flight or my magic elixir of Pepto-Bismol and dramamine that's doing me in," Innes replied to the diplomatic security man, part of the fourteen-person delegation being dispatched to investigate Mortimer's murder.

Bob hated the meal, stale salad and rubber chicken. He hated the movie selection, some airhead comedies and a B-grade flick about dancers in New York. He hated most of all traveling with delegations. The government had to do everything by committee. No wonder so little ever got done. This was the worst kind of delegation, however; a mish-mash one comprised partly of bureaucrats from domestic agencies like the FBI and Justice, novices to international travel who required babying the whole time.

The rest of the group, from CIA, Defense, and State, looked to Innes like the pasty-faced, per diem-gouging, anal retentive types that typically populated traveling government committees.

He fought not to be included in the team, but lost out on three counts: he worked in the office of the Secretary, he spoke fluent Italian, and he was available.

Innes's job was to provide all-round support to the head of the team, the self-important legal advisor brought into the Department a crusty Boston law firm. He was to coordinate arrangements with the embassy, act as notetaker at meetings with Italian officials, write cables and interact with host country authorities.

Whisked through immigration and customs at Rome's Fiumicino Airport just after sun-up, the group was taken directly to the embassy where it was briefed by Baldwin, Kobalski and CIA station chief Hempstead and sent on its way directly to the first meeting, with the Interior Minister. Hotel check-in would have to wait, usual for such travel.

Great, thought Innes to himself. No food, no shower, no rest. Vomiting appeared to be a distinct possibility.

Renowned Italian hospitality averted catastrophe, however. In the high-ceilinged baroque meeting room of the former palazzo that housed the Italian Interior Ministry, rich strong espresso and assorted biscotti were served to the delegation. Wafts of the coffee's aromatic vapors enticed the senses, its ingestion shot life back into weary limbs and foggy minds.

"It is with great sadness and shock that I receive you here today," began Ambrolini, an urbane politician descended from Italy's former royal family. Innes recalled that he was a rare straight arrow among Italian politicians, unbesmirched by involvement in the country's pervasive corruption.

"Since I spoke with Mr. Baldwin yesterday, we have uncovered little new information, but the investigation continues. If we look closely at the facts, we find the following: Ambassador Mortimer was without his bodyguard, he was found in a section of the city that foreigners usually do not venture into and he was killed at approximately 2:00 am."

An aide pointed to the location of the murder on a mounted map of the city of Rome. Two other display boards exhibited black and white photographs of the body and surroundings where it was found.

"A key question is, what was Ambassador Mortimer doing out in that part of the city without protection, without his driver, all alone?" asked Ambrolini. "We know it was not robbery; his money and valuables were untouched."

In paced deliberate motions, Bernard J. Scher pulled a pipe from his worn tweed jacket, patiently loaded the tobacco, not once lifting his eyes from the task at hand. Only after two calculated puffs did the State Department's chief lawyer fix his zinc irises on the Minister.

"Now, the way we see it, this assassination of the President's envoy to this country comes on the heels of the bombing of the Egyptian embassy, a plane hijacking to Sudan, the unexplained escape from one of your high security prisons of Abu Khalid Jihad -- key hitman for the Front for the Liberation of Palestine -- and a spate of threats against American military personnel here by al-Qaida and assorted exiled Saudi radicals, all within the past four months," Scher pontificated, totally ignoring the line Ambrolini was pursuing. "I don't think that I need to emphasize that Roland Mortimer was a staunch supporter of Israel, had conducted assiduous fund-raising among Jewish voters in his state. This alone would mark him as a target for Middle East Muslim extremists."

The Minister stiffened. "I see what you're getting at," he said. "But this case has none of the hallmarks of a terrorist attack. If you will bear with me for a moment, our experts will outline for you the details." He gestured to a uniformed police officer. "Major Arno, of our domestic intelligence division, will give an analysis of --"

"What measures have you taken in the last twenty-four hours to track the movements of and collect intelligence on the Islamic radical groups and Middle East crazies that are running around freely in this country?" Scher demanded as he calmly placed his briar on the conference table exactly equidistant between his reposed arms.

"Believe me, Mr. Scher, we will pursue all leads--"

"Pardon my bluntness, Minister, but while your people are tracking down 'all leads' the perpetrators are getting away. Let's face it, the current political climate here is not exactly conducive to getting quick action against evil-doers." Scher was alluding to the political turmoil Italy was going through over corruption scandals rocking the government and mafia murders of judges and mayors in the south.

His carefully calibrated coolness melting steadily, Ambrolini retorted, "While we are speaking frankly with each other, I would like to note that Ambassador Mortimer associated himself with people which an ambassador normally does not befriend. My government has gone to exceptional lengths to protect the late ambassador's reputation. We all know his fondness for *putane*, for reckless behavior, for prowling around bars and bawdy houses. This man invited trouble."

"God knows, he escaped our purview all the time, never wanted to cooperate with security," added a nodding RSO Kobalski, trying to be helpful.

Scher shot a frosty gaze at Kobalski with the implied message of "Shut your big trap you dumbass."

The meeting went nowhere.

After five days, with the investigation going in circles, the embassy was divided between those who bought off on the Italian scenario and those inclined to believe that terrorists had greased the ambassador. The security types leaned toward the former, while the intelligence people largely supported the latter. Chargé Baldwin tried his best to be an impartial searcher of the truth, while simultaneously seeking to avoid an open split with the Italian government. Innes had had it. The cables he drafted back to Washington reflected divisions and ennui. It was 6:00 pm, he had put the finishing touches on that day's cable to Washington ("Mortimer Sitrep: No Leads as Italian Authorities Go After African Gangs").

His conversation with his wife earlier in the day had gone badly. No surprise really. He phoned in to check on things. Davey had the flu. She was working double shift this week. When would he be back? No Hello darling! How's Rome? How's the food? How's the investigation going? Innes had been wanting to take the family off to Mazatlán for a week. Somehow, it kept being put off. He had to work things out with Carolyn. Start off with a nice dinner at the Balkan Crown, their favorite, the night after he got back. Just the two of them. Line up a babysitter, call in sick on the night shift…hmmm.

He sat slumped at a desk in the political section of the embassy, mulling this over, sipping a warm coke. Colleen McCoy, Ambassador Mortimer's staff aide, entered to shred the day's classified traffic.

"Hi, your cable went out okay. It was the last for the day," she said, more as small talk than to inform.

"Last and useless," Innes said sharply, regretting too late his sarcastic slip.

"What do you think, will this investigation get anywhere? You may as well see this now. It just came in."

She showed him a Nodis telegram from the Department. Nodis -- No Distribution -- was the channel reserved for sensitive correspondence between the Secretary of State and his ambassadors. In actual practice, however, quite a number of bureaucrats had access to Nodises, but photocopies were strictly forbidden. Staff aides, like Colleen, as controllers of the information flow to their bosses, saw most everything they saw.

SECRET/NODIS
TO: AMEMBASSY ROME, IMMEDIATE
FROM: SECSTATE WASHDC
FOR SCHER
ALSO FOR CHARGE
SUBJECT: MORTIMER INVESTIGATION

1. SECRET - ENTIRE TEXT.

2. DEPARTMENT AND WHITE HOUSE REMAIN CONCERNED OVER LACK OF PROGRESS ON THE MORTIMER INVESTIGATION. HOUSE SUBCOMMITTEE ON FOREIGN OPERATIONS IS PLANNING TO SCHEDULE HEARINGS. MEDIA ATTENTION CONTINUES TO BE STRONG. PRESIDENT HAS DECIDED TO FORM AN INTERAGENCY WORKING GROUP TO RESTRUCTURE INVESTIGATION.

3. FOR SCHER: IN LIGHT OF LACK OF EVIDENCE
AND APPARENT INABILITY OF GOVERNMENT OF
ITALY TO GET TO THE BOTTOM OF THIS CASE,
YOU ARE INSTRUCTED TO PREPARE YOUR FINAL
REPORT AND RETURN TO WASHINGTON BY END
OF THE WEEK.

4. FOR CHARGE: IN LIGHT OF CONTINUING LACK
OF RESULTS, REQUEST THAT YOU RAISE USG'S
CONTINUING CONCERNS AT THE HIGHEST
LEVELS OF THE GOI. TALKING POINTS WILL BE
FORWARDED VIA SEPARATE TELEGRAM.
DENNISON

"The papers and the networks are all over the
administration on this thing," Colleen said as she handed
Innes the daily wireless file, a compilation of headline
stories in the major U.S. papers.
"U.S. Envoy's Murder Still a Mystery," declared *The
New York Times*. "State Department Bungles Murder
Investigation," announced *The Washington Post*.
Innes shook his head as he read. "This is bad, real bad.
But you know, they're right. This whole so-called
investigation is a total farce. Both we and the Italians are
barking up the wrong trees."
Colleen looked at him with a start, her ear-length
chestnut hair falling forward on her cheeks. "Do you know
something that the rest don't?"
"No. But they're going in the wrong directions. Scher
seems to have some political agenda. In any case, he's
obsessed by terrorists, and the Italians have Africans on the
brain. Kobalski doesn't know what he's doing except to try
frantically to cover his fat behind. If everybody is so well
aware of Mortimer's meanderings, even though they've kept

some kind of conspiracy of silence about them, then why not just go to his haunts and start asking questions? The guy's dead, for Christ sake. Who cares about his reputation now?"

"Maybe that's just it. Maybe the Secretary and the White House are more concerned with keeping any whiff of scandal from the administration. Next year the President's up for re-election, right? Which headlines would you prefer if you were him? 'Al-Qaida Assassinated U.S. Ambassador' or 'Horny Envoy, President's Pal, Offed by Pimps'?"

Innes's haggard face broke into a smile, the first since he left D.C.

"Tell me this. Here you worked closely with Mortimer for a year. You must've known about his private life. Just the bits and pieces we heard in Washington, sounded like he was the Flying Walenda of the boudoir."

Colleen bit her lip, shifted her eyes as she contemplated. She gripped her left elbow with her right hand as she leaned against a low cabinet piled high with back issues of *La Stampa, Corriere della Sera,* and *International Herald Tribune.* She was clad in a smooth pink skirt ending just above the knee and a simple white blouse. At all of 24 years of age, Colleen McCoy, lost in thought, looked vulnerable and scrumptious.

"I don't know," she began uncertainly. "It's not like he was around all that much when you come down to it."

"You mean he played hooky from the office?" Innes tried to shift nonchalantly in his chair in such a way as to conceal his hard-on. Colleen caught it and stifled a knowing smile. She folded her arms and took three paces in the direction of the ambassador's office which lay across a circular foyer. She stared at the office across the way.

"You know, this has not been an ideal first tour. I've been in for a year and a half, I come to this huge embassy and end up working for a wild non-career ambassador who was a virtual stranger at the office and a public embarrassment." She swung around, arms still folded in front of her.

"I don't know. We really never knew where he would go off to after hours. Even during work hours we didn't know his whereabouts half the time. Joe has kept things on an even keel. Everybody went to Joe -- embassy folks, the prime minister, foreign minister, you name it. This place has been like a ship with a ghost captain. But somehow, we kept it on course."

Innes leaned forward at his desk and shot back the remainder of the stale Coke. He was now limp.

"In the Department we kept hearing rumors of wild parties at the residence and the ambassador carousing at all hours in town."

"He had friends -- outside friends. The drivers apparently know a little bit. They've whispered around that Ambassador Mortimer frequented several bars and other establishments in the red light areas. But it's strange. Since his son died in a car accident last summer, he was spouting off about repentance, 'Jesus loves us.' Religious stuff like that."

"So, the man was full of contradictions. What's his driver's name?" Innes asked.

Colleen looked into his eyes. "Pietro. Pietro Molinaro." Catching on to Innes's thinking, she quickly added, "He's still here, I think. If we run, we might catch him before his quitting time." She took his hand and pulled him out of his chair with a forceful tug. The two raced through the foyer, down the gray marble staircase and out of the chancery toward the motor pool.

They caught Pietro Molinaro just before he headed out of the embassy front gate.

"Signore, Signorina, I have worked for eight ambassadors. Some were good men. Some, not so good. Most okay. Ambassador Mortimer, he was kind to me, always making the jokes. I don't think his heart was into this work, I will tell you frankly. He was not comfortable being America's ambassador. I think, after a while, he longed for people like he knew in America before coming here. His son's death, very bad. I drove him to church in the last few weeks. A Protestant church. He went there to pray." Molinaro, 55, gray, but still slim, obviously gave careful forethought to his statements.

"Pietro, can you tell us where he hung out when he slipped away at night?" Innes queried.

"Eh, you know, I did not drive him normally to unofficial things. Sometimes, he take a taxi, sometimes, friends pick him up. Even he drove himself at times." Molinaro wiped his brow with his chauffeur's cap. "But two, three times, I drove him to a bar in the east of the city. It is called..." He scratched his chin as he searched his brain. "Si! 'La Dolce Vita.' I think other drivers, they take him there too. You ask them."

"La Dolce Vita" was one of several dozen unextraordinary drinking establishments that catered largely to male German tourists, working class northern European visitors on the prowl and the occasional Korean or Japanese traveling businessmen with lots of money but zero sense of what constituted class on the European continent. A really bad jazz band boomed a barely recognizable Al Jarreau tune.

Armed with a newspaper photo of the late ambassador, Innes and Colleen shouted above the din to the bartender and waitresses, asking if they had seen the man in recently. The bartender, a bald middle-aged nonentity with a keenly honed sense of how to mind his own business, simply shook his frowning face as he idly wiped the bar. "No, non mai l'ho visto." Never seen him. Ditto with the waitresses. Either they hit the wrong shift, or here was another kind of conspiracy of silence, or Mortimer had never patronized the place, or at least not frequently.

"Let's try some of the other joints nearby," Innes said.

Colleen checked her watch. It had been a long day. But with a deep breath of resignation and a quick shrug, she indicated, why not?

Same results at the "Il Gatto Nero," "La Casa Bianca," "Il Trovatore," "Dude's" and a handful of similar watering holes that Innes and Colleen wouldn't dream of stepping into under normal circumstances.

"Club Il Oriente é Rosso," "The East is Red Club," beamed down in hot pink fluorescent lights. Ersatz bamboo decked the front. In the window, Chinese parasols flanked an oversized balloon bottle of Tsingtao beer.

"Bob! Let's quit," whined Colleen as she slumped her arms forward in a gesture of exasperation. "I'm tired, it's late and this is getting to me."

"Last one, Colleen. Promise!" Innes grabbed Colleen's hand and pulled her along, her feet dragged like those of a child when being taken to the dentist.

Their eyes needed time to adjust to a murky interior in which a blue haze of smoke permeated the darkness. Dim bulbs enclosed in Chinese paper lanterns, which hung here and there from the low ceiling, provided the only light except for the tiny flickers of candles encased in red glass holders that sat atop minuscule round cocktail tables. A

panorama of a south Pacific beach served as backdrop to
the long curved bar, itself sheltered by panels of rough
thatch in what obviously was some interior decorator's
adolescent vision of an exotic eastern locale. Hostesses,
mostly Asian and decked out in red silk tunics, chatted it up
with a male clientele that reminded Innes of extras from the
movie "Good Fellas." Bethatched private cubicles lined the
walls. A poster mounted next to the stage featured an
enlarged photo of three grinning scantily clad Asian
women, one wrapped around a saxophone, another
caressing an electric guitar, the center one clutching a
microphone with both hands. "The Gang of Three," shilled
the advertisement. "Direct from Taipei!"

Colleen gaped wide-eyed and slack-jawed around her.
"They've got to be kidding. This must be somebody's idea
of a bad joke," she said.

"Hello! Table for two?" asked a thirtyish Asian woman
in English.

"Uh, yes," answered Innes. He signaled to a corner
table.

"You like a drink?" asked the hostess as they were
seated. "Special house cocktail is Kon Tiki Cooler. You
Americans, huh?"

"How about a Ricard straight up and…"

"An Orangina," finished Colleen.

Innes answered her question, "Yes, we're Americans.
Do many Americans come here?"

"Oh, some in summer months," the hostess replied,
obviously pleased to converse with Yanks.

Wasting little time, Innes pulled out the now fraying
newspaper photo of Mortimer. "Ever seen this man in
here?"

"This man look familiar," she responded as she studied the picture closely. "I think Mikki know this man. I get her. You wait. Drinks come in a minute, okay?"

A Ricard, an Orangina and Mikki all appeared exactly eight minutes later.

"Hi, where are you from?" a tired Innes asked in a feeble stab at small talk.

"Thailand," answered Mikki, a diminutive female in her early twenties. Mikki fidgeted, eyes flitted nervously. She held her right wrist with her left hand.

"Well, er, do you know this..."

"Yeah," interjected Mikki. "I see him sometime. He come. Not too often. Only see. Nothing else."

Two tables away, a fat man with bushy black-gray hair snorted. "Eh, Mikki! Ven aca, Mikki! Che cosa stai facendo tu?! Eh!" he yelled, cranking his arm in a gesture to return. Innes recognized instantly the strong Sicilian accent.

Mikki looked anxiously over her shoulder. Her eyes said "I have to go."

Innes pulled out one of his cards and quickly scribbled his hotel and room number. "Give me a call. Please."

"Yeah. Maybe I do," she rejoined; she took the card and stuffed it into a side pocket of her red tunic.

As if on cue, Colleen and Innes looked at each other with raised eyebrows expressing "Bingo!"

It was showtime as the Gang of Three strutted out onto the small stage, clad only in teensy gold G-strings. A greasy emcee introduced them.

A wiry, beetle-browed man with a scowl affixed to his pock-marked face sauntered over from the fat man's table, held a menacing gaze on the Americans, then grabbed Mikki by the arm, abruptly turned and pulled her back.

"Bob, I really don't like this!"

Innes was sold. "Yeah, let's go." He left some euros on the table and the two left.

Next day, the Mortimer investigative team slapped together a final report with a schizophrenic conclusion that shed more confusion than light. The team members were scheduled to catch the Friday afternoon Delta flight to JFK, connecting onward to Dulles. Most of them began breaking away for some rushed last minute shopping. Innes was packing his bags, waiting for a phone call that didn't come. He had to give up. Mike Hammer he wasn't. If Mikki wouldn't call, then so be it. And she didn't.

Innes killed time at Fiumicino browsing half-consciously among the usual displays of perfumes, Rolexes, silk ties, cognacs and whiskeys and overpriced kitsch at the duty free shops. He managed to escape from the rest of the team members, who, on the way to the airport, droned on and on about how the 'Skins would do this season. There was only one thing in the universe that Innes enjoyed doing more than prattling on about ball games and that was getting a root canal without an anesthetic.

He pondered Colleen. She surprised him by showing up at the terminal to bid farewell. "Good luck!" she chirped as she pecked him ever so lightly on the lips, which caused him to have to shift his posture again. "Stay in touch!" she shouted as she rushed back.

Delta 161 was now boarding, announced the public address system. Innes snapped to, slung his carry-on bag over his shoulder and quickened his step in the direction of Gate 47.

"Signore! Signore!" called a female voice behind him.
A hand touched his shoulder. Innes turned to find a
striking blonde with crystalline blue eyes. At five-foot-ten,
she possessed an unself-conscious, radiant beauty.

"Signore Innes?" she queried with a slight inquisitive
nod.

"Yes?"

"I am a...friend of Mikki's," she continued. Her Italian
was broken and accented, Slavic Innes thought.

"I understand you are friend of Morty's," she continued,
switching to English.

"Morty? Uh, you might say that, yeah."

The blonde took a deep breath and pensively poked her
tongue in the corner of her mouth. The crystalline gems
looked briefly to each side as her mind raced to select her
next words, then fixed directly into his eyes.

"I knew Morty." She shifted her gaze to each side every
few seconds. "He was fun-loving, not bad man. But his
friends...his friends, they are very bad, some of them."

They were announcing the final call for boarding Delta
161.

Seeing that time had run out, Innes wanted her to get to
the point. "What is it you want to tell me?"

"Some terrible people were after him. At first, we did
not know he was American ambassador. He did not tell us
this. What happened to him is no surprise, believe me!"

"And...?"

"You should stay out, Mr. Innes. Go home. Stay there.
Drop what you are doing. It is too dangerous. Believe
me."

"What's your name? How can I reach you?"

"No...No. I must go now. You will never see me
again." With her long legs, the woman strode swiftly back
toward the main terminal.

"Wait! Please! Come back! I won't tell anyone."

"*Ciao*, Mr. Innes," she said as she skipped away, enclosing a black fur-lined coat around a shapely frame.

CHAPTER FOUR

"Hey boss!"

"How many times I gotta tell you not to call me that, godammit! You call me that, next thing you know people start calling me the 'Boss of Bosses'! Cut it out, *capisce*?"

Two months after the trial, Al remained testy and as paranoid as ever. After all, the Feds were everywhere. No doubt about it. No telling how many listening devices insidiously picked up every word he said, how many informants the Fibbies may have infiltrated into the structure. Besides, if Al was to exude legitimacy, Mr. Malandrino, or just plain Al, were proper. Boss, *Don* and other such appellations misled, misinformed, tarnished the image of respectability that Al was so carefully cultivating.

The brunt of his wrath was Joey "Bags" Giambonzano. Joey's dad had worked for Al's father, Carlo, who, in the old days, had been known affectionately as "Chick" by just about everybody who was anybody in New York. So Joey, the heir of bequeathed nepotism, had a sinecure for life. Joey, all 135 pounds of him, liked to work out at the boxing gym, hence "Bags." He wasn't too bright, but he was loyal and could be trusted.

"Yeah, sorry there, bo--, I mean Al. Yeah, sure, I'll watch it, yeah."

"What do you want?" Al demanded.

"Our friends from the east, they wanna see youse."

"Dumbass. Not here!" Al then mimed that they should step out for a walk. He pointed a finger at his ear and then to a wall, signaling that the latter could hear.

"Yeah, gotcha," responded Joey as they left through the back door into an alley lined with garbage cans, parked cars and dumpsters.

As they strolled to nowhere special, Joey resumed relating his message. "Our pal there, Yakov, just got in. His people called this morning. Say he wants a meeting as soon as we can swing it. Somewheres safe and secure. Know what I mean?"

"Same place?"

"Yeah, Brighton Beach again. They like it there. With their own kind and all."

"Okay. Tell Yakov I'll meet him at the same place today. Late lunch. But only the three of us know. You get me? Start blabbing over the phone or telling others and you can be sure the goddamn Feds will know too."

"You got it b--, I mean Al. I'll go over there myself, personal. Just like before."

Al was of the new generation of his ilk. With the great globalization of world commerce over the preceding two-and-a-half decades, all businessmen needed to adjust, be flexible, if they were to survive in the world market place. The Japanese now owned Rockefeller Center. The Germans produced Mercedes in Mississippi. Labor unions had given up on picketing over "foreign" auto and tractor imports -- transmissions made in Tennessee were hooked up to engines manufactured in Germany with carburetors built in Brazil, perhaps encased in a body cast in Canada.

Earth-moving equipment assembled in Illinois was the product of "Fiat-Allis."

Along with his counterparts at IBM, GE and Exxon, Al went with the flow, adapted, opened up and reached out. His father's generation had run their businesses in a cozy, ethnic cocoon comprised overwhelmingly of Sicilians, with modus vivendi relationships with the Irish and Jews. Al, on the other hand, was diversified. He had forged fruitful business connections with Chinese, Israelis, Colombians and others. The most promising relationship, however, was turning out to be with emigres from the ex-Soviet Union, many of whom had settled in the Brighton Beach neighborhood of Brooklyn. Unlike the Colombians, who were vicious but not very clever, or the Chinese, who were clever yet unreadable, the Russians combined braininess with ruthlessness. And unlike some of the other groups, they could be trusted to keep a deal as well as their word. The Russians brought with them old world values, something even third generation Sicilian-Americans could feel comfortable with.

The "Café Novoye Rossiya" exuded warmth, especially on a late fall day in New York. Its narrow but long confines were heated by old fashioned radiators. A large brass samovar shared space with a locomotive-like coffee machine at the bar in the rear. Great wafts of steam, interlaced with the rich aromas of Ceylonese teas and Turkish coffee, billowed to the high pale-green ceiling bordered by plaster rococo of the gilded age. The bay windows jutting to the ice-covered sidewalk sweated from the released vapors. Mama Irina Boronova, the rotund jocular proprietor, mothered over her customers, mostly

working men, many taxi drivers, who huddled at the little
tables flush against wainscoted walls.

Yakov was seated at a rear table, waiting for Al. He
cracked a broad smile as Al entered the cafe, Mama
Boronova taking his coat and Bags's. Yakov half-rose from
his chair and extended his right hand in a show of welcome.
Yes, Al liked these people. They had couth, manners,
respect for colleagues. Trust, however, he reserved for no
one.

"Ah, Al! It is too long since we meet," Yakov greeted in
his thick Russian accent. He put an arm around Al's
shoulder, slapped him heartily on the back and embraced
him. "You look too skinny. You are not eating? Come,
we eat blini together. I order already. Mama B., she is
bringing out."

"Hey! I'm trying to lose weight. What're you trying to
do, kill me?" Al slapped his belly, then poked at Yakov's
playfully. Bags took a seat next to Yakov's two poker-
faced aides.

"I want to kill some people, but you are not one," Yakov
said with a stiff smile. The two took seats across from each
other.

"Your trial. My heart was with you," Yakov said, his
unreadable hazel eyes and Cheshire grin illuminating a
broad face.

Al grunted. "You know me. They'll never get me.
Maybe I'm smart. But more important than that, I got
lawyers even smarter than me."

"But you know they won't give up. Same now in
Russia. People demand justice, so government goes after
businessmen. Businessmen, gangsters; Russian people still
do not know difference. They still think like communists.
Anybody who makes money is bad. They want everybody
to be poor, like in old days."

"Yeah, just like here. They go after the businessmen, like me. And then they tax to death anybody who does okay for himself. So, we got government harassment and lots of poor people. But the FBI, the Manhattan D.A., they want to nail me bad, in particular. I've bitten them in the ass too many times and got away with it. They don't like that."

Mama Boronova brought a large plate of freshly made cream cheese blinis and a pot of steaming coffee.

Al waited until she departed and no other outsiders were nearby. "So?" he said.

With a single, curt nod, Yakov indicated that he was ready to get down to business. "Al, business is not so good. In fact, very bad. Last week, DEA hit my warehouses. They find nothing. But I am very worried. Legitimate contacts, they think I am crook. Afraid to do business with me."

"Cost of doing business. After that goddamn trial, people don't want to know me. If it wasn't for some old friends, I'd be out of business completely. Construction keeps me going. Some old customers keep the jobs coming. And I've tightened up running things."

"Yes, I heard. Good move to hire young soldier to handle security."

Yakov always had solid information, excellent sources. Invariably, he knew who was doing what to whom, who was doing well and who not, and why; who was sleeping with whom. This inside knowledge on the part of a relative newcomer spooked Al and imbued in him an element of mistrust toward his slick foreign friend. Yakov placed both hands on the table, leaned forward, looked side-to-side, then unsmilingly locked his eyes on Al's.

"Al, I need that special information like we used to get before."

Al blinked as if sand had just blown in his face. He shifted uneasily, leaned forward inches from Yakov's face. "Look, in case you didn't know, what with all your secret sources, I'm trying to lay low. For all I know, the friggin' FBI may be listening to us through that goddamn coffee pot." Al's jugular and the veins in his temples pulsed.

Sore subject, Yakov could see. Putting on an expression of concerned sympathy, he signaled for Al to calm down. He leaned back in his chair. Bags was instantly alert and jumpy, like a hunting dog at the surge of a flock of ducks. Yakov's two faceless flunkies barely stirred, yet monitored every move with hawk-like attention.

A minute of tense silence followed. Yakov grinned and proceeded to dish out three hot blinis onto Al's plate. Extending his arm to it, Yakov commanded, "Eat. Best in Brighton Beach." He dug in with the table manners of a Visigoth. The others joined in.

After three solid minutes of forks hitting plates and loud chewing, Yakov spoke up again.

"Al, times are not so good. Both of us have problems. Good business requires good information. Contacts to pull strings to make things happen the way we want them. Six months ago, before your troubles, such information flowed like melted gold." Pointing to Al with an up-ended palm, and then back to himself, Yakov continued, "I help you and you help me. Things will get better for us both."

Al looked at Yakov with non-committal eyes as he continued to eat, now more slowly.

"My people, back home, they are ready, but they need important information, they need ..." He searched his brain. "Green light. They need green light that is safe at this end."

Al wiped his mouth roughly with a gray cloth napkin, briskly tongued loose food from his gums and cheeks and, pointing to Yakov with his right index finger just above his dish, said, "Yakov, we've made a lot of money together. We make a good team. You know if I can do it, I will. But right now the time isn't right."

Yakov listened attentively. Mama Boronova interrupted with amiable obliviousness to recommend her currant-covered cheesecake for dessert. Made it herself that very morning. Okay, we'll take five big slices, Yakov exclaimed in Russian without consulting the others.

"I'll tell you what I'll do," Al went on. "Let me get back on my feet, get everything on track. Then, when I feel the heat is off, I'll reactivate some old contacts, make some calls, see what I can do. Right now though, I'm trying to bore the Feds to death."

"Yes, okay." Yakov extended his right hand. The two shook in agreement.

"Dimitrov here," Yakov gestured to a humorless flunky with a nasty scar that ran from the top of his forehead, across the left eye and down to the middle of his cheek. "He will be go-between with your people. Dimitrov is discreet. He is quiet. He will make sure that communications do not break down," Yakov added more as a veiled threat than a mere statement. Dimitrov's rugged face remained impassive, a granite mask.

"Yeah, right. For the time being, have him call me direct. I'm sorting things out right now. Lots of personnel changes."

After protests all around that they couldn't eat another morsel, the table of "business associates" attacked the cheesecake.

Al's paranoia about frequenting the same establishments went by the wayside when it came to Pironi's. In business steadily since the turn of the century, Pironi's was a haunt of several generations of Malandrinos. Al's niece, in fact, had married the son of the proprietor. Al had a semiconscious superstition about the place, that it held a metaphysical immunity. Like some mystical Wagnerian Ring, it kept the Feds at a safe distance. He ordered a pot of espresso and some biscotti.

Richard Anthony "Ricky" Laguzza walked in. Ricky was Al's nephew, the adopted son of Francesco "Little Shoes" Fagliarone, a long-time Colombo stalwart and politically influential *don* who died a natural death at 89. "Uncle Cheech," as he was affectionately known, never had a blood son. After Ricky's widowed father became a fatal casualty in the Riccobene Wars of 1982-84, Cheech took his boy under his wing. What the flashy, young street tough failed to learn in the way of class from the older man, he made up for in a singular lust for getting his own way.

"I just had East-West talks with our pals again," Al said as he shoveled a fourth spoonful of sugar into the demitasse. He signaled for Ricky to sit.

As he took a seat, Ricky straightened his gray sharkskin suit over a muscled frame otherwise clad in a black T-shirt and no socks. "What, the Russians?"

"Yakov. He's getting impatient. Wants insider information again. Told him things are still too hot."

Ricky grunted and slurped his coffee after gulping a cannolli down in one bite. He cast a lascivious eye at a well-proportioned waitress who whisked by with a tray of antipasti. "This gonna be a regular thing, or what?"

"Naw. Too risky. His guy, that, uh, Dimitrov guy. He's the go-between."

Ricky choked, spraying a fine mist of Lavazza on the lapels of his silk Guido Ceruti suit.

"*Minghia!* Uncle Al. Not that guy. He's a fuckin' nightmare on two legs. He's wigged out. He makes me look normal."

"You two have a lot in common," Al said with a smirk. "That's why you're gonna deal with him on my behalf." Al raised a hand and closed his eyes before Ricky could get a word out.

"I can't take any chances. You know that. Yakov says the DEA just raided his warehouses, in Jersey. The heat's on him just like it's on me. I can't afford to be careless. He thinks he's still in Moscow where all the cops are on the take and things are out of control. Let him take all the risks. That's why I need a buffer -- and you're it."

"You saw the job they done on Morty. So, the guy had it coming. But, Christ, they didn't have to turn him into chopped meat. Yakov's okay. For a Jew. We all make money together. But his men, they all did duty in Afghanistan and Chechnya. Made 'em all gonzo. They all got that post … shell-shocked syndrome, or whatever the hell they call it. They'll shoot you dead just to see if their gun works"

Al gestured that he didn't want to hear any more objections. "What're you doing lately? Back to collecting rents. Hustling for Al-Mac Construction. Making sure all our mom 'n' pop bookies keep the payments up."

Ricky looked away.

"I don't know about you, but I'm bored stiff. More important, Al Persico, Barney Bellomo, you think they aren't watching us? They're just waiting to pounce. They see the first sign we're floundering, BAM! They'll hit us so hard, it'll make our heads spin."

"Barney's in the slammer."

"Slammer, schlammer! These guys can run their outfits out of a whale's ass. They smell weakness like a fly smells shit. Believe me. They'll hear about Al Malandrino being on the ropes faster than I will."

Ricky reflected silently for several minutes, his eyes locked onto the sugar bowl as he aimlessly churned the contents with a spoon. He had come a long way since Uncle Cheech rescued him from certain hard time in the joint when he was only seventeen. Cheech worked the system to get Ricky off on a murder one rap. He had kidnapped Joey Lupica, a rival suitor for Ricky's girl, tied him up and slammed him repeatedly in the head with a two-by-four. After Cheech worked his magic, all the witnesses developed amnesia, the prosecutors became anemic and the jury very open-minded. While he possessed as much conscience as a protozoa, Ricky felt eternally loyal to his new family, especially Al Malandrino.

"Okay, Uncle Al. You're right. You're always right. What do I gotta do?"

"You contact Dimitrov. Keep your ears open and be ready to pass messages."

"Sounds like the goddamn 'hot line'."

"You bet, Ricky. This way, we avoid misunderstandings. Who knows, maybe even a war." Al smiled, then devoured a chocolate biscotto.

Pironi's antique, wood-and-glass, lace-curtained door opened. Wentworth's fresh, All-American face poked itself in, the blue-gray eyes scanning the place.

"Hey Chuckie!" Al shouted, waving one arm. "Over here! Whaddya doin', Chuckie? Lookin' out for some tail?" Al winked and nudged a decidedly unenthusiastic Ricky in the ribs as the latter downed a glass of Pellegrino. Ricky half-raised his left arm to deflect his uncle's light pugilistic jab.

Al motioned Wentworth to have a seat. They shook hands. Ricky offered a limp wrist, almost as an afterthought.

"So, you guys have met?" Al asked.

"Yeah," Ricky murmured. "Ran into each other at the Al-Mac office. Wasn't it Chuckster?" Ricky's deadpan eyes challenged Wentworth's.

"It's Chuck," Wentworth corrected him.

"Whatever." His attention was suddenly captured by a well-filled leather miniskirt sashaying on the street outside the window displaying "Pironi's" in gilt, cursive lettering.

Al motioned for Wentworth to take the seat next to him. "So, what's up, Chuckie-boy?"

"It's 'Chuck'!" Ricky interjected sarcastically.

Al shot a reproachful look at Ricky, then turned back to Wentworth.

"Well, Mr. Malandrino…uh, Al, I just needed you to sign these papers to hire two more employees -- newly retired army sergeants -- to help me out on security matters. They'd also double as warehouse foremen to replace two that we fired recently. So you'd be getting twice your money's worth." He handed Al a sheaf of papers.

After scribbling his signature quickly and handing back the documents, Al slapped Wentworth on the shoulder. "You're a good kid, Chuckie. Doin' a terrific job. Anytime you need anything, you let me know. Don't be shy."

"You've been more than generous, sir." Wentworth then excused himself, begging off coffee and biscotti, and departed.

"That kid's a real piece of work, Uncle Al. I can't believe you hired a guy like that."

"What's your problem, anyway?" Al said. "I get somebody who can clean up the mess over at Al-Mac and

you dump all over him. I never saw you shakin' the tree
over there, little nephew."

"It's just that we got Beaver Cleaver working at
Gangsters R Us. He'll get in the way."

"I think I see the problem now," Al said. "You're
jealous! Ol' Chuckie there gets more done in two months
than you did in two years over at Al-Mac"

"Gimme a break. If I wasn't here, all your goombah
competitors would be all over you. Not to mention the
fuckin' Spanish, Chinese and any other greaseball
hoodlums jumpin' out of the melting pot demanding a piece
of the action."

Al gestured that he'd had enough. "Chuckie Wentworth
has what you and I never had: trust. He also happens to be
very good at what he does. Finally, the guy adds
respectability at a time when the businesses -- and I --
really need it. So, I'm not asking, but I'm telling you: Get
along with him. Help him out. When you help him, you
help the family. You obstruct him, you hurt the family.
Capisce?"

Ricky nodded.

CHAPTER FIVE

The "Wen-ching Ho" had been unloaded of its cargo, its crew either at quarters or taking in as much as they could of New York in two nights time. Customs did its thing checking the cargo and cleared the whole lot of canned food and electronic components from China after some cursory checks. Homeland Security was a bit more vigorous. Washington was tied in knots over a veritable armada of cargo ships, fishing vessels and scows from the Orient transporting hundreds of illegal Chinese immigrants to the U.S. This on top of fear, verging on paranoia, that al-Qaida would try to smuggle a "dirty bomb" into the country. After three hours of thoroughly screening the ship's crew and poking into every conceivable crevice, the Feds gave a clean bill of health and departed.

Customs agent Ed O'Meara lingered behind. He had unfinished business.

He met with Ricky as agreed, in the warehouse dispatcher's office at 8:00 pm. Ricky sat comfortably behind the gray metal desk in the small windowed cubicle smoking a cigar.

"Edmund! Lookin' good!" he greeted the customs agent in a voice of mock sincerity. "How's the wife, the kids, the mortgage?" he cracked in barely disguised ridicule.

"Fine, fine," Ed replied impatiently. "Let's get this out of the way, and we can both go home."

"What's the matter, Ed? Job getting you down? Haven't they given you the annual step increase yet? What about that promotion? You a GS-11 yet, Ed?"

"Yeah, real funny Mr. Laguzza. Can we get this over with, *please*?"

"Sure, why not? Just like to keep up with old friends is all." Ricky got up and gestured to himself. "How do you like the duds, pretty spiffy, huh?" He wore pleated dark green trousers held up with bright red suspenders. The crisp blue longsleeved shirt had a white collar which was closed at the neck with a large brass pin. A broad silk tie with a detailed portrait of flappers around a Model-T graced his neck. Ricky was in one of his yuppie moods. He reached down and grabbed a small duffle.

"Here it is, pal" he said as he dumped the contents onto the desk. Fifty stacks of 20-dollar bills rolled out. "Fifty grand, like we agreed. Take the wifey and kiddies to Disney World."

O'Meara was not amused. He was scared. This was the seventh such dealing he'd had with this man. While it was a very lucrative relationship, the briefer his contact with Ricky, the better. Here's this horse's ass cracking sick jokes, risking getting both of them caught in the process. Security's sake demanded no-muss, no-fuss transactions. Besides, he didn't like the greaseball. This guinea wise-guy is jerking me around, a family man, O'Meara thought.

He hurriedly gathered up the cash back into the bag.

"What's wrong? Aren't you going to count it? Who knows, maybe this time, I'm stiffing you." Ricky took a pensive puff of his Nobile as he regarded the customs man with squinty eyes.

"I trust you, Mr. Laguzza," O'Meara lied. He just wanted to get his ass out of there. With Ricky, he felt like a mouse in the presence of a large cat which delighted in torment. O'Meara dealt with him out of necessity. He had six kids, the twins soon to enter college. His superiors cheated him of promotions. And the government imposed de facto racial and gender quotas for recruitment and promotions. The way O'Meara saw it, they could all go to hell. Fifteen years of looking through people's dirty underwear and crawling into the stinking holds of freighters won him no rewards and little hope for advancement. He had to cut his own deals. Look out for his and his family's welfare. And, after the first plunge, no looking back.

"Hey Eddie, you don't wanna know what you cleared for me?" Ricky queried mischievously, gesturing to a dozen cases of canned lychees.

"The less I know, the better, don't you think, Mr. Laguzza?" O'Meara held the bag in his hand and was poised to sprint out the door.

"You got it, pal. That's what I like about doing business with you, Eddie. You ask no questions. Just take your money and run."

O'Meara nodded once and made his move.

"Just one last question, Eddie." Ricky leaned against a file cabinet with the cigar clenched between his front teeth. Nobody else knows about our little relationship? About this transaction?"

O'Meara jerked his head over either shoulder, as if expecting cops to smash in the doors with sledge hammers any second. His heart churned like the diesel engine of a ship accelerating out of harbor.

"You can trust me, always, Mr. Laguzza. Why should I
tell anybody? I'd only be doing myself in."

"I don't know, Eddie. You micks talk up a big storm
when you pour a couple of beers down your gullet."

Outrage momentarily displaced O'Meara's fright. He
instantly recalled his fireman father knocking the front
teeth out of an Italian shopkeeper when the latter blamed
the elder O'Meara and his fellow firefighters for letting the
man's store go up in flames. The Italian had called the
brigade "a bunch of lazy Irish drunks." Ed O'Meara,
however, knew better than to try to live up to his old man's
reputation.

"Like I told you, nobody. I'd like to leave now."

"Hey. Go," Ricky replied easily, one arm crossed over
his chest, the other gesturing toward the door. "I'll be in
touch."

O'Meara scampered away, his head rotating wildly for
any sign of danger. He clutched the duffle close to his
chest.

From the front of the warehouse, a hundred feet away,
Ricky heard a commotion -- loud voices and scuffling. It
was too late to bolt and take action.

"Whoa! Nobody leaves!"

A fat man in an ill-fitting gray suit and felt hat two sizes
too small came sauntering toward Ricky with two other
men in tow. The larger one, a neckless giant, dragged
O'Meara by the collar. Ricky froze.

In big clumsy strides, the fat one ambled up to Ricky as
if he were about to try to walk straight through him. He
halted three inches from Ricky's nose. The goons were
right behind.

"Well, well, well. What do we have here?" the
interloper exclaimed, looking around him. The menace
emanating from this artless baboon was accentuated by

round colorless eyes set too close together atop a potato nose. "Looks like we caught somebody red-handed doin' somethin' that's most likely against the law. What do youse guys t'ink?" he motioned to his cohorts, his eyes locked onto Ricky's face. The goons were expressionless. The huge one holding O'Meara by his collar gaped stupidly from a dullard's face.

"Who the hell are you?" Ricky demanded. "You're no cops. I know all the cops in this area. And you're not Feds either. Feds dress better and don't drool."

"Who am *I*?" the fat guy bellowed. He snickered, made like he was about to throw a look at his henchmen, then crashed his right fist into Ricky's groin. Ricky doubled over, grabbing hold of the desk to keep from falling.

"You guineas are all alike. Think you can bust in here, do business without going through the union."

Ricky coughed into his handkerchief. "What're you talking about? What union?"

Fatso pulled a billfold from his inside jacket pocket, opened it and shoved it into Ricky's face. It displayed an I.D.

"Brotherhood of Teamsters, pal! You do anything on this pier, you gotta go t'rough the Teamsters."

"What the fuck you talking about?"

"Hey, keep talkin' like that, and I'll have to invite the Longshoremen in too. I'm sure they'd be real interested in what kinda deals are goin' down in their warehouses. Let's get down to business fast. No tellin' who else is goin' to stumble in here. All these lychee nut cans. I hear that junkies are really getting off shootin' up lychee nut juice. We know that you have a nice cozy relationship with customs here. We know that some of our finest customs officers get a nice share of the pie. Since the Teamsters transport everything in these warehouses to the distributors,

the Teamsters gotta have their cut too. Just look at it as
your contribution to the pension fund."

"Does Al Malandrino mean anything to you, buddy?"
Ricky demanded as he regained his composure.

Fatso rubbed his chin in mock contemplation. He
pointed a finger upward and raised his eyebrows in feigned
surprise. "Malandrino...Oh yeah, ain't he that dumb guinea
who just barely escaped serious time in the joint? Ooh,
yeah. Sure. Real smart guy. I t'ink I have actually heard
of him. Seems to me he's got this t'ing against unions.
Can't stand 'em. Locks 'em outta all his businesses. Not a
guy for the working man."

"Who do you work for?" Ricky demanded. "Bellomo?
Persico? Who? I think we're going to have to talk with
whoever is supposed to keep you under control."

"Listen you ginzo greaseball piece of shit. I work for
me and the Teamsters. Max Chesny. That's who I am, you
got it?"

Chesny backed up two steps. Without taking his eyes
off Ricky, he began to reach for a two-foot metal pipe that
sat on the warehouse floor.

Ricky prepared to lunge at him and his two cronies.
Every muscle tensed. His eyes bored in on the intruder.

As if in defensive response, the obese Teamster stood up
instantly. He stiffened and shivered.

"Come on, blubberball. I'll take you and your buddies
on," Ricky yelled.

Chesny's eyes rolled upward. His fingers straightened.
His legs trembled. Blood flowed from his mouth and nose.
He seemed to be rising from the ground.

The goon holding O'Meara fell onto his hands and
knees, eyes bulged to the point of popping out of his head.
His tongue protruded from his mouth. The man's head
appeared ready to explode. Ghastly moans emitted from

deep inside his shaking body. Blood-tinged foam gushed over his chin and down his throat, wetting the lapels of his overcoat.

Ricky heard a "Chump!" then a "Crack!" The third goon crashed to the floor. His neck began spraying blood in all directions. A fire ax was planted squarely down his right ear and into his jaw.

Ricky moved fast. He grabbed the pipe from the floor and zonked Chesny smack on the side of the head. But Chesny gave no reaction as bloody vomit oozed from both sides of his mouth. There was the sound of cracking ribs from behind.

Suddenly, there appeared none other than Dimitrov from a stack of crates containing Swedish refrigerators. The Russian had a sickly contented grin on his face as he visibly struggled against Chesny's weight. He was yanking a large knife up the dying man's rear rib cage.

Two of Dimitrov's mates were attending to the other Teamsters, one garroting the big man; the other admiring the handiwork of a quick ax to the head of the third Teamster.

From the rear of the warehouse ran Bags and Herman "The German" Metzger, like Bags, a life-long and loyal employee of the Malandrino clan.

"What the hell...is this?" Ricky demanded.

"We are aborting a contract with Teamsters," Dimitrov huffed as he reached Chesny's shoulder blade.

"Holy Christ!" Ricky shouted.

Dimitrov ignored Ricky. He wasn't quite finished yet. He let Chesny's corpulence drop to the floor. He then methodically commenced to eviscerate his victim. A geyser of blood gushed in several directions, covering the floor quickly in a sticky scarlet mess.

Ricky grabbed Dimitrov's shoulder to yank him backward. The Russian bolted around and flashed a foot-long chromium blade to within a half-inch of Ricky's eyes. He backed off, holding his hands outward from his sides.

The other two Russians held Bags and the German at bay.

"You see this?" Dimitrov asked calmly. Menace and madness radiated from his eyes.

"When I was boy in Murmansk, I work in fish factory. Every day, I clean sturgeon, take out eggs to make caviar. I become like surgeon. Cut quickly and expertly. I do it with eyes closed. Sturgeon knife you can use to shave with." Dimitrov scraped Ricky's three-day growth, instinctively causing him to flinch. "Sturgeon knife cut bones like other knives cut cheese." The Russian broke his trance-like gaze and backed off slightly.

"Ricky, breathing hard, was half bent over, with his hands on his knees. "Next time I have some people over for a cozy massacre, I'll know who to call."

"I will tell you something, dear Mr. Ricky," the Russian said, resuming a distant glower. "We learn in Afghanistan how to kill properly. We, as soldiers, killed with gun -- clean, simple, quick. But enemy kept coming to kill us. When *mujahideen* kill us, they take time. Sometimes they cut off ears, take out eye or cut off nose. Next day, they cut off balls. Maybe they take five days to kill Russian. They slice off skin and tie body to big rock in desert so his comrades can see. Whole companies of Russian soldiers refuse to fight when they see this. They kill commander rather than fight such people. Some desert to enemy, become Muslim. We learn lesson from Afghanistan. We lose war because enemy kills better than us. Now we *Afghantsi* kill skillfully. Teamsters never again bother us. I guarantee you this."

"Let's just get the fuck out of here."

Dimitrov eyed O'Meara, who was slumped against the crates crying uncontrollably. He had vomited all over the duffle bag.

Ricky stiffened. "Don't even think of it. He's useful. You don't know how useful. Without him, we're finished. He's not going to breathe a word about this. Are you Eddie?"

The customs man whimpered. He held his knees tightly and rocked back and forth.

"He knows that if he talks or welches, he's next. Leave him alone," Ricky commanded.

"Okay. But if he betrays us, I fillet him like sturgeon. And his family also."

O'Meara burbled that he understood.

"Bags, Herman. Load this stuff fast. Take Eddie home. Give him a couple stiff drinks first, so his wife'll think he's like this because he's plastered." Ricky locked his eyes onto Dimitrov's. "Okay, Jack the Ripper. Let's leave the talking to Uncle Al and Yakov." Ricky spat, then about-faced and sprinted out.

CHAPTER SIX

Bernard J. Scher was put in charge of the government-wide effort to investigate Mortimer's death. He headed an Interagency Working Group, or IWG for short, comprising State, NSC, FBI, CIA, Defense, Homeland Security and the Secret Service. The IWG met twice a week to compare notes and seek ways to advance the investigation.

The national chairman of the President's party personally phoned daily for updates. Mortimer was a key supporter of the party and President. The party would miss the hundreds of thousands Mortimer raised through the PACs.

Secretary of State Dennison, seen by most Americans issuing sound-bites from breezy links at warm resorts, also wanted to know every detail, any clues that might lead somewhere. Mortimer had made Dennison, as chairman of the Committee to Re-elect the President, look good. In the coming race, he wouldn't have it so easy without Mortimer's golden geyser.

The press was merciless in commentaries on the government's mishandling of the investigation. The *Washington Post* questioned Scher's abilities as an investigator, noting that his hum-drum performance as a

corporate attorney at his old law firm ill-equipped him as
the government's chief diplomatic lawyer. The *Post*, the
New York Times and the Sunday morning talking heads
questioned the administration's assumption that terrorists
did Mortimer in.

While this was distinctly an inside-the-beltway
hullaballoo which held virtually zero interest for the
average American, at election time, political opponents of
the administration on the Hill and critics in the media
would be slavering to turn it into ammunition to undercut
the electoral chances of the President and his party.

Innes tried mentally and emotionally to remove himself
from the whole affair. He had learned long ago to keep as
much distance as possible from fools and their shenanigans
inside the government. Sycophantic office directors and
Deputy Assistant Secretaries pursued with unquestioning
vigor the line laid down by Scher and his ass-kissing staff.
All manner of hyper-ambitious bureaucrats came out of the
woodwork to weasel their way onto the investigation team.
The word around the corridor water fountains was that this
could be "career enhancing" -- governmentese for fast
promotions. His obligatory attendance at Scher's brainless
IWG meetings, however, made Innes a captive. There to
sit against a wall and take notes and report back to his
bosses in the Department's Secretariat, Innes was in on
most things. What he didn't learn at the meetings he
usually could easily obtain through a secure phone call or
an office visit. At the last meeting, he found himself
unconsciously shaking his head in disgust. He caught
himself before anyone could notice.

"What do you mean the CIA has nothing recent on the
Patriotic Front for the Liberation of All Children of Islam?"
Scher thundered at the CIA's Deputy Director for
Operations.

"We don't even know if the PFLCI still exists. At most it had a dozen members, all hotheads at the University of Cairo. But they've all graduated. One is working in New York with Prudential Securities. The others we're still trying to track down. The Cairo Station believes one was tortured to death by the Egyptian police--"

"I want the low-down on the Prudential guy by tomorrow afternoon," Scher shot back. "Now, what's this latest report about the Kurdish Workers Patriotic Brigade threatening to blow up the embassies of imperialist governments who give aid to Turkey...?"

Innes couldn't believe his ears. He looked at his watch impatiently every six or seven minutes.

"We're demarching the Egyptians," intoned the gray-suited Deputy Assistant Secretary for Near East Affairs.

During a coffee break, Innes cornered Claire Norton, Scher's deputy on the interagency group.

"Claire, can you tell me what's going on?"

"'Going on', Bob?"

"I can't believe it's just me who sees we're barking up the wrong trees."

"Whatever do you mean?" Claire replied in astonishment.

"Why are we committing the formidable resources of the U.S. government in chasing after phantom terrorist suspects? We all know Mortimer's reputation. Though no one has the gumption to raise it."

"Ambassador Mortimer's personal life may have not been saintly, but it's irrelevant to this investigation," Claire answered officiously. "Besides, why sidetrack a serious investigation by getting the media into a feeding frenzy on marginal issues like Mortimer's personal foibles?"

"When I told Scher about what I found out before I left Rome, it was like I was giving him my mother's recipe for blueberry muffins. He turned off completely."

Claire Norton was the same rank as Innes. She, like most of her female thirty-something peers in the Foreign Service, was immaculately burnished and behaved, and unmarried. Every hair always in place; her outfits were replications of the Brooks Brothers and Nordstrom suits of her male counterparts. She reminded Innes of female Coldwell-Banker agents who sold homes only in certain elite neighborhoods in the northwest quadrant of the capital. Claire punched all the right tickets. She was on the threshold of promotion to the senior ranks. Her positioning herself to be selected as Scher's deputy on a major task force was a strategic move.

"Do you really think Mortimer was zapped by some raghead zealot?" Innes asked almost in desperation.

With a plastic smile and a practiced upbeat delivery, Norton responded in measured tones, "We believe that there are enough indications to lead us to suspect strongly that terrorist elements are behind the assassination of Ambassador Mortimer." She sounded like a junior press spokeswoman reciting the party line, Innes thought.

Scher reconvened the meeting.

"The Strike Force for Bosnian Salvation," Scher began in a dramatic, paced presentation that would have the participants think that this Balkan splinter group had just gotten hold of the bomb. "DIA tells me that they have threatened to carry their message, quote, 'to wherever necessary and by whatever means,' endquote. I can't understand why they haven't been entered on Interpol's watch list."

"We're demarching the Swiss," chimed a Deputy
Assistant Secretary for European Affairs with no
explanation.

"Islamic crazies are crawling all over Italy," Scher
continued. "The Italians are so gummed up in Government
of the Month antics, they can't be trusted to investigate a
parking ticket." A wan smile unfolded across Scher's pale
face.

As if on cue, all attendees in the conference room broke
into a collective chuckle. Also as if on cue, they stopped.

Innes excused himself.

Back at his work station in the Ops Center, he slumped
into his chair, plunked his elbows on the desk and closed
his eyes as he rubbed his temples in deliberate, circular
motions. "Frigid career bitches," he murmured.

"What'd you say, Bob?" Robin Croft asked cheerfully.

"Uh, nothing, nothing really. Just losing my marbles
again, that's all. What's up?"

"Well, were you mumbling something about your wife?
Anyway, she called. There's not much really going on.
France's trade minister is calling us names again. Some
Argentine military guys making noises about the Falklands
again. Here's a *Reuters* piece that just came over the
ticker."

Datelined Ankara, it was titled, "Russian Diplomat
Slain." It went on, "A Russian diplomat was found
murdered today just outside the Turkish capital. The slain
envoy's mutilated body lead police to suspect an attack by
Chechnyans as an act of vengeance against Moscow."

Innes was momentarily lost in deep thought. His chin
rested in a palm. Croft carefully watched for a reaction.
An extended "Hmmmm" rumbled from inside her
supervisor.

Fidgeting, Innes riffled through the other press tickers stapled to the *Reuters* article. Just beneath the Ankara dispatch was a *New York Times News Service* story out of New York headlined, "Three Teamsters Officials Murdered." The sub-heading read, "Killings Have Hallmarks of Gangland Hit; Teamsters Deny Mob Ties."

CHAPTER SEVEN

The headquarters of the FBI sits like a proud young dowager, its face exhibiting strong clean lines and a full blush complexion. Self-confidence, direction and rectitude radiate from a form anchored in stolidity, if not grace. Most of all, it exudes power. Situated two blocks from the White House on Pennsylvania Avenue, the premier law enforcement agency tasked with protecting Americans from all manner of evildoers, is still named, in huge brass letters, after J. Edgar Hoover. It is an irony lost on no one.

Over seven thousand bureaucrats report there each day. They track criminals and spies, they categorize finger prints and analyze evidence, they track the bank accounts and travels of secret agents, terrorists and mobsters. They type and they file and do forensics research and test weapons. Those who rise the fastest move along with the sexy issues.

Since 9/11, tracking down terrorists was fetching promotions and citations left and right. Drugs and associated money laundering never hurt any special agent's career. And doing anything to make the mafia's life harder would win recognition and occasionally awards. Counterintelligence, however, was keeping the best and brightest away in droves. With the end of cold war and blooming of democracy in former communist states, there were fewer spies, fewer embassies to have to watch closely, fewer schemes by foreign governments to parse out. The Counterintelligence Division had atrophied as agents trained in Russian or Hungarian or Polish were transferred to Miami, New Orleans, L.A. and smaller cities to pursue Islamists, inter-state car theft rings, white collar banking fraud, small mobsters and crazies issuing threats against anything, everything and anybody.

The irony is that letting the guard down allowed Robert Hansen to engage in a 15-year secrets-selling spree to the Russians in what was described as the "worst intelligence disaster in U.S. history." Thus burnt, the Bureau made the wise decision to offer some incentives to attract and keep good agents in counterintelligence.

Speedy Donner was one such agent. As a Russian specialist, he still had plenty to do. Donner's real given name was Peter. He acquired the moniker Speedy Petie in high school. He always seemed to be the fastest in everything. Ran the swiftest in track. Liked to drive suped-up hot rods. He was the first to be accepted by a university as well as the first to get a degree. He was the first among his peers to marry, the first to have a child, and the first to get divorced. His superiors liked Speedy because he saw before anyone else in the government the new dangers posed by the reconstituted Russian KGB, now broken up into several separate components, the CIA counterpart known as the Foreign Intelligence Service -- in Russian, *Sluzhba Vnye Shneii Razvyedki*, or SVR. As the former Soviet Union crumbled and frayed at the core as well as at the edges, it was Speedy who, in a memo to the Director, predicted that Russian officials would be increasingly looking out for their own personal aggrandizement. Diplomats and spies, he maintained,

would flock to Western intelligence services to be recruited
-- for remuneration, of course. Others, however, could be
expected to become renegades, free-lance criminals, as well
as sellers of state secrets. The Director of Central
Intelligence, who was shown the memo, praised Speedy in
a letter to his counterpart at the FBI, for demonstrating
"foresight in predicting that former servants of an ex-
superpower living in an ideological vacuum with little in
the way of monetary compensation would inevitably be out
for themselves in their deep disillusionment." He added
that Speedy was one of the first to raise alarm bells about
the possibility of Russian nuclear scientists selling their
expertise to the likes of Iran's mullahs or North Korea's
Kim Jong-il.

The fact of the matter was, Speedy simply loved his
work. He adored Russian language and culture and was
obsessed with piecing together the personal lifestyles,
motivations and beliefs of ex-Soviet officials. If they
shipped him off to Des Moines to chase after bank robbers,
he would just shrivel up and die. He therefore resolved to
be the best in CI.

Innes kept in touch with his old college roommate. The
bonding went further than that. As graduates of the State
University of New York at Geneseo, they were often the
butt of jokes and smirks from their colleagues in the elite
government services in which they worked.

They agreed to meet at Rio Lobo on upper Connecticut
Avenue for their monthly pig-out lunch of Tex-Mex.
Speedy, naturally, arrived first.

"How's work?" Speedy asked.

"Shitty. I work for fools. How about you?" Salsa
dripped down Innes's chin as he wrestled with a Taco
Grande.

"I also work for fools. But they like me."

"Who you going out with these days?"

"You know Heidi Klum?" Speedy was plowing through his Tres Burritos de Texas methodically, nary losing a crumb.

"You mean the model?"

"Yeah. And do you know Maria Sharapova and Charlize Theron?"

"Uh, I know who they are, sure." Innes's eyes followed a clump of chili as it escaped his lips and went splat onto his lap.

"Nobody like that," Speedy finished.

"How's your kid?" Innes asked.

"Sore subject."

"Okay, now that we got all that out of the way, I have a business-related question.

"Shoot."

"You know anything about a Russian diplomat who was murdered the other day in Ankara?"

"Never went out with him."

"Cut out the wisecracks."

"I saw the same press reports, but since it's out of FBI's bailiwick, we're not getting anything on it. And we're not asking either. If you're interested, how come you aren't asking the CIA? They're supposed to know everything."

"I thought you would ask for me. I've been getting the run-around from them. In any case, you know everybody who works the Russian beat."

"No sweat. I'll get a full report to you tomorrow."

"Great. How about a beer after work, say 6:30 at The Pub in Georgetown."

"I'll be there. By the way, how's the wife?"

"Sore subject."

Speedy neatly wiped his mouth and placed his fork and spoon on his clean plate. With his sixth paper napkin,

Innes caught a rivulet of grease before it reached his elbow. Molten cheese anchored his dish to the table cover.

"Terrific chow, as always," Innes declared, smiling.

"You bet." Speedy looked at his roomie with amusement.

Innes was pulling the regular eight-to-five shift at the Ops Center. The watch officers rotate duty to even out the burden of night shifts and to give everyone the chance to work normal hours.

Robin Croft had just placed on his desk the morning's take of telegrams from embassies, CIA stations and military commands around the world. She gleaned that which she felt was important, messages that Innes, in turn, would bring to the attention of the Ops Center Director or various Assistant Secretaries, perhaps after seeking additional or late-breaking information via secure voice communications or classified e-mail or FAX.

Pawing through the take, Innes made a comment or asked a question about several of the items.

"What's this about the French trade minister calling us names again? Somebody oughta fire that guy. Shred!" Innes held the confidential cable from Paris at arm's length, as if it were putrid, and unceremoniously dropped it into a burn bag.

"And the Mexicans are massacring Indians again. They should be ashamed to be our neighbors. It's all in the papers anyway." Embassy Mexico City telegram number 13251 followed the French minister into the burn bag.

Robin enjoyed Innes's sense of humor, a commodity sorely lacking in a building in which too many people took themselves far too seriously.

"I'll try to get the world to cough up some better news next time," she said in mock seriousness.

"You can start with Bernard Scher." Innes puffed up his chest and set his mouth into a frown of grave pomposity. "What's the latest with the Terror of the Terrorists anyway? Has he gotten down to Sudanese kindergartens yet?"

"Not sure. But people on the Hill aren't letting up. Senator Scofield announced late yesterday that the Senate would order the General Accounting Office to investigate the Mortimer case if the administration couldn't do it properly. And the *Washington Times* has another one of its scathing editorials skewering the State Department for being namby-pamby on the case."

"Anybody from the IWG call me?"

"Nope. Oh, I almost forgot. The secretary took a phone message for you from Embassy Rome." Robin handed Innes a yellow message slip. It said, "Please call: 'Colleen. 02-595-003-291.'"

Innes found an empty cubicle allowing privacy, and punched the number.

"Hello? Chargé's office," came a chipper female voice.

"Colleen?"

"Bob?"

"One and the same."

"Guess what? I've been assigned to Bangkok. I'll be in the political section. It's a great job."

"Oh, uh, sure. Congratulations." Innes wondered why she was calling him with this news. Bangkok. Hm. Great. Never see those gams again.

"Yeah! And I'll be starting ten months of Thai at FSI." FSI was the Foreign Service Institute in suburban Virginia where U.S. diplomats underwent language study and other training.

Innes sat up with a start.

"That's terrific. Show your face around here after you arrive. We can talk about old times. I know a great oriental night club."

"Can't wait," Colleen replied hesitantly, playing along. "It'll be sooner than you think. I arrive this coming weekend. I'll give you a call then."

Innes caught himself grinning ear to ear as he replaced the receiver. Then forced himself to ask why. A good new-found friend's coming to town, he tried to convince himself. It'll be very useful to get a firsthand readout on how the investigation is playing out in Rome. She's a fine young officer. I'll give her some helpful career counseling tips so that she can avoid some of the pitfalls I made, he thought unpersuasively. Innes was clearly struggling with himself.

Alexander Vladimirovich Starenkov. SVR *Rezident* in Ankara. Twenty-five-year veteran of Moscow's espionage service. Distinguished himself in Kabul. Was rewarded with a plum assignment as deputy *Rezident* at the Soviet Mission to the United Nations, where he was discreet and regularly foiled the FBI's efforts to monitor his movements and communications. Did a stint as an aide on national security matters in Putin's NSC-clone foreign policy advisory board. Forty-seven, married, two kids. Otherwise, an enigma. He was so discreet that it wasn't till Speedy Donner got his file from the bio shop at Langley that he even remembered the name.

Innes read the dossier quickly but thoroughly. Speedy had sanitized it of highly classified information, but would answer Innes's questions fully based on what little information was available on this man.

"Looks to me like this guy was a real pro, not a hotdogger," Innes said as he accidentally dropped a fry onto the file cover.

"I promised my date in the bio office that I'd return the file *sans* grease," Speedy said tartly.

"A date, huh? Guess she hasn't caught on that you live up to your name as a lover."

Speedy launched an onion ring at Innes's nose.

"What was his reputation in Turkey?" Innes asked.

"He hadn't been there long. Had the cover of commercial counselor. The Turkish service told our station chief that Starenkov was actually a very energetic commercial officer. Worked hard to promote Russian exports. Was all over the Turkish business community."

"Think he was trying to develop cut-outs to steal high tech stuff from us?"

"No evidence. He mainly cultivated Turkish agro-business types. Food exporters on the one hand and farm machinery importers on the other. Reading about this guy really puts you to sleep. Sort of a spook Al Gore."

"How many foreign commercial officers are you aware of who've been literally torn apart for trying to sell more tractors?" Innes asked.

"That's the thing. Neither the Turks nor we nor anybody else can figure out what this guy was into that would land him into this kind of end."

Their young waitress asked if they wanted another pitcher of Rolling Rock on draft, the favored brew among university students on a tight budget. Customers nursing their drinks generated neither profit nor tips. Speedy and Innes got the message. They ordered another pitcher.

"The Turks are ready to conclude that some crazed Chechnyan or Azeri did a job on him. Caucasus peoples are like that, they keep reminding us; wild, violent, vengeful. The Turks should know. They've had a lot of experience of their own slaughtering their neighbors to the east."

"What's Moscow's reaction to all this?"

Speedy promptly emptied his glass of Rolling Rock, set the empty glass squarely down on the cardboard coaster and fastidiously dabbed his lips with a cocktail napkin.

"They're outraged, of course. Turks say they're being hit up both in Moscow and in Ankara for results to their investigation."

"And?"

"And the Russian government is convinced that Armenian crazies did it – not Chechnyans. They hate the Russians; the more so since it became public that the Russian army has been channeling arms and ammo to the Azeris covertly. The Turks don't mind pinning the blame on the Armenians either, but they need at least some circumstantial evidence first. The Russians are pressing the Turks to go after members of something called the Armenian Redemptist Army in eastern Turkey."

"Christ. Doesn't this sound familiar," Innes intoned.

"What do you mean?"

"Bernie Scher…uh, I'll tell you later. What do you think yourself, Speedy?"

"Hey, remember me? The 'they're-all-out-selling-themselves' theoretician? Everybody in the USG, and probably in the Russian government too, still thinks in cold war terms. An intelligence agent gets shredded to pieces. Oh! Must've been a political murder."

"So, okay. Who would do in a quiet, competent Russian family man who was out to help his country's economy and -- by the way -- was also a spy?"

"I don't know, but I'm working on it. I'm just willing to bet it wasn't political and that it wasn't random violence

either. Ergo, he sold himself to somebody out there and
whatever the deal was, it went sour and they creamed him.
Either that or he just got in the way of some sweetheart deal
already in progress."

Innes looked at his watch. "Geez, 10:00 already! My
wife'll kill me. She's supposed to be on the night shift by
now."

"How is it with you and Carolyn anyway?" Speedy
asked.

"Like I said before. Sore subject."

They paid the bill and left, agreeing to stay in touch on
any new developments concerning the late Alexander
Starenkov.

Innes and Colleen met at the Nok Lek Restaurant, on
Glebe Road, several minutes from the FSI campus at
Arlington Hall Station. Colleen was eager to plunge herself
into everything Thai, starting with the food. They took a
stab at ordering several dishes, neither having much
familiarity with Thai cuisine. Nok Lek, or Little Bird in
Thai, like so many ethnic restaurants, was a family-run
operation. They took up the suggestions of Mrs. Somphat,
wife of the owner, and ordered a couple of other dishes on
a hunch. Coverless formica-topped tables with simple
folding chairs lined either wall of the narrow eatery, lodged
between a Payless shoe store on the one side and a CVS
Drugs on the other in a drab '60's-era shopping center. It
was a favorite among the Southeast Asia hands at FSI.

The first course was *tom yam kung*, a hot and sour
shrimp soup served in a kettle kept warm by a small can of
sterno in its belly.

"Bob, I'm glad we're together again," Colleen said. She touched Innes's hand slightly. "I still think of our little escapade in the netherworld of Roman nightlife. And you?"

Her interest made Innes feel good. In retrospect, their little adventure into Rome's less notable nightlife now seemed amusing. It was something they shared, a bonding experience.

"Hm. Work's a grind and things aren't so hot at home." Innes averted his eyes downward and fidgeted with his napkin.

Colleen's face was the definition of feminine caring. Wordlessly, she urged him to open up.

"You know what I think of the Mortimer investigation. On the one hand, I'm convinced that those boneheads are mishandling it. On the other, they won't let me disengage. What makes it worse is that I can't help but think that there's much more to it than meets the eye. Just a gut feeling that I can't let go."

"And at home?"

Mrs. Somphat brought the first course, *satay*, barbecued strips of chicken on a stick served with a sweet peanut sauce.

Innes picked one up, dipped it into the sauce and began to nibble as he focused his thoughts. As a Presbyterian Yankee, Innes was not given to sharing his personal affairs with others, even close relatives and friends. Stoicism and internalization of emotions were his nature. He studied Colleen's face. Her pouty pink lips and wide, hazel eyes exuded curiosity and concern. Her hands were folded demurely in her lap. She invited trust. Somewhere in his mental firmament, Innes thought that this was a woman in whose soul he could get lost.

"Oh, it's pretty complicated…" Innes caught himself.
He looked deeply into Colleen's eyes and pondered for a
moment. "Actually, it's pretty simple, I guess. Carolyn and
I have grown distant. I don't know if it's the crazy work
hours we're both putting in, or the constant moving from
post to post, or contending with the Beltway rat race, or
some combination of everything."

"Do you discuss things with each other?"

Innes reflected a second. "I suppose we've gotten out of
the habit, when I think about it."

"If you let it drift, it'll only get worse--"

Innes interrupted and in a rapid staccato, said, "We
married while still in college. I try not to dwell on it, but I
often can't help but think that we married too young. We
grew together, but then began to grow apart. I can't put my
finger on it, but the closeness is gone. We each do our own
thing. We're only going through the motions now.
Anyway, ten years and two kids later things just aren't the
same any more." Innes felt a rush of blood to his head. He
had rarely confided his innermost emotions to anyone. But
he welcomed this chance to get off his chest feelings that
had been gnawing at him for months, for years. It was
cathartic.

The main courses arrived, a spicy green curry, a clear
rice noodle and shrimp salad laced with little red peppers
and *tom yam kung* soup. Famished, each dug in
enthusiastically.

They ordered a second round of iced coffee. Innes
stared at Colleen's face. "You know something? You don't
look well."

"What do you mean?" Colleen asked as she took another
large swig of the iced drink.

"Your face. It looks flushed. You all right?"

"I feel fine," she insisted.

Innes reached over and placed his hand on her forehead, then her cheek. "Yeah, you feel like you've got a fever." Innes asked for a glass of ice water. Colleen seconded the order.

Colleen pulled her compact from her purse and studied her face in the tiny mirror. She raised her eyes to Innes's face. She then reached over and felt his cheek. She began to chuckle.

"What's the matter?" Innes said, taking another large gulp of cold water. He reflexively grabbed Colleen's compact and looked at himself in the little mirror, half expecting to see a noodle in his hair or a pepper in his nose, considering the way she was laughing between mouthfuls of plain rice and swigs of ice water.

"We're both burning up!" she blurted in a mixture of mirth and agony.

"You can say that again."

"We've o.d'd on hot peppers," she said, fanning her extended tongue with one hand.

Innes greedily gobbled several ice cubes. "This stuff sneaks up on you."

Observing the scene like a little girl who had just pulled a prank on her friends, Mrs. Somphat went to their table bearing a plate of sliced, fresh pineapple and bananas. "Here. You eat this now. It take the fire away," she ordered her clients between giggles.

Innes and Colleen devoured the fruit.

Colleen had to return to class. Innes was late for the office. They paid the bill and exited Nok Lek. Almost oblivious to the press of time, they stood in the parking lot each waiting for the other to bid farewell. She mentioned how she dreaded going back to Dr. Praman, the "Terror of Thai Tones." He mumbled something about the stack of papers Robin Croft had assembled for him; the more crises in the world, the higher the stack got. An awkward silence fell on them. As if on cue, the Bangkok-bound junior officer and the despondent diplomat glanced at their watches.

Colleen took a step toward him and looked up at him. "Bob, this was nice." She took his hand and pressed gently. "Don't let it all get you down. You're too nice a guy. Don't give in."

There was a tingling inside that Innes hadn't felt since he was an adolescent. Her earnestness and caring struck deep. He paused as he searched her face. "Can we do this again? I really enjoy talking to you. I mean I feel we have a lot in common. Actually, what I want to say is–"

"Yes. Just call. Or I can call you. Or--"

"Next Saturday. After I finish the morning shift. The zoo? How about it?"

Colleen's face brightened. Strands of her auburn hair waved in a gentle breeze. "Yes. One o'clock?"

"Yes. One o'clock."

CHAPTER EIGHT

They locked in passionate embrace. It was as if the
world were about to self destruct and this was the last
chance to experience physical human love. There was such
little time. No one should know. It was clandestine, yet so
necessary. It started languorously, then accelerated rapidly.
The long anticipation had made her nervous. At first she
was awkward, maladroit, but with the intensity increasing,
she lost herself in the act. He applied himself expertly,
assertively. He was considerably older. She was very
young, very fresh. She had put off this moment repeatedly.
Finally, she gave in, gave all of herself. Now he was on top
of her. His weight was oppressive, yet the vigor of his
passion drove her naturally, almost unthinking.

The surroundings were less than ideal. A cheap hotel
room in an undesirable section of the city. Drab, colorless
curtains she could see, along with a worn, colorless carpet.
A sagging bed with gray sheets and stained pillows. He
quickened and became forceful. Oh, God, let it be finished,
she screamed in her mind. The traffic noise from the street
was distracting, annoying. A bus belched grumpily as it
pushed through the tight alleyway three stories below. The
radio was on. The Bee Gees ran through one of their weird,

falsetto tunes of the mid-70's. She struggled to control her emotions. Finish. Finish. Now. Now. I must think of what will come, she shouted silently to herself. Make him finish. Help him to finish. She concentrated, her face contorted, shut out reality. Her eyes rolled back into her sockets, the lids and brows scrunched unrevealing as to whether the cause was deep pleasure or deep pain. She moved as she was supposed to. Now! Now! Now!

He collapsed and remained on her, unmoving, but breathing hard. Her head exploded in a supernova of emotions, the intense energy of which was being channeled into one direction as she began to regain herself: Go! Go! Get out!! This was wrong. Wrong. Yet she remained frozen. Tears streamed along her cheeks. She sobbed almost soundlessly.

Finally, he stirred himself and raised his wet body from her. Immediately, he reached for his watch and squinted to see the time. He sprang from the bed and leapt to the tiny bathroom. After three minutes he returned to the side of the bed and looked down at his conquest as he zipped his trousers.

"You were good, very good. You pass." He touched her cheek roughly and laughed hoarsely, cruelly.

She had turned on her side and was staring blankly at the grinding radiator.

"Go see Sasha. He will tell you what to do next."

She remained silent.

"Did you hear me?"

"Yes." She was still.

"Go to Sasha. I think we can take you on." He put on his jacket, opened the door of the little room. "We must do this again sometime!" His voice was mocking, denigrating. And he slammed the door.

She came from a good family. Her father had a
supervisory position in the Rostov Oblast public health
administration. Her mother was an accountant at a steel
plant. Her paternal great grandfather was a senior
functionary under the czar, a fact which the family was
proud of, but kept hidden during the seventy-three years of
Soviet communism. She completed four years of
university, having obtained a degree in accounting,
following in her mother's footsteps. Yet times were hard in
Russia. Very hard. Making ends meet on the equivalent of
forty dollars a month was impossible. People scraped, stole
and hustled.

Lydia Puchinskaya was in the same boat as everyone
else. She could labor in a legitimate job -- her mother
pulled strings to get her a junior bookkeeper's position at
her factory. And try to buy and sell this and that on the
side just as most of her friends were doing. But for a bright
lady of 22, the gritty, industrial southern Russian city of
Rostov, on the Don River, offered nothing but bleak
uncertainties. The old social welfare net was gone.
Everyone was out for himself. With the collapse of Soviet
communism, there came a monolithic vacuum. No
direction for society. Nothing to believe in.

Lydia contrasted this with the incredible glimpses of the
outside world which she saw on television and in the
movies. She saw a documentary several months ago on
Paris. The reporters zoomed in on shops that were stuffed
with wonderful meats, sausages, varieties of breads, cheese,
toys, clothes. They filmed the City of Light's beautiful
broad, tree-lined boulevards which channeled the
metropolis's plethora of nice cars and chic people. But
what truly captured Lydia's imagination were the fashion
shows. How breathtaking, the beautiful women clad in
cutting-edge fashions. Gold, black, silver, tropical

splashes. And their hair done up so daring or so simple. But two things struck to her core: the absolutely self-assured expressions on their faces, as if to dare the world to call into question their individual self-worth, and the air of assertive freedom. People were giving their adulation not only to the young models' beauty, but also their style, their sassiness, their ease of movement under obvious pressure to perform well. Lydia wanted the chance to aspire to such marvelous things. She wanted out of Russia.

And, while Sasha was not exactly a white knight in shining armor, he did come to her rescue. The tall, handsome Sasha with the velvety voice and fine manners and seemingly limitless quantities of both charm and money to sway a girl. Sasha, in his ankle-length mink coat and black BMW, blowing into gray, torpid, decaying Rostov like a devil's wind into the desert, sweeping up anything that lay in his path. No one had to ask what his profession was. Object of both envy and scorn, Sasha was representative of the new class of post-communist entrepreneur in the new Russia. A clever young man who knew how to advance in a system suddenly devoid of controls and in which everyone had a price. A master of *blat* -- "pull," influence. In the Dodge City of the new Russia, the Sashas were both sheriff and bad guys. With money and muscle they cajoled or threatened government ministers and kiosk vendors, generals and janitors. The distinction between mafia and mere capitalist was a vague blur. The now chatty newspapers screamed mafia at them. But, like the new class they sensationalized, the papers themselves now hustled for income. Anything to sell a story.

"Lydia of the Lillies," Sasha breathed so sweetly. "Come with me to Moscow and I will give you work," he promised so earnestly.

"I won't ask questions," she replied solemnly. "Just take me from here."

He was intoxicated with her beauty, he confessed. She was too smart for a bumpkinville like Rostov.

She went with him, leaving only a farewell note to her family, promising to stay in touch.

Sasha treated her like a princess. New clothes. Fine restaurants. The ballet. For a week.

Then came the terms.

Beautiful Slavic women were making good incomes in the West working as "escorts." A young lady who was in great demand could pocket up to $5,000 a month. And we're not talking about plying oneself in sleazy bars, Sasha assured. No pimps. And no worry about being made to go out with undesirable men. You choose. Wealthy, successful men in Berlin, Amsterdam, London, Milan and, yes, Paris. Industrialists, bankers, diplomats. Sophisticated men who desired the comforting company of a charming lady as they made their rounds and went on travels to the fleshpots of the world. And the key thing, Sasha was careful to point out, Lydia would have contact with people who could open doors for her in the fashion business or movies. All Sasha asked was that she commit herself to a year as an escort. After that, she could continue or part company on a handshake. Naturally, Sasha and his representatives took their commission, which would be explicitly understood from the outset. After all, the escort service arranged passport, visas, transportation and lodging.

Lydia accepted. Sasha turned her over to Borin, one of his aides. She didn't like Borin from the outset. He was square and fat and ugly and smelly and rude. Borin told her that she had to pass a test. He took her to the Hotel Oktober, near the train station and feted her with greasy sausage and cheap vodka. He then informed her that he would administer the second "interview." Upstairs to the dingy room. What happened after that was a blur. Was it force on his part, or resignation on hers? Maybe a combination of both. In any case, she knew it all had all been too good to be true. Sasha, the sweet-talker. "Compromise," she counseled herself. Every goal in life has its price, whether in Russia or out. Father always said that life was full of compromises.

The visa line was long and slow. It usually was on Monday mornings. It seemed that all of the riff-raff of the fallen Soviet Empire spilled into the consular sections of America's embassies and consulates in the Newly Independent States on Mondays. And while the proportion of the human mix varied from post to post, invariably Russians jostled with Ukrainians who rubbed elbows with Armenians who waited with Uzbeks and Georgians and Azeris and a few Balts and on it went. Stale sweat and the lingering scent of horrible Russian cigarettes and not unoccasionally liquor breaths permeated the air. They nervously clutched their applications for "B-2" tourist visas, "F-1" student visas, "immediate relative" immigrant visas and so on, knowing that fully eighty percent could be expected to be rejected. The so-called non-immigrant visas, for people who claimed to want to stay only temporarily in the U.S., such as tourists, businessmen and students, were given to those who could prove beyond a reasonable doubt that they would return to their home country. This was a difficult proposition for people who lived in a conglomeration of failed economies, some racked by unrest, where the urge to seek a new life abroad was strong.

It was nothing new for Edna Hoff. Eighteen years on the visa line in such places as Manila, Port-au-Prince, Mexico City and Dublin gave her a keen eye for determining who was a good bet and who wasn't.

The consular section at U.S. Consulate General St. Petersburg was a sterile, all-business set-up where queues of anxious visa-seekers waited patiently for hours for their shot at one of the American consular officers who stood behind the thick bank teller windows which separated them safely from humanity. And the $100 dollar non-refundable application fee in a country where the average monthly wage was only double that tended to discourage frivolous petitions. But hope, rooted in desperation, springs eternal.

Akhmet Ulamov, a Kazakh taxi driver whose family had moved to Saint Petersburg when it was Leningrad, was classic. Twenty-nine, divorced, modest income, shared a cramped two-bedroom flat with two other families.

"How long do you want to visit the U.S?" Edna queried, despite the fact that he had already written his response in the little box soliciting the same information on the application form.

"Three months," Ulamov answered, merely echoing his written answer.

Edna had a reason for repeating questions. Applicants sometimes would display nervousness over this particular question -- a dead giveaway that they weren't telling the truth, that they actually intended to stay indefinitely. Ulamov kept a straight face.

"And how do you intend to support yourself?" Edna asked, with emphasis on the "how".

"Like I put down on the form, personal savings --"

Edna cut him off. This was her way of dominating the interview and keeping the applicant off guard. If there was anything she hated, it was an uppity applicant.

"Have you ever been in trouble with the law?" Edna's tone of voice rose with this question as she glared down her long nose suspiciously at Ulamov.

"No. I said so already on the --"

Edna didn't like Muslims. They constituted most of the criminals in Saint Petersburg, along with the Georgians and Armenians.

"You say you aren't married. Have you ever been married? And if so, why no longer?" she insisted on knowing, apropos of nothing in particular.

"Yes...I mean, no. I am not married, I am di--"

Never married herself, at 45, Edna could spot a phony flirt a mile away. Men often tried to charm her in a cheap tactic to gain her sympathy in the visa interview. Some sent her flowers and chocolates. A couple even tried to give her jewelry. Some called to ask for a date -- oldest ruse in the book. Edna knew of several female colleagues over the years who were stupid enough to fall for such blandishments. They issued visas to lovers who would then abscond to the U.S., never to be heard from again. A couple were fired for malfeasance.

"Where do you plan to travel while in the U.S?"

"New York, Disney World, Oklahoma City."

"What's in Oklahoma City?" Edna demanded.

"My brother lives there. With his family. I want to visit them--"

"I see," Edna declared with finality. Abruptly terminating her interrogation, Edna bent her neck downward, her thick glasses a mere four inches from Ulamov's application, upon which she scribbled furiously.

She raised her head and, with a smirk of triumph, curtly informed Ulamov that his application for a tourist visa was rejected. "I regret to inform you that you have been found ineligible for a non-immigrant visa under section 214(b) of

the Immigration and Naturalization Act: failing to prove
that you have a permanent abode outside the United States
to which you intend to return. Good day," Edna rattled off
swiftly. She'd said this at least ten thousand times during
her career. She would repeat it perhaps sixty times this
day.

"Next!"

With no time to digest the verdict, a perplexed and
crushed Ulamov was shown the door by a security guard.

The young blonde woman stepped gently up to the
window and cracked a faint, polite smile as she passed her
passport and tourist visa application through the slot.

Edna was immediately suspicious. Young women
anywhere were potentially bad visa risks. They often had
beaux in the U.S. with whom they planned to marry. Or,
they merely wanted to get to the Land of Opportunity
whereupon they would aggressively hunt for a husband. A
tourist visa avoided the red tape and time involved in
getting the requisite fiancée visa which was created for
such a purpose. Edna was sick and tired of seeing good
American males being snatched up by opportunistic foreign
females. This was a pet peeve of her fellow sisters in the
Foreign Service.

"Hmmm." Edna scrutinized the documents with a
hardened, studied eye, flipping the pages of Lydia's fresh
passport vigorously. A new passport was often an obvious
tipoff that the applicant (a) had never traveled before; or (b)
was seeking to hide past travels. Either way, the person
could be susceptible to violating her visa status once in the
United States. Edna couldn't abide her hard-earned tax
money going to subsidize the welfare costs of illegal
immigrants.

Without lifting an eye, Edna blurted in a barely audible monotone, "How long do you intend to remain in the United States?"

"Three months," Lydia replied without hesitation.

"And what is the purpose of your visit?"

"To see America."

"What cities do you intend to travel to?"

"The art museums of New York, Washington, Chicago and San Francisco."

The woman's composed, self-assured delivery irritated Edna. This Russian girl obviously was not intimidated. There was something else. She was beautiful. Blonde tresses done up in delicate curls. Her upturned nose wiggled ever so slightly when she spoke. Edna once read somewhere that this feature drove many men to distraction. The woman's deep-set, sea-blue eyes radiated a serene earnestness. Her blemish-free face was barely made up. The pouting lips required no rouge.

Edna was five-feet-eleven, 120 pounds, with the angular face of an imminent crone, crowned with a thatch of straight, ear-length hair of an indeterminate brown, streaked with grays. Her coke-bottle glasses, with an elastic neck strap, concealed pale gray eyes.

Wasting no time, Edna demanded sternly, "Do you have a fiancé in the U.S?"

"No."

"Are you planning to--"

"No. I have no plans to marry an American," Lydia interjected calmly.

Edna despised such impertinence from mendicants. She refused eighty percent of applicants and was proud of it. In her mind this was the only way of keeping America from being overwhelmed by job-thieving, welfare-collecting, men-stealing migrants.

"I regret to inform you that--"

Lydia cut her off. "Please see my references." She slipped a letter through the window.

"Edna dear," it began. "This is to introduce Lydia Puchinskaya, the daughter of a good friend, a wealthy businessman, former party man, from Rostov. Lydia is an art student who wishes to see the great museums of America. I will call. With affection, Pavel."

This indeed was an important reference. Pavel was Edna's lover. She might be all business at the office, but at home, Edna was a woman. Being with Pavel, whom she had met at her yoga class, was quite a sensitive thing. American officials in Russia still operate under a "non-frat" -- non-fraternization -- policy. This means no love affairs with the locals. The KGB might be gone, but in name only. Sexual seduction remained a tried-and-true means of recruiting spies. But Edna was as tough and discerning as they came. She could smell an ulterior motive a jail sentence away. Eighteen years of visa work honed the sixth sense for such things. With so many of the good, eligible males in the Foreign Service -- there weren't many to begin with -- being snatched away by calculating foreign females, why, heck! Smart, dynamic and lovable ladies should not be expected to live like nuns. We're human too, she had concluded firmly.

And Pavel was so sweet. So innocently boylike. And, at 25, athletic and six-foot-two, a serious hunk. He dabbled in yoga, and had quit after only the first class. His passion was dancing. He, in fact, taught Edna how to dance.

Pavel never asked for any favors for himself. Indeed, he invariably tried to refuse Edna's gifts -- unheard of in this broken society of conniving schemers. But once in a while, he would recommend for a visa a special friend, usually female. But they were of impeccable credentials and from good families. She approved the visas, certain that Pavel wouldn't send any ringers. Pavel was a real Prince Charming. Just like his brother, Sasha.

CHAPTER NINE

Too many things had been getting under Al's skin. Not enough to make him go back to his den and devour cannolli before the boob tube. But enough to give him sour stomachs and restive nights in bed. He had bags under his eyes and popped fistfuls of antacids. Knowing from experience Al's ferocious temper during these down periods, his people tried to keep some distance, treading lightly around the boss and speaking only when spoken to. If problems came up -- God forbid -- if they could be deferred, they were, until Al's normally jolly, generous humor returned.

Problems plagued his business dealings with the various ethnic groups with which he had assiduously forged links over the years. Sectional rivalries in the Latino outfits were hurting business. Colombians and Dominicans were fighting it out over turf over crack distribution in the Bronx. Al's Chinese counterparts in Manhattan were unable to bring under control the growing Asian youth gangs which were extorting and threatening Vietnamese, Thai and Chinese shopkeepers around the city. Many of these small scale business people were suppliers of Al's businesses, or had cooperative arrangements with Al's territorial capos. When the Asians suffered, Al also suffered as profits went down and the complaints from his people rose. Along 125th Street in Harlem, city authorities had cleared out illegal vendors. Al had provided the seed money to Harlem business cohorts to get the vendors started and supplied in return for eleven percent of the receipts, now dried up. Even the Irish, Jewish and other politicians with whom he had carefully cultivated discreet and mutually enriching relationships over the years were not returning his calls. The *New York Post* was running a series of investigative articles documenting the cozy relationships between city politicians and alleged organized crime figures, making the former suddenly gun-shy.

Even his right-hand man, Ricky, was falling down on the job. Smitten by a red headed co-ed philosophy major at NYU, Ricky was busy squiring the young lady on vacation trips to St. Kitts, Stowe and Las Vegas.

The only shining exception in this miserable picture was Wentworth. The young man now had Al-Mac Construction Co., Inc. running like a finely calibrated machine. In fact, Al-Mac was the one business free of problems. As efficiency increased, so did contracts and profits. Things were running so smoothly there that Al began to worry that his newest acolyte might be getting bored despite the frequent fat bonuses Al bestowed. The lad was unquestionably trustworthy. Nonetheless, Al carefully kept him out of his other enterprises, preferring to use Wentworth as gloss on his ongoing program to portray himself and his wide-ranging commercial realm as clean and legitimate. He came, however, to depend on his ex-Marine more and more in face of the compounding problems and Ricky's goofing off.

Al's most reliable business partners, the Russians, now also fell into the same jinxed category of problem-makers.

It was six weeks since the last meeting with Yakov. Al passed word that he wanted an urgent conference.

A private upstairs room was set aside at Pironi's. Al wanted to confront the Russian on his own turf this time. Whether out of growing paranoia or prudence, Al took precautions he had never taken before at Pironi's. He made the reservations under an alias. He told only Ricky -- just back and visibly fatigued from a gambling-cum-sex binge in Las Vegas -- and Wentworth in advance that the meeting would take place. Bags and Herman "The German" were given much shorter notice. They were Wentworth's muscle on the security side.

With Bags at the wheel, Al, Herman and Wentworth drove at a leisurely pace to the lower Manhattan address in an unassuming, maroon Buick Lucerne. Al told Wentworth only that he needed to discuss financial and other business matters with an associate and wanted to ensure that no competitors were tuning in. He instructed Wentworth to sweep the meeting room for bugs. Wentworth, Bags and the German were to wait outside while Al and Ricky met with Al's counterparts upstairs.

Al washed down a couple of Tums with a glass of cold Brioschi. "Where the hell is that son of a bitch nephew of mine?" Al demanded to no one and everyone as he nervously paced the meeting room. "Those goddamn Russians will be here in ten lousy minutes and that no-good-for-nothing, shit-for-brains, jerk-off nephew of mine is off doing God knows what!"

Bags, never a master of tact, replied, "Geez, Al, could be he's shackin' up with that college chick again. You never know, yah know?" He finished with a pointless shrug and a dumb grin.

Al stopped in his tracks, wheeled around, held his face six inches from that of Bags' and glowered at the unfortunate flunky. The sight of Al's big, bloodshot eyes boring in on him without so much as a blink and his nostrils flared like those of a wolf about to pounce a prey caused Bags to take a step backward. Sensing fallout from an imminent multi-megaton explosion, Herman turned his shoulder away from the blast site. "I think I better go outside and keep an eye out for Ricky. Yeah, that's what I'll do," Bags said. The diminutive lieutenant flew down the stairs, barely avoiding smashing into a platter-laden waiter climbing the steps.

Ever the epitome of cool, Wentworth ignored Al's blustering and proceeded to sweep the room methodically with his electronic detection equipment.

Al shook his head and slowly turned to Wentworth. He visibly untensed. No explosion after all.

"Chuckie, you sure what you're doing will do the job? The FB-…uh, I mean the…my competitors got all kinds of the latest technology. The last thing I need is for them to--"

"Al, I used to do this in our embassies. The CIA and NSA trained us in counterespionage. We were taught all the sophisticated m.o's of the Russians and Chinese. I know what I'm doing."

"Just asking. That's all."

"Somebody will have to ensure that your visitors aren't wired, or that any of them are even carrying portable radios, calculators and other electronic devices. I can sweep them bodily, if you wish." Wentworth pulled out of his black, leather satchel a "magic wand" -- a hand-held instrument used to check a person's body for metal and electrical items.

"No. I want to make them feel at home, unwind; not make them think that they're here for a colonoscopy. Get my drift? And when they arrive, I want you to keep an eye on Bags and Herman downstairs. Make sure they're doing their job and not getting distracted by re-runs of the 'Flintstones'."

"Sure. I'll finish up at nineteen-hundred."

"Wha'?"

"Seven p.m. In five minutes, I'll finish sweeping the place."

"Yeah. Right. Nineteen-hundred."

At seven sharp Wentworth packed up his gear and proceeded down the stairs. Al had resumed pacing back and forth, his nervous tension radiating like electricity humming from a power line. Suddenly, he bolted toward the stairwell. Cupping his mouth, he yelled after Wentworth.

"Chuckie! You know what *calamare* is?"

Wentworth turned at the bottom of the stairs. "Ate it all the time in Rome. Why?"

"Do me a favor. Go in the kitchen and make sure those greasers in there aren't mangling the *calamare*. Should be crisp, not overdone, and light on the oil."

"Roger that, boss!"

"Hey, one other thing."

"Yes?"

"Soon as that no-good-for-nothing nephew of mine shows up, holler. Okay?"

Pironi's was packed. Unusual for a Tuesday night in February. This made Al that much antsier. After all, the object was to keep this meeting as low key as possible.

Al's greater circle of goombahs also patronized the place. But lower Manhattan's Little Italy was fast becoming a suburb of Chinatown and not many ordinary Chinese knew Al or his associates. Twenty years previous, if you had a business dinner on or near Mulberry Street, chances were good that all the city's families would know about it, if not the content, by breakfast the following day. But as the community dissipated, the likelihood was less.

Like a medieval baronet, Tony Acquello made a point of visiting every table every evening to check on his guests. Tony was owner, manager, maitre d' and sometimes alternate waiter and assistant chef when the need arose. He inherited the place from his father-in-law, Frank, whose own father, Angelo, had started Pironi's in 1911. The family had kept the restaurant in continuous operation since, closing only for Christmases and on November 22, 1963 when Jack Kennedy was killed. As to the latter event, every ginzo gangster in New York swore on the Madonna to Frank that the mob had nothing to do with it. Many of the old-timers, after all, had had lucrative dealings in the old days with Joe Kennedy. Furthermore, why would the mob want to rub out the first Catholic President, himself a son of immigrant stock? Wise guys might not be great at a lot of things, but one thing they were good at was remembering who was good for them and who was not.

Like his father-in-law, Tony was a paradigm of discretion, an essential ingredient for a successful restauranteur to the rich and infamous. He hired his help with this in mind. The long-termers were generously tipped by regulars like Al. Patrons knew that they could hold sensitive meetings and carry on business at Pironi's without worrying that a vain, loudmouthed host would be blabbing about it all over town. Conversely, Tony knew that such trust meant good business from regulars and the parvenus. Violating that trust could be painful -- physically as well as financially. It was that simple. Whatever problems some of his clientele had with the law, that was their business and Tony was happiest the less he knew, though he invariably knew a lot simply through osmosis. Give me your tired, your weary, free-spending nouveau riche seeking refuge from the authorities. In return, I'll guarantee you a reasonably safe, quiet and comfortable place to conduct your affairs, nefarious or otherwise. But leave me out of it. That was Tony's code. And, by the way, the food was the best in town.

The establishment itself was little touched by the passing of time. The bar, first way-station before dinner for many of Pironi's clients, occupied the left side and featured the restaurant's original, ponderous, curving, dark oak bar. Oak wood panels, carved elaborately *a fin de siècle*, lined the walls. A brass tube rail skirted the perimeter. The centerpiece behind the bar, a large fish aquarium with little medieval castles, was flanked by scores of liquor bottles -- Strega, Galliano, Vermouth Rosso, Sambucca and assorted "digestivi" being prominent. A small clip stand offering little bags of "Beer Nuts" for a buck stood forlornly off to the rear left, sharing little noticed space with a large jar soliciting donations for some crippling children's disease. A framed homily on the bar's mirrored rear wall read, "Old Age and Treachery Will Beat Youth and Idealism Every Time." The half-Irish, half-Sicilian bartender, Ralph Madden, had been in Pironi's employ for the past ten years. Always ready with a naughty joke and sympathetic ear, he knew the favorite drinks of half of Pironi's clientele without asking. The overall atmosphere was somber yet warm, almost musty, of another era. Unprepossessing old-fashionedness.

The dining area followed the same unpretentious, atavistic style. Simple white linen cloths covered nondescript tables adorned with generic candle lights. The walls featured frescoes of the island of Capri and classical Tuscan landscapes painted by some mediocre artist many years before. Framed official portraits of the President and the Pope occupied equal positions over the swinging doorway to the kitchen. A few autographed publicity photos of quasi-famous show business and sports celebrities hung in the waiting area near the entrance. "To Frank and Tony. Great food and service. Your pal, Al Martino," read one black and white glossy. Aging waiters and corpulent waitresses whisked food and dirty dishes efficiently.

The customers resembled the establishment: dark, modest, rumpled, self-satisfied, alert. By habit and dress, they were as much at home in this habitat as forest creatures were in theirs.

The older males wore dark suits, often with no necktie. They were straight-backed and stately. Old Worldly. Several sat at small corner tables -- familiar, staked-out perches habitually occupied by individual regulars. They read their newspapers -- *Wall Street Journal, New York Times, Italo-America* -- reading glasses cocked upward, their faces held at a comfortable distance, as if the reading material were infused with some unpleasant odor. Most nursed a demitasse of espresso; some with an accompanying shot glass of Grappa; others with a tumbler of sparkling cold Pellegrino with a twist of lemon. None was accompanied by a female.

Occasionally, two or three could be seen huddled closely together engaged in animated conversation, spoken *sotto voce*, punctuated by lively hand gesticulations. Was it business they talked about? Or the Old Days? Or, their grandchildren? If you asked Tony Acquello, he'd answer with a silent shrug of the shoulders. But the answer would be "yes" to all of the above.

The younger males, ranging from a few twenty-somethings to those in their forties, most falling in the middle-aged category, generally were slicker, shinier and shiftier looking than their elders. They had stiff, blow-dried haircuts and wore shiny suits, as often as not timeless. Chest hair was in. Sedateness was not. These often were escorted by females who appeared to fall into one of two categories: bleached blondes with big boobs and love handles or permed anorexic brunettes weighed down with oversized jewelry. The conversations were loud and centered on football and politics. Johnny Walker Black with soda on the rocks and dry martinis predominated among this group.

Tony hovered at Carl Giovanezza's table. Carl was with his wife, of the dark-haired, anorexic variety. Carl himself had no hairline to speak of, his graying, wavy locks anchored firmly into his forehead in a semicircle. A former stevedore, he worked his way up the ladder of the Longshoremen's Union, gaining five pounds every step of the way. Carl never smiled, probably not because he didn't want to, but because the peculiar physiognomy of his hardened Calabrian face simply wouldn't permit it. What Carl lacked in articulateness he made up for in vociferousness. But in the same matter-of-fact tone, he might talk about the correct way to de-bone *calamare*, as how he had sent his former rival in the union, Stan Janoszewski, on a one-way cruise in a cement canoe. Stan used to be good friends with Jimmy Hoffa. Anyway, Carl grunted to Tony how fine the linguini with clam sauce was this evening. "Can't be beat!" he growled. Ever the diplomat, Tony complimented Mrs. Giovanezza on the amethyst broach, the size of a baby's fist, which hung heftily from her bulimic neck.

Next stop was the table of Johnny Diosordi. Known by friends and acquaintances by his boyhood moniker of "Johnny Blues" for the color of his eyes, Johnny was the complete opposite of Carl Giovanezza. Thin, wiry and given to talking too fast for most human beings to understand, he made his mark in the garment trade. Or, to be more precise, persuading garment manufacturers to buy fire insurance from him. His wife, an unnatural blonde with equally unnaturally large breasts, remained glued to her cell phone most of the evening while chug-a-lugging Tia Marias. She, by appearances, had an oral fixation. Johnny, a voracious eater, as is often the case with small, thin, fast-talking men, devoured an antipasto, cheese manicotti with meatballs, veal Fra Diavolo, a salad and two baskets of bread. Soaking up the last traces of sauce with the last crust of bread, Johnny muttered with his mouth full, "Hey, Tony, thish ish great shtupp. Fantashtik. Never better!" Washing it all down with the last drops of Montepulciano d'Abruzzo, Johnny then asked disingenuously, "Hey, Ton', need any fire insurance?" Seeing shock setting in in Tony's face, Johnny guffawed and playfully boxed his host in the stomach. "Hey, just kiddin'! Heh, heh! Hey, Ton' what's for dessert?"

Tony continued to make the rounds. Eighty-year old Sam Dellanova, once the king of juke box operators and reputed fixer of horse races, graciously complimented Tony on the "greens and beans" -- escarole and cannellini beans cooked in oil and garlic. His doctors approved of this particular Italian soul food dish. Good for the bowels, they said.

Tony was nearly bowled over by a young man barreling off the stairway. It was Wentworth.

Regaining his balance, Tony asked politely if he could offer any assistance.

"You the manager?" Wentworth asked breathlessly.

"I own the joint. What can I do for you?"

They shook hands and exchanged names. "I need to check on how the vittles are coming along for the party upstairs."

"Vittles?! Vittles??"

Wentworth blushed.

"Hey. The *calamare* will be excellent just like always. Al always worries about the *calamare* when he's hosting guests."

"How'd you know--?"

"Like I said, I own the joint. Some things I don't want to know about. But customers, I always know who's coming. So, like I said, the *calamare* will be delicious. So will the veal and *cavatelli a pesto*. I got some great almond cakes which you'll love. Russians really like Italian pastries--"

"But, you're not supposed to know..." Wentworth was awestruck.

"Hey, like I said--"

"Yeah, I know. You own the place."

"One detail further, Chuck." Tony jerked his head toward Bags and Herman at the bar, nursing Cokes, eyes glued to "Tuesday Night WWE-RAW Wrestling."

"My clients, a lot of them carry around their own security. I can appreciate that. All I ask is that you keep them presentable and at a safe distance from the rest of the customers. I run a respectable place and I don't want to scare people away. Know what I mean?"

Wentworth nodded.

"Anything else?"

Wentworth shook his head. This man impressed him.

Tony caught Wentworth as the latter began to move toward Al's TV-fixated henchmen.

"Don't worry about those Russians coming here. I got them going upstairs the back way. Nobody'll know." He finished with a wink.

Impressive.

A few minutes after seven, through the upstairs dining room window, Al saw two cars pull into the rear parking lot. The lead car was a black Lincoln Town Car, the second, a dark red Cadillac Deville.

"Fuckin' Russians!" Al said. "Here I'm trying to do things quiet and they pull in like some kinda gypsy parade."

He was beside himself. An important meeting was about to take place, at his request. And his *consigliere* was nowhere to be found. Al thought, should he merely fire Ricky, or garrote him slowly? Blood is blood and business is business. When you combined the two, results were often disastrous. Italians are hung up on family, Al tsked. They never learn.

Out of the Lincoln emerged Yakov, resplendent in a black seal skin coat and matching fedora. The driver rushed to open the left rear door. A pair of shapely legs thrust out first, followed by a hatless head of radiant blonde tresses done up in a complex hairdo of delicate braids held in place with tiny pearled pins. Clad in a black evening dress that stopped short of the knees, the woman pulled up a full-length coat of dark fur, mink, Al thought. He had never seen Yakov with a woman. And the Russian rarely talked about them.

Out of the second car leapt Dimitrov, easily identifiable by his stiff posture, quick, furtive sideward glances, resembling a carnivorous lizard, and, of course, the nasty gash across his face. Another flunky stood by, hands thrust deep into a discount rain coat, also very alert and on guard.

Al saw Wentworth appear from the restaurant to greet them, shaking the hand of each business-like, except for the woman's, whose hand he held lightly in an upward motion. Very gallant. Wentworth spoke some words with Yakov and motioned the retinue toward the rear entrance. He could be a protocol officer in a foreign ministry.

Al was mildly concerned about Wentworth's involvement with this crowd in these circumstances, but found himself yet again grateful for the young man's stabilizing intervention into a situation almost out of control.

Bags and Herman waited passively, but on guard, at the rear entrance door.

Four wine buckets at each corner of the elaborately set table chilled *Bolla Soave*, to be served with the antipasto. Two waiters and a wine steward stood by quietly. Tony, in his usual, efficient way, had seen to all the details. The room, set aside for reserved parties, had none of the atmosphere of the restaurant proper. Comfortable but functional.

Al fidgeted, alternatingly preening his hair and straightening his collar with each hand. *Ricky'll be looking for work, I swear,* he thought. *Damned spoiled little peacock. He'll be sweeping floors and cleaning toilets at Al-Mac.* These thoughts, emanating from true, heartfelt anger, nonetheless, resonated hollowly within Al's brain. He needed a back-up whom he could trust completely, and Ricky was it despite his undependability in other areas. He also had been the cut-out maintaining communications with the Russians, through Dimitrov. In the bottom of his heart at this moment, Al felt vulnerable.

He heard the shuffling of feet up the stairs. Al awaited his guests at the top of the stairwell, next to the door to the private room.

Yakov led the troupe, hat in hand, his face sporting a stiff smile. Seeing Al, he skipped up the remaining upper six or seven steps and embraced Al with a bear hug.

"Old friend!" he exclaimed. "In Russian, we say, 'When old friends meet, spring cannot be far away.'"

"In Italian, we say, 'When old friends meet, it's time to eat!" Al motioned him into the room.

Yakov wagged an admonishing finger at Al. "Always make jokes, you funny guy!"

The blonde was next. She was even more dazzling up close. Tall, erect, regal yet demure. The golden hair, fairly blinding in its radiance, framed a face of strawberries and cream complexion, the natural blush of which was accentuated from the cold night air. A black satin dress with traditional Russian filigree around the upper breast formed deliciously over her tall, lush figure. But it was the marvelous, beaming, deep blue eyes that commanded Al's total attention. Riveting and inviting, yet betraying a hint of sadness or guardedness. Al couldn't be sure.

"May I introduce this, my gracious lady," Yakov gestured. "-- Lydia Yekaterina Puchinskaya."

Al gently kissed her hand, more out of instinct than conscious intent. He knew how to squire a lady, but wasn't so much into continental manners. This was that rare female who, through vibes of some sort or other, triggered a mechanism in men that caused them to behave either like Lancelot or Genghiz Khan. Gallant or wantonly lustful.

"Very pleased. Though I'll never be able to say your name," Al said.

Al then correctly shook Dimitrov's hand. The warm feeling instilled in him by Lydia was immediately replaced by an icy chill. He had never taken a liking to this Russian. And after Ricky related to him the incident at the warehouse, gory details and all, a cold dread added itself to his instinctual dislike for the man.

Wentworth brought up the rear.

"What do you want me to do, boss?" he asked.

Al faced a dilemma. No Ricky to be seen. He wanted somebody to share the table with him from his organization, if only to impress on Yakov that he headed a solid and united outfit. One elementary lesson he learned long ago was that you never, never betrayed any hint of weakness to your rivals or potential rivals. Those whose organizations exhibited cracks invited destruction.

Yet he had gone out of his way to keep Wentworth apart, on the clean, "legitimate" side of his affairs. After all, that was the reason he'd hired him.

A solution hit him like a lightning bolt. Keep Wentworth around till Ricky showed up. Ricky could be sloppy, but, in the end, he really never let his uncle down. Al would keep the conversation on small talk until Ricky arrived. Then he'd quietly ask Wentworth to attend to other matters elsewhere.

Al put his hand on Wentworth's shoulder and spoke softly into his ear, "First of all, don't call me boss. Chuckie, stick around for a few minutes. Have a drink. Look important, but don't say much. I'll have something else for you to do later. Got me?" He winked. Wentworth gave a single nod. Ambassadors and generals used to do this to him. He knew how to be a good aide.

They took their seats. The wine steward promptly poured the Soave.

Al lifted his glass. "To old friends. *Cent'anni!*"

Forgetting protocol, he clinked glasses first with the Princess of Russia, as Al thought of Lydia.

"*Nazdaroviye*," Yakov returned the toast. "May old friends find new business."

Al could see what was coming.

Wentworth followed orders and kept silent, except when spoken to. Al had introduced him simply by his name, leaving a question mark in the minds of the Russians as to his true position in Al's structure. Dimitrov glared at him intensely. Lydia sat directly opposite Wentworth. They smiled politely at one another.

The antipasto arrived. Marinated eggplant, oil cured olives, sliced prosciutto and salami, sardines, sun dried tomatoes and red peppers on a bed of romaine and arugula. Al served his guests personally.

After some small talk, Yakov began, "Now, Al, I think you know what is on my mind. But first, I let you to talk about why we meet tonight. For example, some problems of supply--"

"Hey, you got problems, I got problems, everybody's got problems. Don't worry about it now. Let's have a good time. *Mangia!*" Al saluted them with another raised glass.

Yakov's face betrayed puzzlement.

Dimitrov, ex-fighter of the Hindu Kush and professional survivor of Russia's cutthroat mafia wars, squinted as if confused. His radar-like eyes coldly locked onto Al's face, minutely scrutinizing every move and gesture, studying him as a cobra does its prey.

Wentworth attacked the antipasto lustily. He and Lydia continued to exchange polite smiles.

"Your associate here." Yakov gestured at Wentworth. "Mr..."

"Wentworth," he responded.

"Ah, yes. You are new," Yakov said knowingly. "Your duties include...?"

Al interjected before Wentworth could answer. "Yeah. Chuckie here's been with us, what, nine months?"

Wentworth nodded.

"He's been working on special projects, haven't you Chuckie?"

"Ah yes. I see. And, so, where then is Mr. Ricky tonight?"

"Also working on special projects. He should be joining us real soon."

Dimitrov took it all in silently.

The two bosses reverted to talking about New York politics, conditions in Russia, the weather and other non-business-related matters. Al kept looking at his watch. Just where was that goddamn nephew, anyway?

Lydia's eyes kept meeting Wentworth's. He reciprocated. Each smiled faintly. Gentle wafts of a delicate perfume came his way, carried on invisible currents.

The next course, piping hot bowls of *stracciatella* soup, was served neatly by Tony's efficient men.

"You make me eat borscht. Now it's my turn to take revenge," Al joked.

Yakov maintained a jovial demeanor, but his impatience, mingled with confusion, was making itself felt.

Dimitrov definitely picked up that something was not quite right in the Malandrino camp.

Wentworth broke the ice with Lydia in a quiet side conversation.

"Do you speak English?" he asked.

Her cheeks reddened and dimpled ever so slightly with a gentle smile and responded in a voice which was neither high nor very low in pitch. "Yes. I studied English for twelve years. I love English. More than French." She spoke as much with her expressive eyes as with her mouth.

Goose bumps erupted across Wentworth's skin.

"And I *love* America!" she added.

Wentworth's scalp tingled.

The door swung open, banging against the inside wall. In sauntered Ricky, dressed in a loud, silk turquoise suit, shirt open to reveal a nest of dark hair. Over this he wore a bold camel hair coat with a huge curved collar.

Al's eyes shot at his nephew, reflecting anger and surprise, but tempered with relief. *Looks like a stinking pimp,* Al thought.

"Hey, sorry I'm late everybody," Ricky offered with no further explanation. He took a seat next to his uncle.

With a slight nod from Al, Wentworth excused himself. A similar gesture from Yakov excused Lydia. Ricky cast a lingering leer over Lydia. The two went downstairs to wait in the restaurant lounge by the bar.

"Now we get to business, yes?" Yakov asked.

"Yes," Al said. "We got some problems we need to iron out. For some reason, this is the season for problems. But with my Russian friends, these are few."

Yakov nodded assent. "Only three years we have done business together. In three years we make more money together. Every year, all of us at this table, we have become richer. *Druzhba i brastvo*, friendship and brotherhood -- but not communist kind!"

Al chuckled.

"Yakov, I want to raise an issue of m.o.--"

"What?"

"Modus operandi. The way we do things in our organizations. You know, habits, practice. That kind of thing.

"In any case, this incident at the pier a little while back."

"Yes. Teamsters man who cannot mind his own business."

"Yeah. The guy was a jerk, had no business butting into our affairs."

"Now he is no longer problem," Yakov interjected self-contentedly, brushing his palms together to indicate that, like a ball of lint, Max Chesny was easily disposed of.

Ricky started, only to be caught by an impatient signal from Al to keep quiet, an act lost on neither Yakov nor Dimitrov.

The diners fell silent suddenly as Tony's waiters removed the soup dishes and served steaming plates of *cavatelli* lightly covered in a heavily garlicked green pesto sauce. The silence persisted as Al's beloved fried *calamare* and a fine red Bordolino, personally selected by Al, were served. Long experienced with Pironi's special clientele, with their eccentric need for strict privacy, the headwaiter whispered to Al that he would be on call at the bottom of the stairs.

Al cocked an ear toward the door, listening intently as the waiters shambled down the steps. Satisfied that privacy was ensured, he fixed his sight on Yakov's face.

"Look, I know that in Russia it's Wild West time, that anything goes and everybody's out for himself. The place has just opened up. Nobody's on top and there are no codes of conduct.

"It used to be that way in this country too. Back in the '20s and '30s people were machine gunning each other in the streets. They talk about how some cities are 'dangerous' today. You should've seen Chicago back then. My old man used to tell me about Luciano and Capone and all those old gangsters. How they could buy any politician, judge, cop. And how they let their temper get the best of them, then go out and chop their enemies down -- shoot them, beat their brains out, set 'em on fire, throw 'em out windows, or off a bridge with cement overshoes. Those

were crazy times. But it was Prohibition. After FDR
repealed Prohibition, those wiseguys who didn't behave
themselves went to jail, like Capone. The rest of them
grew up."

Yakov listened carefully and nodded.

"Today, some of those old ways have come back. Drugs
take the place of Prohibition. And it's the Salvadoreans, the
Asians, the Colombians who are cutting each other, and
innocent people too, to pieces. There's no rules. As a
result, there's chaos. And chaos is not only bad for life
expectancy, it's also bad for business."

"So, Al, you are telling me that in our line of business
we can all be gentlemen."

"I didn't say that. What I'm saying is that we who are
more established learned from our past mistakes. We have
a code, rules--"

"Al, I admire your success. We all have much to learn.
Yes. Let me tell you two stories of my experience. In bad
old days, under communists, I knew a young man, his
name, Oleg Korataev. We belong to gang called *Valiulins*.
He, I and another man, Sasha Graber, we work together to
make money. We smuggle radios, cameras, ladies
underwear, anything that Soviet people want but cannot get
because stupid communists don't let them. We have friends
then in KGB and police and city government. We pay
them, they turn blind eye. We don't get rich, only
communists get rich. But we do okay.

"In 1992, we send Oleg to America to set up network.
Then we send Sasha. We call Oleg, '*Oleg Grozny*' -- Oleg
the Terrible -- because he was powerful and made people
do what we want. Oleg was boxer. He also was good with
knife."

Yakov nodded in Dimitrov's direction. "But Dimitrov is
better with knife. No, best." Yakov devoured the

calamare, washing it down with glass after glass of Bordolino.

Al recalled how Yakov and the other Russians went through bottles of vodka without even getting dizzy much less passing out. Wine must be like water to them.

"If somebody does not pay debt on time, we send Oleg. He always came back with the money.

"Sasha, on other hand, we call him 'Alexander the Diplomat.'" Russian gangs have troubles, they fight each other, we send Sasha. He is, how do you say, smooth talker. Everybody trust Sasha. He negotiates peace treaties -- like Andrei Gromyko.

"So, these men do very, very well in Brooklyn, also they go to Chicago and Toronto. Sasha even has night club -- right in Brighton Beach.

"One day, no money comes in. They collect 'insurance' money from shop owners and pay eighty percent to me at end of month. So, I call Oleg. No answer. I call Sasha. Sasha says, 'Oh so sorry, boss, but we quit. We now on our own. Bye, bye. And he hangs up phone.

"Few days later, *Oleg Grozny* gets one bullet to back of his head near subway station. Not much time later, Mr. Sasha dies on street in Moscow. Forty bullets from machine gun to his chest. Then, we find third rebel, young man named Yanik, here in Brooklyn. He gets four bullets in face. Police find body in garbage dump later."

Yakov again brushed his palms together. "No more problem for us.

"Second story. Mr. Naum Reichel, not friend, not with our organization, but competitor, again here in Brighton Beach. He becomes very bold, very arrogant, very stupid. He tries to make Russian restaurant owners to pay protection money to him. This is not approved by us. Madame Boronova tells us about this man. Then we learn that he and his little punk helpers begin to sell heroin in neighborhood.

"Next thing to know, Mr. Naum Reichel is walking on Brighton Beach Avenue and two men shoot him in chest and stomach. But these men are young and green, not *Afghantsi* like Dimitrov. They shoot badly. Mr. Naum Reichel lives.

"But shortly after, in Berlin, another man, a Russian, is beat up very badly. So bad that doctors say his face requires many operations and he will be ugly forever. He also loses spleen. This man is Simeon, brother of Naum.

"Mr. Naum Reichel lives, but he knows that old business days are past. He goes away to open flower shop in Pittsburgh.

"In all these cases, police ask questions of Russian people. They talk to witnesses. They investigate. But nobody sees nothing. Nobody knows nothing. FBI advertises for *stukachi*, informers, in Russian-American newspaper. But nobody calls them.

"Point of story, Al, is this: fear is stronger than persuasion. Gentlemen lose. Bad guys win. We Russians, we understand this. This is our history. At pier, we protect our interests and your interests. We guarantee that nobody bothers us again. Not Teamsters. Nobody."

Yakov accentuated this last remark with a half-salute of his wine glass before gulping the contents.

"You're all nuts!" Ricky blurted.

He was checked by a look of sharp rebuke from Al.

"My dear Ricky," Yakov continued. "Your mafia is almost finished. Little by little, the authorities destroy you. Even Gambino family is no more. John Gotti – he was a mere peacock. Pathetic. You lose because you become soft, like rest of American society. At the same time, FBI becomes more tough. Now mafia exists only in movies. This will not happen to us."

Al sat back, contemplating the Russian, and drummed his fingers on the table. The *tap-tap-tap* of his fingertips was the only sound in a room as silent as a crypt. And the others remained as still as corpses.

Finally, Al shifted in his seat, leaned forward, and said, "This is what I propose, Yakov. From now on, if you want to carve your enemies up like Thanksgiving turkeys, or to pump ninety-nine bullets into somebody's face just to prove a point, go ahead. As long as they have no connection to me or my organization. But if you want to do a job on somebody of mutual interest, you consult me first. Agreed?"

Yakov took a moment to absorb this, lightly rubbing his lips with a thumb and forefinger. "Yes, okay. You still are angry for what we did to your traitor friend, Mortimer, yes?"

"Christ, Yakov. You don't just go around cutting out the guts of officials, much less an American ambassador. Morty had it coming, like I said before. Ricky was going to take care of him, in our own way. We would've brought him down without killing him. Would've wrecked him politically and financially. He would've been horseshit to all his muckedy-muck friends in politics, Wall Street, his home town. We were going to circulate pictures we have of him with little girls down in Mexico. Through some friendly reporters, we were ready to expose his links to drug traffickers. Hell, he would've ended up blowing his own brains out. We could've made it happen. We're experts."

"Risk of revealing connection with us was too great," Yakov said bluntly.

"Bullshit. Listen to me my Russky friend." Al's
jugulars pulsed. He held an index finger straight to
Yakov's face. "This is my country. You have no right
going around pissing all over it. Mortimer was yellow and
he was greedy. You got it right. But he might have come
back to us. The information tap that your asshole buddies
in the KGB, or whatever it's called now, couldn't get
enough of might have resumed. We would've tried to
blackmail the son of a bitch again. If that failed, then we
were going to make a train wreck of his life."

Al whispered to Ricky to get the waiters to serve the
next course. Ricky went quickly downstairs where he
found the headwaiter dutifully standing by. The latter
scampered off to the kitchen.

Turning to go back upstairs, Ricky caught a glimpse of
Wentworth and Lydia in the lounge engaged in animated
conversation. He went over.

Studiously ignoring Wentworth, Ricky put on his best
Brad Pitt smile and bent down toward Lydia, placing one
hand on the back of her chair.

"Hi. Miss...Lydia was it?"

"Puchinskaya. Lydia Yekatarina Puchinskaya," she
replied formally.

"Lydia. Pretty name. Can I buy you a drink, Lydia?"
He abruptly signaled a waiter to come over.

"As you can see, Mr...Prick? I have already
something." She tapped her glass of Gimlet."

"Rick. It's Rick."

"Oh," she giggled. Her face flushed. She turned
innocently toward Wentworth. "I thought you said that he
was a prick? I do not know this word. Is it a funny one?"

Wentworth stifled a laugh. Ricky was not amused.

"Butt out Wonderbread!"

The headwaiter tugged at Ricky's sleeve. "Mr. Malandrino wants you, like right now, Mr. Laguzza."

"Yeah. Okay." His eyes bored through Wentworth, who returned a defiant Marine's gaze.

"One word of advice, Lydia. Stay clear of poor white trash Southern crackers. We got better in this country."

Turning to Lydia, he added, "You need anything -- anything -- call me. I can make things happen in this town." He handed her one of his legitimate business cards and hurried back upstairs.

"Did I say anything wrong?"

Wentworth burst out laughing.

Ricky re-entered the upstairs dining room. There was a chill, a low-grade tension in the air. They were silently into their *vitello francese* -- veal in a butter-lemon sauce. As Ricky took his seat and fixed his napkin on his lap, Al furtively jerked his chin upward and put an index finger together with a thumb in the Sicilian gesture for "What gives?!" Ricky shrugged and commenced to eat.

Amid the chomping, slurping and gulping, the only voice to be heard was that of Jerry Vale crooning "Amore, Scusami" over the music sound system.

"The other thing I wanted to bring up," Al broke in without warning, his attention fixed on his plate, "is how come the supply of junk has suddenly dried up? It's been, what Ricky? A month, two months? A lot of people rely on us for a dependable supply. We've always been noted for offering a quality product for a good price on a reliable basis. Lately, we haven't been living up to our reputation. As a result, there's anger and mistrust. The Chinese start relying totally on their own sources and stop doing business with us across the board. The Latinos automatically assume we're doing a job on them. So they start slicing up everybody in sight, like in a Rambo movie. I got a double Excedrin headache times a hundred. I haven't been able to get a straight answer out of your guy here." He nodded at Dimitrov. "So, what gives?"

Yakov stopped eating, shifted uneasily.

"Al, I must offer apology. I also have headaches over this unfortunate development. Problem was at other end. At first, I don't know exactly where. I think that maybe competitor in Russia is double crossing me. I go back, with Dimitrov, to Moscow. My colleagues, they also don't know nothing. They say problem is in Azerbaijan. Maybe war there has stopped supplies from transiting. Maybe war in Afghanistan keeps them from getting out at all. I send Dimitrov to Baku. They tell him, problem not with us. Is in Turkey.

"To make long story short, we go to Turkey. Supplies always go through Turkey after Azerbaijan. We have SVR friends in embassy. SVR is new name for KGB. The ones in Ankara embassy, they work for us. So, they say, new boss, he does not approve. He tries to stop SVR to be in business making money. 'To protect Russia is our duty,' he says. 'Business of SVR is not *business*.' He asks Moscow to investigate, to arrest his own men there in Ankara, Turkey. Also in Russian consulate at Istanbul.

"Believe me, Al, such people are very rare in Russia now. Honest people. Patriotic people. They earn maybe a hundred, two-hundred dollars a month in Russia. Still they play by rules. Fools. Anyway, I go back to Moscow to talk to SVR friends. They try to stall investigation that Starenkov demands. But they tell me they cannot fire SVR *Rezident* in Turkey. If they try, he will go to Russian Duma and to newspapers to spill the peas."

"Beans."

"Yes, Al, all of the beans. This democracy is good for us in most ways. But in other ways, is pain in ass. If in America, freedom is another word for nothing left to lose, in Russia it is another word for everything to lose, including your money -- or even your life."

Perhaps aware of the effect the wine was having on him, Yakov stopped and stared into his glass pensively as he slowly swirled the contents.

"And?" Al asked.

Yakov's enigmatic Cheshire grin creased across his face. He looked Al in the eyes, the smile faded.

"Comrade Starenkov becomes no longer problem." Again, he brushed his palms. "Finished. SVR is now again our partner in Turkey. Comrade Starenkov is victim of Chechnyan fanatics, or maybe Armenians. In any case, he is victim of one of Russia's many little enemies left over from old Soviet Union republics. So says SVR to leadership."

Al stared a moment at Yakov. This was a very dangerous man, he pondered. A man so ruthless and so lacking behavioral limits cannot be trusted. Italians had Honor, Respect, *Omertà*, a code for doing things. But these Russians were little different, after all, from the soulless Colombians or Vietnamese or the road warriors who roamed the desolate cityscape of the South Bronx.

"So, supplies resume?"

"Immediately."

They shook hands.

CHAPTER TEN

As was too often the case, the call came at home at 1:00 am. Innes got more than the normal share of off-hour calls. It was one of the growing number of reasons for his wanting to get through with his assignment in the Ops Center and move on to a less demanding job, one with predictable duties and hours such as political officer in a boring, cushy embassy in Europe. This was the only clear thought in his fatigued brain as he picked up the receiver.

At the other end was one of the junior officer drones doing the night shift. He apologized for waking Innes.

"The White House called earlier. They asked the Secretary to go over to brief the President on the latest on the Mortimer murder investigation. The Secretary asked Scher to go along. Scher, in turn, wants you to accompany to take notes, etc," he said.

"And it takes this long to let me know?!" Shaking off sleep, Innes caught himself. "Uh, right. Sure. What time?"

"0800 sharp. Secretary Dennison wants to be briefed beforehand at 0700. Scher wants his people assembled at his office at 0600 on the button. Sorry buddy."

"Uggh."

"What is it this time?" Carolyn yawned, barely stirring from her side of the bed.

"The President wants to be briefed on the Mortimer thing. They want me to be there."

"Will you be home by supper this time?"

This rankled Innes. Had he replied that Jesus Christ called personally to let him, Robert Woodruff Innes, be the first to know of His Second Coming, her reaction would have been exactly the same.

"That's up to the Commander-in-Chief, dear. I'll have to let you know." The sarcasm dripped from his voice like a corroding acid.

Carolyn muffled a grunt and faded back into slumber.

The scent of fresh coffee permeated the office of Bernard Scher. A colorless, functional government workplace, the importance of its occupant was nonetheless made clear by its comparatively larger size, its window view and the obligatory ego wall hung with diplomas, awards certificates and photos of Scher shaking hands with presidents, popes and other potentates.

Sitting in a rough semi-circle were Scher's deputy, Marc Glaston; Dennison's chief of staff, Harrington Fell; the chief of diplomatic security, Ralph Torres; the deputy CIA director, Tom Hunter; the FBI's director of investigations, Dominic Berlucci; Innes's boss -- Operations Center director Bill Platten -- and Innes himself. Each clutched a styrofoam cup of cafeteria coffee, except for Innes, who nursed a can of Coke. All looked sleep-deprived.

Scher sat in the most comfortable chair, an overstuffed GSA-issued item of mediocre quality and design. He puffed on his ever-present pipe. The billowing hickory smoke made at least half of the attendees, stomachs growling from lack of breakfast, nauseous. In the confines of his own office, the State Department's legal advisor, who apparently viewed himself as above the law, chose to ignore the ban on smoking in the building and no one had the temerity to challenge him on it.

"As you all know," Scher began, "the President has asked to be briefed on the Mortimer investigation. I want to get the latest and to pick your collective brains on where we should be going from here. At seven-forty-five I'll head out to the White House with the Secretary. I will brief him an hour from now, just before we depart. Mr. Innes, you will be notetaker. The rest of you will brief NSC staffers on details while we're with the President."

What Scher failed to mention was that the Mortimer murder mystery was leading nowhere and wouldn't go away. Congress kept asking nagging questions as to why no leads had been uncovered, and second-guessing the sincerity of the President and the competence of the concerned government agencies in resolving the case. Major newspapers found the case grist for attacking the administration for its policies on terrorism. With a recession on its hands, legislative gridlock in Congress and a foreign policy lacking in direction, the White House, eight months before a presidential election, didn't need any more political problems than it already had.

"Tom, what do we have on Middle East terrorists?" Scher asked. Hunter proceeded to review a panoply of the usual suspects: al-Qaida, Hamas, Hezbollah, Syrians, Iranians, PLO renegades, muslims of varying political persuasions, both domestic and overseas, even Sri Lankan Tamils, who were neither Middle Eastern nor Muslim.

Innes rubbed his fatigued face with both hands. He'd heard it all before. The investigation of the Mortimer case

was quickly becoming the biggest, running bad joke in
Washington for a good reason. His boss, Platten, gave him
a sharp look and signaled for him to take notes.

"Thanks Tom." Turning to Berlucci, Scher asked,
"What's the scoop on that guy at Prudential?"

Berlucci drew a blank, then said, "You mean the former
Egyptian student?"

Scher stared at the ceiling and fidgeted, advertising his
impatience. "Yes," he said in a tone of voice he reserved
for slow children and stupid bureaucrats. "The radical
Islamic extremist who Homeland Security managed to let
into the country." The last point was a cheap shot at the
agency whose Immigration and Customs Enforcement
screened aliens at the nation's border checkpoints.

Berlucci shrugged. "The guy's clean. And he's making
a load of dough. Married a nice American girl. They're
pursuing the American Dream in the suburbs."

Scher's utter contempt filled the atmosphere in the
cluttered office with the volatile tension of a fuel-air
explosive just before ignition. He looked icily at Berlucci,
puffed methodically on his pipe.

Scher turned to Torres. "How about you?"

"The RSO in Rome reports that the Italian police are
getting increasingly worried about rising numbers of
Kosovo extremists popping up on Italian soil. As long as
Kosovo is denied formal independence, they're worried that
the Kosovars will become the next Hamas and will start
tossing bombs all over Europe."

Platten added, "State's European Bureau agrees. They
see a return of Balkan terrorism along the lines of the
Serbian and Bosnian anarchists before World War I."

Scher's face lit up. He leaned forward. "That's
interesting. *Very* interesting. What solid evidence do we
have?"

Torres and Platten looked at each other, then to Hunter, then back to Scher.

"We've made it a top collection priority for our stations in Europe," Hunter replied.

"Meaning you've got birdshit," Scher sneered. "We've *got* to develop some solid leads fast. We *have* to show that there is momentum to the investigation, that State and the other agencies are pushing ahead, meticulously sifting through the evidence, leaving no stone unturned. I want the public to see our efforts in a positive light so that they'll draw comparisons with the 9/11 investigation."

"As for the FBI, we see no evidence, circumstantial or otherwise, to link this murder with Kosovars. Or with any other organized political grouping," Berlucci said.

"What are you getting at?" Scher demanded coolly.

Berlucci turned his palms upward and shrugged as to indicate that it was obvious. "In law enforcement, whenever we exhaust leads in one area, we open another channel of investigation. And we broaden the circle of possible suspects, to include people who wouldn't come to mind at first blush. Right down to the victim's grandmother, if necessary." With his wrestler's physique and agile mind, Berlucci radiated confidence and competence. "And not least important, nobody's come forth to claim credit for the killing. Nobody. Usually, these groups jump out of the woodwork to claim responsibility. This leads us to believe that even the craziest of the crazies don't see a political hook they can latch onto in the Mortimer case."

"I think he has a point," Innes said. "It's clear that we aren't getting anywhere in the direction we've been heading. Maybe Ambassador Mortimer was the victim of other -- more conventional -- perpetrators with entirely different motives from what we've been looking at."

Platten looked reprovingly at Innes. In the hierarchical
State Department culture, subordinates were expected to
leave all the talking to their bosses. And the greatest sin
was to question or contradict the party line as laid down
from on high.

Scher looked at his watch, put down his pipe and shifted
in his chair.

"Look. Until somebody can show me solid evidence to
the contrary, the leads we're pursuing are that Ambassador
Mortimer was killed by politically motivated elements.
Anti-American elements, terrorists, who, for whatever
hare-brained political agenda, wanted to hit at this country.
This is the most logical tack. I can't be having this
investigation going off in nineteen different directions
looking at Mortimer's Aunt Tilly or anybody else who
doesn't fit a logical profile of an envoy killer. The media,
not to mention Congress, will devour us. And the President
won't stand for it. We have to show results. And the
sooner the better."

He then laid down a framework for briefing Secretary
Roy Dennison and the President: the investigation was
going great guns; all legitimate leads were being pursued;
the list of probable suspects was being narrowed as the
intelligence agencies continued their relentless collection
and analysis of data; and the pressure would be maintained
on the Italian government to follow suit leading up to
arrests as soon as possible.

Innes had been to the White House before. When he
was younger, he joined as one in a cast of hundreds of
government workers invited to act as cheering, flag-waving
greeters on the South Lawn to welcome third-tier foreign

leaders -- the presidents of Finland, Cameroon, Paraguay came to mind. On a more substantive level, he'd attended meetings at the NSC, both in the Old Executive Office Building, adjoining the White House, and in the West Wing. He had attended a reception in the Rose Garden in 1988 commemorating "Captive Nations Week," a big deal for President Reagan in those days before the communist bloc evaporated. Innes, however, had never seen the Oval Office or any other inner sanctum in the power house on Pennsylvania Avenue, nor had he ever met a president much less briefed one.

The entourage met in the State Department basement. The Secretary of State arrived first, having zoomed down in his reserved elevator. The others scrambled down the stairs, victims of the Department's chronically malfunctioning lifts. Scher accompanied Secretary Dennison in his dedicated, armored vehicle. Armed Diplomatic Security guards followed this car closely in their own armored Chevy Blazer. The rest squeezed into two of the Department's small fleet of chauffeured dark blue Crown Victorias. They unconsciously took their places in strict rank order, which meant Innes was crammed into the last limo along with Marc Glaston, Platten and Berlucci.

With cops diverting traffic and the DS Chevy's emergency dome light whirring, it was a five-minute drive through the three blocks to the west gate. Having been precleared, they entered after a cursory inspection by the Secret Service uniformed guards manning the entrance.

On the way, Glaston said something about how the intel agencies needed to hustle more and get results quickly on this case. Without missing a beat, Berlucci told him not to hold his breath. Innes had an instant liking for the FBI man.

Dennison, Scher and Innes were ushered into a West Wing conference room. They were joined by Defense Secretary Wilkins, CIA Director Levin, FBI Director Karlson and Chief of Staff Selmur. Each took his seat, again according to hierarchical rank. Innes sat against the wall behind Dennison and Scher. Scher sat at Dennison's right elbow. He kept up a non-stop patter in a low voice. Innes caught "no need to worry," "just a matter of time," and "no doubt it's political."

Two aides arrived, young staffers, a male with a shock of brown hair hanging over his forehead, about 30, and a black female, somewhat younger. Each was decked out in J. Crew *cum* L.L. Bean attire. She appeared to try to offset the preppy image with oversized, jangling earrings made somewhere in the Third World.

Next entered a smug-looking character in a light, double-breasted suit and silk shirt, whom Innes immediately recognized as Nicholas Horvath, the President's National Security Adviser. They all shook hands. The youngsters identified themselves as Wynn Kearnan and Prudence Harding, special assistants to the President for domestic constituencies and public liaison, respectively -- members of President Corgan's "brat pack," infamous for their combination of activism and inexperience.

The meeting's host strode in unannounced and with such naturalness that several of the attendees almost overlooked him. In his wake was his chief of staff, Howard Selmur. The President took his seat and asked for a quick summary.

Drawing from Scher's earlier briefing at State, Dennison proceeded to explain to President Corgan that, while there were no big breaks in the case as yet, the investigation was going forward at a vigorous pace, etc., etc.

Henry Corgan listened patiently, leaning back in his chair, twirling his reading glasses. He had a reputation as a no-nonsense, let's-get-down-to-brass-tacks politician. His p.r. spin doctors had to soften a cutting, aggressive image which, according to the exit polls, cost him votes in the last election, especially among women.

"Who did it then?" he asked simply.

After a pause, Dennison stated with forced confidence, "Well, the intel people and FBI are narrowing the field of probable suspects."

Corgan cut Dennison short, fixed his eyes on Karlson and asked, "Is that so?"

Sensing an awkward moment, Karlson collected his thoughts. "Mr. President, we've got a long way to go in this investigation."

"You mean you got zilch, is that it?"

Karlson nodded. "Mr. President. We need to broaden the scope of inquiry. Maybe terrorists are responsible. Maybe not. We need to take a fresh look at other possibilities."

"For instance?"

"Criminal. Personal."

Dennison's stomach was churning. "Mr. President, to go off in these other directions would only invite more criticism from the media. Without some proof that--"

Corgan stopped him. "Look, gentlemen -- and lady -- all I want is results. We can't have this dragging on with absolutely nothing to show. One of my ambassadors gets knocked off. Hell, he gets butchered. And we can't find squat."

Kearnan, Harding and Innes scribbled furiously in their notebooks.

The President looked at Horvath. "Nick, I want you to stay personally on top of this. Stay in touch with Misters

Levin and Wilkins as well as with Mr. Dennison and Mr.
Karlson. Whoever else. I want a status report at my
morning briefing every day."

The meeting was over. It had lasted barely fifteen
minutes. Corgan was gone in a flash.

The others huddled.

Dennison, Levin, Wilkins and Scher went off to one side
with Horvath and Selmur. Dennison was driving home a
point animatedly as the others listened intently with their
arms folded.

Innes went to the young presidential assistants. They
asked him his views.

Innes recounted his escapade in Rome, how he thought
Scher and company were chasing wild geese, that, once the
truth -- whatever it was -- about Mortimer came out, it
might be unsettling to the administration. They scribbled
away. They asked that Innes stay in regular touch with
them on developments.

"That depends on my bosses," he said, pointing to the
klatsch of self-important functionaries at the other side of
the room.

Bob Innes was seeing more of Colleen. Frequently,
their get-togethers were over lunch, the time most easily
available, and safe, for Innes. The more they saw each
other, the more they laughed. She began teaching him
Thai. During a stroll along the elm-lined Reflecting Pool
one Friday in late winter, she taught him, "*chan rak khun*,"
I love you. Caught speechless, he stopped, looked deeply
into her soul, put his arms around her gently and kissed her.
The world was spun faster and faster. It must have been,
for they both toppled to the ground, which created yet more

laughter, and a second kiss, this time anchored in the earth. Joggers, passing tourists and old people feeding the pigeons laughed with them. "Atta way, you lovers!" shouted a tattooed Vietnam vet manning a nearby POW/MIA awareness kiosk.

Their hushed passion blossomed when they held each other during increasingly frequent rendezvous at her small apartment in Arlington. He didn't want to leave her side during these trysts, to face the walking dead at his workplace, the cold woman to whom he was married, the loveless life that sucked him deeper into self-doubt and despair. The white softness of Colleen's neck held the warmth and mystery of womanhood; her eyes, the inspiration of love; her hands, the strength of beauty. In her he could get lost forever.

For Colleen, it was a forbidden love, one with only question marks at the end of the road. But she chose to suspend thinking about these troubling enigmas and decided to live and love for the present. But she prayed to God that it would all somehow work out in the end.

In her small bed, they stroked each other tenderly.

She turned on her stomach and propped her chin in one hand. "My grandfather from County Mayo used to tell us Irish legends and tales. My favorite was of Cuchullain, a grand knight, and his lady, Emer. They lived in the wondrous and peaceful land ruled by King Conchobar."

"Did they live happily ever after?"

"It wasn't so simple. He had to end a relationship with another woman, and she had to contend with the disapproval of her family. Together they defended the kingdom from foreign enemies. They almost died doing so."

"What kind of--?"

Deep in thought, she signaled Innes to keep quiet. "I'll never forget what they always said to one another after a harrowing adventure: She: 'May God make smooth the path before you.' He: 'And may you be safe from every harm.'" She looked at Innes with a bemused expression.

Innes smiled back.

Silence enveloped them like a cold fog.

Stark reality rudely raised its formidable head. Alas, it was not olden times, nor could they inure themselves from the hard facts of modern times. And Innes was married. With children of his own.

Colleen turned on her side. She tried to conceal the tears streaming down her cheek onto the pillow. Innes stared into space for answers that were not there.

CHAPTER ELEVEN

Innes wrote up a detailed summary of the presidential briefing. He concluded with a recommendation that the investigation change course and begin to delve into facets of Mortimer's personal life. He added highlights of his own side investigation in Rome, but left out any reference to Colleen, for her own protection.

His report won eager reception, but not from his superiors. A stick'um note plastered on Innes's computer screen confronted him as he dragged himself into his cubicle at 7:30 am. "See me NOW," it announced in red ink. It was signed "Platten."

Innes sensed a changed atmosphere in the Ops Center. People took discreet notice of his presence, some following him with their eyes. It was the feeling one had upon showing up with a black eye or a bad haircut. The attention people paid was not positive, however subdued it might be.

Robin Croft's was the only face reflecting overt sympathy. "Bob. I just want you to know that I'm behind you. If I can be helpful, just let me know."

With the profound uncertainty that comes with facing a firing squad, Innes shuffled into Platten's glass-enclosed cubicle.

Platten didn't look up from the stack of morning traffic.
His face was as gray as his thinning hair.

"Ahem," Innes coughed nervously.

"I know you're here," Platten said stiffly.

Innes felt awkward. Memories of fifth grade and the
principal's office swept through his mind.

Platten tossed a document across his desk. "What is
this?"

"My memo."

"Your memo."

"Yes. That's right. My memo."

"Who else has it?"

"The usual suspects."

"This is no laughing matter, mister!"

"Sorry. I circulated it around for clearance. Seven,
eight offices, I guess."

"Multiply that by at least ten. The photocopiers are
working overtime as every secretary, every staff aide, every
bored civil servant with a dirty mind cranks out copies of
your memo."

"I don't get it," Innes said.

"You don't *get* it, huh? How about this?" Platten
snatched up Innes's memo and clutched it with both hands
before his eyes. "Our investigation turned up numerous
incidences of sexual misconduct by Ambassador Mortimer.
For example, at a February 13, 2006 banquet, he chased a
16-year old girl, the daughter of a prominent Italian
industrialist, to her hotel room and tried to break the door
down. As a result of liaisons with Roman prostitutes, Mr.
Mortimer contracted herpes. Only the direct intervention
of the Italian leadership prevented a newspaper from
printing the allegations of a Brazilian transvestite who said
s/he had..." Platten flung the memo to the floor. "Just
what was in your mind? You can't write such drivel--"

"It's true."

"How the hell do you know?!"

"Our investigation?"

"*Our* investigation?"

"I mean, my investigation -- that is." Innes cleared his throat. His body erupted in beads of cold sweat.

Platten let out a deep sigh and shook his head. "You digressed from your instructions, Bob. As we speak, DS agents are swooping down on office after office in a vain effort to confiscate and destroy copies of your memo. Lie detector tests are next. Dennison's personal orders. It goes to show how furious the Secretary is over this. Not to mention Scher."

Innes looked away. Images of fishing on sparkling Adirondack lakes rushed into his brain. Escape. Escape from the Washington Circus of Pathos and Paranoia. He wasn't crazy. Nor wrong. They were.

To Toby Wheeler, it was all very amusing and, by the way, a great story. It didn't take forty-eight hours for a draft to land on the desk of the diplomatic correspondent of the *Post*. Wheeler was a thoroughgoing professional who knew the meaning of constraint as well as opportunity. But inside his devilish little soul, he relished the prospect of making the White Washington Establishment squirm a little. As a rare black reporter on a lily white beat, he'd encountered more than his share of slights, gross misassumptions regarding his abilities and scoops slipped to colleagues from competing papers simply because they fit the established profile of a "diplomatic correspondent." A black face, southern drawl and a degree in communications from Southern Baptist University just didn't cut it. And the denigration wasn't limited to American society. When the *Post* sent him as a young reporter to man the Moscow bureau in the waning days of the Soviet era, Wheeler saw first-hand how unenlightening seventy years of communism were for the Russian people in the area of race relations. He'd been spat upon, denied service and called nigger.

It broke on a Monday morning, good timing for stretching a story over a week of otherwise slow news. *Slain American Envoy Linked to Organized Crime*, proclaimed the headline. Wheeler went on to recount the content of Innes's report, augmented by interviews with government officials both in Washington and overseas. It painted a picture of a gross incompetent, Roland Mortimer, appointed as U.S. envoy to a major ally, whose leaders essentially ignored him. The story of Mortimer's chasing an underage ingenue to a hotel room made it into the report as well as the late ambassador's nocturnal outings alone into Rome's less savory entertainment areas. The *pièce de résistance* was an exposé of Mortimer's reported links to organized crime figures -- set against his cozy friendship and strong political ties with the President and a host of other senior administration officials. Finally, Wheeler reported on Dennison's clumsy attempts to quash the story, this following on a botched and misdirected investigation.

An accompanying editorial on the op-ed page denounced the crony system of political payoffs that resulted in sending unqualified ambassadors to represent America abroad. It ended by calling the Senate to task for turning a blind eye in the confirmation process.

Dennison and the White House mobilized the p.r. machinery. The investigation was continuing apace, they told reporters. All legitimate avenues would be vigorously pursued, they assured. There was no evidence that

Mortimer had links to organized crime, they said solemnly. Yes, he led perhaps not the most circumspect personal life. But these were the 2000's after all. Mortimer was a true patriot and served the President loyally and capably. Blah, blah, blah.

Innes felt like vomiting as he read the headline and first few paragraphs the next morning. The children's breakfast burnt in the toaster. Carolyn unplugged it just in time. She read the story and remained silent for several minutes. "Guess you're going to have an exciting day at work," was her unhelpful comment as she poured coffee for herself.

Innes was given the OES account. The Oceans, Environmental and Scientific Affairs Bureau was a necessary, yet bit player in the Department of State. Most Foreign Service officers shunned duty in a bureau manned by techno-geeks who were fascinated by such things as fisheries, cooperation on weather reporting, saving the whales and negotiating scientific exchanges. Innes started chugging "Jolt" cola -- "All the Sugar and Twice the Caffeine!" -- to stay awake. His previous duties were divvied up among Robin Croft, who no longer worked for him, and several others. Innes realized that he was being sidelined to bureaucratic Siberia. He actually welcomed some boredom and predictable duties, but pondered the likely end of his career.

A week later, the voucher office called Innes to inform him that a "routine" review of his travel vouchers over the past seven years showed that he owed Uncle Sam at least $4,000, that he should pay this initial amount within 30 days or face having it docked from his salary.

His career development officer, "CDO," in human resources called.

"Bob, I don't know how to say this, so I'll just give it to you in one shot. The system has 'identified' you for a twelve-month stint in Somalia. You'll be humanitarian affairs officer."

Somalia was a desolate country racked by years of civil strife and run by warlords with a reputation for going after U.S. government personnel with literally murderous tenacity. "Humanitarian affairs officer" was a grab-bag appellation for one who monitored starving refugees, human rights violations and mine-clearing operations.

"There'll be a lot of travel in-country, so you won't be stuck in the office all the time," the CDO continued. "Oh, but your family can't go. They'll have to stay back here. But you'll get separate maintenance allowance to cover some of their expenses."

"What the hell is going on, Dan? One day, I'm on the Secretary's staff, handling the sexiest issues out there. Next day, the 'System' slam-dunks me in a putrid cesspool like Somalia!"

"Fair share, buddy. Remember?"

Theoretically, all U.S. diplomats were required to take turns serving tours in hardship posts, hence "fair share."

"We all know that 'fair share' is a joke. How many hardship tours have you served?"

"This isn't about me, Bob. Look, I've got instructions. I'm passing them on. You don't like the assignment, you have the option of quitting."

"This isn't an assignment. It's a death sentence."

"Your call, buddy."

"Somebody wants me out -- whether dead or alive."

The CDO hung up.

Innes got no satisfaction from the quasi-union nominally defending the labor interests of Foreign Service employees. Its vice president wanly advised Innes not to fight an assignment, citing "the needs of the Service." As for the voucher matter, he said that it was a "private matter."

Carolyn called to say the IRS had sent a certified letter informing him that he was to be audited. The auditors requested a ton of information on Innes's claimed deductions going back, yes, seven years.

Innes's reduced assignment in the prestigious Ops Center ended abruptly. He found out one morning when he showed up for work and encountered a young woman sitting at his desk. She was as embarrassed as he was surprised. Straight from junior officer training, she had been assigned to his job. She timidly handed him an envelope marked "Diplomatic Security." It contained a pink slip of paper signed by "Agent D.S. Warren" curtly informing Innes that his top secret security clearance had been suspended pending "further investigation," offering no further explanation. Innes's torpid CDO sympathized, then promptly let him know that, until the security problem was cleared up, Innes was assigned to processing Freedom of Information requests -- the unclassified aspects, effective immediately.

Innes's world was falling apart. "When it rains, it pours," which is what the union guy told him, just didn't cut it. Why now? And why in spades?

Family life fared no better. His relations with Carolyn went from cold to hot war. The shouting made the kids cry which, in turn, made Carolyn cry, which made Innes that much more irritable. He increasingly sought refuge at Colleen's, then stayed, returning to his own house only to see the kids. Colleen fretted over him. She tried desperately to console him, but he kept sinking deeper and deeper into despair. He would lay his cheek on her breast and weep. As she stroked his hair, she wept with him.

Innes came from a long line of stubborn yeoman farmers. He recalled when, as a boy, his family dairy farm in Ontario County, in upstate New York, was to be seized and auctioned off by the bank because his father couldn't make the mortgage payments on time after two years of drought. The elder Innes's neighbors and many friends in the surrounding communities chipped in to pay the bank off. Just in time for the rains to resume. Inneses could always rely on friends in times of trouble.

He called Speedy.

The special at the Okura was red roe *sashimi*. Speedy, always game for interesting food, wasn't so sure about this, or Japanese cuisine in general, being mainly a ribs-and-chops, burrito-and-beans, pizza-and-burgers type of guy. But Innes's arm-twisting got him to relent. Innes ordered for both of them.

Speedy regarded the tuna *sushi* with deep suspicion. "Looks to me like fish bait." He sniffed at it and grimaced.

Innes told him how to eat it, lifting a piece with his chopsticks. "Look, you dunk it into this soy sauce and just eat it." He did so, washing it down with a small cup of warm *sake*.

Speedy bravely followed suit. He immediately went into a coughing fit which sent several pints of extra blood coursing to his face. His head looked like it was about to burst. He grabbed his cup of green tea and gulped it, then involuntarily sprayed it all over the table. This aroused the attention of the other diners.

Catching his breath, he gasped, "What was that little piece of green shit?"

"Oh, just *wasabi* – Japanese horse radish. You should've just mixed a little in the soy sauce, not swallowed the thing whole. I should've told you. Sorry."

When the sushi arrived, Speedy asked to see the menu, and ordered chicken teriyaki.

Innes explained the cascade of problems suddenly confronting him. "They're after me big time. It's obvious," he said.

"It sure looks that way," Speedy said, deep in thought. "But can you prove it? Henry Kissinger once said that" -- he lowered his voice and affected a German accent -- "'These people play for keeps.'"

"He's right."

"You bet he's right. But Washington types are also as stupid as they are clever. Despite Watergate, despite Irangate, despite all the cases of big shots trying to do in whistleblowers, they never learn and they do the same stupid things over and over again."

"So? What should I be doing?"

"At this point? Hang in there, but also be prepared to press your case outside of channels."

"Hmm." Innes played with his food. "Anything new on Mortimer?"

Speedy sank his teeth into a teriyakied chicken breast. "Afraid not. But Dom Berlucci has taken direct control over the investigation. This is good. State and CIA are flubbing up. But more than that, now that it's front page news, the Director wants us to pull out all the stops, whether the White House likes it or not."

Innes nodded, mulled it over in his head.

"Berlucci wants to talk with you. Your memo knocked his socks off," Speedy said.

Innes dropped his head. "The Ontario County DMV must have it by now."

"He told me to tell you that nobody needs to know about it. All he wants is to pick your brain. That's all. You'll be protected."

Innes pondered a moment. With his chopsticks he slowly demolished the block of tofu in his *miso* soup. "I don't know, Speedy. I'm trying to cool it."

"You can't let go and you know it. Besides, what have you got left to lose? They can't fire you. And they can't fire at you." Speedy chuckled at his own sick pun.

Innes looked up, and slowly nodded.

CHAPTER TWELVE

The lovemaking was never tender. But it was, mercifully, always brief. Eastern European males tended to be that way, in Lydia's experience. When they came to America, they changed their outlooks in many ways, these phallocentric men from the Old World. They learned to be more superficially outgoing, a must in the American business milieu. They chilled out, especially those that emigrated to California. They dressed down, studiously acquiring the subtle habits and nuanced gestures of American informality. They burnished their accents to fit in better. "Hey, John! What's happenin'?" replaced "Good day Mr. Smith. Are you well?" in their new American-English lexicon. Yet in the bedroom, they reverted to Ivan the Terrible, or Vlad the Impaler. In the bedroom, females were to be conquered. Outside, they were to stand demurely behind their man.

As was customary, he turned on his side and fell fast asleep, snoring deeply. In an hour or two he would awaken, hurriedly wash up, dress and scurry out the door. And he would be back, within a week's time. They would dine clandestinely at a handful of upscale establishments where the maitres d' knew him and would provide a private

room, away from the glare of publicity, the earshot of
Washington gossipmongers, the prying of the malevolently
ambitious. Discretion was an essential hallmark of the
President's National Security Adviser. The public and
private personae may not square, but God help him if the
latter overwhelmed the former to its detriment.

So, it was not all wham-bam-thank-you-ma'am. Like
most vain men, particularly of Horvath's social origins and
oversized ego, the President's right-hand man liked to talk,
mostly about himself, or his role in saving the American
civilization. And dutifully, she listened, commenting only
in support of him.

As with most men, he talked a lot about his boss.

"He's surrounded by all these kids. Whiz kids from
nowhere who happened to be backing the right candidate at
the right time. They're not idealists nor ideological.
They're like all the other cynical yuppies who came of age
in the '80s and '90s. They're out for themselves and they
don't want to put in the time necessary to gain the
experience to function effectively." As a creature of Old
World culture, Horvath was acutely hierarchical and
dismissive of youth, especially in the realm of politics.

"Foreign policy. Humphh! What foreign policy? The
man is totally impervious to grand strategy. Tells me it's
'un-American.' Can you believe that? There are plenty of
wolves out there just waiting to eat us alive. He really
never has read any of my books. He took me because he
wanted a Harvard professor to lend respectability to an
administration populated with backward nincompoops. I've
tried repeatedly to sell him -- to explain to him -- my
theory on controlled inevitability, the central thesis of
which ..."

At such points in the monopologue, Lydia would tune
out and let the tape recorder do its job. Yakov saw to it that

the latest state-of-the-art listening and photographic gear for clandestine recording was installed in the classic Georgetown townhouse he set her up in.

"Russia. Putin's days are numbered. We all know that. He's pissing off too many players over there. The cookie-pushers at State want to give him the farm. The Pentagon, however, wants to prepare for the next cold war. I have prepared a list of seven options. If Corgan bothers to study them between his preoccupations with tax reform and immigration and covering his big ass with Congress..."

Lydia day-dreamed of Rome, the fine living, the exuberance of the people. She thought back further to grimy Rostov, to her mother and father and her old friends. She had gone back for a visit a few months earlier. Girls she went to school with, girls who were beautiful, with clean complexions, bright eyes and velvety voices punctuated by spasms of giggles, were now married, or divorced, with kids, lazy husbands and lives that ground them down, wrecked their beauty and their souls, as only Russia could do. Their every waking hour was devoted to survival. Their faces drained of loveliness, their spirits devoid of spontaneity, their hearts sapped of hope, they merely carried on, certain only that the next day would be like the previous. Lydia shuddered. There but for the grace of God ...

"As far as I'm concerned, people deserve the leadership they get. So it is with you Russians. And we have to deal with it." There was an edge to his voice. Horvath, a refugee from the 1956 Hungarian revolution against communism and the Soviets, retained a visceral dislike of Russians. Lydia concluded that he got a vicarious pleasure out of screwing them. This, plus his affinity for European, particularly Slavic, women, made for very complicated emotions in an overeducated, insecure man who thought

very highly of himself. She further concluded that he felt
the rules did not apply to him -- including those which
forbade U.S. officials sleeping with nationals of states with
"hostile intelligence services."

"And so, my little Russian *tsvetok*, who are you seeing
besides myself?" Horvath stood looking out the bedroom
window onto the brick sidewalks and elms of 31st street.
He was naked and held his hands together in front of his
groin.

Lydia tensed. She lay on the bed still, carefully
modulating her breathing. While she had been getting
accustomed to his mood swings, Lydia still had not found a
way of dealing with Horvath's unpredictable temper.

"I've told you already. I see only you."

He remained unmoving before the window. Lydia could
nonetheless hear his breathing pick up.

"And what are you telling other men about me?" He
slowly turned around, keeping his hands in place.

Lydia would not look away. She held her gaze onto his,
refusing to show any sign of weakness or fear.

"Nicky, I see only you."

"Many people have underestimated me over the years.
They think I am a fool who can be easily manipulated. But
I have showed them who is smarter, braver."

"You are very smart. And very brave, Nicky. But you
also must be more trusting."

"Trusting?" He slowly approached the bed. "Trust is a
luxury of fools. Trusting fools become slaves. Or they
die!"

"Nicky, I don't like when you get like this. Please lower
your voice." She especially didn't like the idea of this kind
of scene being recorded.

Horvath leaned down on the bed, his face inches from
Lydia's.

"If I had been trusting, I would never have shown all those smartasses at Harvard who was best. If I had been trusting, I would be eaten alive by the bureaucracy and the media. If I had been trusting, I would have been a loyal slave of you Russians."

Lydia pulled the covers up over her bosom in a move of instinctive but futile protection.

"I threw Molotov cocktails at Soviet tanks in the middle of Budapest. At fourteen, I killed a Russian! I watched him struggle and scream, covered in flames from one of my little bombs. And you know what? I wasn't scared. I wasn't repelled. I wasn't stunned. Oh, no. I was amused. I *laughed!*"

He reached down with one hand and grabbed her by the throat. Saliva foamed from the corners of his mouth. His face flushed and his neck pulsed.

"I laughed my guts out. Watching this Russian, maybe nineteen, twenty years old, dancing an agonizing death reel. In the street where my mother bought bread and flowers. And I was the orchestra. I provided the music…with my fire bomb."

"Nicky! Stop it!! Stop! Nicky!!" She was losing consciousness.

With his free hand, Horvath swung long and hard, crashing his fist into Lydia's face, the impact of which made her fly off the bed. He remained motionless, the memory-provoked grimace on his face frozen, the terrifying eyes looking at Lydia, but not seeing her. Holding the side of her face with one hand, she picked herself carefully from the floor, watching him warily while trying to keep from passing out. She grabbed a pillow from the bed and held it to her body as she made a gradual retreat toward the bathroom. She felt blood drip from the corner of her mouth.

Realization pierced Horvath's face. The grimace melted into astonishment, then fear. He reached out with one arm.

"Lydia. Oh Lydia…I'm so…sorry. Please…"

From her dresser top she snatched a hand-mirror and smashed it against the side. She grasped a long, narrow shard and held it defensively in front of her.

"Lydia, I want to--"

"Stay away from me. Or I'll stab you!"

He stepped toward her with outstretched arms, utterly vulnerable in his nakedness. Tears streamed down his face.

"I said stay away from me!" she screamed. "If you touch me, I'll cut you. And then I will tell the reporters that you sleep with Russian women and that you beat them! How will your president think of that?" A twisted snarl transformed her soft face into a beast-like apparition. "So, you hate Russians? Do not try to push Russians around. This Russian will fight back!" She brandished her crude blade, it having drawn blood from her tight-gripping palm. She dashed into the bathroom and slammed the door, quickly locking it. Holding fast to the basin, Lydia saw herself in the mirror, cheek swollen and bleeding, her tear-soaked face contorted from hysteria. She covered her cheek with her injured hand, adding more blood to her facial wound. She sobbed uncontrollably in the sink. She began reciting an Orthodox prayer her mother had secretly taught her when she was a girl.

Horvath tapped on the door. "Lydia, I'm sorry. Please come out," he pleaded.

"Go away!!" she screeched. "Go away…" Her voice dissembled in panicked weeping. She heard him exit the room and descend the stairs. The front door of the townhouse opened and slammed shut.

The ride from Washington to the Hamptons was seemingly endless and fraught with uncertainty. She sat the four hours staring out the window of the chauffeured black Lincoln, silent and anxious. The driver, a burly Siberian named Pyotr was solicitous, asking her several times if she needed to go to the toilet or wanted a bite to eat. She only shook her head in response. She held a hand over the swelling on her cheek, hoping the warmth would expedite the healing. Pyotr looked at her sympathetically through the rear view-mirror.

Her thoughts again took her back in time. Was it escapism, self-analysis, self-pity? It wasn't important, really. She saw herself, the Lydia of ten years romping in the meadows, strewn with yellow and purple wildflowers, singing and running, trying to launch a kite with her father. Her mother sitting on a blanket sorting the picnic food, laughing and shouting encouragement. The foothills to the Caucasus, beyond Krasnodar, were beautiful in the summertime. Wonderful places for family picnics and for kids to run free, away from the gray city with its factory air, away from crowded flats, away from the cautious people leading plodding lives. Those days of family outings, swathed in the yellow glow of the summer sun and the warm love of a family trying to retrieve authenticity out of a milieu of stale, state-imposed conformity. Her father's vivid stories. He could paint a canvas in one's imagination. Tales of knights and princesses, the stuff that socialism endeavored to eradicate from the people's collective consciousness. And he told true tales passed onto him from his grandfather, a loyal servant of the last tsar. Stories of palace splendor and court intrigue, of brave cossacks and treacherous priests. Accounts of the richness, and harshness, of pre-revolutionary rural Russians as well as

the unreal grandeur of St. Petersburg. Grand balls in
Moscow and Petersburg, folk fairs in the countryside.
Stories of love, unrequited and consummated. *Oh, great-
grandpapa had things to tell. And, oh, papa, how rich you
made us by keeping alive the flame of fantasy and history.
Were I only born in those days, a girl in Old Russia when
people still could dream and be their true selves...*

"We are here, Miss," the Siberian said.

The Lincoln passed through an iron gate manned by two
cement-block guards, Tatars or Chechens, Lydia thought.
A television camera and some kind of electronic sensors
pointed at them from the arch above the gate.

Up a winding, oak-lined driveway, there appeared a
magnificent hybrid chateau with doric columns, flying
buttresses, gothic windows and huge iron lanterns hanging
from a ten-meter-high entrance. Waiting to open her door
was a butler, at least a man dressed in black tails and
exhibiting a formal demeanor. She was ushered into a
chandeliered marble foyer lined with medieval tapestries
featuring warriors fighting in some long-lost battle. Two
additional grave, heavyset guards stood with arms crossed.
Their eyes scrutinized her from head-to-toe. They parted to
allow her to pass into the next chamber, of white marble in
grandiloquent *belle époque* design. Two large, gilded
chandeliers sported winged cupids blaring horns, an
oversized fireplace on whose weighty mantle perched on
each side two, black-marble, half-robed Greek goddesses
gazing longingly heavenward. Occupying the middle of
the mantelpiece was a tilted glass globe. A bright red
carpet covered the floor. Curved, silk-cushioned Louis
XIV furniture graced the chamber. The butler motioned for
Lydia to sit on a gold-upholstered regency-style sofa.

A plump woman entered and, in a heavy Ukrainian
accent, asked what madame wished for a refreshment.

"Tea," Lydia replied with a fleeting smile across her injured face.

She fidgeted as she sat there alone, in this magnificent room of this splendid mansion. She felt so out of place, like driftwood from some desolate northerly latitude washed up on a golden, tropical shore.

The portly Ukrainian woman returned ten minutes later with a brass samovar from which she poured steaming, black tea. At Lydia's nod, she added a spoonful of dark honey.

Lydia was left alone for what seemed like hours. She sipped the piping hot tea. It warmed her inside. The heat radiated outward, an inner sun rekindling life.

A brass-framed glass door swung open, pulled by the silent, faceless butler. In strode Yakov. He smiled warmly and kissed Lydia's hand, then seated himself in a matching chair on the sofa's right.

"*Gospozha* Lydia Yekatarina, you are as beautiful as ever," he beamed. He used the traditional, pre-revolutionary address for Miss. Her father called her 'gospozha' as an endearment. *Tovarishch* -- comrade -- was rarely heard within the confines of the Puchinski home.

Yakov was so deceptive, so falsely enticing. A python circling its prey ever so gently. A dead feeling permeated her body when she was in his presence. Here was a Potemkin man, she thought, a man superficially charming, but who exuded no life, only a frigid emptiness.

"My dear Lydia, I want to thank you for making this long journey at my request." In fact, she had no choice.

She forced a smile. "This house is so magnificent. It's a fairy tale place."

He swept the premises in a wide arc with his eyes, obviously proud of this acquisition. The Ukrainian maid returned with what appeared to be a glass of lemonade for

Yakov. The latter, sporting gray riding pants and a black turtleneck sweater, was clearly in his element as lord of the manor.

"You know, this belonged to an American robber-baron. He used it only as his summer home. They called these mansions, 'cottages.'" He directed his gaze suddenly onto her. "Can you believe it? A 'cottage'!? Such wealth they had, these robber-barons. We had nothing like this in Russia. Yes, Peter the Great turned St. Petersburg into Paris of the East. But he was only one man and was a tsar. In America, anybody can be a tsar if he puts his mind to it. It's all out there to be gotten. And the astonishing thing is that ninety-nine percent of Americans don't see it. It takes outsiders. They see. They come from nothing. Therefore, they can see everything as an opportunity. Can you imagine?"

She looked at him silently, waiting for him to get to the business at hand and dreading it.

"Are you happy in Washington?"

"You are most generous, Yakov."

"Yes. I brought you here from Rome because I saw with these same outsider's eyes that you are special. People, men, trust you and confide in you. You have a magical effect on them."

Lydia stared into her tea cup while he said this. Then looked up at him, her face saying, *Okay. So what's the point then?*

As if upon some telepathic command from Yakov, in strode Dimitrov. He handed Yakov a small tape recorder. Dimitrov stood stonily silent behind Lydia. She tensed. Her heart began to pound. If Yakov's aura was one of coldness, this man's was of pure malice.

Yakov pressed a button. Nicholas Horvath's tortured voice emanated from the machine. "Lydia. Oh Lydia...I'm so…sorry." Her frantic threat followed. "I said stay away from me! If you touch me, I'll cut you. And then I will tell the reporters that you sleep with Russian women and that you beat them! How will your president think of that?"

Yakov stopped the recording. His face grimaced as if in pain. The air was dense and volatile.

Lydia's thoughts raced with her quickening heartbeat. The cup that she grasped began to shake as a tremble entered her hands. She decided to take the offensive. Her speech was barely audible.

"Yakov. I was frightened. I was--"

Yakov nodded at Dimitrov. In a quick motion, the latter's coarse fingers grabbed her hair and yanked her head backward. The other hand produced a silvery blade which he held tightly under her jaw. She held her breath, knew better than to struggle.

Yakov was shaking his head. He lifted himself out of his chair, fixed his eyes downward while pointing his right index finger upward opposite his ear in an admonishing gesture.

"Lydia. Lydia. Lydia. You don't listen to me. You don't appreciate all I've done for you. You don't take my advice. You don't follow my instructions."

Before Lydia could protest, Dimitrov locked his grip tighter on her hair, driving sharp pangs into her ears and neck. She felt the blade press harder against her larynx. Any more and the skin would break. She knew it.

"You disappoint me, Lydia. You disappoint me very, very much. Without me, you would still be just another decaying beauty in another lost corner of Russia with vanquished dreams and a bitter life."

She could barely breathe. The pain and the panic strangely did not dilute her full comprehension of his words nor of the realization that her life may end violently within the next several seconds. She released the teacup which tumbled and shattered to pieces on the floor.

"In return for providing you with comfort and a new life, with everything your heart would desire; in return for my request that you be warm to one of the most important men in Washington, you threaten to hurt him. You threaten to *hurt* him and then to tell everything to the *press!*"

He turned on his heel and looked at her squarely. "Are you insane?! Do you want to risk everything that I have given you?! Tell me, my little small town slut, do you wish to *die?!*"

She said nothing.

"What am I to do?" Yakov asked exasperatedly. "I can no longer trust you. You reject my generosity. What am I to do?"

Lydia shut her eyes. In her brain, she began to prepare for her death by reciting the prayer her mother had taught her. She returned mentally to the Caucasus meadows. She was wearing a frilly yellow dress and was dancing in a circle with other little girls, all giggling in a rapture of innocent girlhood joy. The sun was a gentle warm and the fragrance of spring wildflowers in their braided hair further lifted their spirits. The borderless deep blue sky blanketed them. The distant mountains smiled upon their frolicking. *Oh! Such sweetness. Leave me here. Where I can again be free, joyful and innocent. Leave me!*

An eerie smile came to her face. She felt at peace. In a deliberate movement, she leaned into Dimitrov's blade. He quickly withdrew it. Yakov moved with a start. For what seemed like an eternity, they gazed at Lydia in puzzled wonderment.

She opened her eyes and looked directly at Yakov with bitter defiance. He seemed at a loss.

Finally, he stuttered, "I…I am a patient man."

"You are also an impotent man who is incapable of love," she spat.

In a flash, Yakov lunged at her, grabbed her by the shoulders and hurled her downward. She crashed into an end table holding a large vase of flowers, which smashed onto the floor, breaking into a thousand fragments.

"You *shall* do my will!" he bellowed. "If you do not, I will scar you for life. And I will search out everything that you love -- your mother, your father, your teachers, your pets -- and I will kill them. Do you understand?!"

Sprawled on the white marble floor, Lydia covered her eyes with one hand and nodded understanding.

"Now get her out of here! Take her back." He pointed a finger at Lydia. "You will rest and heal and you will go back to Horvath. You will call him to apologize for your actions and you will beg him to return." Yakov turned and sauntered out.

CHAPTER THIRTEEN

The tension in the smooth-lined wood and marble Security Council chamber virtually buzzed like a fractured power line on the verge of snapping. In the minutes preceding convening of the UN's highest body, the five permanent representatives and ten nonpermanent delegates converged in last-minute consulting and lobbying, tugging at coat sleeves, murmuring in ears, driving home points with fingers. The diplomat's hallmark, a sympathetic hearing tempered by a demeanor of careful noncommitment, marked the faces of those on the receiving end.

A group of aggrieved ex-Soviet republics -- Russia's "near abroad" -- banded together to seek the world body's condemnation of Moscow's frequent military interventions within their borders. The Moldovans linked arm-in-arm with the Georgians, Armenians, Estonians, Kirghizians, Tajiks and the independence-seeking Chechens to bring their complaints of Russian aggression before the UN Security Council. Given a free hand to intervene up to then, Russia was losing credibility with the international community, which was losing tolerance for Moscow's actions.

One of the jokers in the deck was that the current chair of the Security Council, Ghana, was unpredictable and could steer proceedings in either direction. Behind the scenes, ambassador Akobo complained to his SVR case officer that the cash-strapped Russians weren't paying him enough to help their cause.

It was crucial for Russia that she not be alone in opposing, and vetoing, the draft resolution calling for immediate troop withdrawal and Russian noninterference in the affairs of her neighbors. The overwrought Russian UN ambassador, Grigori Kirilenko, worked the "Perm Five" energetically. The British, seeing parallels to their involvement in Northern Ireland, were likely not to support the resolution. The French, likewise, were cool to it in light of their own promiscuous military interventions in Africa. The two ciphers were the Chinese, who deplored big power interventionism, and the Americans.

The American representative, Harriet Cortez, listened carefully, but maintained the familiar stoic expression of noncommitment. It was evident that she lacked instructions. Washington sources attributed the American silence to internal divisions over policy toward Russia. Policy gridlock. Not an uncommon occurrence in this weak administration. It caused Kirilenko to lose hours of sleep, despite five or six vodka nightcaps each evening. Moscow was pulling out the stops on this resolution, which attacked the heart of Putin's foreign policy. The Foreign Minister called Kirilenko almost hourly for status reports and to issue new instructions. After a week of exhaustive lobbying, Kirilenko was ready to give up the ghost, convinced that the Chinese would support the resolution, along with the Third Worlders on the Security Council. A yes vote from the U.S. would go far to isolate Russia diplomatically and further isolate Putin. The potential then for a right-wing backlash and collapse of democracy in Russia was a terrible reality.

The death knell of Russian democracy, however, was premature. The Friday morning vote went in Moscow's favor, with the Chinese abstaining, the French and British voting against the resolution, joined by the Americans. In her explanation of vote, Ambassador Cortez, reading a prepared text, stated that peacekeeping was a pillar of UN efforts in the post-cold war era, that all nations bore a responsibility to make peacekeeping work, and that Russia was doing her part. She called on Moscow, however, to seek a UN mandate before undertaking such actions in the future. Only three Third World governments supported the resolution in the end. Ghana abstained, Akobo still in a snit.

Kirilenko accepted congratulations from his staff, then promptly locked himself in his office, poured himself a triple vodka and fell into an instant stupor. Two floors above him in the Russian UN mission building on East 67th Street, SVR *Rezident* Anatoly Gorygin leaned back in his chair contentedly. His first instinct was to phone his friend Yakov to thank him for the unique inside information he provided the SVR on the U.S. administration's deliberations on this matter. But he knew better. American intelligence eavesdropped on all phone conversations to and from the mission. No. He would wait till his next meeting with Yakov in a safe location.

Dennison flew to New York the day after the vote to give an address before the Council on Foreign Relations. Except in the fall during opening of the General Assembly, when he and a small army of U.S. diplomats camped out at

the Waldorf to carry on chock-a-block meetings and
consultations with foreign dignitaries, Dennison stayed at
his Fifth Avenue penthouse whenever he was in town. As
an investment banker when not working in government,
Dennison called New York his home and pulled in big
bucks in an old money Wall Street firm, Dickerson,
Dennison, Renfrew and Pratt.

He kept the morning free. On arrival at his apartment,
he told his security detail that he wanted to catch up on
some rest whereupon he retired to his bedroom and secured
the door. The Secretary of State then changed into slacks, a
sweatshirt and sneaks, donned a knit cap and a polyester
parka and slipped into a side servant's entrance which led
through the kitchen and thence out into a hallway. A cargo
elevator conveyed him to the tradesmen's entrance. He
dashed out onto 57th Street where a gray Buick LeSabre
collected him and proceeded through the Queens Midtown
Tunnel, into the functional, low-rise neighborhoods of
Astoria.

A half-hour later, the LeSabre pulled up to Sal and
Vicki's Deli on Broadway. Dennison jumped out of the
vehicle, entered the shop through the front door, walked
briskly past the capacolas, provolone, sopresattas, past the
brewing cappuccino and fresh almond cookies, beyond the
single restroom and into a door leading to a back room. A
self-assured-looking fat man sitting in the corner
acknowledged Dennison's presence with a slight nod. The
young counterman kept focused on making a "Hero
Napolitano." The Secretary familiarly turned right and
ascended a set of low stairs. As soon as he reached the top,
the door opened. It was Bags.

The little room, cluttered with stocks of meat cutting
equipment and paper products, was illuminated by one
ceiling fluorescent bulb. A small formica kitchen table

with plastic-covered chairs occupied the center of the room.
Standing by it with his right hand outstretched was Albert
Joseph Malandrino clad in a stiff, three-piece blue suit and
tie. The paradox of a formally dressed mafia don greeting
the U.S. Secretary of State in a backroom of a marginal
delicatessen in a working class neighborhood of Queens
apparently hadn't occurred to either man as they warmly
shook hands and sat down to conduct their business. Al
dismissed Bags.

"Mr. Secretary, it's great to see you again." Al was
clearly ill at ease and, unusually, at a loss for words.

Dennison mumbled something about it also being nice
to see Al again, glanced conspicuously at his watch, and,
fitting for the venue, wasted no time at getting to the meat
of the matter.

"Al, as I promised when we saw each other last month, I
got for you the information you requested." He pulled out
of his parka a large yellow envelope stamped, "Department
of State, USA Official Business Only."

Al accepted the envelope with both hands and a wide
grin and, with a meat dressing knife, opened it. He pulled
out the thick contents. On top was an analytical study
marked "SECRET" and titled, "'Changing Drug Trafficking
Patterns: Counternarcotics Operations Reassessed',
Directorate of Intelligence, Central Intelligence Agency."
Beneath it was a lengthy confidential Department of State
cable captioned for restricted distribution from U.S.
Embassy Moscow, the subject of which was, "The Future
of the Putin Administration: Implications for U.S. Policy."
There were notes of Cabinet meetings with the President,
DEA reporting, Coast Guard operational plans, an FBI
memo outlining efforts to increase law enforcement
cooperation with Italy, Germany and Russia against
organized crime and a couple of Presidential Decision

Directives setting forth U.S. policy on Russia and on arms
control.

"Mr. Secretary, it's always a pleasure." He produced a
black attaché case and slid it across the table to Dennison.
The Secretary did not tarry in prying it open and examining
the contents which he counted quickly but efficiently.
Twenty stacks each containing one-hundred crisp $100
bills.

"Mr. Secretary--"

"Al, at this point, let's dispense with formalities once
and for all. Call me Roy."

"Yeah, right. Uh, Roy. You know, I followed the
debate on that Russia thing at the UN yesterday. It went
good. I was worried that Washington wouldn't let you go
along with it. Me and my clients were really enthused with
the outcome. I don't know how you pulled it off, but--"

"Al, let's cut the bullshit. I didn't do it because I'm
Vladimir Putin's Number One Fan. And this time, I'm not
asking for the usual kind of payment. I sweat bullets on
this one. I had to fight a battle royal with Secretary
Wilkins at DoD and CIA Director Levin. And that bitch
ambassador at the UN, Harriet Cortez, lobbied the White
House hard to support the resolution. Said, as a Cuban
refugee, she knows freedom and Russian interference better
than the rest of us. Fortunately, the President's NSC
Adviser was my ally. The President required a real hard
sell. Our argument that a vote for the resolution could spell
doom for democracy in Russia and help revanchist,
hardline elements there finally swayed him. I can't be
sticking my neck out like this too often. This one comes
with a high price tag, Al."

Al studied Dennison's patrician WASP face carefully.
He had been doing business directly with this man since
Mortimer's demise, some six months now. But he didn't

feel comfortable about it. Here was one of the most senior
people in Washington in charge of the most sensitive and
prestigious area of government, foreign policy. And he
was selling secrets to the mafia for money. In the back
room of a Queens deli no less. Now he was about to raise
the ante. It was a paradox that deeply disturbed Al. We
were all creatures, and sometimes victims, of our respective
cultures. By a stroke of fate Albert Joseph Malandrino was
born to Italian immigrant, blue-collar parents and raised in
a scruffy neighborhood where everybody hustled for a
living. To keep the neighborhood clean, safe and protected
from outsiders -- as a sort of SDI, a missile defense shield -
- certain individuals took on the responsibility of
maintaining an ancient, transplanted code. The greater
risks incurred naturally entitled these centurions of order to
greater rewards. Contrary to the claims of some *stragneri* -
- strangers, outsiders -- like the public prosecutors and
sensation-mongering newspaper reporters, the *dons* and
their *caporegimes*, lieutenants and soldiers were not
parasites on society. Rather they were guardians of a way
of life based on time-tested, ancient and moral traditions.
A pre-destined warrior caste. They were a necessity. Al
was born into it and accepted it.

But the Dennisons and their ilk had had three-hundred
years to wash out the binding vestiges of their Old World
ways. They were looked upon, and up to, by the newer
immigrant groups literally as "the Americans," the model
citizens for the rest of society. Al liked history in school
and he listed ,as among his heroes Thomas Jefferson,
George C. Marshall and Dean Rusk, all former Secretaries
of State and pillars of the WASP Establishment. He also
considered himself to be a patriot. But, while his success
was owed to playing the game according to his rules and

not those of the Establishment, this was different, almost unholy, like taking bets from a bishop.

"Well, Mr. Sec--, er, Roy, our business relationship has always been to our mutual benefit. Name your price and I'll see what I can do."

Dennison sat with one arm over the next chair and with one leg crossed over the other, richly self-assured and unjustifiably fearless. He focused intently on Malandrino. Behind the icy blue eyes cold calculations were going on, like a missile's computer dispassionately selecting a target. After several moments of such reflection, Dennison leaned forward with both elbows planted on the table and his eyes locked onto Al's.

"Al, you know that we both work in risky and dangerous environments. We're always having to protect our behind while, at the same time, moving forward and negotiating the shoals ahead. One slip and we're sunk. We've each got internal enemies as well as outside adversaries. You've got people in your organization to keep in line. So do I. You've got to contend with rival competitors within your own loose constellation of families. I've got Congress and other Federal agencies. You're constantly having to deal with outside gangs that want to diminish the power of the Italian-based network. I have to deal with foreign threats. We both have to fight the media as well. I think you'll agree with me that they constitute a serious menace to our respective work."

Al had become more relaxed. He sat back taking in every word of Dennison's homily. The Secretary spoke the same language as Al. Indeed, they were both purveyors of power who used their power to safeguard essential interests.

"And sometimes we do what we've gotta do to make sure things go in the right direction," Al offered. "Just like

Uncle Sam went after Castro. We went after Joey Gallo.
Bad apples."

"Exactly."

"Who are you after?"

Dennison leaned back and took a deep breath. "You
read the *Washington Post*?"

"'Fraid not, Roy. But I watch CNN and the networks.
And my pals are all talking about these stories about our
late friend Mortimer. About his ties to 'organized crime
figures' and to your boss too."

"You're quick, Al. And very perceptive. How'd you
like an ambassadorship to a nice place?"

Al snickered at this tongue-in-cheek suggestion. "Hey.
God knows I'm paying you enough. I deserve a nice job
like that after all I've been through. Naw. Money's no
good and I got no patience for the government."

Dennison laughed. "See? You *are* a smart fellow."

There was a light tap on the door. Bags entered briefly
to deliver two cups of foamy cappuccino and then departed.

"But you've got the picture. This guy, Toby Wheeler,
keeps digging deeper and deeper. He's good at what he
does. Eventually, somebody's going to talk. He'll stitch
pieces together and be able to blow the lid off things. Then
the Congressional committees will kick in. Next thing you
know, we're dead meat. And you and I can swap jokes in
jail."

"Let me get this straight, Roy. For today's take, I give
you two-hundred grand. But for the UN vote, you don't
want any money. You want a favor."

"That's correct."

"Just like when we took care of Mortimer."

Dennison became flustered. "No! Not 'just like'
Mortimer. You know I didn't condone what happened to
him! That was wrong. Just plain wrong!"

"I admit things got out of hand. I didn't want it to happen that way either. But the people I contracted it out to, they got carried away. I've straightened them out. Don't worry. But you, Mr. Secretary, gave the nod."

In a carefully modulated voice, Dennison said, "Mortimer had to be removed from the picture. I couldn't fire him. He was getting loony. All of a sudden, finding religion. Said he lived a 'sinful life' too long. Needed to change and all that crap."

"That's no reason to grease a guy."

Dennison was making an effort to stay calm. He stirred his cappuccino languidly, staring at the cup, pondering his next words.

"Mortimer was planning to change parties. And put his considerable fund-raising and campaigning talents to use for the opposition."

"Christ. Do you guys play hardball, or what?"

"There's more. Having found God, the son of a bitch was going to tell the press everything about how we do things. 'Bring down this administration,' he said. Reveal all the details about all the less-than-kosher ways we obtain and channel funds. About our links with crime figures. Including you, Al. I told you that then. Don't start getting amnesia on me. Jesus, he actually told me that he was going to write a book about it. And donate the royalties to the Nebekhenezar Church of Salvation. What would you have done in my shoes? Shit, Al, you had your own reasons for wanting the guy out of the way."

Al contemplated Dennison carefully. He had this man in his palm. He could make him do anything he wanted to. But his stomach churned queasily. Who said government was a license to steal? Also to kill. The Ollie Norths and John Ehrlichmans were boy scouts. Mere patsies and chumps set up for a fall. Dennison and his cohorts might also stumble and be exposed one day. But chances were better than even they wouldn't be. History had found out only a fraction of the nefarious deeds of our leaders. Politics was just another racket and the government just another gang to deal with.

"Yeah. Mortimer had to go all right. No argument there. Who's next?"

"This Toby Wheeler fellow..."

Al leaned forward on the table suddenly, his fists clenched, eyes wide and defiant.

"Look, Mr. Secretary. Roy. Contrary to what you read in the magazines and see in the movies, we, and certainly I, am not Murder Incorporated. When we go after a guy, he's either a traitor or a rival who's declared war on us. Just like how the government does it. What we don't do is go after any swinging dick and knock him off just because he's saying nasty things about someone else!"

Al paused and, with a low voice, added, "And we don't do Uncle Sam's dirty work either."

The air in the little room seemed dense, as if the molecules were converging at the speed of light and the accumulated pressure would explode the atmosphere.

Finally Dennison stirred. He appeared intimidated and weakened. In a barely audible voice, he said, "I only want him hurt. Put out of action."

"So, I see. You want the guy alive, but not functioning. Is that it?"

Dennison nodded mechanically.

"So, then, what else is there in it for me?"

"Self-preservation, my friend. Same as me. If we don't act, we each face destruction."

Al untensed. "Yeah. You're right. You don't need an Ivy League education to figure that one out." Al shifted gears. "Let me ask you one question."

Dennison nodded.

"You're a rich guy. Very rich, I would guess. You come from a nice, old family. Am I right?"

Dennison nodded again.

"Why would a guy like you be on the take for cash? You don't need it. How much richer do you need to get?"

Dennison shook his head. "Al, I'm not 'on the take.' You don't get it, do you? This cash that exchanges hands from you to me doesn't stay with me. I don't keep it."

Al looked at him quizzically.

"The campaign season begins, next year is an election year, remember? Congress has tied our hands on campaign funding over the years to such an extent that they have undermined the Constitution's intent for free and fair elections. You don't think the other party isn't up to its own shenanigans? We know they are. So, we have to counter that with our own measures. You're naive if you think that fifty million conscientious citizens marking the box on their tax return for a three-dollar contribution to the election fund is going to make everything democratic and peachy. This is not Plato's Republic, Al. It's America."

A smile of comprehension forced itself onto Al's face. As Dennison was preparing to leave, Al called out, "One last question, Roy. After Wheeler, then who?"

"One thing at a time, Al. One thing at a time."

The U.S. Secretary of State ventured back out into the cold, busy streets of Astoria.

CHAPTER FOURTEEN

The government always takes crackpots seriously. It has to. They pay taxes too. And the system is set up in such a way that the taxpayer is always right. This is especially so in the area of government information. Armies of graying, semiretired bureaucrats are paid millions to pore over yellowing files on everything from U.S. diplomacy during the Russo-Japanese War to CIA plans to kill Fidel Castro. Armed with black pens, they excise anything deemed to be potentially damaging to living sources or posing a threat to U.S. national security. Millions of man-hours are spent on this process at costs that would have drained the exchequers of previous empires.

"I, Mrs. Thelma Tucker, of no. 2 Sacajawea Lane, Austerlitz, North Carolina, request all the documents that our goverment (sic) has on US-Isreal (sic) relations, including all secret treaties to help the Jews take over the Holy Land. Thank you and the Lord Bless You." Bob Innes pressed the heels of his hands into his brow, rubbing his sore eyes to increase the blood flow. He had been in the Freedom of Information Affairs, or "FOIA," office for three weeks and it was taking its toll on him. Bureaucratic Siberia will do that to a person and this particular gulag was pretty much as bad as it got. He faced the immediate prospect of forwarding Mrs. Tucker's request to the overworked people in the office of Arab-Israeli affairs. As they rode herd on a volatile Middle East, monitored terrorist attacks in Gaza, sought to cool tempers of mutually mistrustful Israeli and Palestinian leaders, fought interagency policy turf wars, and contrived yet more ways of getting the Saudis, West Europeans and Japanese to cough up yet more cash for aid programs, the small, elite corps of Middle East specialists would have to find time to examine hundreds of aging documents for the reading pleasure of Mrs. Tucker.

Thelma Tucker was too much this day. Innes needed to escape. He and Colleen met for an early lunch at Mama's Soul, on New York Ave.

"Bob, you don't look good. You're pale and easily distracted. When was the last time you got a haircut?"

"Hey, lay off." Innes's face was directed downward at a mound of French fries, which he ate one at a time with his fingers.

"Please don't talk to me like that. I love you. I care about you. I just want to help you. You know that."

Innes grunted. He undistractedly munched more fries.

Colleen put her hand on his. "Oh, Bob. I worry about you. Whatever happens, please don't let it affect us."

He slowly turned his face toward hers. "This isn't like I was passed over for promotion, or my car died, or I have a toothache. It's much more than that. My life is being scrambled and turned upside down. It affects everything."

"We'll fight it. Together. With lawyers, if that's what it takes."

Innes looked at her with lifeless eyes. "They're out to ruin my life, Colleen. And they're clever about it. I can sue. It'll take years and money that I don't have. In the end, it'll all be a muddle, I'll have been ruined and bankrupt and my so-called career will go from being a bad joke to living hell. It already has."

"Then leave. Quit. Do something else while you're still young enough!"

His brow furrowed as his fingers held one fat fry between his front teeth.

"No." Innes looked as if he were lost in a trance.

"What do you mean, 'no'? Hello-o, Bob? Are you there, Bob?" She waved a hand in front of his face.

"No. I'm going to fight them. They can't get away with it."

Colleen looked at Innes worriedly. "Bob? Are you okay? What are you thinking of, Bob? Please, nothing dangerous. Maybe you should seek help. From a shrink." She rubbed the back of his neck.

Life returned to his eyes. "What? No, Colleen. I'm not fantasizing about bringing a chain saw to work and ripping the lunch line to pieces or anything like that."

She looked anxious. "Yeah? Okay. What *are* you thinking of?" she asked hesitantly, almost afraid to know.

"Why am I in this mess now? Christ. Only the public library isn't after me. Yet. My memo. They, whoever 'they' are, see me as a threat. I got too close to the truth on the Mortimer investigation. 'They' don't want it resolved. There's something terribly putrid in all of this."

"You think there's a cover-up?"

Innes pushed his plate away. He blinked impatiently. His brain was in overdrive.

"Remember when we were in Rome? You said that the administration might not want Mortimer's murder resolved. It's an election year and the last thing a weak administration needs is a sordid scandal involving a darling party hack."

"And Bernie Scher's chasing his tail. Then your memo gets leaked."

"And that's when the roof falls in on me. There's something about Mortimer that some very powerful people want to keep very secret. And it can't just be his libidinous activities in Rome, or the fact that he was useless as an ambassador. Those things were hardly secret."

A pre-adolescent black boy entered the restaurant and boldly commenced to hawk a variety of newspapers to the clientele. Several were the *Globe*, one of the tawdrier tabloids normally sold in vending boxes -- now empty -- in the neighborhood.

"Slasher cuts women's hearts out! Hey, read all about it, mister. Slasher be on the loose! Know how to protect yo' lady, mister. How 'bout it, man?"

Innes looked as though he'd been struck by lightning. He yanked a buck from his pocket and gave it to the kid in return for a paper.

"Bob! You really are out of your mind, aren't you?" Colleen scolded.

Innes eagerly devoured the front-page story about a slasher who maimed women. He then put the paper down and appeared lost in thought.

Colleen got up and grabbed Innes's arm. "Come on, my dear! We're going to see a doctor, now!"

Innes broke her grasp. "Hey! I'm fine. Really," he protested. He grabbed her forearms and held them as he looked at her eye-to-eye.

"Look how Mortimer was killed," he said.

"More like obliterated. Cut to ribbons and then some." Colleen shuddered.

"Late last year three Teamster guys were killed the same way in New York."

"Bob, that's par for the course in New York."

"And then a few weeks ago, a Russian SVR guy -- their spy agency -- was also murdered, in Turkey. They could barely recognize him, so badly was his body mutilated."

Colleen's raised eyebrows punctuated a questioning look on her face.

"Don't you see? Two diplomats are cut up, one American, one Russian. Three mob-connected Teamsters are also cut up. And each case is a mystery. No leads. No suspects. No motivations. There's a pattern. I don't know it fully, but a pattern emerges. And somebody's afraid I'm getting too close to discovering it."

"Are you sure, Bob? Maybe we ought just to cool it for now. You need rest. Let's go."

Innes wouldn't be budged. Colleen perceived a moonie-like quality about him.

"Three elements emerge in the pattern: there's a criminal angle; there's a Russian connection in there somewhere; and the same perpetrator is killing these people."

"And somebody in our government knows what's going on but doesn't want anyone else to know," Colleen added.

"Russians. Hmmn. An espionage angle perhaps?"

"Who? The Russian SVR guy, okay. But not the Teamsters. And certainly not Ambassador Mortimer."

"Why not Mortimer? As for the Teamsters, I can't figure the connection yet."

"No. Not Mortimer. He may have been a jerk. But he was also a patriotic American. I knew him. Worked for him, remember? I would've noticed something fishy. I think." Colleen was confused and distraught. The thought that her first boss in her budding diplomatic career might have been a traitor deeply disturbed her. Her mind raced through the past year. The possibility that she may have been an unwitting accomplice to a spy panicked her.

"Let's not get ahead of ourselves," Innes counseled, suddenly a fount of reason and caution.

They paid the bill and left.

Colleen wasn't sleeping well. Nor was she eating steadily. This and her deepening anxiety caused her to lose ten pounds. She was falling behind in her Thai language lessons. Innes had become obsessed with his conspiracy theory and this added to her worries. He showed signs of manic-depression. His rantings and intensity called to her mind weird people who made a vocation out of trying to prove the CIA killed Kennedy or the government was covering up what it knew about UFOs.

Could Mortimer have been anything other than a lecherous, bumbling fool? Had she missed something? After a year of working as his personal aide, surely she would have picked up on any truly suspicious activity on his part. Then again, she was a 24-year old, first tour junior officer, not a hard-bitten counterespionage specialist. If he was a spy, what would the inevitable investigation reveal about her role? At best, an unwitting naïf. At worst, a dimwitted nerd totally oblivious to clear signs of malfeasance. These apprehensions ate at her.

Her friends were becoming concerned over her. When they asked what was bothering her, she would simply mumble, "Nothing," and clam up.

Amy Chen entered the service with Colleen. They became fast friends and kept in touch from their respective postings. Amy, now working in Protocol, was afraid for her friend. She insisted that they have dinner at her place. Just the two of them. Amy would make Colleen's favorite -

- Cantonese coconut soup and spicy tofu with mixed vegetables.

Colleen picked at her food, occasionally forcing a wan smile in order to appear amiable.

"Amy, I know why you invited me here tonight. And I really appreciate your making my favorite dishes.
But...I'm all right, okay? Don't worry about me. I've got a few things on my mind right now, but I can manage."

"Nonsense, Colleen. We're almost like sisters. We even menstruated at the same time when we were in junior officer training." She laughed.

Colleen couldn't help also laughing.

"So, what is it kiddo? Love?"

Colleen put down her chopsticks and rubbed her eyes with the backs of her hands.

"Oh, Amy. You don't miss anything, do you? You know everything."

"Hey. There's a Chinese saying that goes, 'He who is half Teaches and half Hakka is like the moon and the sun -- cold and hot, a contradiction of mystery and power.'"

"Huh?"

Amy giggled. "Never mind. Who is he?"

"Amy. It's...He's...Where do I begin?"

"Let me guess. He's married."

"Separated," Colleen added quickly.

"Oh good. Not a totally hopeless cause then."

Colleen went on to describe her falling in love with Bob Innes, their having worked together on the Mortimer case, his travails and increasingly strange behavior. Then she stopped.

"So, you get to the bottom of what's eating at him and help him work it through. You're strong enough for it."

Colleen nodded feebly, but kept her eyes averted.

"There's more. Colleen, tell me what it is. Get it off your chest. Let me help you. You can't go on like this. You're wasting away. You and your man will end up in a loony bin together. Or worse."

"God, Amy. I don't know what I'm into. If I'm in trouble and getting sucked in deeper. Or, if I'm just imagining things. I'm afraid of telling anybody lest I drag them in or they conclude that I'm becoming crazy. But I'm afraid to tell anybody. If Bob is right, people could get hurt."

"If you don't unburden yourself, you'll just continue on your present course. And that spells disaster for you. And your lover."

Colleen knew that her friend was right. She then went on to recount everything she knew about Mortimer, her helping Innes to investigate the case independently, his ill-fated memo and tribulations and her present self-doubts.

"Amy, I'm so confused. And I'm so afraid." She broke into uncontrollable weeping. Amy comforted her in her arms.

"One day at a time, baby. One day at a time."

Growing a year older every twelve months was a bummer. But birthday parties were another thing. Ever since he could remember, Toby Wheeler loved birthday parties. He liked the gathering of friends, poking fun at the birthday boy or girl, the sharing and caring. But the thing he especially loved about birthday parties, and he kept it secret, was birthday cakes. Wheeler got positively giddy over vanilla cake with lots of sugary frosting. He would pig out on cake. If his wife didn't watch him closely, he would get sick to his stomach after getting second, third

and fourth helpings. It was just one of those things. A
simple human fallibility. Marion rapped her husband on
the knuckles with a spatula as he was surreptitiously
fingering frosting from their daughter's coconut and cream
birthday cake sitting on the kitchen table.

"Hey! What's that for, you crazy woman?"

With one fist on her hip and the other brandishing the
spatula rapier-like at her husband, she answered, "I don't
want my man to be a fat slob. Nor do I want him having a
heart attack just because he can't discipline himself around
food, and particularly junk food!"

Wheeler shook his head, but couldn't suppress a smile.

"Man-o-man. Other men got loving wives who feed
them well. Me. I had to marry Attila the Hen."

"Well, Mr. Frosting Fat Ass. If you can't stand the heat,
you can get out of this here kitchen!"

Without warning, he sprang at her. With his hands now
firmly around her waist, Wheeler planted a fat, wet kiss on
his wife's lips. Caught completely by surprise, she
succumbed, getting cake icing in his hair as she embraced
his neck.

"There now. Am I still Mr. Fat Ass? *Darling?*"

Her face reflecting both love and exasperated humor,
Marion let out a short laugh.

"I don't know what you are. You're just a silly man. My
silly man. *Dear!*"

The doorbell rang. She broke from his embrace.
"Courtney's little friends are here! We've got to get
moving." Marion rushed to answer the door, to usher in the
first of a dozen little kids coming to celebrate their
daughter's sixth birthday. With her hand on the knob,
Marion admonished her husband one more time with a
shout, "Now you stay clear of that cake, you here me?!"

"Yeah, yeah." He licked the spatula.

The kids o.d'ed on sugar, having devoured the cake, inhaled the jelly beans and guzzled Sprite. They were now venting the resultant burst of energy on games, notably "Twister" and pin the tail on the donkey. A dozen cacophonous little voices squealed "Old McDonald," "Big Bird, Where Are You?" and, of course, "The Birthday Song."

Wheeler genuinely enjoyed playing with the kids, allowing them to ride on his back and gamely acting as a stationary target for Courtney's new Power Ranger Zapper gun.

The effect of two hours of six year-old mayhem, however, left Wheeler with a throbbing headache and a need for some fresh air. With Marion's ready permission, he took leave for a stroll. Marion was grateful that he had blocked out time to spend with his family and even to take a stroll in the neighborhood. It wasn't only his birthday cake cholesterol intake that worried her. She was concerned that he'd been putting in too many hours on his story about organized crime's inroads into government. The phone rang constantly. Wheeler had to meet sources at weird hours in the outer suburbs. His editor was constantly at him to develop further leads. The consequent stress made him irritable and listless around the house. But Courtney's birthday snapped him out of it. For Wheeler, family came first.

Wheeler quickened his pace through the maple-lined streets of his neighborhood, a bucolic enclave nestled against Rock Creek Park containing ranch houses occupied by affluent black professionals.

God, he loved this place. It was the perfect antidote to a scruffy little pig farm in Texarkana, where he was raised.

As he sprinted along the street pavement, determined to burn off some of the megacalories he had ingested that afternoon, his mind turned to his recent discussions with Marion about having another baby. A son this time. Hmmn. And more occasions to eat birthday cake!

The blow came much too fast for Wheeler to realize what had happened. It was only when a neighbor almost ran over his sprawled body in the middle of the road that his situation was known. Marion and Courtney held his hand in the ambulance ride to the hospital. He had a faint awareness of this. After an initial going-over in the emergency room, Wheeler was examined carefully by doctors. He had incurred a severe blow to his fourth cervical vertebra, Marion was told. It was too early to know whether there was damage to the spinal cord. They injected him with something to arrest such damage. He would need to stay perfectly still for days. Then they would be able to tell whether he suffered permanent paralysis.

"Another mugger attack, I suppose," offered the attending physician sympathetically.

"I don't know. I don't know," was all a shaken Marion could offer in response.

CHAPTER FIFTEEN

It was 11:00 am and Horvath, seated behind his
hundred-year old oak desk in the National Security
Adviser's office in the West Wing, clasped his hands before
his face in a meditative fashion. He was contemplating
how to direct that afternoon's briefing of the President on
military options concerning "Major Regional Conflicts" --
"MRCs" in Pentagonese. The Joint Chiefs would be doing
the briefing. He had little tolerance for the military. There
was something about their clear-eyed, can-do, gung-ho
attitude that he found disquieting. He had seen that attitude
in the eyes of the Iron Guard when he was a kid in Hungary
during the war. He could recall hearing the screams of
Jews from his neighborhood being hauled off by the
Hungarian Fascists. He saw the same autonomic behavior
among the communists who followed the Fascists, and in
the eyes of the hated Soviet occupying troops. When he
hurled those Molotov cocktails as a teenager, he aimed
directly at Russian eyes, if he could get close enough.
Despite control by a democratic government and the
trappings of a citizen-force, the American military too were
a culture unto themselves and therefore were capable of
anything in the right circumstances. They understood only

control and discipline. He must control the military.
Nicholas Horvath, witness to history.

His secretary brought in that morning's mail. She
opened and screened all official correspondence, tacking on
a self-stick note here and there reminding him of an
upcoming meeting with a correspondent, informing him
that she had passed on a copy to another office requesting a
draft reply, and so on. Anita was as efficient as they came.
And discreet. She would forward on to her boss unopened
anything explicitly marked "Personal." Thus, the large
brown envelope in that morning's take, marked "Strictly
Personal," arrived on his desk intact, unopened.

The STU-III secure phone rang. It was CIA Director
Levin.

"Nick, you've seen today's *Post* article on Zimbabwe, I
take it. All this shit that Mugabe's dishing out about how
we had plans to overthrow him. This is a heads up. The
President may get saddled with questions from the media or
Congress. I know that Senator Presser is on his high
horse..."

"Uh huh, uh huh," Horvath kept murmuring half-
listening and half-daydreaming. He reflexively reached for
a letter opener and lazily tore the top of the big business
envelope.

"...we've prepared some press guidance. Basically, it
throws cold water over all this nonsense about trying to
overthrow..."

Horvath slowly reached in and pulled out the contents of
the envelope, though his gaze was fixed absently on a large
map of the world on the opposite wall.

"...I'll fax it to you. Please let me know your
reaction..."

"Yeah, sure, be glad..." Horvath's heart stopped. Ten
thousand bells and sirens shrieked in his brain. His eyes

bulged from their sockets. He felt that he would pee his pants that very moment.

Staring back at him were photos of abused female faces. Mug shot-like. Russian women. Whom he had beaten. Beneath their swollen faces were typed their names: "Marissa Vassileva." "Nina Turcheva." "Olga Galinska." "Lydia Puchinskaya." There were other photos. Of him strolling hand-in-hand with one of the women. Kissing another in a doorway. Making love on a couch. Receiving oral sex in a bathroom. There was a cd as well.

The sweat poured from his face and armpits. He felt dizzy. He stifled the sudden urge to vomit.

"Uh. Uh. Dave. Yeah. Sure. Uh. Can I call you back?" Horvath, shell-shocked, slowly replaced the receiver on the blinking, compact secure phone unit. He sat there frozen. The jolt was such that he was incapable of even panicking. He sat paralyzed. It seemed that a darkness was closing in all around him. *Oh, let it not be! Not be! No! No! No!* He buried his face in his hands.

His intercom buzzed. It was Anita reminding him that he had a luncheon appointment at the Maison Blanche with the Scandinavian ambassadors. He snapped to. But was weighted down by a complete loss of energy.

He hurriedly shuffled through the photos looking for a note, a letter. Something. But there was none. He clutched the cd. Turning his head wildly like some forest beast on the alert for predators, with trembling hands, Horvath stuffed the disk into a small stereo on a side cabinet, frantically put on earphones and pressed the start button.

It seemed an eternity for the sound to come on. It was of a woman screaming. He heard his own voice issuing calm warnings not to struggle. He sounded like a crazy man. Something made of glass smashed. "Stop! Stop!"

the woman cried. He recognized it as belonging to a young
Byelorussian woman he'd been seeing. The sweat
continued to pour off Horvath's brow.

There was a slight pause as the first recording segment
ended. The next segment came on. He heard Lydia's
voice. "Stay away from me, or I'll stab you!...This Russian
will fight back!" Then there was his own pathetic voice.
"Lydia, I'm sorry. Please come out."

He couldn't take it any more and stopped the machine.
In his panic and despair Horvath struggled to focus his
thoughts. Somebody was out to blackmail him. That was
clear. *Oh, Horvath! You thought you were so smart.
You're nothing but an idiot. A stupid, insane fool! And
now you will pay.*

The torture was in the waiting. The blackmailers didn't
have to write a message to him. They'd be contacting him
presently. A real professional job. Horvath was extremely
thirsty. And he needed to relieve his bladder badly. He
bolted out of his office and rushed to the mess across the
way in the ornate Old Executive Office Building. After
doing his business, he thrust his head into the men's room
sink and repeatedly threw cold water on his face. In the
mess, he bought a cold Coke and chugged it. Nearby was a
pay phone. Assured that no one was noticing, he lumbered
over and pressed a number into it.

"Hello?" Lydia answered.

"Lydia, it's me. What the hell is going on? Who put
you up to it?" he demanded.

"I don't know what you mean, Nicky."

"Like hell you don't, you rotten bitch--"

She hung up.

With frenzied hands, he dug into his pocket for another
quarter and pressed as if his life depended on it.

"If you don't speak to me like a gentleman, I will hang up again," she warned.

With great effort, he tried to calm himself. "Lydia. I need to see you. *Urgently.*"

"What about?"

"I think you know."

"No, I don't."

Horvath took a deep breath. "Never mind. Can I see you tonight?"

"Okay. I will be here."

Horvath was little more than a zombie for the rest of the day.

She opened the door without uttering a word, turned and walked slowly away from him. The image of her swaying gently forth, hips moving, that sleek body swathed in a black, form-fitting cocktail dress, would have driven him into a frenzy in better times. He followed this time like a scared puppy dog.

She led him through the simple foyer, through the hallway lined with oil paintings, into the living room. Horvath hadn't felt so frightened and humbled since he was punished by the headmaster in his grade school.

Sprawled comfortably in an overstuffed, patterned arm chair was Yakov. Opposite him, to the rear, was Dimitrov. In another armchair by the fireplace was a third Russian. None rose as Horvath entered.

Yakov sported his trademark Cheshire grin. With his left hand, he signaled Horvath to take a seat next to him. Horvath dutifully obliged. Lydia sat demurely at the far end of the room, her eyes fixed forlornly away from the others.

"With your permission, I shall dispense with introductions and small talk," Yakov began. "Let us get to business."

"Who are you? KGB?" Horvath stammered.

Yakov took a moment to study Horvath. Again, the serpent sizing up its prey.

"To answer your question, no. There is no more 'KGB.' Is gone forever. With Soviet Union."

"Then who are you? What do you want from me?"

"Ah, but I am being a terrible host. Please. A refreshment." Yakov gestured to a tray containing bottles, glasses and an ice bucket. "I have Egri Bikaver. Slivovitz. Even Unicum. All straight from Hungary."

It made Horvath's blood boil. Only Russians knew how to humiliate with kindness. Horvath hesitated. Yakov mumbled an instruction to Dimitrov. The latter poured the potent Slivovitz apricot brandy into a small vodka glass and handed it to Horvath. The latter took it and slugged it down. Dimitrov poured another.

"Please not to preoccupy yourself that we are spies. I assure you we are not."

Horvath shook his head as if not comprehending.

"We are...entrepreneurs. We provide services...for a fee. And you have a problem. We can help you with your problem."

"So, then, you are..."

"Friends. From now on we are your friends. You can always rely upon us. And we on your cooperation."

"And you are Russians."

"We are newcomers. Here to pursue the American dream."

"I fought against Russians. In Hungary. From the United States. I will not betray my country!" Horvath said bravely. Nicholas Horvath, freedom fighter.

"Ah, yes. The little guerrilla fighter. And my father was there. He helped liberate Hungary in 1956. And my uncles drove out Nazis from Budapest in the Great Patriotic War. So, my friend, we have something in common. And so, we meet today."

Horvath paused to collect his senses. "What do you want then?"

"Information! No surprise there, *tovarishch.*"

"And if I don't cooperate?"

"But you will. You have your family, yes?" Yakov leaned forward. "But more important. You have career. You have reputation. You have money. In America, nobody sacrifices these. Are you prepared to spend the rest of your life as a poor mouse? As a man of shame? As nobody, with no respect, no money, no future?"

Horvath gazed at the floor, speechless.

"Of course not!" Yakov continued. "So, we work together from now on. You fulfill our requests and we help you whenever you have problems. Like today." Yakov saluted Horvath with a glass of vodka and knocked it back.

"Now. Here is Mr. Smith." He pointed at Dimitrov. "And there," gesturing to the third Russian, "is Mr. Jones." Mr. Jones was Igor Rokovsky, SVR colonel, an American specialist. In the course of his regular duties at his embassy, Rokovsky, like many of his colleagues, moonlighted for extra cash as a free-lance agent. Yakov had recently taken him on. "Mr. Jones will be your contact. And your friend."

CHAPTER SIXTEEN

Colleen had just finished a grueling two hours of Thai. The tones, four of them, were the hardest thing to master. "Ma," for example, could mean horse, dog, or come, depending on the tone placed on it. Likewise, "kai," could mean near or far. And on it went for nearly every conceivable monosyllable.

She went to collect her mail and messages from her pigeon hole. A single yellow telephone message slip was there. "Call: Mr. D.S. Warren," it said, and listed a phone number.

She called. Mr. Warren, in the bureau of diplomatic security, asked her to come by to answer a few routine questions. They probably wanted to update her clearances, she thought.

D.S. Warren occupied a small partitioned cubicle in State's annex office building across from the Department on E Street. Mr. Warren himself was one of those security functionaries who instilled insecurity and fear by feigning calm and congeniality. Furthermore, his J.C. Penney blue, three-piece suit and brylcreamed hair made him a dead give-away as a security man, or at least the stereotype that most "substantive" officers had of them.

"Miss McCoy. Like I said on the phone, I have just a few routine questions I'd like to go over with you." Colleen could never figure out whether, by using "Miss" in lieu of "Ms.," the notoriously sexist security guys were advertising their contempt for feminism, or were simply as slow and plodding as everybody liked to make them out to be.

"It's come to my attention that you claim to have some special information concerning the murder of Ambassador Mortimer."

Routine questions, my eye, she thought.

"I don't know what you mean."

"Well, you reportedly have stated that you believe the ambassador was killed for something he did, or people he knew. Is that right?"

A little inner voice told Colleen to be on guard. "I have no idea who killed him, or why. That's your task to resolve, isn't it, Mr. Warren?"

"Is it also true that you believe our government is seeking to cover up the circumstances of his murder?"

It hit Colleen like a ton of bricks. Amy! Her good friend and confidante had leaked what Colleen had told her about the Mortimer case.

"Why are you asking me these questions?"

"Like you said, it's our job to investigate. If you have some relevant information, we'd like to know."

"I told the RSO in Rome everything I knew."

"And about this alleged government cover-up?"

"Beats me."

D.S. Warren was visibly irritated. "Okay. Let's move on." He opened a dossier and studied it for a moment. "You are currently cohabitating with Mr. ...Robert Innes. Is that correct?"

Colleen blushed. "What business are my personal affairs of yours?!" she shot back.

"Everything, Miss McCoy. We're security, after all."
He resumed examining the dossier, slowly turning page
after page. "Relax. It's strictly routine. The regs state that
you must report to us any long-term, steady romantic
relationships. We all have to."

"I don't believe this is happening!" Colleen protested.

"Here are two copies of Form OF-174, 'Report of
Relationship.' One is for you. The other for Mr. Innes.
Please complete them and return them by the fifteenth."

"And if I don't?"

"You risk having your clearances suspended. No
security clearance, no Bangkok, Miss McCoy. Please
cooperate. On the other thing, we know that you've been
insinuating that there's more to Ambassador Mortimer's
death than is apparent and that you believe there is some
kind of conspiracy to squelch it. Does Mr. Innes believe
this also?"

Colleen rose. "Mr. Warren, I think that ends this
conversation. If I have any divine inspirations on the
Mortimer case, I'll be sure to let you know." She turned
around abruptly and walked out.

Colleen immediately called Innes. "Bob, this is eerie.
And it frightens me. Now everybody knows what we
know. And think. If they're out to mess up your life, what
will they do next? And now to me?"

Innes paused to reflect. "Toby Wheeler."

"Huh?"

"The *Post* guy who was doing those stories on Mortimer
and criminal connections with the government."

"What about him?"

"He's now off the story."

"Oh?"

"He's in the hospital. Somebody attacked him. He may never walk again. What a coincidence, huh?"

Colleen needed a moment to collect her thoughts. "Bob. This is getting really scary. Should we go to the papers? Or to Congress? Or sit still? Or what?"

"Berlucci."

"Who's Berlucci?"

"I'll explain later. Gotta go now."

Dom Berlucci agreed to see Innes immediately. Innes ran the five blocks to FBI headquarters. He arrived on time, but out of breath and perspiring. He related the latest happenings to the FBI man.

Berlucci listened intently while Speedy took notes. "Bob, you and I see eye-to-eye on Mortimer's death. The guy was involved with some definite sleazeballs. It's criminal. No doubt about it. The Director has asked me to go full steam ahead on developing leads. But all this business about a cover-up and some cabal within the administration to do people in. I don't know. Sounds pretty far-fetched. What proof do you have?"

"I guess it's only circumstantial at this point," Innes replied. "But look at it. After my memo gets leaked, everything in my life takes a nose-dive. Then Toby Wheeler gets hit. Now they're after Colleen."

Berlucci looked skeptical. "And Scher? Is he part of this...this conspiracy?"

"Scher? Scher's just an idiot. Maybe they're using him to throw monkey wrenches in the works. Otherwise, he's just one of those guys who runs in circles all the time. And he's a vain egotist trying to make a name for himself."

"So then, who's pulling the strings?"

Innes rubbed his chin, searched his brain. "I don't know at this point. Maybe...Dennison. And the White House."

Berlucci shot a quick, doubtful glance at Speedy. He strained to appear attentive.

"You guys think I've gone off the deep end, don't you?"

"I didn't say that."

"But I can read it on your face."

"Bob, look. Work with us on the criminal investigation. Drop this other stuff. We'll eventually get to the bottom of this case. That's our business."

Innes nodded in resignation. "Yeah. Right. Uh, I'll be in touch. Okay?" He got up to leave.

Berlucci stood and approached Innes. "Bob. Cool it. And keep your head low." Berlucci poked a punch playfully at Innes's chin and smiled. "You got anything to pass along, contact Speedy here. He knows how to reach me."

"Sure." Innes departed without making any assurances.

Innes called the young presidential aides he'd met at the White House briefing, Wynn Kearnan and Prudence Harding. "I don't ask you to buy on to my thesis at this stage," he told them. "But the President should know that his people, especially Dennison and Scher, are botching the investigation. I think Dennison, at least, is doing everything in his power to sidetrack it. The White House can turn things around by banging heads and reassigning tasks."

The staffers listened carefully, yet noncommittally. They promised to pass his views along.

And they did. In a joint memo to Nick Horvath, who promptly passed it along to his friend, Roy Dennison. "Thought you'd like to know what's going on in your Department!" Horvath scrawled jokingly in the margin.

CHAPTER SEVENTEEN

The day had started out particularly badly for the
Secretary of State. The U.S. special envoy had delivered
the Secretary's peace feelers to the Iraqi Sunni leaders the
previous day. In typical Arab fashion, the envoy was
received cordially and listened to attentively. Plenty of
photographers and reporters were on hand to record the
scene. All smiles. Quotable platitudes abounded -- "Peace
Through Dialogue," "Weaving the Tapestry of Mutual
Understanding," "Expanding the Foundation of
Democracy." The NIACT cable Dennison had just finished
reading was a dispatch from Embassy Baghdad detailing
the massacre that same day of two Sunni villages by Shiite
bands. The latters' leaders denounced American trickery in
trying to lull the Shiites into a Sunni trap. They furnished
to reporters the full text of Dennison's peace feeler. The
media were having a field day. Once again, the inscrutable
denizens of the Levant had dumped egg all over Uncle
Sam's face.

Senator Weems, chairman of the Senate Foreign
Relations Committee, had just slashed the foreign aid
budget for Pakistan and all of sub-Saharan Africa, and was
making threats of going after aid for Israel next. It was

being whispered in the corridors on the Hill that the octogenarian, ex-boll weevil, Democrat-turned-Republican was suffering from early Alzheimer's and had it in for South Asians, Africans and Jews.

The *New York Times* had printed its umpteenth editorial decrying "disarray in our foreign policy" and calling on the President to implement a "shake-up in his foreign affairs team."

Horvath's memo followed. He still had an hour before his scheduled meeting with the Greek foreign minister to listen to the latest tirades from Athens against Albania, Macedonia, Bulgaria, Turkey, northern Cypriots and all of Greece's other ancient enemies going back to the time of Pericles. Dennison asked to see security chief Ralph Torres right away.

"Ralph, what the hell is going on here? Here's one of our officers going around blabbing about gangsters, Russians, conspiracies, corruption, a dead ambassador who might as well have been Al Capone's godson. The guy's obviously unbalanced."

Torres fidgeted nervously. D.S. Warren was with him. "Sure. We've pulled his clearances. Scher's fired him from his team. Human Resources has reassigned him to a no-brainer job. That's about as far as we can go."

"Well, then fire the son of a bitch! Have him arrested. Or, better yet, committed!!" Dennison exploded.

Torres exchanged an uneasy glance with Warren. "Mr. Secretary, we can't fire the man."

"Why the hell not?!"

"Uh, well, for one, there's no cause."

"Treason! Insanity! Think of something, goddammit!!"

"He doesn't fit the picture for treason, or more accurately, espionage. Why, we couldn't even nail Felix Bloch. As for insanity, Med would have to diagnose that--"

Dennison pointed a finger at Torres and spluttered, "You get Med to call him in for a physical. Today!"

Silence.

Dennison began to compose himself. "Okay. All right. What else do you have?"

"Derek here called in his girlfriend, another FSO, and she was totally unforthcoming."

"Have you talked to his Aunt Beatrice yet?" Dennison asked.

"No," Torres replied, not catching the sarcasm. "But her friend, another female FSO named Amy Chen, told us that Mr. Innes and Miss McCoy are talking about going to the media with their story. Apparently, Innes is already talking to the FBI independently about the case."

Dennsion looked at them incredulously.

"Again, they feel that there's a major cover-up of the Mortimer murder and--"

"Wait a minute. We've now got a girlfriend. She won't talk to you. But she's willing to blab to the papers. But not talk to you...And she has a pal who does talk to you. Is she living with Innes as well? Who is this Innes guy, anyway, Charles Manson? How many others are under his sway?"

"Not exactly, Mr. Secretary. Uh, Miss Chen, she came to us because she was worried that her friend, Miss McCoy, was losing it, and that Innes had a screw loose and was a bad influence on her."

Dennison slammed his fist on his desk. "That's it! See? Amy's got it! She's right! And she's a Foreign Service officer, part of the team, for crying out loud! The guy's nuts! At the very least he's a troublemaker. Now, I want you guys to go back to the drawing board. Bring in Med. Bring in the lawyers. Bring in the fucking Forestry Service, if that's what it takes!! We can't allow one loony officer and his gullible girlfriend to go around making all kinds of crazy accusations and continue to suck on the tit of Mother America. Got it?"

The two cowed security men mumbled something about looking into it further, got up and scampered past the waiting Greek foreign minister and out into the maze of State Department corridors.

The football terms flew freely and carelessly. "This will ensure a level playing field." "The best defense is an offense." "This will be a Hail Mary pass nobody'll forget." "If the other party wants to scrimmage, we'll scrimmage. We can afford the best linebackers." And on it went. Middle-aged men, unsure of their virility, commonly turned to jock-talk to simulate an all too rare experience for many of them: genuine male bonding.

The President's chief of staff, Howard Selmur, and Secretary Dennison reverted to such banter during their biweekly luncheons, as if to reassure one other that each was just one of the guys.

"The other side is starting earlier than we expected. They think they've got a chance at it this time around. The way they're attacking us at this stage, we've gotta hit back, and hard," Selmur asserted, slamming fist in hand to emphasize the point. "I'm steering the money to our PACs as soon as I get it. But it's going to be crunch-time before we know it," he declared as he picked at his *crevettes marinières*.

"Wait a minute," said a confused Dennison. "Aren't PACs supposed to channel funds to the parties? Not the other way around?"

"Yes. But for special action projects, it works the other way." Les Nigauds was bustling with the usual clientele of legislators, lobbyists, diplomats, powerbrokers, would-be kingmakers, and the merely pretentious.

"'Special action projects,' huh? Don't tell me it's called 'SAP' for short -- in good bureaucratic fashion?"

"Roy, the President didn't make you Secretary of State for no good reason."

"Hah. Hah. Well, I just sent two-hundred thousand to the Caymans account," Dennison said as he signaled the waiter for another Tanqueray martini, straight-up, with a twist of lemon.

"It's already spoken for. You've got to get more."

"What do you mean?"

"Like I said, it's gone." A plastic smile bloomed on Selmur's jowlly face as he waved back to a senator on his way out of the pompous but "in" eatery on tony lower Connecticut Avenue.

"Gone where exactly?" Dennison demanded, suddenly losing interest in the martini and his *escargots à la Créole*.

"In case you haven't heard, an election year is coming upon us, my friend. Things are gearing up. Ever heard of the New Hampshire primary? The Iowa straw poll?"

"Howard, don't patronize me!" Dennison hissed, trying to keep his composure. "And, besides, our guy doesn't worry about primaries. It's the election he's -- and we've -- got to worry about, remember?"

Putting his fish fork back on his plate, Selmur donned an expression of indulgent patience, the look a parent gives to a child who doesn't quite get it. He locked his fingers together at chin-level. "Roy. Have you been watching the news? This Roger Jalbert will lock in the nomination. No doubt about it. He's young, handsome, charming, wounded

war veteran, family man. The media are calling him a
'Cajun Kennedy.' This is a real contender."

Dennison sipped his martini nervously.

"Gallup is going to announce tomorrow that the
President's approval rating has sunk to 34 percent. Ergo:
We've got to gear up the PACs, the state and local
campaign committees, the media advertising. The whole
shebang. And, with the way things are going, we're already
late in the game."

"Christ. Why didn't you domestic guys tighten things up
a lot earlier?"

Selmur glanced to each side, then leaned forward
slightly to capture Dennison's undivided attention.
"Russia's going to hell in a hand basket and rampaging all
over its former republics, the Iraqis just spat in your face,
NATO is on the verge of paralysis, the President was
upstaged at the last economic summit and the fucking State
Department can't develop one single, solitary lead on who
butchered one of its ambassadors. Now, I ask you, where
does the administration look the weakest?"

Dennison gulped. His cheeks reddened. "Don't give me
that shit, Howard! If Corgan would get off his duff and
take a foreign trip now and then, or make a major foreign
policy speech between elections, maybe, just maybe, the
public might start getting the impression that their President
cares about what's going on around him. Horvath tells me
he's lucky if he sees the President once a week. You tell
me where the problem really lies."

Selmur pondered this a moment, then resumed his initial
point. "What we need is more rainmaker Mortimers. And
the Three C's: cash, cash and cash. And that's both our
jobs, my friend. Unfortunately, our buddy Mortimer is
irreplaceable, at least for the foreseeable future."

The waiter exchanged the finished appetizers with *Coquilles St. Jacques* for Dennison and *cuisses de grenouille Provençale* for Selmur, which they attacked lustily.

"Speaking of Mortimer," Selmur continued, "the heat seems to be off since that black reporter got mugged."

"Yeah...But there's a new twist I'm worried about."

"What's that?" Selmur slurred as he chomped on a fat frog leg.

"I've got one officer, maybe two now, who's making noises about a government-organized crime connection in which Mortimer was just one player."

"So, fire 'em"

"Can't. The regs won't allow it. Not unless he's caught selling secrets or stealing Uncle Sam blind. I've had him taken off Scher's group and pulled his clearances." Dennison snickered. "The son of a bitch is now processing Freedom of Information requests. Trouble is, he still won't let up. I'm pretty sure he was leaking stuff to Toby Wheeler."

"What about Scher?" The sommelier replenished their glasses with a St. Emilion, Château Trotteville, '90.

"Scher's like an obedient lap dog. He's bucking for a higher job in the administration. He knows on which side his knish is buttered."

A light bulb went on in Selmur's head. "Your little troublemaker there. You say you can nail him for espionage. Why don't you make it happen?"

Dennison was closely scrutinizing the dessert cart.

"What do you mean?"

"Set it up. Frame the twerp. I know a couple of Cubans who can help you."

Dennison selected the *tarte a la crème framboise*. Selmur's idea broke his concentration. He turned to

Selmur. "Howard, I don't care what the rest of the world says about you. You're okay in my book."

A simple *café au lait* topped off the meal.

They were old hands at this stuff. They were taught by the best at CIA. And constantly keeping one's eye over a shoulder at all times for twenty years made one vigilant and cautious. Castro reportedly put out a contract amounting to one-hundred thousand dollars on each of their heads. An abiding obsession with anonymity, however, made them elusive targets.

Getting over the shaky plank fence and up to the sliding rear door was easy. With a rubber truncheon, Ramirez crushed the neck of a neighbor's terrier before the creature could manage to get out the beginning of a bark. They procured much of their equipment, like the truncheons, from surplus sales of the Royal Ulster Constabulary and South African riot police. They used the best.

Morales drilled three holes into the aluminum sliding door frame, using his silent, high-speed battery-powered drill, a gift from an ex-Stasi officer, now free-lancing, whom he had befriended in Berlin after the wall came down. The door opened easily and the two Cubans scampered into the Arlington townhouse. The place was just moved into, with boxes and trunks strewn about. Innes and Colleen still had a lot of uncrating to do.

They stashed the papers into an old steamer trunk that had been in the Innes family for seventy-five years.

As stealthily as they entered, Ramirez and Morales slithered back out, taking care to stuff the canine's body into a rucksack and taking it with them back into the night. Not a trace. Not a sound. They were gone.

CHAPTER EIGHTEEN

The UN Security Council vote in Russia's favor had pleased Yakov tremendously; he even felt proud as a Russian. And the stash of secret documents that Malandrino handed over knocked his socks off. All of this showed to his SVR friends that he could deliver -- big time. They were impressed. So impressed that Gorygin got headquarters in Moscow to spring for $700,000 to hand over to Yakov through a cutout in the Bahamas. The SVR chieftains predictably groused about their tight budget. But this package deal, made possible by the American Secretary of State, was a great bargain, and they knew it. As had become customary in these bigger transactions, Gorygin skimmed $90,000 for personal operating expenses. New York wasn't getting any cheaper after all.

Yakov asked for another meeting with Malandrino. This time on neutral ground and private, which suited Al. Both men were leery of pushing their luck with the law, the media or anybody else with a less than charitable curiosity in what the Italian-American and budding Russian mobs were up to.

The aircraft hangar at LaGuardia was closed for repairs. The cold drafts and gray, utilitarian surroundings

compelled both men to dispense with pleasantries and
banter and to get right down to business.

"Al, now I know what that old president meant when he
said, 'Business of America is business.'"

"Coolidge."

"Yes. In any case, Al, vote at UN was…how do young
people here say?…Yes, Awesome!"

"Al Malandrino has friends and he can deliver. But he
doesn't come cheap."

"Of course. Which is why we are here." Yakov
snapped his fingers. Dimitrov appeared out of the shadows
and produced a small zip-lock bag. Yakov unsealed it and
invited Al to sample the white powder inside.

Al begged off and ordered his "chemical man" to check
it. The latter placed a minuscule amount on his tongue,
then nodded back to Al.

"Number One, Super Grade A heroin, my friend,"
Yakov assured. "From Afghanistan. There is no better.
But it is potent, eh? The consumers love it, but they must
use less. This must be made clear. Or they can die of
overdose."

"So, where is it and when can I expect delivery?"

"In seven days. But I must know which port."

"Bayonne…in Jersey. I've got the skids greased. Ricky
here will work out the details with your guy. The ship will
dock at a pier we designate and be unloaded normally. In
the warehouse, the stuff then gets broken out and special
handling. Customs is taken care of already. Oh. And don't
worry about no Teamsters or any other pains in the asses
like last time. We divide the product right there at the site,
then go our separate ways. Sixty-forty split like usual."

Yakov had a questioning look. "You mean we take
sixty, you take forty, yes?"

"Wrong, pal. Other way around."

"Al, I thought we agreed sixty for me, forty for you split. After all, is our heroin."

Without batting an eye, Al replied, "And they're my ports." The gauntlet was thrown. The two just stared at each other.

Al broke the tense quiet. "Yakov, I'm nobody's fool, see? I could ask for a hefty cut of whatever your *compadri* are giving you for the papers and the vote. But I'll take it out of the junk instead. Street price for the stuff you bring here is good. Real good. So, don't feed me any shit about the cut. You'll take forty. We all come out real good in the end."

Yakov pondered this a moment. "Okay...for now. But maybe it will change in future."

Al ignored this.

Yakov pulled out of his vest pocket a sheet of paper. He studied it briefly, then handed it over to Al.

"What's this?"

"Wish list for more information. For next time we meet."

Treating the list as if it were a parking summons, Al handed it to Ricky. "You can't just waltz in here and push a bunch of demands on me--"

"Not demands," Yakov interjected. "Al, I would like you to listen."

"Who says I don't listen? Let's get one thing straight. You can make requests and I can consider them. But don't start pushing me around. After all, this is my turf. You stick to Brighton Beach. Everything will be fine."

Yakov didn't know if Al was just having a bad day, or if something more serious was developing. He drew a deep breath. "Al, I ask only that you look at them and, if you can obtain information on them, fine."

Al retrieved the paper from Ricky and glimpsed at it. Neatly typewritten on a plain sheet, it contained a list which included "notes of Cabinet meetings," "position on expanding NATO," "position on aid to Russia," "travel plans of Secretary of State for next six months," "budget figures for intelligence collection on Russia," "timeline for developing next generation of strategic bomber." Altogether, there were some 50 such collection targets.

Al shifted uneasily in his steel chair. He didn't mind the first such transaction. In fact, he gave it little thought. It was done almost as a favor, a sweetener for a larger, more lucrative deal. He had not anticipated that it would lead to being a regular feature of his relationship with Yakov. Al pulled apart and bent into a new shape an abandoned paper clip that lay on the metal table that separated him from Yakov.

"Listen pal, you give me dope and I give you access and protection. We split the proceeds. That was the deal. Period. A special favor like the UN vote deal I can throw in once in a while as...an extra."

Yakov remained a steely calm. The squeak of metal against metal echoed against the rafters as a cold breeze snaked through the cavernous structure.

"But I'm no friggin' spy, see? I love this country. It's made me what I am today. Do we understand each other?"

"I think so," Yakov replied. "We have other sources." He took back the list and stuffed it into the inside breast pocket of his jacket. He produced a stiff smile and resumed the business discussion. The Russian swept the moment of tension under his mental rug. Dimitrov stood in the shadows like a granite pillar.

"Al, we must prepare for possibility that product from Afghanistan will be interrupted from time to time. I have made arrangements for heroin from Burma to come here

across Pacific Ocean. Also, ten tons of Thai marijuana.
Thai grass is best. Consumers pay top dollar for it. Is
much more powerful than anything grown in Americas."

This piqued Al's interest. "And you need the same kind
of facilitation now on the West coast."

"Exactly. Can you arrange it?"

Al jerked his neck toward Ricky, inviting a reaction.
Ricky shrugged to indicate, "Why not?"

CHAPTER NINETEEN

Lydia contemplated suicide. She had it all planned. She would obtain heroin through a prostitute-friend who had connections. She would put on Rimsky-Korsakov -- her favorite: Scheherazade; draw a hot bath, sit in it; inject herself with the heroin -- enough for five doses; and she would then lie back and dream of picnics in the foothills beyond Krasnodar. Her last sweet dream.

Her prayers at St. John the Baptist, only blocks from the Russian embassy, went unanswered. The drama of the Russian Orthodox mass was a temporary escape. She prayed to her grandfather Boris, pleaded for guidance. Nothing.

She continued to see Horvath. This loathsome man was so like other men: weak and vulnerable beneath a facade of strength. And she no longer had illusions about herself. She was a whore. Plain and simple. And her pimp was Yakov, whose tools of coercion were limitless.

She had a choice. Reject Yakov and face unspeakable pain prior to a death devoid of dignity. Or end her life her own way -- an opiate and Scheherazade.

The phone rang.

"Lydia? This is Wentworth...er...uh...Charles, I mean
Chuck...Wentworth."

His boyish awkwardness made her smile and wipe away
her tears. He told her how he enjoyed talking with her that
night at Pironi's. He hoped she didn't consider it "forward"
of him to request her phone number. Would she like to
accompany him to a Bluegrass concert Saturday night?
He'd take the train down.

"Yes. I would," she said softly. "I would."

He treated her like a lady, a special lady. He exhibited
an old-fashioned solicitousness. He opened doors, helped
her with her coat, made sure she was comfortable and at
ease. Lydia thought back. How long had it been since
she'd been with a real gentleman? Volodya. All of
nineteen and strapping in his crisp Red Army uniform. So
long ago.

Wentworth visited every weekend for a month. They
shared a liking for art, spending hours together at the
National Gallery and the other museums of the capital. He
introduced her to his favorites: the Americans, Thomas
Eakins and John Singer Sargent. The discipline of detail
and studied composure of their subjects very much
reflected Wentworth's own demeanor, she came to realize.
And she told him so. She, in turn, became lost in the
diffuse moods of the Impressionists. He said she looked
like she just stepped out of a Cézanne painting. They
laughed.

He showed her another favorite, Thomas Cole's
"Voyage of Life." Four allegorical paintings, the first
depicted infancy in the form of a cherub entering a bright,
pure world full of wonder. The second, of youth, showed
the opportunities and challenges of life in the form of a
castle in the sky. The third, of middle age, portrayed the
vicissitudes and punishments of that stage in the voyage.

Finally, old age and death were seen as an old man in a damaged vessel at the end of the river of life supplicating himself before angels who beckoned heavenward.

Tears began to stream down Lydia's face.

"Lydia. What is it?" Wentworth took her gently into his arms.

She turned her face away. "Oh, it is as it should be."

"What is?"

"The Voyage of Life."

Wentworth looked utterly perplexed.

"If you do not -- on purpose -- complete the voyage as planned for you, what happens then?"

"You mean if you take your own life?" Wentworth said in a barely audible voice.

"Yes." She sobbed in a handkerchief.

"Well, I don't know. The Bible says that those who take their own lives cannot enter the kingdom of God."

Lydia pressed against Wentworth's chest and cried on his shoulder. Her body trembled. A guard approached and asked if she needed a doctor.

Lydia raised her head and stifled her weeping. "No. I am…really…all right." She wiped her eyes. They departed the gallery.

They strolled to the Tidal Basin. The Japanese cherry trees were in early bud. The bright afternoon sun dissipated the coolness of the day. Lydia stopped at the concrete edge of the basin and looked out on the water with pain in her eyes.

"Lydia, you must tell me what's bothering you."

"Chuck. You are so kind, so warm and good to me." She turned to him and continued haltingly. "I think I am falling in love with you."

Wentworth stood looking at her. She was intrigued by a bemused half-smile on his face. An enigmatic male Mona Lisa. Slowly, he came closer to her and touched her hair.

"That's good. You should be happy." He embraced her and kissed her softly.

"There's so much you don't know." She again turned away. "My life…my life is so…complicated."

"The only way to deal with problems is to share them with those whom you trust and love."

"Oh, but Chuck, these problems are so huge and so unbelievable. I feel trapped and there is no way out. The hurt is so great that I have wanted to…" She stopped herself.

Wentworth held her firmly by the shoulders. "Lydia. What is it? Let me help you. You can trust me."

She grabbed his hand and pulled him away from the Tidal Basin. She stopped under a cherry tree and folded her arms tightly in front of her as if suddenly chilled by an itinerant breeze. "Chuck, I am a very bad woman. So bad…you will not believe."

He placed his fingers on her lips. "It can wait." They strolled silently, hand-in-hand across the Mall, past the Lincoln Monument and the Vietnam Memorial. The rambling, sterile State Department building confronted them like an oncoming storm.

Wentworth paused and reflected.

What are you thinking?" she asked.

"The past. My past. What a distance I've come."

Innes no longer blended into the gray mass of civil servants all around him. Until recently he was just another close-cropped, superficially chipper, frustrated diplomat plodding the maze of corridors and cramped offices of the faceless-ambitious. Now he stood out. Hair streaming down his neck, over his ears and forehead, a faceful of stubble, jeans, Levi shirt and construction boots caused people to assume he was the guy to fix the toilets or to wax the floor. His former workmates shunned him. He ate alone in the cafeteria. He realized that he'd become a white collar leper. Screw them all! He fancied purchasing an earring. A pirate in the Fudge Factory!

Colleen stuck by him, knowing that this too would pass. Robin Croft remained loyal as well.

Innes spent long lunch hours sitting on a bench at the Reflecting Pool to escape the Thelma Tuckers of the world. The Lincoln Memorial loomed nearby at the west end of the Mall. He enjoyed reading Dostoyevsky under the budding elms, with Honest Abe peering out sagely from his massive seat anchored in the ages. The great Russian master's "House of the Dead" struck a special chord. Innes could relate to those in a tsarist gulag. He didn't wish to hurt Colleen. His mind wandered. He closed his eyes and savored the first fresh breezes of spring. Sensing that he was being watched, Innes opened his eyes and looked about. Just the usual crowds of joggers, strollers, tourists and goof-offs like himself. He closed his eyes again. *I'm becoming paranoid. Why would they surveille me? Don't start losing it Innes!* He entered that twilight zone between consciousness and slumber.

Rome. Airport. Colleen. Gift shops. Seductive perfume. Beautiful Slavic woman..."Signore Innes?"

Innes jerked awake. She was there. Directly in front of him. Leggy, blonde, mysterious. Wrapped in a black, fur-lined coat.

"Mr. Innes?"

"Yeah."

"Do you remember me, Mr. Innes?"

"Fiumicino." Innes rubbed his face and pushed his hair back with his fingers. "You…warned me about Mortimer."

"Yes. For your own good…and safety."

"What are you doing here? Who are you? How'd you find me here?" Innes sat up and took Lydia in with wide eyes.

She sat beside him. "It is, as you say in English, a long story, Mr. Innes."

"Call me Bob. And you are…"

"Lydia. Lydia Puchinskaya. I am Russian. I live now in Washington. I phoned the State Department. They told me that you worked here. I have been observing you." She giggled. "I am not a spy. I have only seen you when you go to work and when you come out here, at lunchtime. I wanted to choose the best moment to talk to you."

Innes nodded deeply, taking it in.

"I have information. Very important information which I want to give to you."

"Me? Concerning what? Mortimer?"

"Yes. And more. About some people. Also important."

Innes's long dormant mental computer began clicking. He became alert, his mind raced.

"Wait. Don't tell me. Criminals and spies and the U.S. government."

She nodded.

"And Russians. You're Russian. Mortimer. Was he a spy? Who killed him? The mafia? SVR? Pimps?"

"Bob. We need time. Can you come with me? I want you to meet someone. Another American. We can discuss this. All of it. Do not be afraid."

They flagged a taxi.

Al's generous bonuses were making Wentworth a moderately rich man. He and Lydia took a suite at the Four Seasons in Georgetown. There they could be reasonably sure that the rooms weren't recording studios. After the initial shock that came with Lydia's revelations about herself, Wentworth resolved to help her. He'd asked her to marry him.

Innes knew he had seen Wentworth somewhere before. They shook hands. Before Innes could ask, Wentworth replied, "Marine detachment, Embassy Rome, 2000 to '02. Lieutenant Charles Wentworth. Now just Mr. Wentworth. Call me Chuck."

"Now I remember. Small world."

"Bob, Lydia's in a real fix. She's got some serious dirt on some significant people in this administration. She, we, need help."

"Hold on. Why me?"

Lydia sat close to Wentworth on a sofa. "In Rome, I remembered that you were the only American who seemed to know where to look for the truth on Ambassador Mortimer," she said. "You were the only person who was interested in the truth. When I spoke to you at the airport, I warned you to not pursue your investigation. I did not want you to get hurt."

"By whom?"

"By Russian mafia."

"Did they kill Mortimer?'

"I believe so."

"What about the Italian and American mafias?"

"I am not sure."

"SVR?"

"Russian mafia and SVR are the same, Mr. Innes."

"CIA?"

"No. I don't hear much."

"Hear? Through whom?"

Wentworth and Lydia looked at each other. He took her hand and nodded for her to continue.

"Horvath."

Innes squinted. "Horvath? You don't mean the President's National Security Adviser?"

"Yes. Him."

She proceeded to recount Horvath's recruitment by Yakov and her role. She described the Russian mob's criminal inroads in the U.S., starting with her own illicit visa, and Yakov's involvement.

"Yakov is not what we call *Vory v Zakone* -- a kind of Godfather. But he wants to be." Conspicuously missing was any mention of Al. Wentworth needed time to sort things out in his mind about his boss and his future relationship with him. He and Lydia decided that part could wait a bit longer. Besides, neither knew anything about Yakov's dealings with Al. For all Wentworth knew, they could actually be legitimate. But he had his doubts.

"Why are you telling me all this? What do you want me to do with this information?"

Wentworth leaned forward. "She wants out. And we want to get married."

"And have five children," she added. "And live in South Carolina where I will make pies between making babies."

They looked lovingly at each other, holding hands tightly.

Innes fell back in his chair and massaged his forehead with his fingers. "Oy veh!"

Berlucci didn't want them to come to FBI headquarters. He asked Innes to come alone to receive instructions on where they would all meet. It was an aging, nondescript apartment building on upper Wisconsin. There the FBI had a safehouse flat. He gave Innes the code with which to get through the front door. Innes was to arrive fifteen minutes ahead of Lydia and Wentworth. On a busy rush-hour morning, Innes arrived at 9:00 sharp. Wentworth and Lydia -- he sporting large shades, she a floppy hat -- slipped through the door precisely a quarter of an hour later.

With Berlucci were Speedy and a special agent named Hanks whose specialty was Russian and East European crime gangs.

Innes recapitulated what he had told Berlucci and Speedy at headquarters, bringing Hanks up to speed.

"Tell us about this Yakov character," Berlucci said without further ado.

"Yakov is a very dangerous man. And very clever. He reaches to the top and is frightened by no one," Lydia answered. The apartment was obviously not lived in. Its circa 1975 decor and drawn curtains did not put her at ease. Neither did a large, whirring tape recorder in front of her on the coffee table.

"What do you mean by 'reaches to the top'?" Berlucci probed.

"He stops at nothing to get what he wants. He has seduced some very important people in your government."

"You mean recruited?"

"Yes. He traps them. Then he makes them do his will. He forces them to give him information."

"What kind of information?" Hanks asked.

"I don't know. I never see it. But I believe secrets of your government."

Berlucci and Hanks looked at each other gravely.

"Is Yakov SVR, you know, formerly KGB?" Speedy asked.

Lydia smiled and looked at the floor. She held her hands demurely in her lap. Wentworth sat in a chair to her left. "I am not expert on these things. But in Russia we see now no difference between SVR and mafia."

"Can you name names?" asked Berlucci.

"Yes. Nicholas Horvath. Senator Rory MacDonnell. General Cordner..."

"Jack Cordner? Deputy Army Chief of Staff?" Speedy interrupted.

"Yes, him." Lydia went on to name several additional officials holding high positions in the Pentagon, State Department, CIA and even one in Justice, as well as several members of Congress and their staff.

"How does Yakov entrap these people?" Berlucci asked.

"Different ways. Mostly through women...such as myself." Lydia looked away and wiped her eyes and nose with a handkerchief. Wentworth reached over and gripped her forearm. "I am not the only Russian woman who works like this for Yakov. He has houses for us. Nice houses. He also has Ukrainian, Byelorussian and Polish women. Also in New York. Also in Rome and Berlin."

"Are you his girlfriend?"

"No. He likes to show off beautiful women. But he is not capable of loving a woman. He is impotent."

Speedy was mesmerized, frantically jotting notes.

Berlucci appeared to hesitate for a moment, then asked, "Any FBI people? Has he entrapped anybody from the FBI?"

"No. At least I know of none."

Berlucci appeared relieved.

Innes spoke up. "Do you know the name Dennison?"

"Yes. He is your foreign minister, yes?"

"But, has Yakov recruited him?" The FBI men leaned forward in their chairs.

"I do not know. I am not sure."

Innes nodded pensively. His brow furrowed in concentration. The session continued till past midnight.

CHAPTER TWENTY

Horvath looked nervous. Normally, Dennison's White House counterpart would attack his food with gusto. This luncheon, he barely picked at his salad and declined wine, opting instead for two double vodkas.

Horvath talked languidly and disjointedly about Africa and Japan. He appeared distracted. Unusually, Horvath wasn't noticing the shapely waitresses of Les Nigauds.

"Senator Weems says he's going to try to slash State's budget. Has it in for us more than ever, the son of a bitch," Dennison said. "I've got a contact who's sleeping with his top legislative assistant. He tells me that Weems is trying to pull in his chits with foreign leaders to get their businesses to buy more tobacco from Weems's state. I'm passing the message back that if he goes after our budget, I'm gonna gin up the anti-tobacco lobby and embarrass the fucker to blue blazes."

Horvath was hearing, but not listening. His mind was focused on the previous evening. He had rendezvoused with Yakov through a now set procedure. He walked his Samoyed in Rock Creek cemetery where Dimitrov picked him up and drove him off to a safehouse near Dupont Circle. Yakov ordered him to recruit Dennison. When

Horvath protested, Yakov flashed an evil grin which made very clear what the alternatives were. "Don't worry," Yakov added. "He's as squalid as you are. It will be a cinch."

"Roy, how're things looking for the campaign? What are the plans for organizing things?" Although he was one of highest officials in the administration, Horvath, as a foreign policy professional from academia, didn't normally get involved in party matters or domestic affairs.

Dennison was surprised by Horvath's abrupt change of subject. "Well, uh, not too good so far. The President's way down in the polls. People are already deserting. It's going to take a lot of money this time around. Much more than before."

"Where's it going to come from?"

"That's a difficult point. But we're working on it."

"What is needed?" Horvath persisted, "Hundreds of thousands? Millions? What?"

Dennison fished out and gobbled the green olive from his martini glass. "More like the latter. Why?"

"Oh, I don't know. I just thought that I'd do my bit this time."

Dennison blinked. "Do your bit? What do you mean? Campaigning? Speeches? You haven't really been the garden variety political partisan, Nick."

"With funds. Contributions. You know."

Dennison looked at him hard. "Nick, we're talking big money. Really big money. Your government salary and your pension or whatever you get from Harvard isn't going to make a dent. Nice of you to offer though."

"I can find 'big money' for you." Horvath cleared his throat.

Dennison looked dubiously at his lunch mate.

"I know a rich...uh...financier. He wants to help."

"Who?"

"He, uh, wants to remain anonymous for now. But he's willing to give a lot." Horvath mopped the sweat from his forehead.

"Just like that. That's it? Is he angling for an ambassadorship? That's no problem at all. Does he have a college education?"

"No. Nothing like that. He wants information."

Dennison pondered this a few seconds.

"Information, like inside information? On the administration?"

"And more."

Dennison quickly caught on. "Tell him it's a deal. But it won't come cheap."

Horvath couldn't believe his ears. Just like that. The Secretary of State just agreed to sell state secrets, no ifs, ands, or buts. "Roy, you sure you understand me? What I'm asking?"

"You bet. Ohh! Look. We don't have to give away the store. We selectively pick out some marginal stuff. Stuff that's in the papers every day. Add to that some made-up stuff on the President's thinking, crap like that. Listen, I know politics. The important thing is to get the best guy re-elected. You have to bend the rules sometimes. You don't think the other side's not up to their own tricks? What's that theory that made you famous? 'Controlled inevitability'? It's like that. We steer events to the desired outcome, making it look inevitable, but sacrificing as little as possible along the way. This is what makes democracy stronger and healthier."

"He wants to know your travels over the coming months."

"Piece of cake. Here." Dennison fished out a piece of paper from a jacket pocket. "Take this. It outlines where

I'm scheduled to go till mid-August. Of course, surprise trips come up. Others get dropped, and so on. Uh, that'll cost your friend ten grand. There's other stuff I'm getting that you're probably not. You name when and where for delivery every week and I'll name the price."

He slapped Horvath on the shoulder. "Hey! Welcome to the rough and tumble club of domestic politics. But it's all hush-hush. Got me?" Dennison winked as he gulped the last of his martini.

The Secretary of State suddenly took a keen interest in counternarcotics policy. He wanted the troubled administration, of which he was a key player, to make some headway in a high-profile area like drugs. He called back to Washington for urgent consultations his ambassadors to Afghanistan, Bolivia, Colombia, Pakistan, Burma, Thailand, Laos and other countries where narcotics production or trafficking figured prominently.

He held pow-wows as well with the chiefs of the major law enforcement agencies involved with fighting narcotics trafficking, and with top Coast Guard, Pentagon and intelligence officials. He put State's public affairs machinery into overdrive to get media coverage. He got other governments to agree to send their foreign ministers to an international conference on counternarcotics cooperation in Miami in June. As a preliminary step, he obtained their consent to broaden intelligence-sharing on the drug trade. Dennison designated the State Department's Bureau of Intelligence and Research to be a repository of this data, as well as CIA, DEA, NSA, Coast Guard and Defense Department narcotics intelligence. And he tasked the Bureau with providing him with a seemingly endless stream of not only finished analytical overviews, but also raw intelligence. This included top secret plans to interdict couriers and knock out production labs, and transcripts of high-tech electronic eavesdropping of American and foreign crime figures. The workabee analysts who put it all together could only scratch their heads as to why the Secretary would want so much detailed data. But they and his staff dutifully packaged the stuff in black binders embossed with the gold State Department seal and passed it up the chain.

No Secretary of State could escape having to lug work home. Dennison was no exception. Each evening a black attaché case bulging with a treasure trove of narcotics intelligence accompanied the Secretary home. The same attaché returned with Dennison to the State Department every morning -- empty.

Al's problems were compounding, despite his best efforts to set things straight. He phoned Dennison's office for the eighth time in two days.

"The Secretary's office," answered the "personal assistant" -- the glorified term for secretary -- a woman in late middle age with an accent straight out of National Public Radio.

"Yeah. Look. This is Mr. Goodnough again," Al answered, using the pseudonym he and Dennison had concocted for their phone conversations.

"Yes. I remember, Mr. Goodnough. The Secretary has been very, very..."

"Yeah, I know. 'Busy.'" Al countered impatiently.

"I assure you that Mr. Dennison will get back to you--"

"'…when he gets a free moment.' But you got to understand, this is an urgent private business matter--"

"'…which requires his immediate attention,'" she retaliated.

"Like, right now," he snapped.

"The Secretary is aware. Good day!" The personal assistant abruptly ended the call.

Al slammed down the receiver. He sat, arms folded on his desk, glowering at the phone. Erin McNamara, Al's own "personal assistant," was afraid to breathe. It usually took twenty minutes to a half-hour for his temper to cool. Until then, everybody at Al-Mac steered clear of their boss.

The phone rang. Erin picked up the receiver. With trepidation, she squeaked, "Al, it's for you."

Snapping out of his hypnotic state, Al asked quickly, "Who is it?"

"Mr. Leventhal at Coralsco Supplies--"

Al jumped from his chair and exploded, "Tell him to go to hell!! I'm not talkin' to nobody today! Got it? Hold all calls. Tell 'em I've gone fishin' in Calabria. And if that goddamn Dennison phones, tell him I said he's a worthless windbag. And screw him and the ugly whore who gave birth to him! Tell him he's fulla shit and…"

Erin ran from her desk fed up, leaving Al screaming at the walls. The employees at Al-Mac Construction had an instinctual urge to take a collective coffee break. They streamed from the building like a herd of gazelles sensing an approaching lion.

The only human being on the planet daring enough to approach Al during such outbursts, Ricky, calmly entered his uncle's office with his hands in his pockets.

"Uncle Al." He shrugged his shoulders. "What is it?"

Al paused and focused on Ricky. His breathing eased.

"That fuckin' Dennison. Won't even return my calls."

"Why not?"

"How the hell do I know? Maybe he's playing in a polo tournament with his no-good-for-nothing, blue-blood friends. Maybe he's decided he doesn't like Italians after all. How'm I supposed to know what motivates the prick?"

"So, screw him. What's the big deal?"

"What's the big deal?! The big deal is this! The inside information that *strons'* gets us equals money. Get it?" Al threw a stack of correspondence toward a corner of the office, creating a small devil-wind of paper. Ricky didn't move.

"Mr. American Flag and Apple Pie ain't deliverin' any more. That rotten hypocrite cut off the pipeline. Now we got no more low-down on what the Feds are up to. They planning on a bust somewheres? We don't know squat about it. The other families'll think we're chumps. All that coordination the government's always doing with the Colombians? Now we got nothing to feed to our buddies in Cali. They find we got nothing, they won't waste another minute on us. They'll drop us like a hot *gnocchi*. Our supplies dry up. Our customers go away. My credibility goes zip! That means we're outta business. We're back to juke boxes and numbers. Get it?"

"So, let's pull the plug on the prick. Let the world know what he's been into. Let him sink," Ricky said.

"Humph! You gotta lot of learning to do, *nipote*. Don't you see? We got him and he's got us. We go down together. He had the *cozzi* once to tell me that what we got is 'mutual assured destruction.' Just like in nuclear war."

Ricky pondered a moment. "Why do you think he's stopped?" he asked.

Al slumped into the overstuffed, dark leather sofa opposite his desk and twirled a toothpick between his teeth.

His gaze was distant. "Somebody, or something, got to the son of a bitch," he said calmly.

"Who?"

"I don't know. It sure ain't his conscience. It's something else. I don't know."

CHAPTER TWENTY-ONE

"Mr. Ambassador, it's the Secretary! On line one." H. Carter Wells liked a lot of things about his veteran secretary. But her excitability wasn't one of them. Obviously, if the Secretary of State called, you dropped everything and paid close attention. But, short of a nuclear war, the cool-headed Kentucky colonel just wouldn't get flustered. His granddaddy used to say that Wells men honed the trait from being under fire at Antietam. Brothers of the Wells family had fought on both sides. It could be your own kin throwing all that lead at you. Best to be cool.

"Mr. Secretary, the Thai are on board. Foreign Minister Wichit assured me last evening that he will attend the conference. The Thai government is giving one-hundred percent cooperation."

"Great job, Carter," Dennison replied. "I don't have to remind you that a lot is riding on this conference. I've got a commitment from the President that he'll give the keynote speech. This has got to come off without a hitch and make the administration look good in the process."

Wells promised that he would do his part.

"Now Carter, there's one other thing. To pull this thing off, we don't want to be airing dirty laundry. It'll give the wrong impression, if you know what I mean."

The American ambassador to Thailand knew exactly what he meant. Dennison had given him an earful in Washington the week before. Only in the house of mirrors of American politics would your superiors urge you to violate your conscience for the sake of image. Wells wanted to clean house in his DEA shop in the embassy before the corruption and incompetence got out of hand.

"Mr. Secretary, I feel strongly that the DEA chief here should be sent back. He hasn't been sober since he got here. As a result, that whole shop is out of control. Half are banging in doors, acting like this was the South Bronx instead of a sovereign nation. The other half are either sleeping at their desks or, I fear, are on the take. We just have too much incontrovertible evidence."

"I empathize," Dennison lied. "Just contain it for now. Give it some more time to resolve itself. Stay in touch with my staff. In the meantime, we've all got to concentrate on getting this conference off the ground. The President's credibility is at stake. We can't have a key player like Thailand suddenly losing faith in us. Are we on the same wavelength here, Carter?"

Wells bit his lip till it bled. "I understand, Mr. Secretary. I'll keep working at it. But something's got to be done."

Dennison's attitude irked Wells. Could the man be that stupid? And why would the Secretary of State take an interest in the nitty-gritty of how he ran his embassy? He shook his head. Micromanagement and lack of vision had marked this as one of the least competent administrations in history. It was exceedingly frustrating to a seasoned professional like Wells. If there was any truth to the old saw that a diplomat is paid to lie for his country, it was certainly the case now. Wells felt hypocritical defending this fumbling crew.

Across town in the deteriorating Russian embassy, Oleg Konstantin Vladimirov nervously waited by the phone. The SVR *Rezident* chain-smoked Marlboros and just stared at the phone. Silence.

The intercom buzzed. The Thai Minister of Trade wanted "Commercial Counselor" Vladimirov to attend a briefing the next day on a trade fair the Thai were planning to give later in the year.

"No!" Vladimirov yelled at the young SVR aide.

"No? Sir?" the aide asked timidly as he held one hand over the mouthpiece. "It's Minister Khamhaeng himself on the phone, sir."

"Uh. Uh. Tell him I'm talking to our Foreign Minister right now. I'll get back to him shortly," Vladimirov said distractedly.

He looked around his office. The cheap, flowered wall paper was fraying, the furniture upholstery was threadbare. A lamp was broken and the vintage air conditioner made a loud, grinding sound. He hadn't been paid in four months. His staff was dispirited. Some of the embassy wives, his included, had become Baptist zealots in the post-communist freedom.

He loathed cover work. He didn't know squat about commercial work and couldn't care less. The real embassy commercial officer was an embittered, drunken Kazakh assigned to Bangkok to interact with his "fellow Asians." Half the time, he was getting laid in Patpong, Bangkok's no-holds-barred sex district. Indeed, half the embassy's male staff hung out there now. No more controls. No more cause. The women found religion and the men turned to sex.

Vladimirov glanced at the official photo portrait of Putin high on the opposite wall. "Shithead," he muttered. *Number One Shithead of a government of shitheads.*

The phone rang.

"Mr. Vladimirov? This is Arthur Klausen, of Westerbury Electronics, Inc. I am interested in export opportunities to Russia. Could I make an appointment?"

"Certainly. How about Wednesday at three o'clock?"

"Fine. See you then."

Vladimirov put down the receiver gently. He sported a broad smile. "Arthur Klausen" was the cover name for George Dexter, DEA special agent at the U.S. embassy. "Wednesday," fourth day in the week, meant the fourth pre-designated rendezvous point -- a grubby little cafe in the eastern part of the city whose specialty was Lao food. "Three o'clock" signified the third day of the week, Tuesday. They had earlier agreed to schedule such meetings at 12:30 pm, lunchtime, a normal time to leave the office. The SVR insisted on such circuitous communications in the interest of "operations security." Anyone listening in on the conversation would merely hear a businessman making an appointment with the Russian commercial counselor.

Vladimirov liked working with Americans, despite more than a decade of scheming against them in Germany, Tokyo and New York, among other places, during the late cold war years. Now Russia and America were friends. But Russia was broke and America was not. Socialism was dead. Capitalism was the victor. Time to cash in.

"Sir," Kurtaev, the young aide, said. "Any outgoing transmissions today?"

Poor Kurtaev. So bright-eyed and bushy tailed. Thinks he actually has a future in this business. I haven't the stomach to shake him and tell him that there is no longer a cause, that what we do now here is meaningless; that we serve a government of assholes, in perpetual lock horns with a Duma of fools, all competing for power in a truncated, bankrupt country, an orphan of a hollow former empire. Kurtaev, youth is wasted on this. A young Russian with any brains should live for love and truth, not a sharashka -- *a sham operation* -- *such as this.*

"No, Kurtaev. Thank you. Go home early. Spend more time with your wife."

It would be only this one deal, Vladimirov told himself. A cool half a million dollars from Thai narcotics producers, through their middle man, Dexter. Another half-million from those on the receiving end, Semion Mogilevich, the number one *Vory v Zakone* -- literally "thief-in-law" -- the top made man in the Russian mob. Possessing a degree in economics, he is also known as the "Brainy Don." Commercial Counselor Vladimirov would arrange the delivery via cargo ship. He had put the whole thing together. He'd build a sprawling dacha on the Black Sea. The kids would go to foreign universities. He and his family could live comfortably and without worries. *Just this one time.*

The phone rang again. "Call from New York, sir. Mr. Yakov," Vladimirov's secretary said through the intercom.

Vladimirov hesitated, then picked up the receiver.

"Oleg Konstantinovich, long time no hear, eh?"

"Ah, yes, I've been meaning to get hold of you. You know that I have this aversion to phones." The connection was crystal clear. Yakov ignored his barely veiled message not to conduct business via the open phone line.

"We have a business agreement, my dear Oleg. I have made all the necessary arrangements with my partners at this end," Yakov said, referring to his deal with Malandrino to ensure passage of the heroin and marijuana shipments through a western U.S. port.

"I see." Vladimirov was beginning to hyperventilate. "Uh, you see. I wasn't certain that you could help us in marketing the, uh, caviar. In the meantime, another broker has come along who has firmed up all the arrangements, including, uh, customs formalities."

The silence that ensued from the New York end didn't mask Yakov's wrath toward the SVR *Rezident*. After what seemed like an eternity, Yakov responded.

"We don't tolerate double-crossers, Oleg. When you make a pact with the devil, it's a contract for life. And if the rumors that I hear are true, I will make sure that you are worse than useless to Mogilevich. Do you understand me?"

Vladimirov quickly hung up. He pulled a bottle of Johnny Walker Black from his desk and poured a large glass, spilling some with his trembling hands. He gulped it down and poured another.

All that Ambassador Wells could do was to shake his head in amazement. He took off his reading glasses, set them on the report and looked across his desk to Harry Crestow, the embassy's chief of security.

"Does anyone in their shop know about this?" Wells asked.

"No one. We did it all ourselves. Even the Station doesn't know. Just as you instructed."

"Good job, Harry."

"What now?"

"Stand by. We'll talk again tomorrow."

Crestow departed. Wells called for his secretary to take dictation. "This is a cable -- back channel, Pamela..."

SECRET
TO: THE WHITE HOUSE IMMEDIATE
FOR NSC ADVISER HORVATH - EYES ONLY - FROM WELLS
SUBJECT: CORRUPTION IN THE BANGKOK DEA
      OFFICE

1. SECRET - ENTIRE TEXT.

2. TO MY GREAT DISTRESS, WE HAVE UNCOVERED GRAVE MALFEASANCE IN OUR DEA OFFICE. OUR SECURITY PEOPLE HAVE POSITIVE PROOF THAT AT LEAST ONE DEA OFFICER HERE IS CONNIVING WITH THAI GANGSTERS AND CORRUPT THAI OFFICIALS TO SMUGGLE NARCOTICS INTO THE UNITED STATES. WE DO NOT KNOW THE ESTIMATED VALUE OF THESE DEALS, BUT GUESS THEY REACH INTO THE TENS OF MILLIONS OF DOLLARS. THE DEA SHOP HERE HAS BEEN IN A CONSTANT STATE OF DISORDER SINCE THAT AGENCY'S CURRENT BANGKOK OFFICE DIRECTOR ARRIVED HERE NINE MONTHS AGO. INCOMPETENCE AND CORRUPTION REIGN IN THE LARGE DEA OPERATION HERE. IT HAS NOW REACHED A POINT WHERE IT IS ONLY A MATTER OF TIME BEFORE THIS STATE OF AFFAIRS BECOMES KNOWN, WITH ALL THE CONSEQUENT REPERCUSSIONS THAT REVELATION WILL HAVE ON U.S.-THAI

RELATIONS, TRUST ON THE PART OF CONGRESS,
AND OUR COUNTRY'S IMAGE BEFORE OUR OWN
PEOPLE AND THE WORLD.

3. I REQUEST THAT THE WHITE HOUSE GIVE ME
THE GREEN LIGHT TO IMMEDIATELY REMOVE
THE DEA CHIEF AS WELL AS OTHER DEA
OFFICERS ON WHOM WE HAVE INCRIMINATING
INFORMATION. SECRETARY DENNISON IS AWARE
OF MY VIEWS. I TAKE THE UNUSUAL MEASURE
OF CONTACTING YOU DIRECTLY ON THIS
MATTER OUT OF MY CONVICTION THAT ACTION
IS REQUIRED AND IS NEEDED NOW.
WELLS

Horvath wasted no time alerting Dennison about Wells's
cable. They met late at night at Dennison's sprawling horse
ranch in the rolling hills of northwest Maryland.
Dennison's study fit the classical stereotype of an
establishmentarian's inner sanctum: an old oak desk with
an antique brass lamp. Bookshelves packed with
moldering tomes on the law and history. Walnut
wainscoting, dark green wall covering. Paintings of race
horses lined the room. A dozen or so ego photo portraits of
The Secretary in the company of the Aga Khan, some
foreign presidents, a king or two, Mother Theresa, Bono
and other luminaries, each bearing a personal handwritten
encomium to "My friend, Roy."

"What do I do, Roy?" Horvath asked anxiously.

"Send a message back thanking him for the information,
adding that you're 'taking it under advisement' or some such
baloney like that."

Horvath took the snifter of Hennessy eagerly and swallowed half. He wiped perspiration off his forehead with a cocktail napkin.

"I can't just put the guy off. He'll smell something funny. He'll go to the Hill. Or, worse, the media. Who knows? Oh, Christ! Christ! This is getting out of hand! What do we do?" Horvath finished the brandy, then helped himself to another.

"Get hold of yourself!" Dennison commanded.

Horvath slumped into a high-back, brown-leather chair. "I don't know, Roy. I'm under so much pressure lately. And now this."

"What about our new friends? Have you told them yet?"

Horvath took another swig of Hennessy. "Hah. 'Our friends' are eating us alive. Like something out of a science fiction movie."

"Bullshit. We control things. We just use them. We toss them a few bones and they throw back kings' ransoms at us."

"Yeah. Just like turning tricks. We're whores, Roy. Whores!" Horvath stared misty eyed into space.

Dennison planted himself squarely in front of the President's National Security Adviser, bracing his arms on the chair's armrests.

"Listen, Nick, and listen good. We're in this together. And it's not like we're crooks either. This is for a good cause: re-electing Dan Corgan President of the United States. Sometimes, in order to make an election freer, you've got to alleviate the constraints. In this case, it's money."

Horvath began to cry uncontrollably with his head almost in his lap.

Dennison grabbed him by the shoulders and shook him. "Snap out of it, goddamn it!"

Horvath blew his nose. "You know, I came to this country because I wanted freedom. Freedom to do and say what I wanted. Freedom to vote for the person I thought was best. Now, look at me. I'm no better than those communist stooges in Budapest, cynically manipulating the system. I fought them! Now...look at me."

"Listen up, my friend. We're both in this deep. You call your contact. Give him the cable. Tell him we stand ready to do what we can to put a lid on Wells and that whole mess out there." Dennison shook Horvath again, harder. "*Do you hear me?*" he shouted.

Horvath slowly nodded.

He was indistinguishable from any other Swiss businessman disembarking the Lufthansa flight into the sweltering Bangkok heat, coolly determined to conquer the vast, mercantile reaches of booming Southeast Asia. Clad in a pressed, pin-striped, three-piece suit, clutching a black-leather brief case, clearly focused through wire-rim glasses, he marched forward into Don Muang airport -- shiny and efficient, like him.

"Rudolf Schnitzler, Geschäftsmann/commerçant" read the red-jacketed Swiss passport. The bored immigration officer processed him through quickly. Customs wasn't interested in examining his baggage and waved him through.

In the rear-view mirror, the taxi driver couldn't help but notice one particular feature on "Herr Schniztler": a nasty gash across his face.

Dimitrov checked into the Arnoma Swisshotel. A desk clerk handed him a package which had arrived two hours earlier. He opened it in his room and pulled out the components. Within minutes, he assembled a stripped down 7.62mm Dragunov sniper rifle with scope and test-fired it, unloaded. He went about methodically opening the secret compartments on his matching leather bags. From his suitcase's all-metal bottom, he carefully slid out one mirrored dagger and four small throwing knives. Schnitzler/Dimitrov was ready for business.

Despite his smoking habit, Vladimirov was an avid jogger. It was one of a number of new tastes and pastimes he'd acquired during his three-years at the Soviet UN mission in New York in the early '80s. Others included Nintendo games -- he had quite a collection -- and an affinity for chili dogs.

Every day at dawn Russia's top intelligence officer in Thailand would pull his creaky frame out of bed, don his prized J. Crew jogging suit and trot to Bangkok's only sizeable public recreation area, Lumpini Park. He would jog around the ponds and sculpted gardens and return to shower and change before the heat of the tropical sun reached its full morning strength.

While the running made him feel good, the city's polluted air, laced with the putrid smell of stagnant water in the remnants of canals, and garbage awaiting collection, made him somewhat nauseous. But he soldiered on down the jagged sidewalks, into Bangkok's congested streets when the sidewalks ran out, past the capital's proliferating skyscrapers, through crowds breakfasting at open-air sidewalk stalls.

Vladimirov used this time of exerted energy to organize his thoughts for the day ahead. These days it wasn't so difficult on the work front. The *Rezident* hadn't received a

non-routine message from Moscow in weeks. The collapse
of the communist regime in 1991 had removed a cause to
serve, and the severe budget shortfalls made operations
virtually impossible anyway. Moscow paid little attention
to Asian outposts such as Bangkok, even regarding things
like personnel matters. So, morale at the embassy was
worsened by not knowing when one was scheduled for
reassignment. *Need to ding Moscow again with another
cable.*

Ambassador Chayevsky was a good man -- for a Putin
supporter. He and his wife worked assiduously at trying to
keep embassy morale above the meltdown level by holding
discussion and reading groups, organizing outings and
arranging Russian cultural events for the Thai. *Make sure
to sit down with him this afternoon to exchange ideas.*

*Henry! Now there was one crackerjack son with a
future. So smart -- Moscow University has already
accepted him for its law program. But it is best to get him
into Harvard or another outstanding American University.
After all, I named him after Henry Kissinger, unbeknownst
to the paranoid KGB. Ha! Ha! He should also study
history. And American literature. Must talk to him tonight
over dinner.*

As he did every morning, Vladimirov rounded a small
hillock in a far, secluded corner of the park with plenty of
shade trees. There he would pause and do stretch exercises
before returning to his apartment.

The blade came so swiftly that he saw the blood spilling
from his groin before he felt the pain. Another slash caught
him in the upper neck, just under his lower jaw. The jogger
slumped into a growing pool of warm blood. There was no
death struggle, little pain. It came that quickly. Dimitrov,
after all, knew his business. Like a wisp of the city's smog,

he metamorphosed and disappeared as silently as he had
come.

On Wireless Road, the American Ambassador's
residence was one of the few remaining traditional Thai
structures in Bangkok. Encircled by a moat and swathed in
lush shade trees, the expansive wooden house, with its
canopied windows and inviting verandas and entrance
ways, stood in stark contrast with the concrete and chrome
high-rise office buildings which, over the years, have
grown across the cityscape like a malignant disease.

As he did every afternoon just before dinner,
Ambassador Wells played a couple of sets of tennis on the
courts adjoining the residence, in full view from the street.
Today, his opponent in a singles match was a senior Thai
palace official.

It was deuce and Wells, drawing on his notorious
competitive streak, was determined to hammer home a tie-
breaker hard enough to cause his opponent to lose his
nerve. It was one of Wells's secret tactics which he never
revealed to anyone, except his daughter, Lauren. *Got to
practice with her tomorrow.*

Back arched, right heel up, right arm stretched taut like a
fishing rod. On three, he would bring up the ball with his
left hand and smash it for all he was worth. *One...two...*

"Crack!" The percussion of the Dragunov 7.62mm
could barely be heard above the din of Bangkok's insane
traffic.

Wells fell to his knees and clutched his head, a ragged
hole in which revealed skull and brains. He was dead
before falling forward face-down onto the court surface.

Nary a wrinkle in his Swiss businessman's suit, Dimitrov/Schnitzler methodically dismantled the rifle and stowed it in his black attaché case. Calmly, he walked to the stairwell from the roof of the Deutsche Bank building, catty-corner from the U.S. ambassador's residence, and promptly joined a Nestlé's public relations event on the ground floor. After an hors d'oeuvre and a slug of coke, he departed unnoticed through a rear exit onto Ruam Rudee Avenue. Another face in the crowd.

CHAPTER TWENTY-TWO

"Another U.S. Envoy Murdered," declared the
Washington Post. "American Ambassador to Thailand
Victim of Assassin's Bullet," informed the *New York Times*.
CNN's star foreign correspondent, Kristin Armour, flew
out from Jerusalem to cover the story. Wells's murder
stunned Washington. The shaking of heads would soon
give way to the pointing of fingers. It was now open
season on the State Department by Congress and the media.
Senator Weems seized on the Mortimer and Wells killings
to call for abolition of the Foreign Service as an
independent entity and for turning embassy security
entirely over to the Marines. Dennison faced a virtual
rebellion in the ranks of his diplomats. Hundreds signed a
petition demanding revamping of diplomatic security.

Dennison made Bernard Scher point man for dealing
with the attacks. He appeared at every noon press briefing
to reassure the nation that the government could adequately
protect its envoys, that "vigorous" investigations were
proceeding expeditiously, but that the sensitivity of the
means precluded him from revealing details. His self-
important way and condescending demeanor made him the

target of media attacks. The *New Republic* compared President Corgan with King Lear.

Dennison and Selmur urged the President to go on the offensive in order to defuse the media criticism. Corgan wanted another full briefing before deciding what to do. The same cast of characters -- minus Bob Innes -- met again in the West Wing. Corgan exhibited a grave demeanor. He carefully reviewed his briefing notes as the others sat uneasily, awaiting a signal from the Chief Executive that the briefing should begin. Corgan sat there, reading glasses cocked on his nose, turning each page slowly. It was as if he didn't realize that there was anyone besides himself in the conference room. The cleared throat, the shifting in old wooden chairs added to the general unease in a room that was deadly quiet. The President paid no mind as he continued to review his briefing materials oblivious to those in his presence.

Finally, Corgan stopped, took off his glasses, sat back and pondered, inserting a bow of his spectacles between his teeth. His captive audience looked at their president expectantly and uncertainly. Then he spoke.

"Well?"

The curtness of this remark generated instant anxiety in the group. Like pupils seeking to avoid being picked on by the teacher, they averted gazes, froze and, contrary to their usual natures, sought to be totally inconspicuous.

The President looked right at Scher. The latter fidgeted, his trademark cockiness gone.

"Ahem. Ah...what we have here Mr. President is a case of...er...I mean...a situation in which it is apparent that...that, uh, any number of groups could be responsible. We know, for example, that an Iranian cell has been active in Bangkok for some time." He turned quickly toward CIA

Director Levin. "Dave, why don't you give us a wrap-up of what your people have found on that cell."

Levin's eyes widened. He gulped. The surprise hand-off virtually paralyzed him.

"Yes. Well. In 1994, an Iranian terrorist cell attempted to make some big splash by loading a stolen truck with high-powered explosives. Almost by fluke, the Thai police uncovered the plot and arrested those responsible."

Silence. The President just looked at Levin, without comment. Levin shifted nervously in his chair.

Secretary of Defense Wilkins stared at the conference table top, his hands folded together as if in prayer. One could almost hear him imploring the Lord to spare him from attention.

"But the Marines are responsible for embassies' physical security," Levin blurted. Sweat poured from his brow. "Perhaps the Defense Secretary has something to say on this matter." Levin appeared grateful that all eyes were now diverted to Wilkins.

The Secretary of Defense bolted upright, his eyes flitted around the room like those of a cornered animal.

"Uhuh. Right. We're, uh, we're, uh..." He adjusted his tie, which at the moment felt like a tightening noose. "We a-- a--" he stammered. Wilkins blew his nose. "We are awaiting full details from Bangkok."

Dennison interjected. "What the hell do you mean? You received the same seven-page cable we all did from the embassy yesterday."

"I'm waiting for a report from the Marine detachment there!" Wilkins spat back.

"Are you kidding? What difference is that going to make? The RSO incorporated everybody's input--"

"Gentlemen." Corgan signaled an end to the bickering. "Let me explain what's going on here." He placed his

reading glasses on the table and leaned forward.
"Somebody or some persons out there have murdered two
United States ambassadors. Men I personally nominated.
Men who had my full faith and trust. I'm flying to
Kentucky on Friday to personally give the eulogy at
Ambassador Wells's funeral. I have to face his grieving
family. Not only that, I have to face an increasingly critical
press and American public. What do I tell them all? 'We
have no idea who's behind these murders?' 'Maybe it was
Iranians? Or perhaps al-Qaida? Or God-knows-who?'
You can bet your last government perk that Congress is
going to get into the act big time. And I needn't remind
everyone that it's an election year." He paused a moment.
"I need answers. First, I need to know whether there's a
connection between the two incidents. Second, I need
leads." He looked at Scher. "Solid leads."

"Mr. President, we at the Bureau see a pattern." FBI
Director Frederick Karlson, a decorated ex-Marine and
pioneering Illinois attorney general, was never one to hold
back, be it before North Vietnamese bullets or Chicago
Latino gang leaders.

The others reacted as if a hot stock tip were about to be
revealed. Corgan nodded for him to continue.

"Twenty-four hours before Ambassador Wells was
killed, the Russian intel chief in Bangkok was murdered.
Knifed in the abdomen and throat. Very professional job."

Levin's expression betrayed his ignorance of this event.
Dennison frantically searched his memory as to whether
he'd been briefed on it.

"It could be pure coincidence," Scher spluttered without
forethought.

Without acknowledging Scher's presence, Karlson told
the President, "On August 14th, the SVR *Rezident* in
Ankara was similarly murdered. Swiftly killed, cut up

almost beyond recognition. Messy, but a professional job. The perpetrator, or perpetrators, clearly meant to send a message via the brutality."

"What's that to do with our ambassadors?" Dennison demanded.

Still keeping his attention on the President, Karlson continued, "Not long before that, we lost Ambassador Mortimer. Same m.o. But the brutal message in this and the Ankara incident was being directed not against us or Moscow."

"Who then?" asked Levin.

"We're not sure at this stage, but we've got some ideas."

The conference room was noiseless as its occupants processed this information.

"And you see a connection," Corgan said.

"I do."

"Then what's the glue linking them all together?"

"Simple, Mr. President. Crime."

Corgan's interest was piqued. Dennison hung on this word and leaned forward as far as he could to catch Karlson's next words. As if in telepathic lockstep, Horvath and Selmur did likewise.

"Can you elaborate?" Corgan asked.

"Organized crime."

"As in mafia?"

"Or variations thereof. We can provide details in a separate--"

"Mr. President. We simply cannot be pursuing every cockamamie conspiracy theory at this point," Dennison interjected.

"I have to agree with Secretary Dennison," Horvath chimed in.

Doing his best to put on an air of balance and fairness, chief-of-staff Selmur added in a deliberate, bass voice affecting thoughtfulness, "What we have here, Mr. President, is a situation in which any number of possibilities present themselves. We know that there are terrorist organizations which have targeted American personnel. This is documented. Al-Qaida cells are operating in Rome and Bangkok. This is documented. Then there is the theory that organized crime has targeted our ambassadors. This is *not* documented. What reason would they have? A connection between the murders of our envoys and those of SVR personnel? This is *not* documented." He banged the table with his knuckles to add emphasis.

His face transformed itself instantly into an expression of patient bemusement. "I can make the case that Mortimer and Wells were dispatched by...by Satanists. Or...bikers." A contrived chuckle rumbled from Selmur's self-consciously smiling face. This was met by a few snickers around the room.

"We are not scriptwriters for the next Oliver Stone movie here." Selmur's chuckle became a mocking laugh. Others followed suit. An atmosphere of levity permeated the room. Now putting on his best expression of grave solemnity, Selmur added, "But, Mr. President, to go chasing after a flock of wild geese at this stage would open the administration up to public ridicule as well as complicate the investigation."

Extending his right index finger to drive home his point, Dennison added, "Mr. President, nobody said that these cases would be solved overnight. Bernie Scher here is doing a fantastic job of pulling together the interagency investigation. He has at his beck and call all of the foreign affairs agencies, plus the military services. It's only a matter of time before we develop some leads. Just as we did with 9/11."

Horvath nodded solemnly in agreement.

"Hear, hear," rejoined Selmur.

"Why assist the media feeding frenzy?" Dennison
continued. "They will seize upon any doubts that we
exhibit to call us all a bunch of fools. We need to tough it
out and to show action. I suggest that Bernie Scher's team
be expanded and that he be given more direct
responsibilities and powers over all the concerned agencies.
The comparisons we want are with Truman, not Carter."

Corgan flinched at the last comment.

"But, Mr. President, we *are* developing leads, we think
solid leads--"

Corgan cut Karlson off. "I think Secretary Dennison's
observations make sense at this stage. I agree that Mr.
Scher should be given greater authority and resources to
pursue his investigation. The FBI will coordinate with the
Scher team, feeding it all reasonable leads it develops on
these cases. Beef up security at our embassies, especially
for our ambassadors. Furthermore, I want an expanded,
more aggressive public relations and media campaign. The
press and the public must be made to know how much
effort we're putting into this. The 9/11 analogy is a good
one." He turned to Selmur. "Howard, I want you to pull
this all together. And I want all reports on these cases to
come to me through the chief of staff."

Corgan betrayed for a fleeting moment an air of
resignation. "My chief concern now is Congress. If this
drags on, or, heaven forbid, if we lose more diplomats, we
all hang together ladies and gentlemen." He rose, signaling
an end to the meeting.

With a discreet but sharp nudge, an aide prevented Senator Weems from nodding off and thereby giving the press another opportunity to have a field day at the chairman's expense. When he was a member of the House Un-American Activities Committee way back when he was a junior congressman, Weems once called for FBI investigations to ferret out communists in the TV media. He'd never trusted journalists.

"I call this plenary meeting of the Senate Foreign Relations Committee to order!" he declared in his rich Mississippi Delta drawl, interspersed with an occasional whistle as tongue met with dentures. He slammed the gavel down.

The chamber in the aging Dirksen Building was packed. Reporters, Senate aides, academics and the curious jostled each other. Bob Innes and Colleen McCoy stood unassumingly in the back.

All twenty committee members were present, elevated in a semicircle at the front of the chamber. Called to testify were Dennison, Horvath, Levin, Wilkins, Scher and Karlson. A representative of the Foreign Service's labor group was invited to give the views of rank-and-file members.

After the usual welcoming courtesies, Weems began his attack. "Secretary Dennison, within the past six months, two United States ambassadors have been brutally murdered. No one has come forth to claim responsibility for either one. In fact, these slayings appear to be a total mystery. Now, unless you have some revelatory information for us, I think one could safely say that the State Department has failed to do its job in two areas: resolving these murders, and protecting this country's representatives abroad."

In response, Dennison read from a prepared text which was heavy on the Scher "investigation" but predictably light on results. He made heavy hints that terrorists were responsible -- though one shouldn't assume a connection between the two cases, he counseled. He concluded by asserting that the administration was doing its utmost to identify the culprits of "these cowardly acts" and to bring them to "the justice they deserve." With a flourish, Dennison announced the formation of the "President's Select Task Force on Terrorism" under the "able and tireless stewardship" of Bernard J. Scher; it would have "extraordinary powers" to use "whatever means, consistent with the law, within the U.S. government" to track down all leads and ultimately resolve the assassinations "just like we did in the 9/11 tragedy." Finally, he proclaimed a $2 million reward for information leading to the apprehension of the perpetrators of "these dastardly crimes."

"That's a very fine statement, sir," Weems observed. "But until you nail the possum he's gonna get your garden, by which I mean that no matter which two ways you look at it, we're gonna be losin' some more of our people until the State Department gets its act together. So far as I can see, y'all are just hootin' down a gopher hole. Not only have you not narrowed down realistically the likely suspects, you don't have a clue of where to begin lookin'. Which gets to my idea of doing away with all of this elitist, separate Foreign Service nonsense -- fold it into the Civil Service! And turn all security matters over to the Marines..." An exaggerated cough from the committee vice chairman brought Weems back down to earth.

Scher, Levin, Wilkins and Horvath were equally excoriated by the Chairman. A Fox reporter likened the scene to naughty third graders being brought before the school principal to have their knuckles rapped. The labor rep then read an erudite but cautious statement obliquely critical of protection efforts thus far. He pulled so many punches, however, that nobody quite understood what position his organization had and was dismissed. Then came Karlson.

In his couched statement, the FBI Director was careful not to challenge the administration's line. He nonetheless pointed to possible criminal motivations for the murders, but made no mention of the SVR connection, again not wishing to stick it in the President's eye.

"Mr. Director, am I to understand that you believe organized crime may be behind these killings? Furthermore, would you agree that Ambassador Mortimer had some shady connections that may have brought him into danger? That Ambassador Wells was in the middle of trying to clean house in an embassy sullied by corruption? And that there may be a link between the murders of these two officials and those of Russian SVR officers in the same timeframes?"

Dennison, et al. were stunned. There was a commotion in the chamber. Weems banged his gavel to restore order. Horvath was on his cell phone to the White House.

Once the chamber had quieted down, Karlson answered curtly in the affirmative. He ended with a statement that details could be provided in a follow-on classified briefing.

"We'll do just that, Mr. Director," Weems said. He then adjourned the session with a bang of his gavel. Karlson's face was grave as he rose and made his way to Dennison and Horvath.

"The Chairman's an insightful man," he said with solemnity. "That's okay though. The best policy is to be up front with the Hill. If you aren't, they come back to bite your ass off. Their staffers don't miss a thing."

Indeed they don't. Especially when the Director of the Federal Bureau of Investigation himself is feeding them the information.

CHAPTER TWENTY-THREE

Speedy was beside himself. He'd been trying to reach Innes at his office for five hours.

"What do you mean you haven't seen him since eight-thirty? Don't you people keep tabs on your personnel?!" He virtually screamed into the phone.

"Listen Mister! This here office is the Land of the Living Dead," retorted Alfreda Williams, the portly African-American secretary who kept the Freedom of Information Office from total self-destruction. "We got every kinda misfit and retiree-without-a-cause you can think of workin' here. They don't tell me nothin'. Mr. Innes, he's about as smart as they get around here. But he vanishes like a ghost some days. His boss don't care. The boss's boss don't care. And the only reason that I care is that I'm an honest, God-fearing woman. When Mr. Innes gets it in his mind to get himself back over here, I'll give him your message. Now, good day!" She hung up.

"Shit!!" Speedy jumped from his chair and kicked his waste basket as hard as he could, sending the contents strewing in all directions. "Shit! Shit! Shit!"

"Speedy. If you can't control yourself or your language, then go for a jog around the Mall!" his young secretary, Rachel, admonished.

"Yeah, yeah, yeah. Sorry." He collected the trash back into the can. "It's just that I've got to get hold of a friend about something important and they can't tell me where he is. I'm afraid that he's flown the coop. Still no luck at reaching Colleen McCoy?" he asked.

"Speedy, I've called the Foreign Service Institute at least seven times. All they can do is post a message. She's got to pick it up. She can't be in class all the time."

"Right. Well, please keep trying."

Speedy slumped back into his chair. He picked up the classified memo from the State Department. It jarred him every time he looked at it.

DEPARTMENT OF STATE   SECRET
WASHINGTON, D.C.

    TO: Department of Justice, Criminal Division - Alfred A. Cardoza, Assistant Attorney General Federal Bureau of Investigation - Hendrik K. Mallory, Assistant Director

    FROM: Bureau of Diplomatic Security - Ralph W. Torres, Assistant Secretary

SUBJECT: Request for Arrest Warrant for Espionage Suspect - Innes, Robert Woodruff, 096-42-8787

1. Request arrest warrant be issued and arrest expeditiously carried out on subject, who is suspected of engaging in espionage against the United States.
2. Authorized search of subject's home on April 22 uncovered over one hundred classified documents from State, CIA, DIA, FBI, DEA and other agencies concealed

inside a sofa. Twenty-one were Top Secret, others
captioned or specially compartmented. Computer disk
recovered at site contained correspondence with
"Grounder." Notes indicate drop-off and pick-up sites as
well as monetary payoffs. SIGINT confirms that
"Grounder" is a code name used by Col. Yuri Vasilenko,
deputy *Rezident* in Russia's Washington embassy.

In three more pages, the memo detailed Innes's
"increasingly aberrant" behavior following his "substandard
work performance" and "subsequent reassignment for
disciplinary problems." It described his "paranoid
delusions," including "a conviction that the mafia, SVR and
senior administration officials were conspiring to
compromise the country's national security for vague, ill-
defined purposes." Attached to the memo was a section of
Innes's latest physical exam from State's medical unit. The
central theme was that "the examinee exhibits erratic,
antisocial and rebellious behavior not readily linked to any
physical condition." The examining physician
recommended that Innes be given intensive and thorough
psychological testing.

Speedy's phone buzzed. "It's Ms. McCoy," Rachel said.

Speedy lunged at the receiver, almost dropping it as he
snatched it toward his ear.

"Colleen!"

"Speedy! How ya doin'?"

"Colleen, where's Bob?"

"Why, at work. Why, what's the problem?"

"He's not at work. Not in the office anyway."

"Oh, well, he's probably at the snack bar or somewhere.
He'll be back--"

"Listen to me, Colleen. Bob is in trouble. Big trouble.
You've got to find him."

"What kind of trouble?" Her voice was no longer cheery.

"Somebody's out to frame him. They're going to arrest him."

"What?! For what? Who? Why?"

"Colleen, listen to me. Don't go home. Find Bob. Whatever means it takes, find him. Then lay low, both of you. You've got my home number. Stay in contact. Use false names. And, by all means, *don't go home.*"

Toby Wheeler was progressing. Slowly, but steadily. The doctors thought that he would walk again, but only after weeks of being laid up, followed by months of physical therapy. Being away from his work was more excruciating for the *Post* reporter than being incapacitated. The doctors forbade his using a laptop, but consented to his dictating into a small tape recorder -- but only for short periods of time. Innes was his legs now, as well as his interviewer, researcher and typist. Innes spent increasing amounts of time with Wheeler, his surest ally apart from Colleen. The pariah diplomat spent less and less time at his office. No one cared. Least of all he. And he found a new passion in journalism. Wheeler was an outstanding mentor. Innes did the chasing around. Wheeler composed the stories. His series on crime and government was to resume with the next Sunday issue. Colleen helped Marion with the kids, shopping and other tasks. They became fast friends.

The story would be a five-part series. Drawing heavily upon Lydia's information, it would reveal the Russian mob's inroads into the American body politic. It would name names. They obtained a visa photo of Yakov.

Juxtaposed next to one of Semion Mogilevich, the reputed boss of bosses in the Russian mob, Wheeler would describe their competition and the lengths to which Yakov was going to overcome his rival. Information on links with the Cosa Nostra, however, remained sketchy. At this stage, Wentworth, suspicious but still ignorant about Al, wished to dig further into his boss's affairs. He swore Lydia to secrecy. As far as Innes, Wheeler and the FBI knew, Charles T. Wentworth was simply an ex-Marine working for a New Jersey construction company who wanted to help get his new girlfriend out of a jam.

"This is great stuff. We'll really blow the socks off some very important people," Wheeler exulted. "The rot has gotten deep and this'll help root it out. It's overdue." He clapped his hands together.

"Hey! Watch it. They told you to move as little as possible. Don't push it," Innes warned.

"I can't stand being kept in a hospital bed. I want to go home. I want to eat Marion's chicken stew and dumplings with my family. I want to wear normal clothes. I want to sleep with my wife." He yanked at his antiseptic hospital sheets and threw a glump of green jello against the equally antiseptic wall.

Innes moved quickly to keep him still. "Tony, stop it! Continue like this and you'll be Mr. Wheels for the rest of your life. Just bear with it. You've got to heal. In time, you'll be able to do all those things. In the meantime, be a good boy. Hear?"

"Yes, Daddy! But make sure Marion brings me some of her chicken stew."

"You got it."

They heard running in the hallway, followed by shouting. Colleen burst into the hospital room, followed seconds later by a nurse.

"Miss! Miss! You can't come in here. Visiting hours are over! If you don't leave, I'll call security," the nurse threatened.

"But you don't understand. I have to see my...husband." She gestured toward Innes. "It's very important. There's a...an emergency in his family. He needs to know about it immediately." She neatened her disheveled hair and tried to catch her breath.

The nurse paused a moment. "Well, all right. But do it quickly. I want you and your husband out of here in five minutes. Mr. Wheeler needs his rest."

Dispensing with greetings, Colleen said, "Bob, we've gotta go! C'mon." She grabbed his elbow and yanked him toward the door.

Innes resisted. "Hold on. She's just a nurse, not a concentration camp commandant. Take it easy."

"Thus spake Zarathustra!" Wheeler joked.

"Sorry Toby, but this is important. Big trouble is facing Bobby here. I've got to get him away."

Innes jerked his arm from her grasp. "Now, wait a minute! Explain what this is all about. What trouble am I in?"

Colleen relented. "They're out to arrest you!"

"Arrest me? Who?"

"Them! I don't know. The whole dang Washington power structure for all I know. All those big shots you've been pissing off with your investigative digging." She quickly recounted Speedy's warning.

"Bob, this is it. You're being framed. They actually think they can pull this kind of crap in this day and age. It's like none of these dudes ever heard of Watergate," Toby said.

Innes's mind was racing. He wanted to say something, but his mouth froze.

"You can't go home," Toby continued. "You've got to hide. Stay at my house. Something tells me these clowns are stupider than we think. You'll be safe with Marion. But stay indoors."

"What about me?" Colleen asked.

"They're not after you. You can be an asset as a vocal defender of Bob. And so long as there's some press attention toward you, as the girlfriend of an unjustly accused man, they won't dare go near you. But they will keep an eye on you, hoping that you will lead them to Bob. You won't be able to see one another for a while. You have to be prepared for that. Marion can pass messages back and forth, though, through me during your hospital visits."

Innes and Colleen looked intensely into each other's eyes, questioning and reassuring at the same time.

"Are you prepared for this, Colleen?" he asked.

"Are *you* prepared for it?" she asked back.

They embraced.

"Okay you two. Time is short now. Better split. Bob, take the metro to New Carrollton and wait for Marion. I'll write a note to her explaining everything -- it's not wise to use the phones. Colleen, you can deliver it." He began to chuckle.

"Sorry, have I missed something? Is there a joke in this somewhere?" Innes demanded.

"Oh, sorry, no offense. It just struck me. I'm harboring a white man from injustice. A new twist to the underground railroad."

Two days before the *Post* was to run the first installment of Wheeler's exposé, the *Washington Times* broke the news on alleged spy Robert Innes. "Unnamed Administration

sources" gave *U.S. News & World Report* an exclusive for
a feature story. The wire services and Fox News wasted no
time running the story along with Innes's official passport
photo -- compliments of Diplomatic Security. In the
inverse prism of contemporary American journalism,
Innes's dropping out of sight virtually confirmed his guilt.
In an appearance on *Meet the Press* to discuss U.S. policy
on Russia, Secretary Dennison, questioned about the case,
stated earnestly that he could not discuss it in detail
pending further legal actions. He did let on, however, that
"this may rival the Ames affair" -- the CIA official
sentenced to life for spying for Moscow. The *Post's* editor-
in-chief, questioning the veracity of Wheeler's sources,
decided to put a hold on his story.

By now, Innes's face was familiar to millions as his
unflattering, dour-faced passport photo appeared across
television screens throughout America and worldwide
thanks to the 24-hour news channels. Friends were
shocked. Acquaintances and near-acquaintances strained to
recall past behavior by Innes that would strike one in
retrospect as suspicious or incriminating. In the cafeteria
and around water fountains in the State Department, one
heard, "Met him in Rome. Nice guy, but something about
him set him apart. A loner"; "Sure, he's that character who
dressed like a bum. Heard he was abused as a child"; "Oh,
yeah, him. People say he was a lousy officer. And always
chasing skirts too." Colleagues who actually knew Innes,
realizing that having close association with a traitor was not
good for one's career, suddenly developed amnesia about
him. Junior officers who had been supervised by Innes
pleaded with Human Resources to have his name removed
from their fitness reports.

Robin Croft was the sole exception. She called Colleen
to profess her conviction that the allegations simply could

not be true. She, furthermore, offered to be helpful anyway she could in clearing Innes's name.

Mindful of the flak CIA took for failing to reveal Ames during his nine years in the KGB's pay despite numerous giveaways, Dennison went out of his way to proclaim that Innes had been found out only weeks after selling out to the Russians, according to "highly classified evidence." Torres and Warren received awards for their role in uncovering the spy Innes.

Dennison, Selmur and Horvath met to gloat over their successful ploy. Not only did they manage to remove an annoying troublemaker from their midst, they also drew attention away from the Mortimer/Wells cases. In the process, Dennison also managed to draw some luster to himself as well as to the administration for appearing to be on the ball in thwarting foreign espionage. Catching Innes would add to it further.

The sommelier popped open a bottle of Piper-Heidsieck champagne and filled three glasses.

Already tipsy from pre-dinner cocktails, Dennison rose unsteadily from his chair in Les Nigauds' privatest room, lifted his champagne glass and said, "Here's to three clever guys, the sharpest powermeisters in all of Washington. All for one and one for all!"

Selmur followed suit, spilling half of his champagne before adding his own self-congratulation. "Fly like a butterfly, sting like a bee, that's why they call us the Magnificent Three! After we leave public service, I propose we form a lobby outfit called Dreamworks DSH."

Horvath sat staring into his untouched glass, seemingly losing himself in the sparkling liquid.

"Hey, Nick!" Selmur called. "Wake up, buddy. Celebrate!"

"Yeah!" Dennison chimed in. "We're on the way to turning the tide for our man. Corgan will be re-elected and we'll have it made. Instead of collecting unemployment!" He laughed uproariously at his own lame joke.

A waiter brought in a tray of Beluga caviar nestled in a bowl shaped out of fantail shrimps on a mound of glistening crushed ice -- *joyaux de la couronne*, a specialty of Les Nigauds.

The Secretary and Chief of Staff plunged in, immediately destroying the fishy crown jewels in a fit of unapologetic gluttony.

"Hey Nick, dig in!" Dennison said through his stuffed mouth.

Horvath didn't flinch. His eyes remained transfixed on the bubbly wine.

Dennison approached Horvath and slapped him on the back. "Hey, Nick! Nick!! What's wrong, you tired, or what?"

Horvath sat motionless. His lips moved.

"What's that? What'd you say?" Selmur asked.

"*Szabadság*," Horvath muttered barely audibly.

Selmur and Dennison exchanged worried looks. Dennison knelt in front of Horvath and, with his hand, gently shook Horvath's head by the chin. "Nick? You all right? Say something, Nick."

"*Szabadság*," he whispered.

Selmur put down his glass. He grabbed Horvath by the shoulders and shook him hard. "Nick!" he shouted.

A waiter ran into the room.

"Oh, it's okay. We don't need anything--" Dennison began.

"*Szabadság!!*" Horvath shouted at the top of his lungs. But his eyes didn't move from the glass before him.

"Freedom," the young waiter said.

Selmur and Dennison turned to him.

"He said 'freedom,'" the waiter continued. "My father's Hungarian. I spent my junior year there. *Szabadság* is Hungarian for freedom."

"Er, yeah, we know," Selmur ad libbed. "Our buddy here is teaching us some Hungarian. Aren't you Nick, ol' pal?" Selmur affectionately massaged Horvath's shoulders and then patted him on the back.

Picking up the charade, Dennison added, "That's right. He's not having much success though, ha, ha." He placed a comradely arm around Horvath's shoulders. "Poor guy. Can't hold his booze. Better get him home to the little lady."

Selmur winked at the waiter. "Everything's fine, son. Think we'll call it a night." He slipped a twenty into the boy's hand. The waiter left the room.

They rushed in front of Horvath, knelt and studied the National Security Adviser's face.

"What do you think, Roy?"

"I don't know. He's spaced out." Selmur waved his hand before Horvath's unresponding eyes.

"He hasn't had a drop to drink," Dennison said.

"Exhaustion," Selmur said worriedly.

"A nervous breakdown, you mean?"

"Don't know. I say we take him home and see how he is in the morning."

"*Szabadság,*" Horvath repeated to his glass.

CHAPTER TWENTY-FOUR

The more Dennison thought about Horvath, the more anxious he became. When he and Selmur dropped Horvath off at his house afterward, the NSC adviser still hadn't come out of his trance. Mrs. Horvath took him and put him to bed. But Dennison worried that Horvath had either experienced a change of heart or that he had truly flipped out. He hoped that Horvath was simply exhausted and would recover quickly. But the uncertainty kept him awake most of the night. At 5:00 am, he phoned Horvath.

"I'm fine," Horvath answered unconvincingly. His voice had a metallic tone.

"Do you recall last night?" Dennison pressed.

"Yes."

"And?"

No response.

"Nick. Maybe you should see a doctor. A quick check-up. Use our medical unit."

"No. Not necessary, Roy. I'm fine." His voice was hollow. Horvath hung up.

Dennison next phoned Selmur.

"Howard, I'm worried about Nick. I just talked to him."

"Did he respond?"

"Yeah."

"Then he's obviously okay. He looks like he could use a break, though. I'll suggest that he take a little vacation. Go off to the Caribbean or someplace with his wife."

"Right. But I don't know. He just didn't sound normal, Howard. Last thing we need now is another Mortimer. Flipping out on religion, or something equally bizarre."

Dennison and Selmur agreed that a close eye was needed on Horvath.

A chauffeured White House car picked Horvath up at precisely 5:30 am, as it did every day. The driver handed Horvath a locked dark leather satchel, as he did every morning. It contained the latest classified cables from U.S. diplomatic posts and military commands worldwide as well as the CIA's and State Department's morning intelligence summaries, and selected news clippings. Horvath placed the satchel on the seat beside him, unopened. His interest was directed instead at a ragged, old, army duffle bag which he held securely on his lap.

The car entered the west gate after a cursory check by uniformed Secret Service guards. Clutching the duffle close to his body, Horvath sprinted out toward the West Wing where his office was located. The driver shouted his name and ran to catch up to him.

"You forgot this, sir," he said, holding the leather satchel with an outstretched arm. Horvath took it without comment. He proceeded past a guard seated just inside the West Wing main entrance. He entered his office and shut and locked the door after him.

At 7:00 he briefed the President in the Oval Office. This morning he had little to say. Horvath told his secretary to cancel all appointments, and to forward no calls. At 9:30, President Corgan left the White House to meet with Congressional leaders at the Hyatt Regency. Minutes later, Horvath strolled back to the Oval Office. He carried the army duffle in one hand, as he would a brief case. Again, Secret Service personnel let him pass freely. The National Security Adviser had virtual free run of the Executive Mansion.

Once in the Oval Office, Horvath quickly opened the duffle and pulled out two quart bottles. He twisted off the caps and proceeded to splatter animal blood all over the President's desk -- originally Teddy Roosevelt's; on the Remington paintings and Catlin prints along the walls, across shelves of books containing original editions of Alexis de Tocqueville's accounts of his travels in early 19th century America, biographies of Jefferson and Hamilton, an early Webster's dictionary autographed by Webster himself, and so on. He smeared blood on a photo of Corgan taking the oath of office. Having emptied the bottles, Horvath smiled admiringly at his work. He snatched the duffle and departed the Oval Office at a leisurely pace.

Horvath proceeded toward the First Family's living quarters. He explained to Secret Service agents manning its access that he wished to leave a briefing paper personally with Mrs. Corgan. He declined escort, adding that he would merely leave the document with staff if the First Lady were not around. Once inside, Horvath ducked into the Rose Suite, facing northwest onto Pennsylvania Avenue, and locked the door. He darted to the windows overlooking the broad, now traffic-free boulevard, and flung them open.

Out of the duffle bag, he retrieved a World War II-vintage German Schmeisser submachine gun. For a moment he paused to admire it. He had used one just like it to kill Russians in '56. He polished the receiver housing with his jacket sleeve. *Szabadság*, he murmured.

Outside along the sidewalk and down the middle of Pennsylvania Avenue, Horvath could see tourists gathering for the White House tour; others gawked or took pictures of the most famous residence in America. Vacationers, office workers and vagrants strolled comfortably in the late springtime sun. An environmental group numbering some dozen or so individuals demonstrated peaceably against the destruction of America's forests.

Horvath raised the Schmeisser, released the safety and took careful aim. Through the bead, his eye saw Red Army troops. Oh, how he hated them. Kill some, his Free Hungary commanders had told their men. Demonstrate to the world how vulnerable they were, and America would come to Hungary's rescue. America would save the Magyars. And freedom would be theirs again. *Szabadság*. They killed Russians, quite a few considering their limited means. But the Americans never came. East Europeans equated America with freedom. The two were synonymous. But the Americans didn't come, they didn't help Hungary. So, like many of his co-combatants, Horvath escaped to America to experience its freedom for himself. And now he knew.

The first burst cut down an old man and his two grandchildren. The second ripped into a klatsch of high school field trippers. The third mowed down four office workers. Another abruptly felled several of the demonstrators. Subsequent shots were wild and scattered. He loaded another magazine and began firing again. A homeless man in Lafayette Park caught a round in the abdomen. A Secret Service guard fell to the ground as rounds caught him in the legs. People were running in all directions. They were scrambling for cover at the base of the White House fence, behind trees and the mounted statues in the park. Traffic on 17th Street flanking the White House and Old Executive Office Building on the west, came to a halt as cars careened into each other; drivers braked in the middle of the street and ducked behind the dashboard. The wail of police and ambulance sirens approached.

Horvath heard someone check the bedroom doorknob to see if it was locked. Then the gleaming blade of an ax cracked through the door, followed by a sledgehammer against the lock. Five Secret Service agents burst into the room with assorted arms and flew to the floor and to the sides. They took instant aim with their weapons. The scene fell strangely silent, except for the metallic clicking sound of Horvath pulling the trigger of his now-empty submachine gun, the barrel of which was buried deep in his mouth.

"Click, click, click." The agents were sprawled on the floor and taking cover behind the poster bed and Victorian chairs. With their guns firmly aimed, a hair-trigger's instant from obliterating Horvath, they appeared stunned at the sight of the President's top adviser on foreign affairs cowering against a wall, with a machine gun jammed into his mouth, mechanically pulling the trigger. "Click, click."

One of the agents, keeping his revolver fixed on Horvath's head, cautiously approached him. Horvath did not react, lost, as he was, in another world. Gently, the agent took the Schmeisser away from Horvath. The other agents surged forward and immediately wrestled Horvath to the floor, stripped his jacket, shirt and belt off, and manacled him. More agents rushed into the room. Two lifted Horvath up like a doll and whisked him out of the family quarters, out of the White House and into a waiting security van. The vehicle, lights whirring and siren screaming, sped out the gate, with motorcycle escorts clearing away the traffic.

Ambulances arrived to collect Horvath's victims, the unconscious grandfather and his little ones, weeping highschoolers soaked in blood, the homeless man writhing in agony; wounded tourists, some limp with shock, others crying with pain; office workers, themselves bleeding, helping the more seriously wounded; the Secret Service guard, his legs tourniqueted by his colleagues, placed on a stretcher. Municipal police sought to untangle the twisted traffic on 17th Street. Multitudes of onlookers competed with aggressive reporters and TV news crews to observe the carnage.

The President called an emergency meeting of what he called the "inner cabinet" -- a core of trusted cabinet officers, most long-time personal friends of Corgan's who had been with him through all of his political campaigns. These included Selmur, Dennison, Wilkins and Levin. Karlson was also invited as was Secretary of Homeland Security Lewison, under whose purview the Secret Service fell.

Corgan appeared pale and shaken. His hands trembled. Was it rage, fear or shock? The atmosphere in the Cabinet Room was one of gloom and palpable horror. Corgan rubbed his tired face with both palms, and ran his fingers backward through his hair.

"This tragedy...this incident...this..." Corgan stumbled for words, but couldn't find them. He stopped, stared at the ceiling as if searching for a thought in the ether. A tear ran down a cheek.

"My wife is safe, thank God. Anything could have happened. Those poor people...How could this happen? How?"

"Mr. President, I am initiating a full investigation--"

Corgan's face flashed anger. "You're out. You're fired. As of immediately," Corgan commanded.

Lewison appeared stunned. "I beg your pardon?"

Corgan raised his voice. "Get out! You allowed this to happen. Go!!"

The withering blast caused the others to cringe. A pallor crossed their faces.

Lewison rose and strode out of the room, shutting the door hard behind him.

The inner cabinet waited in trepidation for their President's next move.

"Does anyone have any insight into what motivated Horvath? What caused him to snap?"

"I know that he'd been under a lot of pressure lately," Selmur responded in his low, considered voice.

"Both work and family, I believe," added Dennison.

"For crying out loud, why didn't you bring it to my attention?" Corgan demanded.

An awkward silence ensued.

Corgan let out a deep breath. "Gentlemen, this terrible tragedy may very well mark the end of this troubled administration. Our dream of a rejuvenated America keeps taking hits as one misfortune after another falls on our...my head."

"Mr. President, at least no one was killed," Dennison said in a voice attempting consolation.

Corgan bowed and shook his head. "A 70-year old nun has one of Horvath's bullets lodged in her brain. If she doesn't die, the doctors say she'll never come out of her coma. Seventeen people are injured, eleven seriously." He picked up the *Washington Post* in front of him. "The editorialists are wasting no time. One has drawn the catchy metaphor of 'the White House taking pot shots at the American people.' A TV commentator went so far as to say the White House has 'formally declared war on America.' We're in trouble, deep trouble. And I fear we're in a downward spiral that is out of control."

The President's men bowed their heads dejectedly.

"All we can do is hunker down, Mr. President," Selmur said. "Launch a full investigation, institute an immediate overhaul of White House security. Call it a terrible tragedy inflicted by a very disturbed man, a man whose troubles no one knew, not even his wife."

"Draw a parallel with previous isolated assaults on the Executive Mansion by imbalanced men," Dennison added. "A rare tragedy beyond the control of anyone. Tell the American people that changes are being made in security and personnel screening and stress that we must put this behind us."

"Then after two or three days, we push the Innes spy case to the front burner. Play up our having uncovered him mere weeks after his recruitment by Russian intelligence. And then announce his arrest. Public attention will turn away from today's event," Selmur said.

All eyes turned to Karlson.

"The Constitution says a man is innocent until proven guilty. Furthermore, we haven't seen enough evidence to seek his arrest," Karlson asserted.

"Get Innes!" Selmur commanded.

The President nodded.

CHAPTER TWENTY-FIVE

Innes sat in the Wheeler living room scanning the headlines. "State Dept Official on Lam - Wanted for Espionage"; "Feds Will Apprehend Alleged Spy, Dennison Assures"; "State Competence vs CIA Fumbling: A Case Study in Effective Counterespionage." He shook his head. "They've got everybody snowed. The greatest con job of the decade and everyone is swallowing it hook, line and sinker," Innes mumbled to himself.

Scher's face appeared on CNN. Exuding confidence with his pipe jutting from his mouth, Scher emitted several well-rehearsed sound-bites: "There will be no repeat of the Felix Bloch case"; "Our Ames is different: it took us only nine weeks instead of nine years"; "We're hot on his trail. It's only a matter of time before we nab this traitor."

Innes felt sick. The weight of the entire U.S. government was upon him and was likely to crush him. The Salem Witches, Sacco and Venzetti, the Rosenbergs, the McMartin preschool family, Richard Jewell. American history was replete with handy victims of the hysteria of the moment, of sacrificial lambs to morally corrupt, self-serving politicians and a gullible public. He was now learning up front and personal how challenging big government's version of truth could be dangerous to one's health. He couldn't use his credit cards nor draw money from the bank for risk of being traced and caught. At this point, Innes feared for his mental health. *National Enquirer, Inside Edition* and *On the Record* had descended on his home town like a plague of locusts, interviewing naive locals about his past. He could have no contact with his family or friends. He missed his kids. What would they think? Surely they were being told that their father was a Benedict Arnold. And he missed Colleen terribly.

Colleen got her letters to Innes via Wheeler. Assuming she was being surveilled, Colleen handwrote the letters, then left them with Wheeler during her frequent hospital visits. Marion picked up the correspondence and brought it home to Innes. Colleen's tone was increasingly fearful.

> *Everybody at State assumes you are guilty of spying. Only Robin Croft and I reject the notion. People don't want to know me these days. They must assume that I'm part of the 'plot.' 'Mrs. Robert Hansen,' someone catcalled the other day. I received my first hate mail. They said they couldn't wait for me to join you in jail. I'm constantly fending off reporters. I've been called in three times by Security. I'm scared, Bob. I find myself looking over my shoulder. I see clean-cut, fit-looking men eyeing me. I assume they're FBI, or State Department Security, or something. Or, it may be my paranoia. What happens now? How can I help? My love for you is only made stronger by this affair. I long to see you, to hold you and to kiss your sweet*

face again. 'May God make smooth the path
before you.'
With all my love,
Colleen

Innes was getting restless. Staying holed up indoors
with no plan of action was not exactly a morale-booster.
And, as a fugitive from the authorities, he jeopardized the
Wheeler family. Wheeler counseled him to be patient. The
Post would deliver him from this evil. It would bring down
this amoral administration just as it had Nixon's. Good
investigative reporting required methodical, persistent
digging. Officials would bolt, they'd rat on their corrupt
superiors. Word was the FBI smelled something fishy. It
was only a matter of time. But Innes became antsier by the
day. He'd already been tried and convicted in the court of
the news media without being able to defend himself. The
FBI was his sole potential ally among the Washington
power giants. He decided to give Speedy a call.

He waited till Courtney had gone to school and Marion
had left for the hospital. He donned Wheeler's large fishing
hat and sunglasses. Checking to see that no neighbors were
around, Innes slipped out the back door and sprinted toward
Nebraska Avenue where he caught a bus. He got off at the
nearest subway stop and took the metro to the Smithsonian,
where he blended in with the masses of tourists. He
entered the Museum of American History and made for the
nearest pay phone. Funny, he thought, only two blocks
from the White House. He got Speedy.

"Where the hell are you?!" Speedy demanded.

"Never mind. Give me a quick low-down on what's
going on. What does Karlson think? Are you guys with me
or in the White House's palm?"

"Bob, I really think you should come in--"

"I haven't got time, Speedy. You've got exactly three minutes before I hang up."

"Okay, okay. Karlson has his doubts about the charges. He has us working overtime to get to the bottom of this thing. Berlucci needs to talk to you."

"Maybe later. Like I said, I can't stay on the line--"

"Bob?" It was Berlucci's voice.

"So what now, big brother? You guys going to help me, or what?"

"Bob, come in. We can't do this without you."

"Do what exactly?"

"Look into this thing--"

"That's not good enough, *compare*. I'll stay in touch." He hung up.

After dinner each evening, Colleen stretched out in the overstuffed chair that her grandfather heired to her, put on the Walkman earphones and listened to Thai lessons on tape.

> *Savat di khun Mali. Phakan pai du nang lue khrap?*
> *Mai dai kha. Dichan tong yu baan wan ni na kha.*
> *Repeat after me:*
> *Savat di khun Mali. Phakan pai...*

Colleen tripped over the words. As she repeated the dialogue, about a young man asking a girl if she wanted to go to the movies, she pictured herself with Innes in a dark movie theater. He had his arm around her as she snuggled up against his neck. The Thai lesson went in one ear and out the other. She couldn't concentrate. All she could think of was Bob Innes, his soft kiss behind her ear, the laughs, the warmth of their bodies together. She smiled but the tears streamed down her cheeks. She tore off the earphones, opened the tape player and replaced "FSI Thai Lesson No. 12" with her favorite jazz singer, Johnny Adams, "Good Morning Heartache," and closed her eyes.

She sang the lyrics with Adams and closed her eyes tighter. As her mind drifted further from reality, she felt Innes's presence. His tall frame stood before her, his face had that distinctive Innes demi-smile. He reached to her. She raised her hand to touch his. He grasped it gently and rubbed it between his thumb and fingers. Her mind surged back from the dream world. The touch was real. Adrenaline shot through her veins like rocket fuel and her heart stopped. She sprang from the chair and opened her eyes.

Standing before her was Bob Innes, just as she had envisioned.

Colleen fell to the floor. She looked up and blinked.

"Hi," he said.

"Is it really you?"

"In the flesh."

"Christ!" She held her hand to her forehead. Her chest heaved.

"Well, nice to see you again too."

She pushed her hair back from her face. "How did you get here?! How did you get in?!"

"By metro." He held a key up. "I used to live here once too, remember?"

"You scared the living daylights out of me." She picked herself up, paused, and threw herself at him. They kissed hungrily. Then after several minutes of tender embracing, she led him to the sofa. Their faces touched.

"Bob, you're in danger."

"I'm being framed."

"I know. But coming here will get you in trouble. You'll only fall into their trap."

"At least I'll finally be able to defend myself, and expose who the real scoundrels are."

"They'll keep you under wraps. In some military prison somewhere. You'll be completely cut off. Even so, what proof can you show that some of the highest officials in this administration are crooks and traitors?"

"Well, none. But I think the FBI may help me out."

"You 'think'?"

"Yes…Maybe…I don't know." Innes rested his chin on clasped hands, with elbows on his knees, lost in thought. Colleen stroked the back of his neck.

"Baby. Let's go to bed," she said. She stood up, took his hand and tugged him upward.

Hand-in-hand they slowly ascended the stairs to the bedroom. In the dark they stood facing each other, glimmers of light from the outside traffic moved across their faces. She pressed against him and rested her cheek against his chest.

"I…," he began. But she hushed him with two fingers on his lips. She took Innes by the hand and brought him to the bed. She lay back and looked up at him. Innes thought how beautiful she was in this state of vulnerability. He placed himself beside her. Gently, they embraced and kissed. How long it had been since they made love. The denial made so delectable this moment. They were impatient, but loved slowly, savoring every second.

Her delicate fingers undid the top button of his shirt, then the second and on down to his belt buckle. The feel of his body released a pulsing energy in her. His gentle hands on her body intensified this primal force. Their pace quickened.

Their lovemaking was at the same time driven and tender. Reveling in this sweet time, Colleen and Innes together harnessed the magic energy and rode it to greater heights throughout the night.

They snuggled languorously in each other's arms. "I love you," he whispered. "Don't ever leave me," she said.

Innes rose upright on his knees. He reached out for her. The invitation to love again made her warm and tingly. She smiled and began to rise to meet him.

The headlights of a turning automobile shone through the venetian blinds, briefly illuminating the room and radiating their faces.

In the flash of a second, Innes became perplexed as he saw Colleen's loving expression turn instantly into one of terror. She thrust her arm out as if to protect herself.

"Colleen, wha...?"

The light also revealed a powerful figure standing just behind Innes. A stone-like male figure with a broad face. A gash ran diagonally across its rough surface.

By instinct, Colleen kicked at Innes as hard as she could with the sole of her foot, causing him to go flying floorward, off to the side. A gleaming blade swooshed through the space occupied only a half-second before by Innes's head.

Puzzlement flashed across the man's face. Innes's sudden involuntary departure had caught him by surprise. He then lunged toward Colleen with the knife. A roll to the left saved her but not her pillow which exploded into a mini-mushroom cloud of goose down. By this time, Innes got his senses back. He picked up a metal vanity chair and brought it crashing down onto the intruder's back. The knife flew from his hand onto the floor. Like a wounded bear, he struck back with both fists, which dispatched Innes hard against a wall. Innes slumped downward unconscious.

His black eyes frantically searched the dark for the blade, but Colleen's movement commanded the attacker's attention. He threw his weight onto her naked body and pinned both her arms down. The more she struggled, the greater his enormous weight bore down on her. The breath was being crushed out of her. She felt herself blacking out. She managed to free one thigh and tried to knee her attacker in the crotch, but missed her mark. This drove the bear into a frenzy of rage. He lifted his head and opened his mouth wide. Some of the teeth were steel caps, betraying Russian dentistry. Again, bear-like, he gnashed at her, trying to sink his teeth into her arm.

A fierce drive to survive seized Colleen. Her face hardened into an expression of steely determination. A portion of her brain underused by humans took over. She reached over to a nightstand and plunged her hand into a box. Before he could react, the assailant found himself struggling for air. A fistful of maxipads lodged in his throat. Colleen yanked her fist from his mouth. The veins in his neck and face looked like they were about to burst.

"Hack, hack!!" The sounds emanating from him were like those of a wounded animal. The man was struggling now for his life. His face was a mask of horror, twisted, red, throbbing, soaked with sweat; saliva frothed from his gaping mouth. He was standing now with feet wide apart, his hands clutching his throat, his eyes about to burst from their sockets.

Colleen sat upright on the bed. She was fascinated by the horrific sight of this terrified, dying monster. The pre-homo sapiens part of her brain exuded satisfaction. It told her that in the constant Darwinian struggle for life, she had triumphed against a stronger foe. In this mysterious corner of her brain, there was a Cro-Magnon Colleen thumping her chest and yowling victory wails. She was oblivious to her unconscious lover slumped on the floor, to the need to call for help, to the world around her. Survival was all she thought of.

"Hack!" He gurgled like an asthmatic. "Aaaannhh." He began to collapse, falling on one knee, and fought to stay alive.

Innes came to and looked up at the bizarre sight of his woman calmly watching a man die of asphyxiation.

"Colleen." He switched on a light.

She slowly turned her face toward him. The expression on it was like nothing that Innes had ever seen on her, as if she had been hypnotized. An eerie grin and blank eyes.

"Colleen!!"

She snapped out of it. "Oh, Bob," she cried, and rushed to him, wrapping her arms around his torso.

The dying intruder, drawing on his last reservoir of strength, clenched both fists, then slammed them against his upper chest. A huge glop of feminine napkins popped out of his gullet and went flying across the room. He fell on both knees and inhaled deeply.

Innes made a move for the phone on the dresser at the other end of the room. Regaining his strength, the intruder sprang toward it as well. Innes grasped the device with both hands and brought it full-force into the man's face. He let out a growl and raised a fist.

The wail of sirens approached. Rotating blue and red roof lights filtered through the bedroom window. The intruder froze, then grabbed his knife and bolted through the doorway and down the stairs. A door opened and slammed shut. Dimitrov fled for all his life was worth across the slick backyard grass and into a woodlot and who knows where.

Colleen and Innes threw themselves into each other's arms.

"Are you hurt?" he asked, examining her face with both hands.

"I don't think so. And you?"

"My head hurts, but I guess I'm okay." He went to the window and opened it. He stuck his head out to see what was happening. Fire trucks arrived after the initial police car. People were gathering on their front lawns and sidewalks. Innes craned his neck to get a better view. He saw tongues of flames and billowing smoke several houses down the street.

He turned back toward Colleen. "It's a fire. Nothing to do with us."

She hugged him tightly. "Let's call the police," she said.

Innes placed his hand on the phone to prevent Colleen from lifting the receiver. "We can't. They'll know who I am. We can't risk it."

"But…Then, what do we do?"

Innes thought for a moment.

There was a knock on the front entrance door. They looked at each other. There was a another knock.

"See who it is," Innes whispered.

She put on her robe, straightened her hair, took two deep breaths and, looking back at Innes, made for the stairs. Innes heard her open the front door. A man identifying himself as an Arlington County policeman apologized for the late-night interruption and asked her if she'd noticed any unusual activity in the neighborhood that evening, any strangers wandering about, that sort of thing. It seemed the two-alarm blaze down the street might have been the result of arson. Colleen, thinking fast, replied in the negative. The officer bade good night.

She went quickly back up the stairs.

"Bob, we were almost killed!" She trembled uncontrollably. She put her fingertips to her temples trying to comprehend what had happened.

"He was Russian. I heard him murmur *govno* during the struggle. It means 'shit.'"

She plopped down on a bedroom chair. "I can't deal with this." The shock was now setting in.

He put his arms around her shoulders and drew her to him. "Colleen, we're alive. We're okay."

She looked up at him. "Who was he?"

"Russian mob. Must be. The question then becomes why, and who sent him?"

"And?"

"Who wants me out of the way big time?"

Colleen made a slight shake of her head.

"I'll tell you who. Dennison and whoever else he's in cahoots with. They're using, or being used by, the Russian mob. The new twist is that they want both of us dead."

"Hoh!" Colleen gasped. She covered her mouth with her hand. "This can't be happening."

"But it is. Anything goes in their kind of power game. One sin leads to another and before they know it, they'll kill to save their reputations and status."

"Wheeler's got to know," Colleen said.

"Yes, but first, we've got to high-tail it out of here. Now."

It was too much for Colleen. Her eyes were wide. She was trying to piece things together. "What do you mean?"

"Like I said, we've gotta split before God knows who else comes back here to finish the job." He knelt and held Colleen by her shoulders. "Colleen, listen to me. We're in danger for our lives. *You* and me. We must run and hide. At least until the evil is exposed. In the meantime, we disappear. And carry out our own form of guerrilla warfare against these guys. Come on, love. Let's go."

CHAPTER TWENTY-SIX

Senator Weems announced that it was high time that the position of National Security Adviser be subject to Senate confirmation, as was the case for all Cabinet-level officials and ambassadors, in order "to prevent the President from appointing another unstable individual to that sensitive position." He planned to introduce a bill to make it law.

The wise old men of the Sunday morning news talk shows tsked-tsked and, in orotund, solemn tones, questioned the wisdom of putting "Ivory Tower academicians into such a high-pressure, operational job." The time had come, they suggested, for recruiting among "our best company CEOs" to fill the National Security Adviser position, those "who've been tested and have succeeded in the equally Byzantine and demanding arena of business." Strangely, the need for a foreign affairs expert didn't enter into the debate.

Faced, on the one hand, with an imminent danger of losing another executive prerogative to the Congress and, on the other, mounting pressure to appoint a dilettante as his principal adviser on foreign affairs, an embattled President Corgan realized that he needed to move fast.

Naturally, Selmur and Dennison were most eager to advise him on this matter.

"Mr. President, we can turn around the spate of bad luck we've endured of late by appearing decisive before the American people," Selmur pontificated in his best bourbon and branch water voice. "Appoint somebody now who is both a practiced foreign affairs expert, and is widely and favorably known by the public."

"Yes, Mr. President," Dennison was quick to add. "Act now by putting the right person in the job, and you stop Congress and the media pundits dead in their tracks. Equally as important, you begin to put the Horvath affair behind you. *Decisive* is the image you want to convey." He punched one palm with the other fist to drive home the point.

Corgan took it all in solemnly. "I agree. But who can I tap who fits those criteria, and who's already been through the confirmation wringer so that we know he's squeaky clean?"

With ponderous nods of their heads and brows furrowed, Selmur and Dennison contemplated with utmost gravity the President's pronouncement on the matter.

"Mr. President, under normal circumstances, what you suggest would be very difficult, if not impossible," Selmur said.

"Indeed, the Senate have their knives out. Our adversaries there smell blood. They're ready to devour this administration alive," Dennison added.

"Only by naming someone who's unimpeachable, beyond reproach, can we keep the jackals at bay," Selmur continued, following a carefully rehearsed script.

Corgan leaned forward. "And?"

Selmur cleared his throat and, crossing his arms before him on the conference table, said, "Roy and I have given this considerable thought, and we think we have your man, Mr. President."

"That's right, Mr. President. It would be at great sacrifice to the State Department. He's one of our top flyers," Dennison said.

"But he meets all the criteria we've discussed. He'd be a shoo-in for confirmation."

"And he has the depth of knowledge, experience and operational savvy to be a super National Security Adviser to you," Dennison added.

"We, our staffs, would get along famously with him," Selmur said.

"All right already!" Corgan interjected. "Who is it?"

"Bernard J. Scher, Mr. President." Selmur replied. "He's your man."

"No doubt about it," Dennison asserted.

A welcome silence followed. Corgan was carefully weighing in his mind their suggestion.

"He's done well as State Department legal counsel, has he?"

"None better," Dennison answered. "Hate to have to give him up."

"And with this Mortimer investigation?"

"Mr. President, it's been Bernie Scher who's straightened the mess out and gotten the effort back on track," Selmur stated with great conviction.

"Yeah. But, there have been no breaks in the investigation. And we've lost another ambassador to a killer. I'm very concerned about both of these points."

"So are we, Mr. President," Selmur said. "But look at it this way. By elevating the man who's responsible for getting to the bottom of these cases, who's been doing a cracker-jack job, who's boosted this administration's standing with the voters, you demonstrate movement in the right direction. We'll be sure to crank up the spokesman and our communications people to get the message across that Scher will have yet more clout to see the investigation through."

"And Scher's a fresh face. We've been talking to him about world affairs. He has a solid grasp of where this country should be going. He'll come up with new initiatives -- in tandem with me, of course -- that will underscore American leadership. Congress will be seized with our new direction in foreign policy and the media will devote a lot of attention to it. The bottom line is this: our current difficulties will be put behind us, including these dead ambassadors."

Following their script to its pre-planned conclusion, Selmur finished with a flourish. "You'll go into the election year in a much strengthened position. Roger Jalbert, or whoever they nominate, will merely be our strawman to knock down like that!" He smacked the inside of his extended forefingers with the heel of the other hand.

"I want to think carefully about this, gentlemen. I can't afford to make any more mistakes with appointments. I need to feel one-hundred percent certain in my own mind that I've selected the right person."

The white glare of the TV cams and the bursting flashes of the still cameras had the power and intensity of a dying nebula, as Innes imagined it. There was a grinning President Corgan, puffy-eyed and slightly stooped, shaking the hand of a cocky, self-proud Bernard Scher. Corgan called the press conference to announce his naming Scher as National Security Adviser. In the background were the smug faces of Dennison and Selmur. They stood behind the President and Scher as stolid sentinels of support and political unity.

"Last waltz in the ballroom of the Titanic," Innes murmured. "You say something?" Colleen called from the opposite end of the *Motel 6* room. She was prying wedges of piping hot, gooey pizza from a large-size Pizza Hut box and placing them onto paper plates.

"What a farce. Scher's just been named NSC Adviser. Corgan has had so much wool pulled over his eyes, he should be baa-ing." Innes popped open another Budweiser. "You want another beer?" he asked.

"No." Colleen looked over her shoulder to Innes. "I'll tell you what I want. I want to eat homemade, healthful food in our own house where we can be cozy, near friends and relations and not worry about being murdered in our bed."

"I know." Innes stared blankly at the TV. "It's the *real* thing," cooed a bikinied beach bunny holding the perfectly chilled can of America's favorite refreshment.

"Nothing's real in this society," Innes uttered.

"Bob, how many beers have you had?"

He snapped out of his fleeting stupor. "Uh. I'm fine."

She brought the plates to the bed and placed herself beside him.

"I was just thinking," he continued as he gingerly picked up the hot pizza and took a bite. "P.T. Barnum, Andy Warhol, Paris Hilton, Bill O'Reilly, the advertising mavens of Madison Ave., Hollywood's faceless corporate moguls, overpaid, steroided baseball players, Donald Trump. These are the Greek philosophers and Renaissance humanists of the American civilization."

Colleen shook her head. "I don't get it."

"Well, a sucker's born every minute. Every American should have fifteen minutes of fame, even if that means

turning sluthood into an art form. Blame Washington and
the power plutocrats for all the nation's ills. Grab as much
as you can get and screw everybody else, but gloss it over
through the mythology of hype. Everybody has a shot at
being rich and famous in the Land of Opportunity, just like
Colonel Sanders and Arianna Huffington. Trouble is, both
are corporate creations, manufactured to sell more fried
chicken and political snake oil."

"What's that got to do with our predicament? Bob, I
seriously worry about your emotional state. Being on the
lam like Bonnie and Clyde is scrambling our brains."

"*Form* over *substance*. That's what I'm getting at. The
whole society's geared toward it. Everything's run by
smoke and mirrors. Just look at those clowns at the White
House. All smiles and posturing unity. The reality is
Corgan's a puppet and his key advisers are the evil
puppeteers. They're all driven in their malevolence or
gullibility by one thing: their own power positions. What I
want to know is where does one go to get a degree in spin
doctoring or the art of image-making?"

Colleen put down her plate. She took Innes's and laid it
aside. She sidled up close to him, pulled his head to face
her and kissed him softly on the lips.

"Will you do me a favor, Clyde?" she asked.

"What's that, Bonnie?"

"Put a lid on it."

Innes chuckled. He wrapped his arms around her and
snuggled up. They had only each other amid their uprooted
lives and uncertain future.

"Bob?"

"Yes?"

"Where are we?"

Innes laughed. "Chamberlain, South Dakota. Why?"

"What's here?"

"Nothing. A laundromat, a bar, two fast-food joints and a couple of motels."

"Where do we go from here?"

Silence. "Follow our noses, I guess."

"How long can we continue like this?"

"Who knows? I'll call Toby again this morning for the daily check-in. Then Speedy. Robin Croft keeps me posted on what Dennison is up to."

"Can we really trust the FBI? What are they doing for us? Nothing as far as I can see."

"I keep the calls down to about a minute and vary the times when I phone. We don't use credit cards; we use the cash Toby wires to 'Jason Hawkfeather.' Toby and the FBI guys are our only hope. We have no choice. Something's got to give. It's only a matter of time."

"Let's just hope that the 'something' isn't our lives."

Innes ran out of answers. They lay together, their eyes searching the ether for hope that wasn't there.

CHAPTER TWENTY-SEVEN

The gold-embossed, black-binder briefing books piled high on the Secretary's desk. They had dry, curt titles which addressed ponderous foreign policy matters of the moment: "U.S.-E.U. Trade Issues," "NATO Expansion," "Iran Security Issues," "Democratization in CIS States," "Peacekeeping in Lebanon," "North Korea." But he hadn't read a single page. And he was due to leave for ministerial consultations with the Western allies in Brussels in 24 hours.

The intercom chirped. "It's Mr. Selmur, Mr. Secretary," Dennison's secretary announced.

Dennison grimaced.

"Mr. Secretary?...Will you take the call?"

"Yeah. Okay." Dennison braced his forehead with his left-hand fingertips and thumb. That 20-megaton migraine he got only in face of the most onerous, intractable problems began making itself felt.

"Roy? You there? Hello?"

"Uh, yeah, Howard. How are you?"

"Not too good, my friend."

Silence.

"Roy? You still there?"

Dennison cleared his throat. "Uh, sure. What's up?"

"Oh, just a little problem. Like, let me see now. Oh yeah! Now I remember. There's this small matter of re-electing the President of the United States. Yeah, that's it. And, uh, we need *beaucoup* bucks to do it. Thought maybe you had forgotten your role as the re-elect chief and behind-the-scenes fund-raiser. That's all."

The pain-threshold was surging toward 50 megatons. Dennison popped a second Advil.

"And one final thing. We may be looking for a new Secretary of State after the election -- that is, if we win."

Dennison loathed Selmur. The more so when he went into his dripping-with-sarcasm routine. Dennison, the scion of an old and distinguished line of WASPy robber barons-turned-respectable-financiers, could not abide being humiliated. Especially by poor white trash of dubious ethnic mix, such as Selmur.

"Horvath was key in this. I need time to...reconstruct the source network."

"Look, my dear Mr. Secretary. Two upstarts in our own party have already announced that they'll challenge Corgan for the nomination. Jalbert has won New Hampshire and Iowa. By all indications, he'll roll on right through and clinch the nomination. He's riding the crest of a cash wave toward victory. We're throwing *$500*-a plate fund-raisers and still we're not getting enough takers. I found my secretary making photocopies of her résumé the other day. Got the picture?"

Dennison didn't like such candor over the open phone line. Anybody could be eavesdropping, and they probably were. It only deepened his contempt for the White House Chief of Staff.

"Howard, I suggest we get together to discuss these matters -- privately."

"You bet your blue-blooded ass. Tomorrow. At my office. Ten o'clock sharp!"

"I'll be on my way to Europe then," Dennison pleaded.

"Correction. You'll be on your way to Europe *after* our meeting. Understood?"

A 100-megaton eruption hit Dennison between the eyes. He scrunched them together, seeking futilely to contain the pain.

"I said, do you understand?!" Selmur demanded.

"Right," Dennison answered and hung up.

After five double vodkas, Yakov certainly felt no pain. Trouble was, neither could he think straight. And he knew it. Life was full of trade-offs, he liked to remind himself.

Mama Boronova looked at him worriedly from her perch near the pastry display case across the room. "*Kukuruzhnik!*" she called as she shook her head in disdain. "You act like a cornball, like some bumpkin who can't handle the big city. Act like an adult. Some example you set for your people." A 180-pound widow, Mama Boronova feared little. She was the only soul in Brighton Beach who dared talk to Yakov like that.

A cell phone tweeted. An underling quickly pulled it from his coat pocket and answered. "It's Yemidgian, boss," he told Yakov while covering the speaker with his hand.

"*Govno!* What's he want?"

"Says you know. He wants answers."

"Shit-eating Armenians." Yakov slugged back another Stoli Gold. "Guess he wants to hear it's secure to 'export' his 'product' here. Tell him I'll get back to him."

The underling murmured into the phone and cut Yemidgian off abruptly. Five seconds later, it rang again.

"Boss, it's Gorygin!" the flunky whispered anxiously.

"The cosmonaut?" Yakov was forming a precarious pyramid of vodka glasses on the table. His drunken face contorted as he strained to focus.

"No, boss. The cosmonaut was Gagarin. This is Gorygin." He leaned over and whispered in Yakov's ear. "The SVR guy here in New York. The *Rezident*." He offered the phone gingerly, as if it were a bomb.

Yakov picked it up clumsily. "Is this the cosmonaut Gorygin?" he slurred. He giggled at his own silly joke. His small retinue of subordinates looked away, at the floor, covered their eyes. Their barely concealed disgust was grounded not only in embarrassment, but also in the knowledge that an aspiring godfather who let his guard down could soon become just another dead gangster.

There was a pause at the other end. "Yakov, are you drunk?" Gorygin demanded.

"Only on patriotism, *tovarishch!*" Yakov made a mocking military salute.

"Yakov, there are some 'trade' matters that we need to discuss. When you're sober, call me back. And soon!" He hung up.

"Goddamn spies! You give them some information and they want more, more, more!!"

The unflappable Dimitrov, standing to the side, deftly sidled next to his boss and lifted him to his feet. He whispered something into Yakov's ear.

"*Da*. You are always right. I'll keep my fat trap shut." He placed a forefinger to his lips, "Sshhh!"

Five hours of deep sleep later, Yakov came to in his Brighton Beach flat. His head felt as if Yuri Gagarin's space capsule had come crashing in on it. Two coffees, a couple aspirins and a hot shower alleviated the pain. Yakov began clearing through the mental cobwebs. The

problems that drove him to drink began to reassert their
massive weight. The loss of Horvath, the prize trophy in
his chain of stolen souls, was too much to bear. The
mother lode of intelligence he was selling to the SVR had
dried up overnight. Moreover, he no longer was receiving
the vital tactical intelligence that enabled him to ensure
risk-free importation of narcotics from his criminal
connections in Central Asia and the Far East. And
Malandrino's terms for providing secure entry left Yakov
with little in the way of profits. He had a lot of retainers of
his own to keep flush. Meanwhile, Mogilevich, his chief
rival in the world of Russian criminality, was breathing
down his neck. If he couldn't take care of his own people,
Mogilevich would begin to steal them away. Or worse,
Mogilevich could bribe trusted cohorts to murder Yakov.

Yakov's mind wandered back to school days in Moscow.
His fourth form teacher, a burly matron who idolized the
pantheon of bolshevik heroes, now denigrated as historical
perversions. "Whenever you encounter problems in your
life," she counseled her ten-year olds, "model yourself after
Comrade Lenin and Comrade General Zhukov. Draw up a
strategy, even when the roof is falling on you. And
counterattack. Without a strategy, you will be defeated. A
revolution within, children. That is your key to life."

Wrapped in a bathrobe, Yakov sat slumped in an
armchair and sipped Perrier from the bottle as he half-
focused on *Wheel of Fortune* on the TV. Happy
contestants jumped with glee at having won small king's
ransoms just for out-puzzling other contestants on simple
words and phrases. "The American Dream," Yakov
murmured. *What a country*, he thought. *Even simpletons
could become rich just by being moderately quicker in
grabbing the nuggets of gold that are out there for the*

taking. For the truly cunning and swift, there is no limit. Do not panic, Yakov. Have a strategy!

He bolted from the chair. "Dimitrov!" he shouted. He opened the apartment's door to the main hallway. Responding to his master's call, Dimitrov leapt toward the door. They almost collided with one another.

"Get me that little bitch from Rostov. Get me Lydia," he ordered.

Lydia gave no protest and betrayed no emotion when she got the call from Dimitrov to pack her bags and catch the next flight to New York. After all, since Horvath went berserk and out of the picture, she found herself underemployed, but still being paid. It was only a matter of time before Yakov dreamed up another assignment for her.

Pyotr, the Siberian who'd driven her to Yakov's place in the Hamptons, was waiting for her at La Guardia and chauffeured her to Brooklyn.

One of Yakov's bodyguards stood at the apartment building entrance. He opened the door and, without uttering a word, escorted her to the elevator and up to Yakov's sprawling flat. He tapped lightly on the door. Dimitrov opened it and ushered her in. As always, his stony face exhibited no emotion.

Yakov, dressed in his trademark black turtleneck sweater and beige riding slacks, was seated on a white sofa in the center of the living room. Before him, on a glass and chrome coffee table, was an ice bucket with a champagne bottle jutting from it; this was flanked by matching vases of garish flowers.

An insincere smile manifested itself on Yakov's face. He did not rise.

"Lydia Yekatarina. Long time no see. Come." He
patted the sofa with his hand. "Time to catch up on things."

Lydia's eyes were alert, but she otherwise displayed no
feelings one way or another. She took confident steps and
gently placed herself on the sofa, a comfortable distance
from Yakov.

"A refreshment after your journey." He pulled the
champagne bottle out of the bucket and uncorked it. He
poured two glasses, offering one to Lydia.

She took it and reciprocated his curt toast.

"Lydia, despite some past…unfortunate encounters, I
want you to know that I respect you and wish to look after
your needs…as I always have."

Lydia listened impassively.

"This unfortunate episode with Horvath…tragic." His
voice was flat, unemotional. "I suppose the pressures of his
job just got to him." Yakov feigned sadness with a shake
of his head. "Yes, tragic."

Yakov's unctuous manner and eyes devoid of humanity
steeled Lydia for what might come next.

"But, the past is past. We must look to the future. I
invited you here today to renew our friendship and to plan
new arrangements that will be mutually profitable to us
both." He stared deeply into her eyes. "Is this okay with
you?"

Lydia forced a faint smile and short nod.

"Good. As you well know, Lydia, my business is
information. The procurement of it and its distribution to
the right people -- for a price, of course, which gets shared
among the relevant associates in my organization." He
lifted his champagne flute and invited her to do the same.
He saluted her and took another sip. She reciprocated.

"You know that Horvath was important to me. Very
important. The information he provided was indispensable.

As a source, he is virtually irreplaceable. I know that you were called upon to put up with much. Horvath was a weak man with unusual fallibilities. I am indebted to you for what you endured." Yakov raised a hand while keeping his eyes fixed on Lydia. Dimitrov stepped forward and placed a stuffed brown envelope in the hand. Yakov thereupon held it out to Lydia.

"To show my gratitude, I give you this bonus."

At first hesitant, Lydia took the envelope. With Yakov's encouragement, she opened it. Inside was a stack of $100-dollar bills. She guessed that there were at least one-hundred of the notes.

"As I said, this is a bonus, for work already done. I am prepared to provide additional such bonuses in return for future assignments."

Her interest piqued, Lydia finally spoke. "You surely have such an assignment already in mind. Otherwise you wouldn't have called me here. I am also not so stupid as to think that I could continue to live comfortably in Washington after Horvath left the scene without receiving other 'assignments.'" Her eyes showed defiance and fearlessness.

"Ah, my dear Lydia. Always so blunt. Always so brave. I respect that. Yes, I really do."

"Get to the point."

The false smile faded from Yakov's face. She had pushed him far enough. But he retained patience.

"As it happens, I do have in mind another assignment. Only you can do it. No one else."

"Therefore, I must charge, how shall I say, a special fee. What is it? Or should I say, who is it?"

Under different circumstances, Yakov, without hesitation, would have slit her throat on the spot and without batting an eyelash.

"I am sure that we can reach mutually satisfactory terms. Horvath had a close, personal relationship with the Secretary of State, Mr. Dennison. Now, with Horvath gone, well…"

"Horvath was your link to him, your only link."

Yakov pursed his lips and said nothing, but his expression said it all.

"And you want me to find that link and to put you back in touch with Dennison. But I presume that you want a direct link this time?"

"Lydia, such talent and perception as yours are Russia's loss and America's gain."

"I will see what I can do. And remuneration will be in…"

"Cash."

"The amount and modalities of payment to be determined when I can confirm that the link can be made."

"This is acceptable."

They shook hands. Lydia left the apartment and took the elevator down. With each passing floor, her heart pounded a beat faster. She felt slightly faint. Had they bothered to search her, she very likely would be dead now. Perhaps it was the tight dress she wore. It gave no hint that an FBI wire was concealed within.

The FBI guys gave Dennison's private home phone number to Lydia. They instructed her to tell Yakov that she had in her possession Horvath's address book, which had all of his key contacts. They taped the ensuing phone conversation.

"Mr. Dennison? My name is Lydia."

"Lydia? I'm afraid I don't know anyone by that name. How did you get my number? Is this a crank call? I'll alert the police."

"I'm a friend of Horvath's. A very good friend."

Dennison's attitude suddenly changed. "Go on."

"I am also a friend of some close contacts of his. Wealthy contacts."

"Jesus!" Dennison blurted, half in relief. "Where and when can we meet?"

"Perhaps New York would suit you better."

"Yes. You name the place. The weekend would suit me. I have personal affairs scheduled there already."

Dennison did his Houdini vanishing act from his penthouse apartment again. Yakov picked him up with his black Lincoln in central park.

There was an awkward silence after the initial self-introductions and handshake. Yakov, intrusive and brash, was at this moment unusually tongue-tied. The U.S. Secretary of State's presence awed him just a little. This would be fleeting, however, as his sense of power over other men further swelled his ego.

But it was Dennison who got down to business first. "Look. I don't know who you are or who you represent--"

"I represent myself and myself only," Yakov interjected tartly.

"I see. Anyway, I want to continue the deal Horvath had made with you. In return for…information, I demand cash, paid immediately and in strict conformance with my instructions. The other demand I make is that our relationship be kept absolutely confidential. And if you think that you can blackmail me, you can forget it. I may not know much about you, but what I do know is that, without me and that which I can deliver, you're over a barrel, a virtual nobody."

Yakov was struck by Dennison's bluntness. So were the FBI special agents monitoring the conversation from the tiny device they had planted inside the Lincoln's dashboard when Pyotr brought it to the "Inside Out Car Wash" in Brooklyn the previous day.

Yakov remained unfazed. "I can assure all of what you *ask*. After all, I am a businessman who has become successful by being careful. Miss Lydia will be go-between. We need never to meet again. I think you will find that I am easy to deal with, Mr. Secretary. Not to worry. It will be a mutually beneficial relationship."

"Good. That's exactly what I want to hear."

"Thank you. And while we are being candid with each other, I will say this. Once the information flow is turned back on, it can never be turned back off, as long as you hold your present position. I *can* blackmail you, and worse. But such devices are extreme. I prefer not to resort to them."

Dennison made no reply. His bluster, so effective when dealing with heads of state, ran up against a brick wall in this man. He made another try.

"Another thing. I deplore violence. A couple of my people have gotten in harm's way because they…they were careless. Mind you, I wanted nothing bad to happen to them. But…they disobeyed and…well, since they didn't follow my, uh, guidelines, other people, I mean, people who they upset or threatened because of their actions, they…"

Dennison was dissembling. He stammered, he sweat. His lips trembled and his eyes shifted nervously. Yakov saw right through him.

"Roy. May I call you Roy? *You* are responsible for the murder of the foolish Mortimer. *You* ordered the killing of your ambassador Wells. *You* demanded that Mr. Toby Wheeler be severely injured. And *you* signaled that you wanted Mr. Innes liquidated. I detest hypocrites. Perhaps it is second nature to diplomats and politicians to delude themselves and others when they destroy other men. I may not be an angel. But at least I am honest with myself. Don't attempt to deceive me, and don't pretend that you are a noble-hearted gentleman. I will not tolerate it. Our business relationship will go much smoother if we are honest with each other."

Yakov's initial awe of his new business partner evaporated like dry ice. He turned away from Dennison and stared out the side window.

The Lincoln dropped Dennison off near Fifth Avenue. Clad in his usual jogger's costume, the Secretary sprinted back home, unrecognized, except for the FBI zoom lenses trained on him.

CHAPTER TWENTY-EIGHT

"The lousy prick had it comin'. Didn't have enough sense to keep his fly closed," Al whispered to Tony "Buckaroo" Musomecchio, sitting in the pew behind him.

The priest swung the incense burner over the dead gangster's coffin and uttered the benediction for the dead.

"Hey. The guy was doin' it for so long, he had a lotta husbands and boyfriends fooled. You got a wife like his, you'd be drillin' everything that moves too." Tony laughed hoarsely, causing the old Sicilian women weeping over the dear departed Carl Giovanezza to crane their necks and glare at the two men disapprovingly. A ten-foot crucifix of the tortured Jesus, his suffering face contorted, blood coursing from his stigmata, loomed ominously over the congregation.

"Cut it out, Tony. You're pissin' off all of Carl's old girlfriends." Tony had to stifle a laugh in his coat sleeve. More reproving looks.

"Hey, let's excuse ourselves. I gotta pee. Whadda 'bout you?" Al said.

In mock solemnity, the two men genuflected, hastily made the sign of the cross and lumbered down the aisle to the rear of the stately St. Francis of Assisi church in the

Italian section of Astoria. Ricky and another retainer were
right behind. A hundred pairs of eyes followed them. The
unmistakable thoughts behind them were that, yes, you too
will follow old Carl to the grave in like ignominious
fashion. Feared and fawned upon in life, thugs were spared
of reverence in death, which as often as not was visited on
them in shameful or sensational circumstances.

They hovered next to the white marble holy water
vessels at the entrance of the church. Candles for the dead
flickered against the dank limestone interior. A dim bulb
shone from a black wrought-iron and glass fixture hanging
by a chain from the vaulted ceiling. The stolid edifice
imbued in the worshiper a sense of something larger and
more enduring than one's fleeting existence, something lost
on these men.

"Who the hell was he humpin' that'd give him a heart
attack? Can I get an introduction? She must be some piece
of *culo*," Tony continued.

"Yeah, yeah. What?! You want a heart attack too?
Better stick to what you got. But, look, let's cut the
comedia for a moment. You said you had something you
needed to tell me. What is it?"

The 5'2" "Buckaroo," who got that moniker from having
run cowboy-motif casinos in Reno in his early days, looked
cautiously to each side, then stepped on his tippy-toes and
placed a hand to the side of his mouth to whisper to his
friend. Al bent down to listen.

"Russians all over the place these days. They're in all
our old neighborhoods, puttin' the arm on everybody we
rely on. Even at Fulton and Javits. People are scared.
Word on the street is that they're gonna declare war on the
Italians. And these guys, they don't follow no rules, see?
They'll kill women, kids. Not civilized like us. To them an
infamia is just another tool to get what they want."

Al pondered a moment. "Where they gonna hit?"

"Don't know. Could be our people -- the *tenienti*, our offices, our cars, our families. Who knows?"

"What about names?"

"This guy, Mogilevich, he's all over the place. But so's the other one, Yakov. Seems they're rivals. A bunch of Russians been getting smoked over in Brighton Beach last few weeks. Seems like they've got a guerrilla war goin' already. We're next. My sources tell me that the idea is, you knock out the top guineas, that stacks the deck in your favor in the war against the other guy."

Al stood staring at the altar. The priest was leading the congregation in prayer. Al pondered, his hands reposed, thumbs outward in his jacket pockets, his eyes focused far away. He rocked slightly on the balls of his feet.

"So, Al. Everybody knows you done business with them Russkis. What gives? How do we protect ourselves?"

Al led his friend to the candles for the dead. "Look at all those little fires," he gestured to the hundred-odd small flames barely flashing their presence in the dim, expansive entrance area.

Tony looked confused at Al's change of subject, but went along. He affected deep interest in Al's line of conversation.

"Each one stands for a soul who's left this earth."

"Yeah, I get it. Like my ol' man. After Don Cuornero done him in during the trash-hauling wars back in '68. But I hope it don't count for Don Cuornero after I greased the son of a bitch with a--"

"Ton'. We're in a house of God."

"Huh? Yeah, right. Sure. I get it."

"You ever heard of Quintus Fabius Maximus?"

"Was he that Puerto Rican Johnny "Blues" whacked when they was getting uppity and trying to muscle in on Johnny's numbers business in Brooklyn?"

"No, Ton'. He was a great Roman general. When the Carthaginians invaded Italy, the hotheads in Rome wanted to rush over and throw their legions against the Carthaginian general, Hannibal. But Hannibal had a reputation for being more clever than the Romans. They lost the first battles against him. But Fabius asked for time. He shadowed Hannibal, engaging in battle only when he had superior numbers and could pick off a few hundred here, a few hundred there. In the end, he exhausted and cornered Hannibal. Later, another Roman general, Scipio Africanus, surrounded the Carthaginians and slaughtered them on their home turf in Africa. These guys became great heroes to the Roman people. They helped make Rome into a great empire."

"Al, you was always interested in that history shit. Always readin' them books and playing out battles on the playground with the other kids. *Minghia!* I remember Sister Francesca rapping your knuckles over that. By the way, we gotta worry about them Carta-virginians here? Lot of them comin' over now?"

Al put his arm around his friend's shoulders.

"Just like the Romans had to be smart in how to handle the Carthaginians, we got to be smart in how we deal with the Russians. We play our cards right, they'll be lighting lots of candles in the Russian churches."

Wentworth worried constantly about Lydia. She told him that, for too long now, her destiny was completely in the hands of others. She had grand dreams of leaving

Russia, of creating a life for herself that was not scripted by the relentless denial of hope that her homeland offered in its troubled times. She had sought hope in the West, where she had always been told freedom to choose was limited only by the constraints of one's imagination. But since she left Russia, Lydia said she had been someone else's property, plaything or tool to exploit others. First Sasha and Borin, then Yakov and Horvath. Now the FBI. She burned to set herself free. Her soul ached for a normal life of raising babies and growing old with the man she loved.

Wentworth made her quest his. He consoled her, comforted her and counseled patience. It was he who convinced her to cooperate with the FBI as their plant within the Russian mob. "Only by doing this can you destroy those who exploited you," he said. And it was the motivation for vengeance that made her cooperate.

But Wentworth was feeling uneasy over his own circumstances. By now he knew all about Albert Joseph Malandrino. How naive could he be! But, the strange, paradoxical thing about it was that he could live with it. He liked Big Al. Malandrino never asked him to get involved in any shady business. Furthermore, he'd been acquitted on previous charges, hadn't he? It could be that Al had been involved in legally questionable activities in the past, but now followed a straight and narrow path. He didn't need to be a crook, after all. Al-Mac and his other legitimate businesses provided a lucrative income. This, of course, was self-delusion. Wentworth was there when Al met with Yakov at Pironi's. He even took care of the security for the meeting. Now he and Lydia were doing undercover work for the FBI. If Al were indeed a mobster, he would go ballistic. Certainly, Ricky would take things into his own hands. Life was becoming precarious for Wentworth and Lydia.

"You seein' anybody special?" Al asked with a smirk over espresso and almond *biscotti* at Sal and Vicki's. Wentworth stifled a jolt of insecurity. Al knew Lydia as Yakov's mistress. Wentworth was connected with the Russian mob as well as the FBI. Double jeopardy. The irony was that he was 100 percent loyal to Al. There would be triple jeopardy if the FBI knew, and peril in the extreme if Yakov was aware of all his and Lydia's connections.

"You know how it is. A date here. A date there. Nothing special, Al," Wentworth answered with a shrug and a boyish blush.

Al pinched and slapped Wentworth's cheek, a sign of affection among Italians. He pointed his index finger at his aide and warned, "You be careful now! Be safe. Also, watch out who you go out with. Lots of shady broads out there, not from good families. You can play with them, but when it comes to the real thing, you want a good girl from good family. Understand? I'll find you a nice Italian girl. The kind that'll look good, cook good and fuck your brains out every night!" Al guffawed. He wiped his mouth, then blew his nose into a napkin. "Hey. We gotta go." He plunked a twenty dollar bill on the table.

"Al?" Wentworth spoke without forethought.

"Yeah? What is it, Chuckie?"

"There's something I have to tell you."

"Okay. Sure."

Wentworth wanted to tell his boss everything. Or maybe, just about Lydia. But a sixth sense got the better of him.

"Chuck. I'm running late for a meeting with some suppliers. Can it wait?"

"Uh, yep. No problem, Al. It's not important anyway."

Sal came over to thank Al for the Florentine silver set he had given Sal's daughter for her wedding.

"Such silver I haven't seen since my grandmother's. *Madonna!* She came over with nothin' but some clothes and that set of silver. My older brother, Joey, got it though. She liked him best..." Sal's hands accentuated his every word, except when he wiped beef blood and grease on the stained white apron that draped over his protruding gut.

Wentworth got up. He signaled to Al that he would summon Bags and the car over.

"Yeah, so when my daughter opens this huge box from you, I couldn't believe my eyes! Just like my grandmother's. First thing I do is invite Joey over to my daughter's house. By the way, they went to Vegas for their honeymoon. Had a great time! They won $630. Can you believe that?..." Al was trying politely to break free.

Wentworth sprinted out of Sal and Vicki's front door. In a split second, another instinct took over, one conditioned by his years as one of the Marines' elite. The familiar ta-ta-ta-ta-ta-ta of an Uzi reached his ears before the bullets did and he plunged to the sidewalk, snatched the Browning 9mm from his shoulder holster, rolled over on his side and instantly lodged six rounds into the chest of a figure who was but a flash in Wentworth's eye. He turned and fired four shots at the getaway car, but it sped off. He rolled to the other side and emptied the remaining three rounds into the forehead of a second figure rushing in his direction. Wentworth dropped the empty magazine and slammed another in its place. There was no deliberation, no conscious thinking process involved. Another Wentworth took over, one steeled and ever prepared, with the automatic reflexes of a tiger on the prowl in unfriendly territory. It was over in a matter of seconds. Two strangers lay dead, one sprawled over a suburban station wagon filled with groceries, with a baby seat in the back; blood gushed from his chest, staining the car's hood and fenders in scarlet rivulets. The other assailant, half of his head blown away, lay askew garbage-filled plastic bags in front of the green grocer adjacent to Sal's.

Wentworth jerked the Browning to another target. Both hands gripped tightly around the weapon, finger taut on the trigger. He was hyperventilating. His face and armpits streamed with sweat. Another instinct held him back this time. In his sights was the owner of the now-bloody stationwagon, a young, pregnant woman with a small girl holding her hand. The woman was screaming.

Wentworth bent his elbows, raising the revolver above his head. He sat up looking frantically around him, ready to lower his arms in a nanosecond and resume firing.

He was only now coming to, seeing people taking cover behind cars and lamp posts, dashing into buildings, or simply running away. Now the realization was beginning to sink in that he'd just shot dead two men, that he himself had come precariously close to a violent death just, what was it, seconds, minutes, hours ago?

He heard voices. "Chuckie. Chuck! You okay?" A hand shook him by the shoulder. He looked up at Al's concerned face and blinked. "Take it easy, kid." Cars arrived and screeched to a halt. Men rushed out. Ricky, Bags, beefy Herman "The German" and other Malandrino acolytes swept over the area with weapons drawn. Two men grabbed Wentworth under the shoulders and gently lifted him to his feet. He saw Herman and another man cautiously poke the lifeless bodies of the attackers. Ricky took charge, barking orders left and right.

Wentworth was pulled back into Sal's. The garrulous Sal hovered speechless and quivering behind the meat and cheese case. Wentworth's handlers lowered him into the same chair at the same table where, minutes before, he and Al had bantered about sex and marriage. Someone found

Sal's liquor cache, poured *strega* into a sundae glass and
plunked it down before Wentworth. Al lifted it to
Wentworth's mouth. "Here kid. Drink this. It'll bring you
back." Wentworth obliged. The potent Italian brandy
burned as it coursed through his gullet, into his stomach.
He shook his head as if to ward off mischievous ghosts.

"You all right, kid? Talk to me." He tapped Wentworth
lightly on both cheeks.

"Yeah." Wentworth glanced down at his body to check
visually whether he was still in one piece. "I'm fine. What
happened anyway? Who...?"

Ricky approached and just stared at Wentworth, a flicker
of awe or admiration visible on his face. He surveyed the
carnage. Bullets from the Uzi criss-crossed just inside the
doorway that Wentworth had exited a mere second before.
Glass shards from the shattered front window sparkled on
the wood floor.

"You do this?" he asked.

Wentworth just blinked, still trying to comprehend what
had happened.

"And those two *ciucciamochi*," Ricky signaled toward
the dead men. "You waxed those guys?"

Wentworth rubbed his face slowly with one hand. A
great fatigue was setting in.

Ricky patted the younger man on a cheek. "I
underestimated you, Wyatt Earp. You did good. Real
good. Uncle Al, I think this boy deserves a new job
description. 'Have gun, will massacre.'"

"Leave the kid alone. Can't you see he's got a lot on his
mind? Cut him some slack," Al said.

"I admire his work, Uncle Al. Really, I do. He's
initiated. We can make good use of him."

The wail of police sirens echoed through the
neighborhood. More vehicles screeched to a halt, these

with spinning dome lights. Uniformed NYPD police converged like gathering shadows. Ambulances arrived as did various unmarked cars whose official nature was betrayed by their blackwall tires and the utilitarian men and women who debarked from them. The squawk of official radios filled the air.

A bevy of the city's finest stormed into Sal's and fanned out. "Who's the guy?" one of them asked. The small crowd of Malandrino men stepped away from the small table where Wentworth and Al sat sipping *strega*.

A plainclothes cop in a London Fog raincoat pulled his badge from his jacket and thrust it into Al's and then Wentworth's face. Two policemen, revolvers drawn, ordered the two to rise with their hands raised and legs spread against the wall and frisked them. "I'm lieutenant Menendez. You're the one?" he demanded of Wentworth. Wentworth could see every pore, every hair on Menendez's angular face. He nodded faintly. Using his pen, a uniformed policeman carefully lifted Wentworth's Browning by the trigger guard and lowered it into a mylar bag.

"I'm bringing you in. And you..." he glared at Al. "I know you." A flash of recognition softened his face. "If it ain't Big Al Malandrino. Fancy this. Guess you can't stay away from us. You're coming with us too. And everybody else who was here!" he announced in a loud voice.

A phalanx of balding, bookish men with briefcases pushed its way in. Ernie Feinstein led the way.

He produced identification for Menendez and declared, "I represent these two men as their legal counsel. Mr. Wentworth is licensed to carry a firearm. He was acting in his lawful capacity of self-defense and as declared bodyguard, in accordance with the New York legal code, to protect my client, Mr. Malandrino. You may question these gentlemen, but you may not jail them without the issuance of an arrest warrant by a competent judge. Before *requesting* my clients to accompany you for questioning at police headquarters, you must read them their rights under the Miranda ruling should your intention be to keep them in custody." The other lawyers snapped open their attachés and produced reams of legal documents.

"Holy shit! Another Dream Team!" Menendez proclaimed.

"We are taking witness testimony to prove that my client, Mr. Wentworth, was acting in self-defense against two armed assailants--"

"Listen to me motor mouth! Shut up!!" Menendez ordered. "It's the police who take witness testimony. Got me?"

With a nod from Menendez, police slapped handcuffs on Al and Wentworth and hauled them outside. A barrage of flashes and cam lights blitzed them. A female TV reporter thrust a microphone into Wentworth's face. "Why did you kill those two men, Mr. Wentworth? Are you a mafia soldier, Mr. Wentworth?" The cops pushed Wentworth's head down and shoved him into the rear of a police van. Al was taken to a separate vehicle. Sal and other witnesses received gentler treatment, invited to enter police cars, the doors opened for them by other cops.

Wentworth's would-be killers were placed into body bags and loaded into an ambulance van. Police found no identification on the men. Neighborhood residents said they'd never seen them before.

Al and Wentworth were released after ninety minutes of questioning, and were ordered not to leave the country

pending the result of the investigation. Al again appeared
resplendent before admiring and curious crowds on the
steps of the courthouse, this time flanked by dour but alert
bodyguards. Wentworth, still stunned by events, stood
silently by Malandrino.

"Hey, Al! Guess you showed them!" yelled a
hardhatter.

"Al! Who did it? Colombo Family, Genovese, or
what?" bellowed a fat woman with tinted red hair.

"Is this the start of another mob war, Mr. Malandrino?"
asked the same female TV reporter from the scene at Sal's.

The Renaissance prince raised one hand, palm outward
to signal quiet. With his other, he tugged at his tie and
buttoned the jacket of his silver-gray, double-breasted
Armani suit.

"I am not under arrest."

Applause erupted from the crowd.

"I repeat that I am not under arrest and neither is my
security man here, Chuckie Wentworth." He wrapped an
arm around Wentworth and hugged him. Photojournalists
zoomed in on the younger man. Al again signaled the
crowd to quiet down.

"What we have here is a case of how a breakdown of
law and order is affecting innocent citizens in what were,
up till now, safe neighborhoods."

"Tell it like it is, Al!!" shouted a uniformed
deliveryman. Others whooped similar encouragement.

"Law and order!! Ladies and gentlemen, what this
country needs is law and order! Tell the politicians to put
their money where their mouths are! Protect the American
people from crime! That's what I say!!"

Amid an uproar of acclamation, Malandrino, surrounded
by his gunsels and with Wentworth at his side, made for the
midnight blue Cadillac at the bottom of the steps. The

specially armored vehicle -- thanks to Wentworth's security
organizing -- was flanked by a car and a van in the front
and a car and a van in the rear, each loaded with armed
men. They sped off.

The newspapers were laid out on the large, round coffee
table in Al's office at Al-Mac, which now resembled an
armed camp. Wentworth stared at them unbelievingly. His
face peered from the front pages of the *Daily News* and the
New York Post. "MOB DECLARES WAR - Failed Hit on
Mafia Boss Signals More to Come," trumpeted the former.
"BIG AL SHOOTS BACK - New York Braces for Mob
War," ballyhooed the latter. Next to the photos of Al and
Wentworth being taken away by police was an inset photo
of the slain men. The *Times*, as usual, had a more staid
presentation on page two of the Metro section:
"SHOOTING IN QUEENS - Italian-Russian Mob Tensions
Lead to Violence."
    Al picked up the *Times* and read aloud. "'Police
investigating the incident report that the two dead men
were members of the Russian mafia, whose influence has
been growing in several North American cities, including
Chicago, Toronto, Los Angeles and San Francisco. The
failed attempt on Mr. Malandrino's life signals imminent
hostilities between the two crime organizations, according
to organized crime experts. Mr. Malandrino was tried and
acquitted last year on a variety of charges involving...'
What is this bullshit? Here I draw hundreds to hear what I
got to say and they don't write squat. But throw out the
same old lies about me? Absolutely. That's what the press
is good at. Recirculating old lies."

"Uncle Al, word on the street is those two guys were Russians all right. But it's not clear whether they were Mogilevich's or Yakov's." Ricky leaned against a picture window overlooking the colorless industrial-officescape of northern New Jersey. He poked at his teeth with a toothpick. "And they're pissed at Quick Draw McGraw here. Lot of folks making contracts on our boy Chuckie. You can be sure of that."

Al stared at Wentworth. In a concerned voice, he asked, "Chuckie, how do you feel about that?"

Wentworth shrugged. "No love lost between me and Russians. Been fighting them for years in one capacity or another." He thought of his security and counterespionage work with the government and now his sheer hatred of Lydia's oppressor, Yakov. He wanted revenge. He wanted Yakov destroyed.

"It's Yakov," he said.

Al and Ricky both leaned forward. "How do you know it's Yakov?" Al asked.

"My sources. He also has government big shots in his pocket."

"Like who?"

"The Secretary of State for one. Dennison."

Al and Ricky looked at each other. It all fit together now. Dennison had cut them off after Yakov had gotten to him.

"Horvath. Nicholas Horvath. The President National Security Adviser who went berserk a couple of weeks ago and shot all those people from inside the White House."

"You mean Yakov got him to do it?" Ricky asked.

"No. But Yakov does kill officials, Russian and American alike. I have reason to believe he put contracts out on the American ambassadors in Rome and Bangkok and at least a couple of Russian intel officers too. Senior officers."

"Chuckie T. Wentworth. I place you in Al-Mac Construction to put an end to goldbricking and petty theft and now you're my own personal CIA. I underestimated you."

"It's what I'm good at. It just takes time. Intel collection is part of a security officer's duties. Know what your enemies are up to before they can act on it. That's the name of the game."

"What do you know about my business? About me?"

"I know that you've had some scrapes with the law. Serious scrapes. That the government watches you closely. And that now the Russian mob is out to liquidate you. And it's my job to stop them from doing so."

"Like I said, Uncle Al. The kid's initiated. He's already made. Nothing to do now but to make it formal."

Al sat back, loosened his tie and contemplated Wentworth, assessing him, sizing him up. It foreshadowed an important decision that Al was about to make.

"Kid. You saved my life back there. I owe you my life."

"Just doing my job, sir."

"No. It's more than 'just a job.' You could've been killed. Easy. You waxed those two goons. Now everybody's got your number. 'Hit man,' they'll call you in the papers. A 'soldier' in the 'Malandrino Crime Family' -- whatever that is. The Feds will be sniffing around you. Your friends won't want to know you. Your family won't know what to think. Your life will never be the same. You realize that?"

Wentworth pondered this. He glanced down at the newspapers bearing his face next to Al's on the front page. He looked back up to Al. "Guess you're right."

"You're part of my family now, Chuckie Wentworth. For good or for bad, you're in. It's forged in blood. I'll protect you, guide you, reward you. You need anything. Anything. You just ask. In return, I want your absolute loyalty. You understand?"

Ricky, still leaning against the plate glass window, added, "Kid, this is a lifetime membership. You don't resign. Ever."

Wentworth's head swirled. Images emerged and blended together. Of an idyllic childhood on the farm, sunny days at school, warm family holiday get-togethers, running on the high school track team, dating sweet southern girls, graduation, the Marines, adventures, hopes, dreams. Where would his life now lead to? Lydia, FBI, mobsters. So unpredictable, and perilous.

He bent forward, with his elbows perched on his knees and hands clasped. He looked up at Ricky, then to Al, and nodded, but said nothing.

Al got up and gestured Wentworth to rise. He took the younger man in his arms and embraced him on the left, then the right. Ricky followed suit. *Benvenuto alla nostra famiglia, fratello*, Al said.

CHAPTER TWENTY-NINE

The S.S. *Garrison McGee* had seen better days. In fact, it was now in the final years of useful service. Riven by rust, patched here and there and everywhere by spot welding and barely able to reach nine knots with its ancient, soot-spewing engine, the hulking WWII-era vessel plied from one lesser port to another, its creaking holds crammed at any given time with plywood from Peru, construction steel from Brazil, cocoa from Ghana, hardwoods from Indonesia. As a spanking new British merchantman in 1939 crewed largely with salts from Scotland and Wales, the ship bore the name HMS Harlech. Now of Liberian registry, its latest changeable skipper was an aging Dane, Viktor Sigurdsen, with a drinking problem; its crew was Nigerian, Greek and Tongan, with a sprinkling of South Americans. The cargo was textiles from Thailand. The port was Galveston, only three nautical miles due north. The ship would anchor for the night and await assignment of a berth the next morning.

For the pair of special ops veterans of the Soviet blue water fleet, it was an easy target. Four strategically placed cemtex charges at the water line was all that it would take to send the old freighter to the bottom with its clandestine cargo of three tons of potent Thai marijuana. It would also send a clear message to Al Malandrino who would stand to lose a bundle on the deal, not to mention his credibility with the distributors who bought the stuff from him at hefty premiums. Yakov would see to it by this action.

The first explosion, more a muffled thud than a big bang, had no effect on the aquavit-sodden captain, who snored steadily in his quarters. Several of the Tongans, island fishermen who were constantly alert to nature's unpredictable actions, however, awoke in their bunks with their ears perked. The second and third detonations sent a shock wave jolting throughout the creaky structure of the ship. It awoke even the nonchalant Greeks. Rust-ridden steel beams snapped apart. Supplies toppled onto the decks. Fire extinguishers bolted from their metal harnesses and clanged down iron stairwells. The fourth charge sent a tremendous shiver through midship, causing it to give a deep and painful groan, as that of a fatally injured giant sea-beast. It seemed that the aged thing even welcomed this *coup de grace*, a quick, lethal blow to put it to rest finally. Crew members went flying through the air. The craft listed steeply to starboard, then aft, as the screw snapped apart. Sea water gushed into it from the four explosion points, then spread rapidly as strained steel plates came loose and cracked under the pressure.

Captain Sigurdsen lay prostrate in his cabin, having lost his balance twice in an alcoholic stupor. He shouted orders vainly from where he lay. Tongans, Greeks, Venezuelans, Africans ran to save their individual lives, some colliding into each other, others fighting over the few life boats that would release themselves from rusted moorings. Quickly the S.S. *Garrison McGee* sank, plunging eagerly into a deep, lightless ocean grave. And entombed with many of the crew within was several million dollars worth of a narcotic weed, the playstuff of a self-centered society that worshipped individual self-gratification.

Flora Dominguez was barely aware of her husband's stealthful sidling into bed. He reeked of liquor and cigarette smoke. She was fed up with Rick's nocturnal bar-hopping and carousing with other women. Maybe she would raise hell in the morning. But probably not. She'd threatened to seek a divorce before, but thus far had not acted on it. Her priest counseled her to try to bring her husband around through gentleness and patience -- "Jesus's weapons," he called them. Surely, the passage of time would reform Rick. But at this moment, in the twilight between consciousness and sleep, Flora had the distant urge to murder her wayward man. Just end it.

But there were the kids. And the surge in cash income in the Dominguez household over the past nine months made life much more comfortable for all. A new Cadillac Escalade, a boat, nice clothes, private schooling and, soon, a new house in the Galveston suburbs dampened thoughts of a divorce, at least for the time being. She was curious as to how a senior customs inspector could afford such luxuries on a GS-14's salary, but was afraid to ask. The good life sometimes had a way of dampening one's curiosity.

But the good life had just come to an end. Two ex-*Spetznaz* troopers, veterans of the Afghan war, saw to that. They moved through the largely working class, Hispanic neighborhood, slithered effortlessly into the Dominguez home through the basement entrance, quietly shut the door to the children's bedroom, silently entered the master bedroom where Rick Dominguez lay in his underwear

snoring away, and expertly severed his jugulars and vocal
cords while keeping his mouth shut in a hand lock-grip.
One of many lethal skills learned from the Afghans. They
vanished like spirits in the night.

The wetness of her husband's blood didn't jolt Flora out
of her slumber until the whole bed was soaked. She felt
clammy dampness in the sheets, moved on her other side,
then began to sense that she was lying in a growing pool of
sticky liquid. She opened her eyes, but looked straight
ahead, afraid finally to awake fully and discover what she
would discover. Her arm was immersed in blood. She
turned abruptly toward Rick. His head was bent sharply
back. The gaping eyes and mouth reflected the last fleeting
awareness of his life -- that of terror. A crescent-like gash
just under his mandible spanned from ear to ear.

Flora bolted upright and released a single loud scream,
then leapt from the bed. She covered her eyes, smearing
them with blood. Hysteria began to grip her, panic would
drive her to lose her mind, lose control. *Stop, Flora!*
Think, Flora! The thought then struck her that it was over.
No more Rick. No more cheating. No more beatings.
Rick's shady dealings ultimately led to this. She thanked
God that the killers spared her and prayed to Him that the
government and life insurance would reward her and the
kids with a lifelong income.

She flung herself out of the room and grasped the
banister to get hold of herself. *The kids! The kids!!* With a
burst of adrenaline into her heart, Flora threw herself down
the hallway to the children's bedroom. Ricky, Jr. and Marta
Luisa were sound asleep. Flora carefully shut the door.
She lifted the phone receiver with trembling hands and
called the police. "Get here quick, my husband's been
murdered," she breathed calmly and hung up after giving
her street address. Flora looked at herself in the hallway

mirror. Intent on keeping her dignity, with deliberation, she pushed back her blood-caked, jet-black hair, took another deep breath and slowly walked to the bathroom. Flora climbed into the shower.

Yakov's humiliation of Malandrino on this dead deal was complete. One shipment of grass sunk and one port of entry scratched.

From his headquarters at Al-Mac Construction, Al followed the latest developments like a general receiving situation reports from the front lines. And the news was not good. Yakov had taken over corrupt officials and labor leaders at the ports of New York and Bayonne, and cargo operations at JFK. Through better collaborative deals or strong-arm tactics, he took away longstanding partnerships and understandings that Al had had with other mobsters around the country. Malandrino-controlled warehouses and safehouses were blown to bits by ex-*Spetznaz* operatives, now Yakov's shock troops. Tough Russian hoodlums with little English were pushing Genovese and Malandrino wiseguys out of Javits Center operations and threatening to burn alive any Fulton Fish Market concessionaires who didn't pay protection money to them. In Brooklyn, Queens, Staten Island and Newark, Slavic pitbulls hurled Malandrino-owned jukeboxes and other novelty machines out saloon and restaurant doors. The deal was easy: do business with Yakov, or risk having loved ones slaughtered or homes firebombed. The press was having a field day. The authorities were perplexed and paralyzed, having devoted few resources to penetrating the clannish community of new Russian immigrants or the associated murky world of Russian organized crime.

Al paced back and forth in his office, barking orders to this capo or that teniente. After the police interrogation following Wentworth's shooting the Russians, Al's paranoia of being surveilled by the FBI returned.

"Get Chuckie in here, goddammit!" he yelled at Bags. He reverted to an old habit when his anxiety level reached crisis proportions. He devoured cannolli, washing them down with potent *digestivi*.

Wentworth presented himself fifty seconds later.

"Where the hell were you? Don't you know a war's on?!"

"Yes, sir."

"I want one of the bubbles."

"Sir?"

"Don't 'sir' me! I'm your boss, not General Schwartzkopf."

"Yes, sir. I mean, yes, uh, yes, okay."

"Just shut the fuck up and listen. Okay?"

Wentworth nodded.

"Get me one of those deals they use in embassies where the ambassador can talk with his people about secret shit without the opposition being able to listen in. I think they make 'em out of glass so's if there are any bugs planted they're visible."

"You mean the secure conference facility."

"I don't care what they call it. Just get me one. Who sells them? How long they take to deliver?"

"You can't just pick one up at Wal-Mart. Only one or two firms make them. They're custom-made and it takes months before they can deliver."

Al blew up. With a swipe of a forearm, cannolli went flying in all directions. "Can't you see the friggin' FBI has probably got this placed wired like a video arcade?!"

"I've swept it four times this week alone."

"They got ways. Even you don't know about.
Technology from NASA. Who knows what they got?!"

Ricky walked in. "What's the matter, Uncle Al?"

"The goddamn Feds gotta be tuned in to this place like it
was a Holyfield-Tyson fight and Mr. sow belly and grits
here can't protect us!"

"Uncle Al, calm down. Chuckie's got this entire
compound tight as a virgin's ass. Take it easy. Lay off the
sugar and booze. It's a dangerous combination. Makes you
hyper."

Al paused, then looked up at Ricky and Wentworth with
contriteness on his face. He ran a hand though his hair.
"Yeah. You're right. I gotta calm down. It's just that,
between the Russians, on the one hand, and the Fibbies, on
the other, we're being brought down. If we don't turn
things around, and I mean soon, we're finished."

"Uncle Al, you were always telling me stories when I
was a kid about those old Roman generals."

Al loosened up and smiled.

"Remember the one who, rather than go head-on at the
enemy, he dogged them, picked them off until they were
exhausted?"

"Hah. Yeah. That's Quintus Fabius Maximus. My
favorite. Smart cookie."

"And how did he know the weak points where to
attack?"

"Hannibal, he wore down. He had good spies and
informants. They reported Hannibal's every move back to
Fabius."

"We've got to think like Fabius, Uncle Al. We need
better information."

"Yeah. You're right. I've got to lighten up and we need
more dope on what that *stronso*, Yakov, has up his sleeve."

Uncle and nephew focused on Wentworth. Immediately catching on, the ex-Marine responded, "Intel. We need good intel."

"How 'bout it Chuckie?" Al asked.

Wentworth hesitated. His immediate instinct was to shield Lydia from further danger.

"You're a made man now, Chuckie. Good or bad, you're in the family now. Everything you've done so far has helped this family. You told us all about what Yakov was up to from your sources. You *saved* the family when you gunned down these two Russians. On the street they're calling you 'Terminator IV.' How about it Chuck? You can deliver, or what?" Ricky gave Wentworth no wiggle room.

Wentworth's heart pounded louder and louder until the pulse blocked out all other sound. His mind raced. *Think! Got to protect Lydia. The FBI. The 'family' will bury me alive if they knew. Think!!* Suddenly, Wentworth's head jerked backward as a thought slammed into his brain like a meteor.

"Al, those Romans. They were always cutting deals to get what they needed."

"Yeah. With the Gauls, the Celts, the Germanic tribes, Greeks. One week they were spilling each other's guts. Following week, they were fighting side-by-side against another common enemy. They did what they had to do to advance Rome's interests. So what?"

"The Russians have us on the run."

Al and Ricky shifted uneasily.

"You -- we -- have a two-front war. One with Yakov. The other with the federal government. One's conventional. The other's a guerrilla war at this stage."

"What're you getting at?" Al demanded doubtfully.

"Just listen to me. At OCS -- Officer Candidate School -- they taught us that multi-front wars are usually disastrous. Clausewitz said to avoid them at all costs. Lord Salisbury said that the enemy of our enemy is our friend. And another British statesman, Lord Palmerston, said that his country had neither permanent friends nor permanent enemies, but only permanent interests. You want to destroy Yakov." *And so do I. More than anything else. To avenge what he's done to Lydia.* "And you want to get the Feds off our backs." Wentworth stood up and came within inches of Al's face. "The enemy of your enemy is your friend. Make a deal with the FBI. Offer to cooperate with them in return for immunity."

Al's nostrils flared. His breathing accelerated. His eyes reddened.

Before he could respond, Wentworth added, "If you don't, be prepared to be crushed from both sides. Just like Rome was in the end."

Ricky stepped forward. "This isn't ancient Rome, but I think the kid may have something, Uncle Al. Let's at least consider it."

"I can be the middleman to broker the deal. They have, uh, I mean, they would have confidence in me because of my background." *And I'll be square with everybody. Get myself at least a little out of harm's way.*

Al said nothing. He turned to the picture window and surveyed the sere yet prosperous econoscape of post-industrial America. He'd spent his life striving to take his slice from the American pie. And his father and grandfather before him. Now it was all at risk. He could lose his empire *and* wind up in jail if he didn't play his cards right.

"All right. You go and test the waters. Make no promises. Just discuss the possibilities. Report back to me immediately after. Got it?"

Wentworth nodded assent. "I'll get on it right away." He bolted out of the office, grabbing a chocolate cannolli as he did so.

Wentworth had trained alongside the FBI at Quantico where they shared a training base with the Marines. The Best. That's what the FBI and the Marines are, he thought at the time and still did so. The Marines and the FBI each was a closed society with its own ethos of fighting pride and fearlessness. They related well with each other. He had never, however, entered FBI's massive headquarters. Escorted by Speedy, he thought how easy it would be to get lost in the 2.5-million-square-foot maze of straight corridors crossing diagonal ones, all flanked with look-alike offices. It might rival the Pentagon as the Washington building easiest to lose one's way in.

They took a private elevator up to the seventh floor where they confronted the imposing Office of the Director, so marked by a simple plaque. A kindly secretary stood and greeted them. "The Director will see you now," she said, and she opened the door.

Standing smack in the middle of the expansive office was none other than Frederick Karlson, a Teddy Roosevelt look-alike clearly uncomfortable in a suit and tie. He extended his hand. His face, however, reflected determination and vigilance. Standing to his side was Dom Berlucci.

"Have a seat young man." The Director indeed was all business. Skip the pleasantries and talk turkey. Just like the Marines.

"My people tell me that you were a Marine officer."

"Yes, sir. And proud of it."

"So was I. Alpha Company, 3rd Battalion, 26th Marines. We went head-to-head with the 304th NVA Division at Khe Sanh. Lost a toe to a booby trap, but otherwise came out of it all right. My people tell me you come here offering some kinda deal on behalf of Albert Malandrino."

Wentworth sensed he was on the defensive. In Karlson's eyes, he must have appeared as another Ollie North, another Marine gone wrong.

"Sir, I want to do what's best for my country. That's all."

He went on to relate how he fell in with Malandrino, that he became aware of Al's true background only recently, his relationship with Lydia and her past. He explained what he knew about Yakov.

Karlson was skimming a file, undoubtedly the FBI's own investigative summary. He flipped the pages and nodded as Wentworth spoke.

Karlson put the folder down and removed his pince-nez glasses. "I'll be blunt, Mr. Wentworth. You're a young man who's mixed up with some pretty evil characters. You're walking the thinnest of wires. If you fall off, you're in a world of hurt. Do you know how much resources your government has spent trying to nail Mr. Malandrino and his cohorts into a tight, dark box? Do you have any idea how many man-hours this agency has devoted over the years to bring Malandrino to the justice he deserves? And now the Russian mob. You're associated with them too, tangentially, through this Russian woman."

Wentworth's rehearsed delivery became lost in a swirl of confused emotions. Duty. Honor. Country. Those were the precepts by which he lived. To be lumped into notorious company made him feel unclean and unpatriotic. He froze up. As the emotions welled up inside him, he fought back tears.

Karlson broke his hard stare. "Okay, young man. What's the deal? I'm listening."

Wentworth summoned old Marine courage and cleared the confusion from his mind with a wipe of his forehead and a stiffened spine.

"Sir, I want to help destroy the growing Russian gangs before they claim any more of our society. I want to see corrupt senior officials be brought to the justice *they* deserve. I want innocents, like Lydia Puchinskaya, to be set free. I believe this can be accomplished and, at the same time, compel Al Malandrino to disengage from criminal activity. If there's a price to pay, I guess that's it. Let Al off the hook in return for his cooperation."

Karlson reflected on this for a moment. "Why should we agree to cooperate with him?"

"Well, I know that you've got dirt on Secretary Dennison and others."

"We've got tapes."

"So did you on John DeLorean."

Karlson winced as though a dentist drill had hit a raw nerve. John DeLorean was filmed accepting drug money by the FBI in '82 to save his foundering car company, but beat the rap through slick lawyering. The Bureau has never lived it down.

Wentworth knew what the FBI Director faced. The prospect of collecting so much detailed and incriminating evidence only to have it dismantled in court before a national audience by some ultra-clever, overpaid society lawyers was one of his worst nightmares, and probably would bring his career to an ignominious end. Wentworth had found his hook.

"But you may be unable to nail them -- and Yakov -- for good without assistance from Malandrino. He's been dealing with all these characters for a long time. He knows them inside out. And, if I might say so, sir, you're in government. Compromise is the name of the game, whether it's labor unions versus management or Washington versus North Korea. Churchill said he'd shake hands with the devil himself if it would help bring victory over Hitler."

Karlson cracked a smile. "You're one smart Marine."

Wentworth smiled in turn. "Thank you sir. Had to be all that training at Quantico alongside the FBI."

"Okay. Here's what we're willing to do. You tell your boss that we want to meet him and discuss the details. If he truly cooperates -- and I mean in the full -- we can talk about cutting a deal. Bottom line is this: he becomes -- read my lips -- ONE-HUNDRED PERCENT legit. We might also want a lot of information on other wiseguys. The more of his ilk he can bring down, the more...open-minded...we're prepared to be."

"I'll do my best, sir."

"Good, get to it then."

"Oh, Lydia, can you put her into witness protection?"

"Seems reasonable."

"And one last thing."

Karlson raised his eyebrows and tilted his head in an expression of impatient indulgence.

"Bob Innes and Colleen McCoy. They're on the run. And I don't understand why. Surely, the FBI isn't after them. It's Dennison trying to do them in, in cahoots with

Yakov. Their lives may be in danger. Can you find them and protect them?"

Karlson looked inquiringly at Berlucci. The chief of Investigations flushed with embarrassment. "I'll get right on it, sir."

CHAPTER THIRTY

Les Nigauds had abruptly fallen out of favor among the Washington power set, such is the fickleness of this inconstant group. The food and service showed it. Nonetheless, there were those diehard loyalists who continued to patronize the place, hoping that by mere dint of their illustrious presence, the schools of flitting politicos would meander back to this particular feeding ground.

"I want *canard canadien à sauce de groseilles sauvages*, goddammit!" Dennison shouted at the uncomprehending Honduran waiter. "Duck! You understand duck?!" He poked the menu with his forefinger. "You can't speak any civilized language and you can't read! Get me the manager! Where's Jean-Marie? I want to speak to Jean-Marie. This is outrageous!" Dennison's face was as red as the raspberry sauce he would get with his duck should his order ever make it to the chef.

"Deplorable. Simply deplorable," Selmur muttered, shaking his head. He was grimacing at his drink. "This isn't a martini. This is toilet bowl cleaner."

A stooped fellow in an ill-fitting black tux came to the table. "Can I help you?" he asked.

Dennison just stared at the man's face. "Who are you?"

"Rini Delopo, the manager."

"Where's Jean-Marie?"

"Oh, he's moved on to *La Grosse Légume* on Capitol Hill."

Dennison's jaw was slack from disbelief. "Delopo. What kind of name is that?"

"Filipino, sir."

Dennison and Selmur looked at each other gravely.

"I'm trying to explain to this, er, gentleman that I want *canard canadien*."

"The what?"

"What do you mean 'the what'? The fucking duck!"

"Ohh! Right. We make a nice Cantonese sauce and fried rice with it. What vegetable would you like? We have snow peas, fried plantains or okra jambalaya." He poised with his pencil and pad, ready to take down the order.

"Jesus Christ." Dennison dropped the menu on his plate.

"Did you say okra? Okay. And you sir?"

"I'm afraid to say," Selmur sneered. He looked up at Rini Delopo doubtfully and, pointing to the item on the menu, said, "*entrecôte normandaise avec pommes de terre au gratin*?"

"Ahh, yes. The fried steak with shoestring fries. It comes with avocado," Rini replied courteously as he jotted down the order. "And some wine? We have a fine selection of California chardonnays as well as chianti and some new red wines from Oregon. Or, if you prefer, the new bartender can make you his special Sangria. He puts in a secret ingredient with a kick," Rini added with a wink.

"*La Grosse Légume*, huh? On Capitol Hill? We'll have to check it out sometime," Dennison sighed. He dismissed Rini with a wave of his hand.

"I've resisted going to that new place. I don't like the symbolism people would draw of our traveling to Congress's turf. I don't like that at all," Selmur said.

"I agree, but what choice have we now?"

"Excellent opening there Roy."

Dennison braced himself for Selmur's hallmark sarcasm. He truly hoped that the fried steak would give the Chief of Staff a massive coronary.

"The way things are going, the President's going to lose the race and retire to Carmel. And guess where that leaves us? Out in political Siberia. I don't know about you, but the notion of sitting out two terms with the opposition in the White House is not appealing. I'm 58. That prospect deals me out. And you too." He flagged down the waiter and carefully mouthed the word "v-o-d-k-a," indicating a double with his fingers against his water glass.

"You can't complain about cash for the campaign. I've got a steady flow coming in. And I found some slick accountants from Miami who are laundering it faster than your mother did your shirts."

The unsmiling Selmur fixed his gaze on the Secretary. "My mother never did shirts."

"Oh."

"We need more. Our traditional contributors are all bailing out. They're not even bothering to cover all bases. They're shoveling it Jalbert's way by the ton. It's Christmas every day in the other camp."

Dennison summoned up feelings that he thought were courage and, putting on a stern face, said, "Money alone isn't going to win this thing, Howard."

"You're right."

Dennison was taken aback by this sudden agreeableness on the part of his White House colleague. "You agree then?"

"Why, absolutely. All the cash in the world isn't going to win this for us as long as Jalbert is riding high in the polls."

"What are the PACs up to?"

"Ah! Screw the friggin' PACs. They're effective within limits. Mobilizing single-interest groups is their thing." Selmur plucked a blossom from the small vase on their table and studied it with a detached interest. As his eyes contemplated the gentle construction of the flower, his mind seemed to move farther away.

"Well, the state party chairmen and organiza--"

"Too late. Jalbert's already swept the primaries. The nomination is his. He'll be the darling of the nation when he wows the party convention in New Orleans next month." Selmur tore one delicate petal from the flower stem.

"I guess the President's got to hustle. Get out on the stump and--"

"Not his style. Corgan doesn't like people. Can't get him to leave Pennsylvania Ave. these days except to go to the golf links or a good fishing hole." He pulled another petal off.

"I know. Pretty bad situation. What if we got some early endorsements…?"

Selmur remained transfixed in another dimension as he pulled the remainder of the flower apart. "You see the movie, *The Untouchables*?"

"With Robert DeNiro? Yeah." Dennison was confused by this twist in conversation.

"Remember the scene where Al Capone has all his associates over for dinner? He walks around the table giving a pep talk…"

"And then bashes in the head of one of them with a baseball bat. What's that got to do with us?"

Selmur remained silent.

Finally, after several uneasy minutes, he spoke. "If we didn't have to contend with pretty boy Jalbert, we'd clinch this election."

"What are you saying Howard?"

"I'm saying what I'm saying, that's all."

"Are you suggesting that we should..."

"I'm suggesting that you might want to talk to some of your contacts about possibilities."

Dennison became indignant. "If you're suggesting violence, count me out. I don't condone--"

"Stuff it, Roy. Who're you trying to kid? There's Mortimer, Wheeler, Wells. Hell, even Horvath. Who else? I'm losing track."

Beet red and breathing heavily, Dennison stammered, "I didn't...agree to any extreme actions being taken against those people. Or anybody! Things got out of control...beyond my means to..."

"Bullshit. You hobnob with some pretty scary characters there, Roy. What do they say? 'You shake hands with the devil only once.'"

Dennison again summoned ersatz courage. "We're in this together! As was Horvath. We sink or swim together, Howard. We've had only the President's...and the nation's...best interests at heart--"

"Shut up! Listen to me and listen good. I haven't said boo or even met any of your...interlocutors. Isn't that what you State Department types call people you talk with? Interlocutors. Hmmm. It depersonalizes people who either kill for you or whom you one day kill yourself -- via the instruments of government and all in the name of 'policy', of course. Funny how the military and intelligence communities have fucked up the language, especially during the cold war. 'Collateral damage', 'peace through strength', 'balance of terror.' To use another strangelovean

term, my friend, I got 'plausible denial.' You don't."
Selmur had that triumphant air of a chess master who had
once again checkmated an opponent.

Dennison came as close to violent rage as he ever had in
his silverspoon life. A bestial urge that rarely invests those
of gentle upbringing seized him momentarily, an urge
which, had it been allowed to run loose, would have had
him tearing Selmur's throat out with his fish knife. As this
urge dissipated, it was supplanted by one of ignominious
defeat. It also was a bestial urge, one of lying prostrate
before a predator in order to signal no threat. Dennison,
blue-blood, Exeter and Harvard grad, Establishmentarian to
the core, felt filthy, shameful, vanquished. As ambition
was shed fleetingly, the remnants of conscience reemerged.
But it was too late.

He lowered his head. "What do you want me to do?"

"Do what you have to do."

"Jalbert to be out of the picture."

"Enhance the President's chances to the max. That's
what we're talking about here." Selmur ordered another
vodka.

"This, all of this, everything we've done so far, can be
blown at the flick of a reporter's laptop switch. We're
playing with fire. State Department security can't tell me
where two renegade FSOs are hiding. And the FBI is
dragging its heels on the case. You saw Senator Weems's
reaction. The hay we made on the case as a diversion from
our other problems is now turning to muck. There are
loose cannons out there aimed right at us." Dennison's lips
quivered. He began to weep.

Selmur looked hurriedly around the nearly empty
restaurant. Then huffed, "Get hold of yourself. Stop it!"

Dennison wiped his face with his napkin.

"You get our Cuban friends onto that case. They're the best in the business. And discreet. We got the money to hire them. Do it! All we need now is two flat-footed bureaucrats on the lam shitting on our whole plan. Do it!!"

The great cathedral which loomed over Innes and Colleen dwarfed them. It was as if their monumental problems had been cast into concrete and gothicized, and now would topple over onto them and crush them under the massive weight. They looked up at the soaring structure and were held in awe. On an unusually clear day, the sun, ripe and golden, cast its final, glowing rays through Golden Gate park and caressed the city on the bay in gentle warmth.

"It's beautiful. And imposing," Said Colleen, craning her neck up at the 265-foot spire.

"Let's go in," Innes said.

The large, gilt bronze doors at the entrance depicted a welcoming Renaissance Florentine scene. "The Gates of Paradise," it was called.

As they entered the church, a cascade of tinkling bells sounded from above. It was as if a guardian angel beckoned them, heralded their arrival.

They felt tiny under the 92-foot high vaulted ceiling of Grace Cathedral, on Nob Hill.

"It makes one feel insignificant," Colleen whispered. "In the grand scheme of things, we really count for very little."

"These gothic cathedrals were meant to do that -- as well as to extol the magnificence of God, of course. It took two generations to build this. Imagine devoting one's entire life to such a project."

More than sixty stained glass windows lined each apse; the holy figures depicted therein seemed to echo the chants and prayers of saints of long ago. The rose window of faceted glass just above the main portal reflected soft pinkish beams that caressed their faces and hair.

Colleen wore her hair tied over her neck. Reddish-brown curls played teasingly on her forehead. The rose light gave her a surreal look.

"You're so beautiful," Innes said. "So beautiful." He touched her cheeks tenderly.

Colleen felt like a teenager again. Goose bumps tingled on her skin. She reflexively lowered her eyes shyly.

Before they could consummate a kiss, the bass strains of an organ commenced a low, solemn wail. They looked up but couldn't see the organist. They looked at each other and smiled. Hand-in-hand, they walked slowly up the darkened nave. They sensed that all the saints, all the apostles and all of the holy people of Christendom looked down upon them, judging them against centuries of both wise and folly human behavior.

The lugubrious lamentations of Albinoni's *Adagio* filled the vast cathedral and echoed from all its surfaces, giving it an even eerier and sadder effect.

"I want to marry you. I want us to wed in such a setting, invoking the ages of the romantic love of long, long ago," Innes said.

Tears streamed down Colleen's cheeks. "Oh, Bob. I love you so much." She threw her arms around him and pressed her head tightly against his neck.

The shuffle of leather sole on stone broke the spell. Still in embrace, Innes and Colleen looked toward the rear of the church. Nothing. "Must be the organist's wife coming to drag him home for dinner," Colleen joked.

They continued up the nave, holding hands. At the crossing, they turned right toward the east transept. The organist stopped playing, perhaps to proceed home for dinner. An old woman who lit candles and said prayers for the dead crossed herself and departed. The whole cathedral was theirs now. The atmosphere was one of stolid peace, of refuge from the myriad burdens of daily existence. A reassuring ethereal presence manifested itself. The two lovers felt secure and welcome in this place. Running and hiding and evading threats were momentarily distant from their minds. They basked in the glow of peace from this structure and of love from each other.

A black cassocked priest shuffled quietly near the confessional at the transept. He looked briefly at Colleen and Innes and smiled. He knelt at a shrine to the Virgin and began to pray. He was dark, tall and broad-shouldered. Innes guessed that he was in his late 30s.

"I don't know what it is exactly," Colleen said. "But, for the first time in weeks, I feel safe. I also feel that we've been on our own too long, Bob. We need to talk to someone we can trust. Maybe we can hide out in a seminary or retreat or something somewhere around here until things blow over. I'm tired of running and having to look over our shoulder all the time."

"I know," Innes replied.

"Let's talk to this priest when he's finished praying. Shall we?"

Innes shrugged agreement.

The priest made the sign of the cross, kissed his rosary and rose.

"Father." Colleen approached him.

The priest turned and faced her. He smiled again. He had Latin dark eyes and wavy black hair.

There was the shuffle sound of shoe against stone
flooring again behind Colleen and Innes. They turned to
see another priest, also olive in complexion and in his 30s,
genuflecting before the high altar. He stood and walked in
their direction.

"Father, we would like to talk to you."

"Yes, certainly," he said. Innes thought the accent was
Spanish.

He signaled with an open palm to follow him. They did
so and approached the crossing, where the other priest
awaited them. He stood erect, his face expressionless.

Innes's mind flashed back to his boyhood in upstate New
York. He recalled hunting with his best friend, Gary Hams.
They would spend hours stalking deer. When they found
one, the boys separated, each moving ever so quietly
through the brush, seeking to flank the animal. Nine times
out of ten, however, the deer sensed the danger
approaching, perked its ears and dashed lithely into the
dark woods. To catch the deer, they learned to think like
them by keenly observing the wind against the brush,
listening to the warbling of birds, and smelling the ground.
That "deer-sense," as Gary used to call it, suddenly
returned to Innes. He tightened his grip on Colleen's upper
arm and halted.

All his senses became magnified, as if some drug were
taking effect on him. The buzz of a fly overhead, the
sounds of San Francisco's traffic outside, the odor of
burning candles, the clamminess of the concrete-enclosed
air each commanded his highest attention. And these
priests. Were they not flanking them? Just as the deer of
Innes's childhood could sense something alien to the woods
in their midst, Innes felt uncertain as to the presence of
these cassocked men in this holy place.

In this heightened state of alert, Innes's ears picked up behind him the ever so audible sound of stiff metal brushing against fabric. His senses told him that this man didn't smell like a priest. Faint odors of liquor and tobacco wafted through the air from his direction. Everything moved in slow motion now. He was aware of every detail of every physical thing around him. The deer-sense in him commanded him to bolt.

Innes used his grip on Colleen's arm to shove her down to the floor. In slow-motion, Innes saw Colleen's expression of fear and confusion as she hurtled downward, her eyes imploring, "Why are you doing this to me?"

Innes turned his head to the rear. Priest Number One pulled a long silvery blade from under his robe. His face was contorted as he lunged at Innes. Priest Number Two produced a revolver with a long barrel and pointed it at Innes. Events moved now in real time.

Innes bent down and hurled his body against the knife-wielder. His 180-pound frame caused Priest Number One to go flying backwards and down to the hard floor. The blade went flying from his hand. Priest Number Two fired two rounds, one of which tore flesh from the arm of Priest Number One. Innes shoved himself rearwards toward the frame holding the dozens of flickering candles to the dead. With each hand gripping the struts connecting the legs, he raised the structure and used all his might to thrust it at the gun-toting priest. The thing knocked the man to the floor, but not without two more shots being fired, this time at the vaulted ceiling. He was covered with candles which ignited his cassock.

The first priest got up, grabbed his knife and went for Innes like an enraged tiger. Colleen picked up a missal and threw it at him. It hit the attacker in the jaw, knocking him off balance momentarily. Innes took Colleen and pulled her away. They ran across the transept, stopped for a second at the presbytery and began to run down the nave. Two more men coming from the main entranceway caused them to stop in their tracks. They looked back. Priest Number One had thrown holy water onto his partner to put out the flames. They felt trapped. Colleen jerked Innes toward the high altar. All the splendor of this magnificent temple of worship would not save them.

"Oh, Lord! If you really exist, *save us!!!*" Colleen shouted at the top of her lungs.

The killer-priests were now back on their feet and bearing down on Innes and Colleen. They looked all around them. Coming across the presbytery right at them were their attackers. To their backs was the glittering high altar -- sacrificial altar, it occurred to Innes. They were aware of the two other men at the far end of the cathedral beginning to make their way up the nave.

"Sacristy!" Innes shouted. "Where's the darn sacristy? All cathedrals have them." He turned left, then right. A white curtain concealed something. Was it a statue? Or a door? "Quick!" Innes hissed, and signaled toward the curtain with his head. They ran for it. He yanked the curtain down. There was a door. It opened. They hurled themselves in and slammed the door shut. Inside the small sacristy were all the accoutrements of the sacred Anglican mass: priests robes, vessels of different sorts, altar boy garments, images of saints, tall candle bearers, incense burners, altar bells.

"Help me, Colleen!" Together they moved a stone statue of St. Francis and propped it against the door. Just then, two bodies slammed against the door. There was the crack of wood, but it held.

Innes picked up another, smaller statue, this one of St. Paul. Like a shot-putter, he stood back, took three steps forward and heaved it into the small window. There was a second assault against the simple door. This one caused the hinges to loosen from the wall. Innes and Colleen stuck their heads out the window.

"It's high. We won't make it," Colleen warned.

"Do we have a choice?"

The crack of gunfire filled the cathedral. The siege against the door halted abruptly.

Innes pulled Colleen to the window ledge. "The tree. We've got to get into the tree," he said. He stood on the ledge and squatted.

"Bob. Noooo!!"

Innes jumped up and forward out the window. His hands caught a branch and held on tightly. He quickly wrapped his legs around it and shimmied toward the tree's trunk. When he reached the sturdy middle portion of the branch, he carefully stood up and reached for the branch above. With his weight pulling it down, the branch's tip touched the sacristy window.

"Colleen! Grab it! Come!"

Colleen made the sign of the cross and grabbed the branch. With her eyes shut tight, she jumped. The branch transported her downward as though she had wings. Softly, she landed on the ground, not believing that she'd made it unhurt.

Innes scrambled down the trunk, the rough bark scratching him and tearing his clothes. Without looking back, they ran down California Street toward the Embarcadero. Out of breath and panic-stricken, they ran as fast as their legs could carry them. They ran on pure adrenalin. Perhaps in the back of their collective consciousness they saw the sea as haven, or perhaps they fantasized that they would stow away on a ship at one of the wharves. Whatever, they were escaping from the

cathedral, the holy place where their lives, for the second
time, had came within a communion wafer's breadth of
violent death.

Morales and Ramirez lay sprawled at the high altar,
blood from their lifeless bodies spread over the floor and
down the steps of the church's most hallowed spot. One
FBI agent looked over them. The other searched frantically
with his eyes from the sacristy window, cursing himself for
losing Colleen McCoy and Bob Innes.

"Why are we here, of all places?" an angry and fatigued
Colleen demanded. "Look at us. We look like a couple of
bums. In the restaurant wall mirror, she looked at her
scratched face, leaf-infested hair and torn dress.

"Nobody will think of looking for us here," Innes
replied.

"Well, I've got news for you, Mr. Flying Walenda, there
are no guest cells at Alcatraz prison. We can't stay here."

Pot-bellied middle-aged men in baseball caps with
cameras slung from their necks, walked with families in
tow, their frumpy women scolding hyperactive children
who were o.d'd on sugar products. Some took long
sideways glances at Innes and Colleen, seated at a corner
table.

"I can't stand it! I want a hot bath, a hot meal and to be
free from pursuing killers!" Colleen hissed. "People must
think we escaped from the zoo." She self-consciously
tugged at her hair to get out bits and pieces of debris.

"Look! You think I don't want the same things? You
think I like this? And as for what we're doing here, what
safer place can we be right now but in jail? Nobody will

think of finding us here. At 5:00 we'll take the last ferry back and then hightail it out of the city."

"Great. Bonnie and Clyde on the lam yet again."

"Okay, Miss Gratefulness and Cooperation. I'm open to suggestions. I suppose you've got some brilliant idea to return us to our nice and cozy former lives?"

"No." Colleen pouted and sulked. "Where next then?"

"New Orleans."

"What?! That's got to be 2000 miles from here!"

"2300, to be exact."

"That's it, Bob." Colleen rose. "I'm going back to D.C. I can't take it any longer. Better to take my chances there. I'll go to the media, to the courts. I'll fight it out that way."

"Nobody'll believe you. They'll take you for a crackpot, the ditsy moll of the spy and traitor, Robert 'Vladimir' Innes."

She plopped back into the chair. In her exasperation, she sought answers. "Why New Orleans? Why?"

"They'll go after Jalbert. At the party convention. It makes sense. They'll stop at nothing to hold onto power. Look what they're doing -- correction, trying to do -- to us. Look at Mortimer, Wheeler. And the murders of the Russian SVR guys, there's a connection. American political bigshots making deals with mobsters in order to rake in enough cash to sway the election in their favor. The mobsters rake in cash from drug deals that the political bigwigs make possible and protect. Take that several steps further. Kill and maim those who get in the way. Somebody's got to break it open, expose it, make the guilty ones face the music."

"And that's us."

"Right."

"I think you misunderstood when I told you that you were like some hero of yore. You're taking it much too literally."

CHAPTER THIRTY-ONE

Something about the archaic decor of the FBI safehouse flat made Lydia nauseous. Whether it triggered painful memories of what passed for modern Russian house trappings or accentuated the increasingly frequent bouts of morning sickness she'd been getting, she could not say. She wanted to tell Wentworth. Oh, how she wanted to! Nothing focused one's thoughts more on the need to plan for the future than having a baby. But she would await the right moment. Get through the final travails that would be required to destroy Yakov and his partners in evil first. This was the important last hurdle to freedom and a normal life.

"…we've been very, very pleased with your assistance thus far, Miss Puchinskaya…indispensable role in bringing these characters to justice…"

She managed only to half-tune in to what Berlucci was saying. *A house in the woods. What color should the nursery be? Oh! Pink flowers and bunnies if a girl, blue with cartoon characters if a boy!*

"…we're very close to bringing this case to closure…it'll be big, very big. Some of the most powerful figures are involved…"

Wentworth touched her hand. It broke her spell. She stared into his gray eyes, a good soldier's eyes. Eyes that reflected directness and integrity. *He'll make such a wonderful father. So loving.*

"Are you okay?" he asked.

She smiled warmly. In his presence she felt as if they were enveloped in a warm aura of love. She couldn't lose him. It was their destiny to spend the next hundred years together. It was God's will.

"Yes. I'm fine," she assured him.

"We want you to return to Yakov and find out what his next moves are. Find out what he's doing with Dennison and any other government officials. Only you can do it. Only you. Lydia? Can you do it?" Berlucci looked at her with concern.

Lydia smiled, but was crying. She looked again into Wentworth's eyes and rubbed her tears away. Turning to Berlucci, in a barely audible voice, she answered, "Yes."

Gorygin detested much about his work. Climbing up the career ladder to become New York *Rezident* required countless meetings with innumerable sleazebags in too many unsavory locales. A family man, he loathed his occasional meetings with Yakov in the Lambda Cinema in Greenwich village. He hated pornography, and homosexual pornography made him positively ill. Despite sitting off in a remote corner of the theater, and despite his averting his eyes from the screen, the sounds emanating therefrom made him sick. He always tried to rush these rendezvous.

Yakov arrived with Dimitrov some fifteen excruciating minutes later. Colonel Rokovsky, from the Washington embassy *Rezidentura*, sat uncomfortably next to Gorygin.

"I'll be brief," Gorygin began. He signaled to Rokovsky, who produced a leather satchel from which he pulled an envelope. From this he took out a stack of enlarged black-and-white photos.

"You know this woman, I presume?" Gorygin said. He shined a small flashlight onto the photos.

The pictures were of Lydia entering and exiting the apartment building containing the FBI safe house, of Lydia kissing Wentworth in a restaurant, of Lydia receiving instructions from FBI agent Hanks in Rock Creek Park.

Yakov's eyes were wide. He scrutinized each photo with studied fascination.

"The building has an FBI safe house. They use it to surveille our embassy. We've known about it for years. The man in the park is an FBI agent. The man she is kissing is--"

"Malandrino's security man."

"Colonel Rokovsky can provide you with more details. I wanted you to be aware that one of your informants may be informing on you."

Yakov's jaw tightened. He looked straight at the antics on the screen, but was clearly focused elsewhere.

Rokovsky, on the other hand, joined his boss in staring at the floor and shuffling his feet impatiently. A gay couple across the aisle was making out at an increasingly vigorous pace. Gorygin always liked to know his contacts' sexual orientation and weaknesses. It helped him assess them as intelligence assets. Yakov was an enigma, however, never letting on any interest in either sex.

"So, comrade, I leave this information with you to act on as you please. Obviously, our interest is self-protection.

Your bad sources become our bad sources. I cannot afford to risk my people and operations over them. Goodbye." He and Rokovsky couldn't rise and depart the place fast enough.

"Dimitrov, what do the Afghans do to traitors in their ranks?" Yakov asked softly.

Dimitrov smiled and merely nodded.

"You know what you have to do. So do it! And bring me a piece of her so that I know that I do not have to concern myself about her any longer."

Bob Innes and Colleen McCoy were greatly on Dom Berlucci's mind, the more so since the Director had asked for a status report that afternoon. With so much on his plate -- Yakov, Malandrino, Lydia, not to mention the hundreds of other cases the Criminal Investigations Division was working on at any given time -- Berlucci had simply not paid that much attention to the runaway State Department pair. Karlson was fidgety. When the pressure was on and the anxiety level rose, the FBI Director became jumpy. His leg shook nervously, he toyed with pens, letter openers; his mouth puckered. He jumped from his desk and padded in circles around his office. Berlucci saw the telltale signs immediately.

"Lots goin' on," Karlson began after Berlucci took a seat. "Big stuff. One slip in the chain and... Well, we aren't goin' to slip, are we Dom?"

"No, sir."

"We've got Russian espionage on the agenda. We've got mafiosi. Most important of all, we've got a political scandal brewing that'll make Watergate look like amateur hour. It's all gotta be handled with finesse, Dom. With keen attention to detail."

Berlucci nodded. Karlson liked him, trusted him. He used his investigations chief to bounce ideas off.

"Those two kids from State. I've been resisting White House and State Department pressure to bring them in."

"There's absolutely no evidence to link them with the Russians. They're good officers. Selmur and Dennison are using them as scapegoats or as diversions from their other woes. We lost them in San Francisco."

Karlson puckered and his leg began to shake. "What happened?" he asked tersely.

"Two pro hitmen were after them. Cubans. We got them. But Innes and McCoy evidently thought that our men were also assassins. They jumped out a church window."

Karlson stopped pacing and gave a long, incredulous look at Berlucci.

"We've got the California field offices out trying to track them down. We've sent a general alert to all the other principal field offices."

"We need those kids, Dom. If the White House guys, or whoever it is, find them first and has them killed, they'll be able to say that they got two 'dangerous spies' on the run. They'd probably plant guns on the bodies to prove their point. Besides, Mr. Innes knows a lot that we don't about all of this muck. And he knows more about how Dennison thinks than any of us do."

"Malandrino's beginning to cooperate. He's already given us a wealth of information on Yakov's start here and where he's going, his contacts, m.o's, subordinates."

Karlson resumed pacing the room. He made a brushing motion by his ear as if a fly had been annoying him. "Bah! That's all well and good. My great-granddaddy fought in

the wars against the Sioux nation. He used to say, 'Listen
to a turncoat, but don't trust him.' You keep Malandrino
talking. But I always get a queasy feeling dealing with bad
guys like him. Maybe I'm in the wrong business. Maybe
I'm gettin' old. I don't know. We'll need really credible
witnesses in a court of law to back up the evidence we're
gathering. Make sure nothing happens to those kids."

"You think they know what Yakov and his buddies are
planning next?"

"Could be. At least an idea. I'm not sure we do."

"I've got the Russian woman sniffing around."

"Watch out for her too. I don't want a bunch of dead
informants in this case."

"Where do *you* think Yakov will hit next?"

"Ongoing criminality out there among the various mobs
doesn't worry me so much as the criminality in the White
House. You keep your resources on Yakov. Find out what
he's up to. Control Malandrino. But if I had to guess
where to anticipate trouble next, I'd guess New Orleans."

"The party convention. Jalbert."

"You got it. Oliver Stone couldn't top this one."

It was just off Fifth Avenue. She couldn't resist. Lydia
entered Baby and Thee Boutique. All she could do was
sigh. Darling Victorian prams, imaginative crib mobiles
made of wood, lambs wool blankets of soft colors, and
dolls and more wooden toys, cute bassinets, music boxes
playing lullabies. Together they beckoned her into an
entirely different world from the one she had been in. So
pure and warm. The miracle of creating another human
being to nurture into goodness. This was what she wanted
most now.

She fingered hand-knit booties and tiny sweaters. She lovingly caressed a life-like baby doll, and admired a rustic wooden picture frame. She imagined a photograph of her, Chuck and the baby filling it. She turned it over. "Made in Russia," said the label. Lydia's thoughts turned to her mother and father, good friends and loved ones. It seemed like centuries ago. How selfish and naive she was. Seek fame and fortune in the West. Leave loving relations for the harsh, cutthroat societies of Europe and America. How silly, and tragic, she was to want to leave Russia. But the harrowing, nightmarish journey would soon end. And she would be free, to spend the rest of her life with the man she loved, free to raise children in a better world.

A hard object against her kidney startled Lydia from her dreaming. She jumped away and turned.

"Oh, pardon me!" said a thirtyish redhead. "I'm afraid I've done much too much shopping today." She smiled apologetically as she pointed to her tote bag stuffed with a cornucopia of baby things. A baby-pack frame sticking out of the bag had poked Lydia.

"Ohh. When is yours due?" asked Lydia.

"Still eight more months. But I can't wait to prepare for when we are three."

"Me too."

Lydia continued her browsing. She inspected soft crib bedding and organic Pampers. And a baby hair care set of tiny brushes and combs, of ribbons -- blue or pink. She ran her fingers slowly through the delicate bristles. Nothing was finer than an infant's hair. Like wisps of heavenly clouds.

She felt a jab in her side again. Smiling, she turned to talk once more to the redheaded woman.

Dimitrov's cold, hard face confronted her. Lydia's heart stopped. Her head spun. It is one of the miracles of the human brain that, in moments of extreme danger, it can process multiple thoughts at supernatural speed. In this nanosecond or two of utter menace, Lydia's mind soberly commanded her to protect her baby. At all costs. Including by killing the threatening predator.

Time stood still. Dimitrov didn't flinch. She heard a click. In his hand, the ex-*Spetznaz* operative held a gleaming commando's knife. He had turned counterclockwise a rotary catch in the front. She stared at the object that she knew was meant to end her life at that moment. Four small barrels revealed themselves. A trigger formed one-half of the hand-guard. She looked up at the Russian. He smiled coldly. Steel caps on his teeth added to his unhuman appearance.

A shot shattered the tranquility of "Baby and Thee." Lydia crumpled to the floor as one .22 caliber bullet tore into her ribcage.

Women began screaming. In various stages of pregnancy, they scrambled for the exit, knocking down displays of talc and oil, dolls and dollhouses, bassinets and bottles.

Lydia closed her eyes. A lightning bolt of pain shot through her side. *Baby and thee. Baby and thee. Your baby will be forever lost. You will be forever lost!* a voice within her screamed.

Summoning a primitive strength, Lydia forced her eyes open. Above her, Dimitrov re-turned the rotary switch on the knife to lock the trigger. He then reached down and pressed the blade tip against her belly.

"Nooooooo! My baby!!" she shrieked.

The crash of metal against bone filled the room. Dimitrov wavered. He appeared dizzy. From behind, Lydia saw the redhead, holding the remnants of an aluminum baby-pack. Pieces of it crumbled down Dimitrov's head and neck.

Regaining himself, the ex-commando lashed rearward, catching the woman in the upper chest. Blood sprayed. Her eyes were wide, her face in shock. She clutched her chest and fell backward.

Dimitrov stood erect and took a deep breath. His thick, black leather boots locked Lydia in a taut grip at her waist. He calmly reached down again with the blade. It gleamed from the overhead fluorescent lights. The gleam momentarily blinded Lydia. Was this indeed how the end would be? A gleaming light to guide her away from the pain of a tortured life? But what about her baby? Are unborn babies guided outward as well?

She shook her head. Frantically, she thrashed about the floor with her hands. Her fingers clutched something. She thrust it upward. At that moment, Dimitrov's crotch became the unwelcome recipient of twelve inches of wooden baby crib mobile. Lydia removed it and slammed it harder on target.

The 190-pound Russian bent over. The blade fell to the floor. He clutched his groin with both hands. The normally expressionless face was the definition of hurt.

Lydia rose. Blood oozed down her left side. She picked up a nail invoice sticker from a nearby cash register and held it to Dimitrov's temple. A crazed, wild look seized her face as she proceeded to cup Dimitrov's other temple with her hand, for better resistance when she forced the nail into the man's brains.

The sound of approaching sirens echoed from the concrete city outside Baby and Thee.

Dimitrov jerked his head back. His eyes locked onto Lydia's. Two primordial beasts gripped in a death embrace. Abruptly, he leapt up. He let out a bellow. He snatched the gun-knife from the floor. Like a wounded bear, he lumbered away, lurched forward and bolted out of the shop.

Lydia fell unconscious. There was no gleaming light this time.

CHAPTER THIRTY-TWO

July in New Orleans reminded the Iraq War veteran of the southern Tigris marshlands. Though a native of the bayou, Roger Jalbert sometimes felt queasy in the heavy humidity and stagnant heat of his home state. It reminded him painfully of the past, the buddies he'd lost to the insurgents during two consecutive two-year enlistments as a Navy Seal in Iraq. Of his own brush with violent death in the marsh delta while on special ops. Tiny bits of IED shrapnel still surfaced from his left thigh and calf as another aching reminder of that period of his life.

"*Laissez les bons temps roulez!*" he declared before twelve-hundred party stalwarts at the Moriol Convention Center. "Good times will return to America. It will return because of the peace and prosperity that President Roger Jalbert will bring to this country. America wants leadership. *Honest* leadership. The old ways of doing things must end. A new wind of change is sweeping this nation. And, with your support, it will sweep into the nation's capital and fill the White House with fresh, clean air. With your support, we will all ride that wind to victory on November 5!"

It was a dry run for the party convention the following day, a "practice bout" one of Jalbert's pugilist-oriented handlers called it. Jalbert's juices were flowing. The fatigue of months of nonstop campaigning temporarily dissipated when he was before a friendly crowd before whom he could lay out his Agenda for the American Renaissance.

And the crowds were friendly indeed. Taken by Jalbert's gaullic southern charm, his looks that women would die for, his dash, wit and intelligent repartee with questioners, America's voters were prepared to deliver a landslide victory to the "Cajun Kennedy." He and his young family electrified a nation that had become tired of drift and bland stewardship.

"So I invite you to join me in bringing about a renewal of this nation, to walk together arm-in-arm -- Americans of all races and all faiths -- down that majestic path to a Renaissance of America's spirit. To rediscover those shining principles of liberty, brotherhood and prosperity for all that the Founding Fathers embodied when this country became free."

The audience jumped from their chairs and delivered a spontaneous, standing applause which, after two minutes, showed no sign of abating. It was an event that had been repeating itself since New Hampshire and in every subsequent primary, each one of which Jalbert swept handily. Christine Jalbert and their eight-year old boy and six-year old girl were brought to the podium. The applause intensified. There were whistles and loud cheers. Jalbert's winsome wife and adorable children had won the hearts of Americans as well.

Jalbert loved to mingle with the masses. He skipped down from the podium to press the flesh. The Secret Service agents assigned to protect him often were caught off guard by the athletic presidential candidate dashing off into the crowds.

The TV news anchors set up in the Big Easy covered his every move -- to the detriment of President Corgan, who was on his own campaign trail. They gushed over the intellect and idealism of Jalbert and devoted overtime coverage to his family -- attending church services, dialoguing with inner city residents, visiting military bases, listening to classical symphonies, dancing Cajun at a parish hall.

And the party professionals milked it for all it was worth. They carefully orchestrated a build-up of positive tension and anticipation in the weeks and days leading up to the party convention in a city finally experiencing its own post-Katrina renaissance. And after that, they would continue the momentum through election day.

By contrast, the Corgan camp appeared lusterless, lame and maladroit. The President appeared tired and embattled. Rumors of health problems circulated. Mrs. Corgan shut herself off. Presidential advisers and campaign staff were strident and devoid of new ideas.

To Yakov, Jalbert was a bug to be crushed. A pretty, flashy bug, to be sure. But one to be destroyed before it got too big. The equation was starkly simple: a Jalbert victory would sweep out of office the dozens of officials that he had so carefully and expensively suborned over a span of years. From Dennison and, indirectly, Selmur, on down. Pundits predicted that Jalbert's winning momentum would sweep Congress as well. Yet more Yakov assets, therefore, would fall by the wayside. Without access to power, Yakov's burgeoning illicit business ventures would become targets of law enforcement agencies and criminal competitors. The intelligence he gathered to sell to the SVR and others would dry up overnight. Dennison didn't need to draw pictures for the Russian parvenu. Yakov seized the opportunity to be catspaw for those who would hold onto power at all costs. It was a continuation of a symbiotic relationship. This particular operation simply could not fail. He would see to it personally.

"I hate Greyhound buses. I hope they go bankrupt," Colleen spat as she and Innes disembarked from their sixth bus since leaving San Francisco two days earlier. It was late afternoon.

"Once our lives are back to normal, we won't have to travel like Paul Muni fleeing the chain gang," Innes said.

"We stink," Colleen protested. She let her K-Mart travel bag plop onto the concrete pavement. She looked at Innes defiantly and blew a wayward lock from her forehead.

"We'll find a room."

"We're broke."

"Maybe Wheeler's wired some funds. I'll check."

"He doesn't give a hoot about us."

Losing his patience, Innes put his face inches from hers. "I've had it with your bellyaching! If you really want to give up, then do it! Go back to D.C. If you make it back there alive and free, do let me know!" He turned on his heel, picked up his duffle and began to walk away.

Thirty seconds later, she was trodding one step behind him to his side. No further verbal exchanges took place.

They took a room at "Madame Toussaint's Pension," just outside the *Vieux Carré*. An abbreviated bed that filled a tiny room in a third-floor walk-up with a communal bath, it was nonetheless a welcome perch from days of being on the run. The mellifluous strains of old-time jazz filled the air. Another sign of New Orleans coming back to life. Showered, Colleen plunked herself on the bed and fell instantly into a deep slumber. The music and the chance to rest put a smile on her face.

"What are you doing?" Innes asked. He shook her. "Get up. We've got to see Jalbert's people."

"Go to hell," she mumbled and turned the other way, burying her head under the pillow.

Innes grabbed the corners of the sheets and, like a magician doing the old table cloth flick trick, yanked hard. Colleen went tumbling onto the floor.

She sat upward. Her wet, tousled hair over her face gave her a wild look. She looked up at Innes with rage-filled eyes. In a flash, she was at his throat with both hands, then pummeled him on the chest. "I'm not going, goddamn it! I *hate* this running around!" She screeched like an angry cat.

Innes subdued her and pinned her on the bed. In patient, succinct words, he commanded, "Stop it. Stop it. Get hold of yourself. We're in this together. Soon it will be all over. *All over*. Do you hear me?"

She stopped struggling and turned her head to the side. She nodded. Then looked directly at Innes. With a breath of resignation, she murmured, "Okay. Let's get going."

Among the many monuments of the American Civilization, the Louisiana Superdome stood out, in its brobdignagian enormity, as one of the most enduring. Eons from now, when America's past would have to be parsed from dust and artifacts, the Superdome would stand, like

Egyptian pyramids or Roman coliseums, defiant against time as mute testimony to a great civilization.

"Wow," is all Innes and Colleen could say as they craned their necks to view the 27-story high, eight-acre structure. "It looks like that enormous UFO in *Cocoon*," Innes observed.

They approached a guard. "Pass?" he asked.

"We don't have passes. But we need to see the Jalbert campaign people," Innes replied.

"Sorry. No pass, no entry."

Innes thought quickly. He pulled out his wallet and removed his State Department building pass. Colleen produced hers as well. "U.S. Department of State. Here for the convention. We need to obtain Superdome passes. Who do we contact?"

The guard studied the eagle-emblazoned, security-stripped I.D.'s carefully, but quizzically. He directed them to the security office.

There, they explained their purpose to a very junior, crew-cutted security aide in a stiff blue blazer.

"Assassination plot? Russians? American officials? Uh, wait here."

A burly, unsmiling, authoritative-looking fellow sauntered into the small ante-room. "You folks got something to tell us about a security threat?" His badge said, "Hefflin, James R., Deputy Chief of Security."

In a nearby cubicle, a female worker was laminating building passes. He placed the finished items into a plastic tray.

The pair again recounted the danger to Jalbert.

Hefflin pursed his lips. "Well, that's very interesting. We'll keep a heightened alert for any threats. We'll especially keep an eye out for Secretary Dennison and anyone else from the White House who might try to infiltrate," he humored them.

Innes could see what was happening. "Wait a minute. You think we're nuts, don't you?"

Hefflin looked down and made a whistling sound as he toyed with a stapler.

"Look, damn it. We're serious here. If you don't warn Jalbert's people..."

Hefflin took his job seriously. "I'll tell you what I'm gonna do. There's some FBI guys here you can talk to. They listen to everybody."

Innes made a halting gesture with both hands. "No. Not the FBI."

"Why not? Are they in on the 'plot' too?"

"We're not sure where they stand. It's best not to include them right now."

Hefflin lost all patience. He looked at his watch. "Well, folks. I'm a busy man. We got a political convention to take care of. Got over 50,000 people streamin' in from all over the country." He showed them the door. The young aide stood menacingly with his arms folded.

Innes and Colleen got up. "You really don't understand. You've got to take this thing seriously!" The aide pushed Innes against the shoulder. Innes swiped his hand away. Amid the scuffling, Colleen snatched two finished press passes from the plastic tray. They were unceremoniously shown out of the complex.

Wentworth, Dimitrov and Laguzza each had little difficulty stealing themselves -- unbeknownst to each other -- into the Superdome, using subterfuges from their respective past training. The morning after Innes and

Colleen were evicted, Wentworth joined the South Carolina
delegation, waving a placard that proclaimed, "Jalbert for
the Future. Spartanburg, S.C." Dimitrov entered as part of
the Buffalo, N.Y. contingent led by councilman Stan
Kominsky. Inside, he donned a guard's uniform and
strutted about with walkie-talkie on his hip as all the other
guards did. Laguzza weaseled passes for himself, Bags and
Herman, through the connections of Vincent "The
Omelette" Scarfomalo, an old pal of Al's and scion of shady
Louisiana business circles. That morning of the first day of
the convention, Bob Innes and Colleen McCoy breezed in
as members of the press. The New Orleans FBI office was
there in force as well, augmented by Dom Berlucci along
with Speedy Donner, agent Hanks and others.

Speaker after speaker after speaker pontificated before
the masses of party faithful. Senator this and governor that
and the reverend so-and-so and a lot of plain nobodies got
their fifteen minutes in the sun of national publicity. All
endorsed Jalbert as the party's candidate for president. The
Son of the Bayou, the Sunbelt Jefferson, the Cajun
Kennedy -- Roger Charles Jalbert captured the hearts and
imaginations of his entire party. A lone contender for the
nomination withdrew in the face of this blockbuster support
for the Louisianan. A motion was made to clinch the
nomination that very evening.

The usual hyper-hoopla associated with American
political party conventions provided the setting. Grown
men pranced around the stadium with a huge, inflated
crayfish. Balloons in the shape of *fleurs-de-lys* festooned
the tiers. Indigenous jazz bands belted out Dixieland tunes.
Bevies of southern beauties, bedecked in skimpy Old Glory
outfits, danced. Showfolk from Hollywood hugged and
kissed and pronounced the dawn of a grand new era.
Multitudes of grinning middle Americans in funny hats

pumped and waved placards with the usual variations of their man for President. Single-night romances were being struck. Network "anchorpersons" preened and performed before millions of television viewers who were otherwise uninterested in summer reruns of reruns.

Among the sea of beaming faces, several reflected different emotions, if anyone took the effort to notice.

Wentworth, clean-cut and bearing a large "Jalbert for President" button on his shirt, plodded up and down the stadium levels seeking revenge. His professional soldier's eyes scanned the crowds mechanically. As soon as Yakov and Dimitrov were confirmed in his mental computer, he would strike with deadly force. To avenge Lydia was his only concern in life now.

Vengeance, not political idealism, drove the Malandrino contingent as well. Feeling powerless in the face of Yakov's challenges, Big Al, acting on a tip that Yakov had gone to the Crescent City, ordered Ricky and his two best men down to search out and kill the two Russians. Ricky surveyed the throngs of conventioneers with binoculars from an upper deck while Bags and Herman weighed into the crowds.

Innes and Colleen likewise mingled and searched, but were at a loss as to what to do should they encounter a familiar enemy face or spot something fishy, except simply to rouse security personnel.

The FBI guys walked, watched and listened, occasionally talking into their sleeves; and "interfaced" with their Secret Service counterparts.

Yakov was beside himself with gleeful anticipation. From his forty-first floor suite overlooking the Superdome, he awaited the signal from Dimitrov. At the moment when Jalbert appeared and took the podium, Dimitrov would say through his walkie-talkie, *Ty nuzhen Rodiny'* -- "The Motherland needs you." He, in turn, would wait ten minutes for Dimitrov to depart and get well clear of the complex before signaling an *Afghantsi* helicopter crew to lift off in a rented Bell waiting in a field on the other side of Lake Pontchartrain. Three Afghan war veterans, one pilot, one armed with an AK-47 and a third munitions specialist, would fly fifteen minutes toward the city center. Flying low and fast, they would follow the flat surface of the lake until they reached the West End, avoiding the nearby Coast Guard Station. Then the chopper would cut east, traverse City Park and make a mad dash for the Superdome. The pilot would hover over the stadium center only long enough for the munitions man to eject the fuel-air burst device, then head out at top speed for the Delta where a fast cigarette boat awaited them to take them to a ship that would deliver them to Cuba. What they didn't know was that, in reality, there was no cigarette boat, nor an escape ship. Yakov would dial a number on his cell phone that would trigger a small explosive incendiary device which would blow the helicopter and its crew to smoky smithereens. Yakov didn't like too many living accomplices. Fewer mouths to reveal the truth. Something he picked up from Comrade Stalin.

The fuel-air bomb, used so effectively against Afghan villagers as well as *mujahidin*, would send a fine mist of high-octane gasoline into the air of the stadium, then ignite. The resultant explosion would be utterly devastating to any living thing within a kilometer radius. The instant fire would devour the oxygen as well as incinerate everything in its domain. A mushroom cloud would rise, the impact of which would disintegrate most structures.

Yakov couldn't wait to see the effect such a device would have in an enclosed area like the Superdome. The power would reverberate, thus intensifying the devastation. The thought of killing 50,000 people gave Yakov a sense of supreme power, certainly. But the big prize was not only elimination of the major threat to his accumulating wealth and influence, Roger Jalbert, but also several generations of future leaders in his vein.

Yakov rubbed his hands and smirked. Immediately after the explosion, Dennison and Selmur would engage the President in calming the nation and appearing as a strong leader. They had already scripted a scenario. Selmur would call in the media. Dennison would arrive at the White House. They would trot out Corgan before the TV cameras and stick under his nose an eloquent speech which would include a sensitive condolence to the Jalbert family as well as those of the other victims. Bernie Scher would be appointed to a special task force to seek out the terrorists responsible for the crime; a bunch of muslim fanatics would be arrested. With the help of some expertly-planted, manufactured evidence and the vengeful mood of the nation, the White House would push for a swift trial, followed by even swifter executions.

Popular Kansas governor -- and probable vice presidential nominee -- Helen Termont stood before the convention. She signaled the ebullient crowd to quiet down. After a few minutes, the raucousness abated, allowing Termont to give the nominating speech.

"The new American Renaissance needs an architect. We stand ready to build according to that architect's plans. Fellow Americans, I give you the next President of the United States -- Roger Charles Jalbert!!"

The convention went wild. "Jalbert for President! When do we want him? Now!" chanted thousands of people in unison.

Jalbert took in the glory. His boyish smile enchanted. Horns hooted, trumpets blared. Confetti fell from everywhere like a freak flurry on a spring day. A band struck up, "Happy Times are Here Again." After ten minutes of cacophonous rejoicing, the multitude settled down. A skillful speaker, Jalbert allowed an expectant pause to stretch a minute before beginning.

"My fellow Americans, I don't know about you, but I'm glad to be here." Again, an eruption of applause.

"I'm glad to be here among you, the best friends and supporters one can hope for. Together, we will remake this great country, bring it back to the exaltedness it used to be in a Renaissance of freedom and prosperity!"

One nearby spectator wasn't impressed. Yakov sat before the TV, exhibiting only an icy impassiveness. The walkie-talkie sounded. *Ty nuzhen Rodiny'*, Dimitrov signaled.

Yakov waited the allotted time. Then pressed the beeper button. The chopper crew would be lifting off immediately.

Dimitrov strode through the crowds with a locomotive-like determination. Those who didn't move in time he merely shoved out of his way. The commotion caught the eye of Laguzza in an upper level. He recognized the graceless gait and death-mask visage of target number two. He ran down.

Ricky intercepted the Russian just before he reached an exit. He smiled maliciously. He had Dimitrov alone finally. Man-to-man. Ricky reverted to what he was best at: the street-fighter. He vividly recalled Dimitrov's skills with a knife against the Teamsters. He pulled from his jacket a Berretta 9mm. But with lightning reaction, Dimitrov, commando of the Hindu Kush, steeled professional assassin, flashed from his belt a 7.62mm silent pistol. He pressed it into Ricky's diaphragm and pumped three rounds. Ricky's face combined surprise and confusion. He clutched himself, but knew he was dying. Dimitrov delivered the coup de grace with a karate-chop blow behind Ricky's neck, making a cracking sound and sending the now-dead mobster to the concrete floor, his open eyes capturing the instant lethality of Dimitrov's blows.

Dimitrov lunged toward the exit door, but was blocked again, this time by Wentworth who had also spotted the Russian plowing through the crowds. Dimitrov jumped to the side to run by the American. But, just as quickly, Wentworth matched his move. The Marine crouched forward and tensed like a cougar about to assault a prey. Dimitrov reached for his silent pistol. Wentworth's foot crashed into the Russian's gut, sending the weapon flying. Dimitrov stood his ground. Again the two men squared off. Dimitrov plunged head-first at Wentworth. They locked together like wrestlers. Muscle matched muscle. Action met counteraction. Dimitrov jerked his head back, then forward against Wentworth's. The impact broke flesh and sent him crashing against the cement-block wall. Blood poured into Wentworth's left eye. He shook his head to regain himself. With his right hand, he tore a red fire extinguisher from its mounting. With both hands, he brought it down with all his strength onto the side of Dimitrov's neck. The Russian tumbled awkwardly down to the floor. He rose on all fours and kept shaking his head, as if he was trying to awaken from a deep sleep. Wentworth picked up Dimitrov's pistol. Standing above the stunned Russian, he took careful aim at the back of his head.

"No! Chuck! Don't do it!"

Wentworth looked over to see Innes and Colleen approaching cautiously.

"Chuck, you don't need to do this."

"I owe it to Lydia."

"This is cold blood. Marines don't kill in cold blood."

Wentworth remained still. He kept the revolver aimed at Dimitrov's head.

"Let the right people handle this, Chuck. He'll be brought to justice. And so will Yakov." Innes took two more careful steps toward Wentworth.

Wentworth jabbed the barrel hard against Dimitrov's ear. "Where's your boss, asshole?"

Dimitrov remained silent.

The muzzled air-pop of the gun sounded. A bullet tore through Dimitrov's left hand, prostrating him. "Where's Yakov, goddamn it?! Next shot will be in your spine. And the last one in your brain, if you don't tell me."

Innes felt nauseous. He couldn't control what was about to happen. Colleen stood wide-eyed and paralyzed in the shadows.

Dimitrov looked up. Even as he faced imminent death, he displayed no fear, no hate, no remorse. He closed his eyes.

Wentworth pressed the weapon tight against Dimitrov's lumbar area. He squinted as he prepared to pull the trigger.

But it was Wentworth who saw stars as the Russian spun around and planted the tip of one boot into his tormentor's stomach. Wentworth grimaced and fell backward. Dimitrov sprang to his feet. From his belt in the back, he snatched a knife and held it upward as he quickly contemplated which part of Wentworth's anatomy to slash first. He had to end this *now*. A storm of hell-fire would soon engulf and consume everything in the stadium.

Dimitrov could die fighting this man, or in the firestorm soon to be unleashed, or he could still possibly break free in the precious few seconds still available.

The thumpa-thumpa-thumpa of a helicopter approached.

In the fleeting moment that Dimitrov's mind was preoccupied, an object came crashing down on his hand. The knife slipped from his grip and fell.

Wentworth wasted no time this time. He shoved the barrel just under the Russian's ear, as he had been trained so long ago, and unhesitatingly pulled the trigger. There was a pop noise as Dimitrov's cranium burst open, accompanied by a fine blood-mist and pieces of gray matter spraying through the air. Dimitrov's body collapsed with a dull thud.

The others stood stone-still. Their minds were racing to catch up with what had just happened.

Colleen stood over Dimitrov's corpse, in her hands the janitor's broom she'd used to knock the knife out of Dimitrov's hand. She looked down at him. She began to shiver.

Innes bent down. "Look, this fell out of his pocket." It was a hotel room key. "Hyatt Regency. Hmm. Yakov."

The three stood in a triangle as in a Mexican stand-off. "Let's go!" Wentworth commanded.

They stepped out into the night. Above, a helicopter arrived and hovered.

They all stopped and looked up at it. The thumpa-thumpa-thumpa became louder. The chopper disappeared over the roof and hovered there. Thumpa-thumpa-thumpa. The trio remained where they were. Seconds passed. They heard the helicopter's rotor blades circling above the Superdome. They waited, but knowing not for what. And waited.

Thumpa-thumpa-thumpa. The sound came close again. The chopper reappeared over the edge and hovered above them briefly, then darted off into the black sky.

A thunderous sound erupted from inside the complex. It was wild applause as Jalbert wound up his speech.

"Let's go," Wentworth commanded again. Innes and Colleen followed him.

Wentworth, driven by bloodlust and revenge for his lover, raced like an Olympian down Girod and across LaSalle toward the towering brick and glass mega-hotel. The ultimate target of his revenge was in that place. Drawing upon all his Marine skills, he would conduct his last search-and-destroy mission, even if it killed him.

Colleen and Innes lagged further and further behind and were compelled to stop a couple of times to catch their breath, their goal of restraining Wentworth becoming more distant.

Meantime, security personnel found Dimitrov's body and alerted the city police, the FBI and Secret Service at the scene. A posse of law enforcement personnel was now chasing after the three. No more time to stop and catch one's breath.

As he approached the hotel, Wentworth began repeating, "4106, 4106," Yakov's suite number. Seeking to avoid attention and especially the police, he entered the parking garage. He went to an elevator and repeatedly pressed the button. He stooped, with his hands on his knees as his chest heaved while he caught his breath.

The door opened. But before he could go in, three large males stepped out. Between two of them was a fourth man, unconscious, his head bobbing back and forth like that of a broken doll's. It was Yakov, out but not dead.

A brick-like hand caught Wentworth on the chest. The men, grave and as stolid and imposing as deluxe refrigerators, glared at Wentworth.

"You go. You go. Not business of you," one of them growled in thickly accented English.

"Is our friend. We take him home," another stated slightly less threateningly. The accents were clearly Russian.

Twenty feet away stood another man. He wore a black silk shirt and a fedora slung low over his forehead. He stood in front of a black Chrysler 300 sedan. As his mates approached, the man looked up. He was stocky and had a broad face punctuated by a brown-gray stubby moustache.

As the men continued to drag Yakov to the car, one of them again looked challengingly at Wentworth. "Go way! Now!!" he ordered. With a conspicuous motion, he revealed an Uzi under his coat. Another opened the rear door of the Chrysler. They shoved Yakov, his limbs dangling, into the back seat; they climbed in after him and shut the door. The bearded man looked for a moment at Wentworth, then got into the front passenger seat. The car sped off with a squeal.

Wentworth stood motionless, his demand for vengeance unrequited. He heard steps to his rear. It was Colleen and Innes. Additional figures were approaching from further behind. Wentworth wept.

CHAPTER THIRTY-THREE

The thing about "America This Week" was that, although its Sunday morning audience constituted a tiny slice of the nation's television viewing audience, that slice counted among its members the most powerful, listened-to and influential makers and shakers in the country. Host Hardon Kennerly had been grilling Washington big shots every Sunday since Watergate. Co-host Jane Silva had joined him just before the arms-for-hostages scandal of the Reagan administration. Like moths drawn to a flame, the powermakers came to Kennerly thinking that they could outwit him or get their message across to the people over him. Those who were of integrity and played it straight got genteel treatment. Those trying to pull one over on him, however, got mauled badly.

Secretary Dennison and Chief of Staff Selmur foolishly accepted an invitation to appear on the program, convinced that they could give a boost to the floundering Corgan administration through their collective eloquence, quickness of mind and verbal combativeness.

Kennerly opened by saying the show was honored to host a "double-header." He graciously welcomed the duo in tones as gentle as the summertime waves along the shore of his native Virginia tidewater home. Without missing a beat, he went on to recount a laundry list of administration failures ranging from high inflation and unemployment to foreign policy disasters. "In the balance," he summed up, "is the survivability of the Corgan administration. Coming up fast in the race for President is Roger Jalbert, a man who says he can and will turn this nation around. Judging by the polls, he's got the majority of the American people agreeing with him. Here to present the administration's views are White House Chief of Staff Howard Selmur and Secretary of State Roy Dennison. Mr. Selmur, what do you have to say about all this?"

In his best Harrod's custom-tailored, dark blue suit and fresh haircut from "Poubelle's of Watergate Stylists," Selmur confidently ran down the major issues, defending the administration's actions on each. He neatly handed off to Dennison who smoothly delivered a rehearsed defense of the White House's foreign policy. They each sat cross-legged and cocky, ready to parry the next verbal thrust.

"On our panel today, we have Jeanette Paredsky of the *New York Times* editorial staff, James Wimberly from the *Cleveland Plain Dealer*, and Toby Wheeler, just back to work at the *Washington Post*. Welcome back, Toby. Hope you're feeling well."

The three journalists took their seats opposite the White House guests. Wheeler was pushed to the center spot in his wheel chair.

The questioning started with Paredsky who asked what the administration was doing to prevent the predicted bankruptcy in seven years of the Social Security system.

Without a crib sheet, Selmur paraded a dazzling array of numbers and statistics. "This President came into office promising a secure future to Mr. and Mrs. America. He keeps his promises," he finished with a flourish.

Wimberly, noting that the U.S. had gotten itself into trade wars with its major trading partners, asked what the U.S. was doing to resolve them.

"As you can see, the Japanese are backing off, opening their markets to more American goods. The French Trade Minister is now in Washington to settle his government's dispute with us over agricultural subsidies. And Canadian labor unions are losing their grip on auto workers, who are striking less and producing more," Dennison explained. "Everything this administration does, it does with the best interests of the American people at heart."

The camera turned to Wheeler. He appeared sullen. He seemed to be concentrating hard on something.

Anxious not to waste precious on-air time, Kennerly prodded the *Post* reporter. "And Toby…?"

Wheeler blinked as if snapping out of deep thought. "Yes. Ah. I have a question on a more abstract level."

Their faces gravely attentive, Selmur and Dennison braced themselves. Sweat formed on Dennison's brow. He had the uneasy, slightly nauseous feeling one gets when confronting someone to whom one has done grievous harm.

"'Tyrants and despots have no right to live…. Who would be free must himself strike the first blow.' Do you know who said that?"

Dennison and Selmur shook their heads. Their anxiety level increased a notch.

"Frederick Douglass. He was talking about a rotten system of governance and the need for those of conscience to challenge it. He said this over one-hundred-fifty years ago. My question is this: are you ready to face up to your crimes against the American people?"

Painfully aware of the cameras boring in on him, Selmur harrumphed; then drawing on his deepest reservoirs of snake oil, said, "Our distinguished colleague from the

Washington Post evidently has some problems with this administration's policies, as is clear from his consistently harsh reporting on us since inauguration day. And since we are quoting great men from the Civil War days, I remind him of what President Lincoln said, 'You can fool all of the people some of the time; some of the people all of the time; but you can't fool all of the people all of the time.' If this administration were as bad as Mr. Wheeler claims, we would have been out of office long ago."

Jane Silva attempted to cool things down. "Well, so the sparks fly as we get nearer to election day--"

"Now is the Day of Judgment, gentlemen," Wheeler interrupted. "Now you must atone for the murders of two United States ambassadors, the derangement of the last National Security Adviser, an attempted plot on the life of Roger Jalbert, and...the paralysis of my legs."

Dennison rose. "Why, I never!" Selmur caught him and forced him back into his seat.

The program director, fascinated with the drama, ordered the crew to continue and a commercial to be postponed. Kennerly gleefully obliged.

"I've invited here today two subordinates of the Secretary who can prove what I say," Wheeler said.

Innes and Colleen joined the panel. Innes held a videotape. "I'm Robert Innes. This is Colleen McCoy. We are Foreign Service officers whom the Secretary and Chief of Staff here have tried to frame as spies as well as to have killed."

The panelists looked at each other in amazement. A murmur rose from the crew. The network's phone lines became jammed.

"You're out of order, young man!" Dennison shouted.

"No, you're out of order, Mr. Secretary!" Innes shot back with his finger pointed at Dennison's face. He handed the videocassette to a technician. "Please watch the monitors."

The screen flickered. Then came the FBI film of Dennison meeting with Yakov. "This is the Secretary meeting with a Russian mafia kingpin named Yakov."

Dennison's voice came on. "In return for...information, I demand cash."

"Here's Mr. Dennison and Mr. Selmur discussing some interesting things over lunch." It was their last meal at Les Nigauds.

Selmur: "If we didn't have to contend with pretty boy Jalbert, we'd clinch this election."

Dennison: "What are you saying Howard?"

Selmur: "I'm saying what I'm saying, that's all. ...I'm suggesting that you might want to talk to some of your contacts about possibilities. ...There's Mortimer, Wheeler, Wells. Hell, even Horvath. Who else? I'm losing track. ...Do what you have to do."

Dennison: "Jalbert to be out of the picture."

Selmur jumped up. "I disavow any responsibility for Dennison's actions!" he bellowed. "This man is a disgrace to the government of the Uni--"

Dennison, summoning genuine courage for the first time in his life, sprang forward and socked Selmur in the jaw. "Liar! Liar!" he shouted.

Above the pandemonium, the sound track continued.

Selmur: "...You get our Cuban friends onto that case. They're the best in the business."

As Wimberly and a soundman restrained Dennison, Selmur spluttered, "Why, he's a crook. It's outrageous! Had I known..."

The monitor, continuing the videotape, showed Selmur smirking at Dennison while chugging a double vodka: "I got plausible denial. You don't."

The director cut to a commercial. From the wings appeared Berlucci and several FBI agents.

"Roy Dennison, Howard Selmur. You are under arrest for conspiracy to murder, conspiracy to commit grievous bodily harm, money laundering, espionage and about two dozen other charges we can read you later." The agents handcuffed the pair. As they were being led away, Dennison paused before Innes and Colleen and said, "You don't know what you're getting yourselves into."

Innes had a look of deep satisfaction. "See you in court, Mr. Secretary."

Speedy knew where to find Wentworth. He was at Lydia's side every available hour at Columbia Presbyterian to see to her recovery from the wound made by Dimitrov's bullet. Speedy lucked out. Bob Innes and Colleen were visiting as well. Though the two had been extensively debriefed following Selmur's and Dennison's arrests, he'd wanted to see his old buddy informally as well as to tie up loose ends with Wentworth.

Lydia's complexion was pink and she was beaming. She and Wentworth were holding hands. They welcomed Speedy as if he were a long lost friend. The TV was tuned in to CNN, with the volume low.

"Speedy, we want to invite you to our wedding," Lydia said.

"Wonderful. I accept. But only if there'll be good food."

"We will marry as soon as I am released next week."

"My family's putting on one of those old-time southern 'ya'll come down' affairs. There will be ribs, corn bread, okra stew, baked ham, hush puppies..."

"Okay, I confirm even before I get the invitation."

"Just leave some for the rest of us," Innes joked.

"Then you'll have to return for the baptism," Wentworth added.

"They've asked Bob and me to be godparents," Colleen said.

Speedy laughed and extended his congratulations. He asked if he could ask some follow-up questions, then produced a folder with enlarged photos and papers.

He showed a photo to Wentworth. "Does this face look familiar?" It was of a sixtyish, dour-looking man with a broad face, bald pate and a moustache.

"That's the guy at the Hyatt. He's the one who took Yakov away. He seemed to be in charge."

"He's Semion Mogilevich. The top dog in the Russian mob, the so-called Red Mafia, now," Speedy noted.

"He kept me from finishing Yakov," Wentworth said bitterly.

"It's more like he saved you the trouble -- and legal problems. Yakov challenged him as tsar of Russian gangsterdom in America. They had a blood feud going back years in Russia. Seems Yakov had knocked off some of his business cohorts, then had to flee here to get away from the heat. Then Mogilevich follows him here. They both discover in America green pastures for their nefarious affairs. Next thing you know, they're at it again. Rival Russian gangs battling it out in New York and other North American cities. Trouble is, Yakov bit off more than he could chew when he took on the Italian-American mafia."

"You think Malandrino made a deal with Mogilevich, as well as with you FBI guys?" Innes asked.

"We strongly believe it, but have no evidence to back it up. In any case, word on the street in Brighton Beach is that they had drugged Yakov in the Hyatt, dragged him away and took him to some location nearby New York. People say that his captors waited for him to regain consciousness, fed him, let him rest. Then, after he was alert and healthy, they bound him naked and dipped him slowly into a vat of acid."

Everybody winced, except Lydia, who stared coldly out the hospital window.

"We'll never find the body. He could be sharing quarters with Jimmy Hoffa in some bridge foundation, or his bones could be at the bottom of the East River."

"What went wrong with Yakov's execution of the Selmur/Dennison plot to kill Jalbert and 50,000 other people?" Colleen inquired.

"Seems Mogilevich got to the chopper crew and bought them off. They cut and ran without doing the job."

"And Mogilevich?" Innes asked. "Sounds like you're saying this Mogilevich character is going to be around for quite a while."

"Or the next guy after he gets his. Whether Mogilevich succeeds or fails, the Russians are here to stay," Speedy said.

"Then what's this -- the risk, the blood, all the effort -- all about?"

Speedy shrugged. "It's the flip side of the American Dream, I guess."

CNN announced that President Corgan was making a special appearance to address the nation. The President came on. He sat at an ersatz oak desk in a mock study with facade bookcases and an artificial fire in a faux fire place.

"Turn the volume up. This should be interesting," Innes said.

Laying on thick the wise old great uncle routine, Corgan began with a homily his father used to tell him when he was "knee-high to a Holstein calf."

Colleen histrionically put an index finger into her open mouth to indicate she was ready to puke.

"Papa Corgan was an infantryman in France during the Second World War. By the way, he returned to his farm after seeing 'Gay Paree.' And he raised seven wonderful children, each of whom did their patriotic duty in defending this country." Corgan riveted his sympathetic eyes on the viewers. "He learned about life from living on a farm. He said that when you have aggressive or other deviant cattle among the herd, you separated them out for the greater good of the herd. It wasn't the farmer's fault that some cattle turned out bad. It was just part of nature's imperfections. So it was with troops in war, he'd say. For the greater good of the unit, you set the bad apples apart and got rid of them."

Wentworth began to hum "Old MacDonald Had a Farm."

Corgan got up from his Hollywood set desk, stepped to the front and sat on the edge. He crossed his arms, glanced at the floor briefly in feigned concentration, then again looked directly into the camera with liquid, cheerful eyes.

"Hold on to your wallets everyone!" Innes warned.

"As you know, two senior officials recently were taken into custody for violating the trust of the American people."

"That's another way of saying, 'Two of my closest advisers were arrested on felony charges," Colleen interjected.

"And how fast we forget about poor Horvath," Wentworth added.

"These men, for whatever reasons, turned out to be bad apples. They contravened their oath of office and to me as your President. But I have taken vigorous action and have instituted a shake-up in the White House staff and at the State Department."

Speedy grimaced. "I'm afraid to hear the punch line."

"I am taking the unprecedented step of appointing concurrently as my Chief of Staff and as National Security Adviser a man who has demonstrated the brilliance, integrity and trust to take on such weighty duties simultaneously. I am naming Bernard Scher, a man whose character and dogged commitment to seeking the truth has won the respect of Congress as well as the Executive Branch and the American people."

Innes's and Colleen's jaws went slack. "He can't be serious," she gasped.

Scher joined the President. They shook hands. Scher was his usual, smug, puffed-up self. Both grinned into the camera as it panned off.

There was stunned silence in the room. Finally, Lydia spoke.

"This country is just like the Soviet Union. I'm sorry, but Brezhnev and the other incompetent mediocrities would feel very comfortable here." She shook her head.

"One difference," Innes rejoined. "The election."

Innes and Colleen left the hospital. Innes walked with his hands in his pockets and his head low. Colleen sensed that something was bothering him.

"Bob. Don't let all that get you down. As you said, there will be payback time in November. Jalbert's bound to win by a landslide. Thing's will definitely look up."

Innes looked at her without saying a thing. He was about to speak, but held back.

Colleen sensed that Innes was struggling with himself. She looked deeply into his eyes. Her lips trembled. "What is it, Bob? Is it...is it...us?"

He gave a short nod.

The dilemma of their relationship would finally be resolved. But it could go either way and the mere possibility that it might end panicked her. Tears welled in her eyes and fell down her cheeks, but she did not avert her gaze.

Innes reached out and gripped both hands on her shoulders. "Colleen. I, uh..."

"Is this it? Bob... Are we...? The knuckles of her clenched fists whitened.

"Carolyn came to see me. She brought the kids. She wants me back. The kids miss me, and I them."

She broke from his grip, turned away from him and covered her mouth with both hands. The noise and commotion of the city faded from her consciousness. There was only Innes and she, and he was fast receding from the picture.

He placed a hand on the back of her neck. "Colleen, I..."

She broke free from him, stepped away and just looked at her lover horrified.

"Colleen." He approached her again, shaking his head. "Colleen. I'm not going back. I want to be with you. I'm divorcing Carolyn. But I'll still be close to my children. I love them too much."

"Ohh, Bob!" She ran into his arms. Their kiss sent the pain away. After a minute, she drew her head back and searched his face.

"Bob, promise me something?"

"You name it."

"That wonderful life we've talked about. Let's do it. Make it happen."

"You mean leave Washington?"

She nodded.

"'And may you be safe from every harm,' milady." They kissed and embraced in the glory of the radiant midday sun. At that moment, they existed only for one another.

CHAPTER THIRTY-FOUR

The victorious prince stood on the steps outside the Federal Building in Brooklyn. The crowd of hardhatters, blue-collar youths and housewives bellowed, "Atta way, Al! Show 'em Al!" Local reporters jostled to ask questions.

Big Al Malandrino, clad in a blue-gray, perfectly fitted Brioni suit, drank it all in. He held his arms up for calm.

As the crowd obliged, Al held up a sheet of paper.

"After years of persecuting me, of violating my civil rights, of impugning me as an Italian-American, a loyal and patriotic citizen of this great country, the Federal government has finally notified me -- in writing -- that I am what I've been saying all along -- a legitimate businessman."

His admirers yelped, hollered, cheered and clapped. "You tell 'em, Al!" "Give 'em hell, Al!"

He waved one hand to solicit quiet. Poking the sheet of paper with his forefinger, Al declared, "The United States Federal Bureau of Investigation has written me this letter 'thanking you for your cooperation in bringing to justice certain dishonest senior Federal officials who, through their nefarious criminal acts, committed a gross disservice to the

American people.' Signed, 'Dominic Berlucci, Chief, Investigations Division.'"

More applause.

"I'm making an announcement. To show that I am a responsible citizen who cares deeply about this country, I am contributing money and people to elect as our next president Roger Jalbert, the best man for the job! God bless America!"